THE DIVINE COMEDY OF
DANTE ALIGHIERI

Il PURGATORIO

THE DIVINE COMEDY OF DANTE ALIGHIERI

WITH

TRANSLATION AND

COMMENT BY

JOHN D. SINCLAIR

II PURGATORIO

OXFORD UNIVERSITY PRESS
NEW YORK

London   Oxford   New York
Glasgow   Toronto   Melbourne   Wellington
Cape Town   Ibadan   Nairobi   Dar es Salaam   Lusaka   Addis Ababa
Delhi   Bombay   Calcutta   Madras   Karachi   Lahore   Dacca
Kuala Lumpur   Singapore   Hong Kong   Tokyo

First published by Oxford University Press, New York, 1939
First issued as an Oxford University Press paperback
by special arrangement with THE BODLEY HEAD, 1961

This reprint, 1972

Printed in the United States of America

CONTENTS

9

CONTENTS

CONTENTS

CONTENTS

DANTE'S PURGATORY

DANTE'S Purgatory is a lofty island-mountain, the only land in the southern hemisphere, at the antipodes of Jerusalem. On the lower irregular slopes are the souls whose penitence has, for some reason, been delayed in life and whose purgation is now delayed. Above that is the gate of Purgatory proper, the place of active purgation, which consists of seven level terraces surrounding the mountain and rising one above another, connected by stair-ways in the rock. On these terraces the seven deadly sins are purged by penances from the souls that have been beset by them. On the summit of the mountain is the Garden of Eden, or Earthly Paradise, from which the purged souls ascend to Heaven.

THE SYSTEM OF DANTE'S PURGATORY

The Earthly Paradise

The Terraces of Purgation

Love Excessive
- 7. The Lascivious
- 6. The Gluttonous
- 5. The Avaricious

Love Defective
- 4. The Slothful

Love Perverted
- 3. The Wrathful
- 2. The Envious
- 1. The Proud

Ante-Purgatory
- 4. Negligent Rulers
- 3. The Unabsolved
- 2. The Lethargic
- 1. The Excommunicate

PURGATORIO

PURGATORIO

PER correr migliori acque alza le vele
   omai la navicella del mio ingegno,
   che lascia dietro a sè mar sì crudele;
e canterò di quel secondo regno
   dove l' umano spirito si purga
   e di salire al ciel diventa degno.
Ma qui la morta poesì resurga,
   o sante Muse, poi che vostro sono;
   e qui Calliopè alquanto surga,
seguitando il mio canto con quel sono   10
   di cui le Piche misere sentiro
   lo colpo tal, che disperar perdono.
Dolce color d'oriental zaffiro,
   che s'accoglieva nel sereno aspetto
   del mezzo puro insino al primo giro,
alli occhi miei ricominciò diletto,
   tosto ch' io usci' fuor dell'aura morta
   che m'avea contristati li occhi e 'l petto.
Lo bel pianeta che d'amar conforta
   faceva tutto rider l'oriente,   20
   velando i Pesci, ch'erano in sua scorta.
I' mi volsi a man destra, e puosi mente
   all'altro polo, e vidi quattro stelle
   non viste mai fuor ch'alla prima gente.
Goder pareva il ciel di lor fiammelle:
   oh settentrïonal vedovo sito,
   poi che privato se' di mirar quelle!

CANTO I

*Morning; Venus; the four stars; Cato; the rush
and the dew*

To course over better waters the little bark of
my wit now lifts her sails, leaving behind her so
cruel a sea, and I will sing of that second kingdom
where the human spirit is purged and becomes fit
to ascend to Heaven. But here let poetry rise again
from the dead, O holy Muses, since I am yours;
and here let Calliope rise up for a while and
accompany my song with that strain which smote
the ears of the wretched pies so that they despaired
of pardon.[1]

The sweet hue of the oriental sapphire which
was gathering in the serene face of the heavens
from the clear zenith to the first circle[2] gladdened
my eyes again as soon as I passed out of the dead
air which had afflicted my eyes and breast. The fair
planet that prompts to love made all the east laugh,
veiling the Fishes which were in her train.[3] I turned
to the right and set my mind on the other pole,
and I saw four stars never seen before but by the
first people; the sky seemed to rejoice in their
flames. O widowed region of the north, since thou
art denied that sight![4]

Com' io da loro sguardo fui partito,
    un poco me volgendo all'altro polo,
    là onde il Carro già era sparito,   30
vidi presso di me un veglio solo,
    degno di tanta reverenza in vista,
    che più non dee a padre alcun figliuolo.
Lunga la barba e di pel bianco mista
    portava, a' suoi capelli simigliante,
    de' quai cadeva al petto doppia lista.
Li raggi delle quattro luci sante
    fregiavan sì la sua faccia di lume,
    ch' i' 'l vedea come 'l sol fosse davante.
'Chi siete voi che contro al cieco fiume   40
    fuggita avete la pregione etterna?'
    diss'el, movendo quelle oneste piume.
'Chi v' ha guidati, o che vi fu lucerna,
    uscendo fuor della profonda notte
    che sempre nera fa la valle inferna?
Son le leggi d'abisso così rotte?
    o è mutato in ciel novo consiglio,
    che, dannati, venite alle mie grotte?'
Lo duca mio allor mi diè di piglio,
    e con parole e con mani e con cenni   50
    reverenti mi fè le gambe e 'l ciglio.
Poscia rispuose lui: 'Da me non venni:
    donna scese dal ciel, per li cui prieghi
    della mia compagnia costui sovvenni.
Ma da ch' è tuo voler che più si spieghi
    di nostra condizion com'ell'è vera,
    esser non puote il mio che a te si nieghi.
Questi non vide mai l' ultima sera;
    ma per la sua follia le fu sì presso,
    che molto poco tempo a volger era.   60
Sì com' io dissi, fui mandato ad esso
    per lui campare; e non li era altra via
    che questa per la quale i' mi son messo.
Mostrata ho lui tutta la gente ria;
    e ora intendo mostrar quelli spirti
    che purgan sè sotto la tua balìa.

When I had withdrawn my gaze from them, turning a little towards the other pole where the Wain had already disappeared, I saw beside me an old man alone, worthy by his looks of so great reverence that no son owes more to a father;[5] his beard was long and streaked with white, and his hair the same, a double tress falling on his breast; the rays of the four holy stars so adorned his face with light that I saw him as if the sun were before him.

'Who are ye that have fled the eternal prison against the blind stream?' he said, shaking those venerable locks. 'Who has guided you or who was your lantern in coming forth from the profound night that holds in perpetual blackness the valley of Hell? Are the laws of the abyss thus broken, or has a new decree been made in Heaven, that, being damned, you come to my cliffs?'

My Leader then laid hold of me and with speech and hand and sign made me reverent in knees and brow, then answered him: 'Of myself I came not. A lady descended from Heaven for whose prayers I succoured this man with my companionship; but since it is thy will to have it made more plain how in truth it stands with us, it cannot be mine to deny thee. This man never saw his last hour, but by his folly was so near to it that little time was left to run. I was sent to him, as I said, for his deliverance and there was no other way but this on which I have set out; I have shown him all the guilty race and now purpose to show him those spirits that cleanse themselves under thy charge.

Com' io l' ho tratto, sarìa lungo a dirti;
   dell'alto scende virtù che m'aiuta
   conducerlo a vederti e a udirti.
Or ti piaccia gradir la sua venuta: 70
   libertà va cercando, ch'è sì cara,
   come sa chi per lei vita rifiuta.
Tu 'l sai, che non ti fu per lei amara
   in Utica la morte, ove lasciasti
   la vesta ch'al gran dì sarà sì chiara.
Non son li editti etterni per noi guasti;
   chè questi vive, e Minòs me non lega;
   ma son del cerchio ove son li occhi casti
di Marzia tua, che 'n vista ancor ti priega,
   o santo petto, che per tua la tegni: 80
   per lo suo amore adunque a noi ti piega.
Lasciane andar per li tuoi sette regni:
   grazie riporterò di te a lei,
   se d'esser mentovato là giù degni.'
'Marzïa piacque tanto alli occhi miei
   mentre ch' i' fu' di là,' diss'elli allora
   'che quante grazie volse da me, fei.
Or che di là dal mal fiume dimora,
   più muover non mi può, per quella legge
   che fatta fu quando me n' usci' fora.   90
Ma se donna del ciel ti move e regge,
   come tu di', non c'è mestier lusinghe:
   bastisi ben che per lei mi richegge.
Va dunque, e fa che tu costui ricinghe
   d' un giunco schietto e che li lavi 'l viso,
   sì ch'ogni sucidume quindi stinghe;
chè non si converrìa, l'occhio sorpriso
   d'alcuna nebbia, andar dinanzi al primo
   ministro, ch'è di quei di paradiso.
Questa isoletta intorno ad imo ad imo,   100
   là giù colà dove la batte l'onda,
   porta de' giunchi sovra 'l molle limo;
null'altra pianta che facesse fronda
   o indurasse, vi puote aver vita,
   però ch'alle percosse non seconda

How I have led him would be long to tell thee; there descends from above virtue which aids me in bringing him to see thee and to hear thee. May it please thee to be gracious to his coming. He goes seeking liberty, which is so dear, as he knows who gives his life for it; thou knowest it, since death for it was not bitter to thee in Utica, where thou didst leave the vesture which in the great day will be so bright.[6] The eternal edicts are not broken for us, for this man lives and Minos does not bind me; but I am of the circle where are the chaste eyes of thy Marcia, who in her looks still prays thee, O holy breast, that thou hold her for thine own.[7] For her love, then, do thou incline to us; allow us to go through thy seven kingdoms. I will report to her thy kindness, if thou deign to be spoken of there below.'

'Marcia so pleased my eyes while I was yonder' he said then 'that whatever kindness she sought of me I did; now that she dwells beyond the evil stream[8] she cannot move me more, by the law which was made when I came forth from thence. But if a lady from Heaven moves and directs thee, as thou sayest, there is no need of fair words; let it suffice thee to ask me for her sake. Go then, and see that thou gird him with a smooth rush and bathe his face so as to remove from it all defilement, for it would not be fitting to go with eye dimmed by any fog before the first minister of those of Paradise. This little island, round about its very base, down there where the wave beats on it, bears rushes on the soft mud; no other plant which would make leaves or harden can live there,

23

Poscia non sia di qua vostra reddita;
   lo sol vi mosterrà, che surge omai,
   prendere il monte a più lieve salita.'
Così sparì; e io su mi levai
   sanza parlare, e tutto mi ritrassi   110
   al duca mio, e li occhi a lui drizzai.
El cominciò: 'Seguisci li miei passi:
   volgiànci in dietro, chè di qua dichina
   questa pianura a' suoi termini bassi.'
L'alba vinceva l'òra mattutina
   che fuggìa innanzi, sì che di lontano
   conobbi il tremolar della marina.
Noi andavam per lo solingo piano
   com'om che torna alla perduta strada,
   che 'nfino ad essa li pare ire invano.   120
Quando noi fummo là 've la rugiada
   pugna col sole, e, per essere in parte
   dove adorezza, poco si dirada,
ambo le mani in su l'erbetta sparte
   soavemente 'l mio maestro pose:
   ond' io, che fui accorto di sua arte,
porsi ver lui le guance lacrimose:
   ivi mi fece tutto discoverto
   quel color che l' inferno mi nascose.
Venimmo poi in sul lito diserto,   130
   che mai non vide navicar sue acque
   omo che di tornar sia poscia esperto.
Quivi mi cinse sì com'altrui piacque:
   oh maraviglia! chè qual elli scelse
   l' umile pianta, cotal si rinacque
subitamente là onde l'avelse.

see esperienza applied to Ulysses in Inf XXVI

see Ulysses canto

not yielding to the buffets. Afterwards let not your return be this way; the sun, which is now rising, will show you where to take the mountain at an easier ascent.'

With that he vanished, and I rose up without speaking and drew close to my Leader and set my eyes on him.

He began: 'Follow my steps; let us turn back, for this plain slopes down from here to its low bounds.'

The dawn was overcoming the morning breeze, which fled before it, so that I descried far off the trembling of the sea. We made our way over the lonely plain, like one who returns to the road he has lost and, till he finds it, seems to himself to go in vain. When we were at a part where the dew resists the sun and, being in shade, is little dispersed, my Master gently laid both hands outspread on the grass. I, therefore, aware of his purpose, reached toward him my tear-stained cheeks and on them he wholly restored that colour which Hell had hidden in me. We came then on to the desert shore that never saw man sail its waters who after had experience of return. There he girded me as the other had bidden. O marvel! for as was the lowly plant he chose such did it spring up again immediately in the place where he had plucked it.

see ulysses canto XXV Info

See I Canto Info

> Dante's ulysses travels this far but does not return

25

PURGATORIO

1. The daughters of King Pierus challenged the Muses to a contest of song and sang of the Titans that fought against Jupiter; Calliope, Muse of Epic Poetry, defeated the mortals, who, for their presumption, were turned into magpies.

2. The horizon.

3. Venus, as morning star, was in conjunction with the constellation of the Fishes, which in spring rises shortly before the sun.

4. Possibly the stars of the Southern Cross, not visible in the northern, inhabited, hemisphere, but seen from Eden in the southern.

5. Cato, fighting in the Civil War against Caesar, took his own life in the prospect of defeat rather than survive the freedom of the republic; he died in Utica, North Africa.

6. The day of judgement, when their bodies will be restored to the dead.

7. Marcia, Cato's wife, who is still in Limbo (*Inf.* iv), was given by Cato to his friend, on whose death she persuaded Cato to take her again, that it might be inscribed on her tomb that she was Cato's wife.

8. Acheron, the river of death (*Inf.* iii).

NOTE

Dante's conception of Hell, as of Paradise, is in its general form traditional; but his Purgatory is his own. The Church conceived of Purgatory as a kind of temporary Hell and, like Hell, subterranean; for Dante it was impossible so to conceive the life of penitence and purgation by which 'the human spirit becomes fit to ascend to Heaven'. His *Inferno* is a picture of the soul's bondage and defeat, his *Purgatorio* of its liberation and victory, and he takes every means to mark the contrast. For his higher theme he needs a higher inspiration, for which he appeals to Calliope, the greatest of the Muses. By her song she had defeated the insolent challenge of the sisters who sang in praise of the rebel Titans, and it is such a song he needs now to tell of the hard-won victory of grace.

In Hell Dante has been an observer, a learner, in no sense identified with any of the sufferers there; it has been his discipline to see the operations and issues of sin, his gain to have been wholly freed from any faith in sin or fear of it in the last reckoning when he left Satan beneath his feet, and his attainment 'to see again the stars'. But in Purgatory Dante is himself a penitent among the penitents. Partly in anticipation, partly in present fact, he shares their experience of penitence and pain, of shame and aspiration, of labour and trust in grace and gradual attainment, of all that belongs to the gaining of the soul's liberty; and in his imagination of Purgatory as a great mountain rising from the sea into the sunshine and bearing a garden on its summit Dante departed from all the traditions of his time. It is opposite to Hell in situation and shape as in character and purpose, and it stands on the earth but rises clear above its earthliness.

The *Purgatorio* opens on Easter Sunday morning. It is singularly characteristic of Dante that he indicates quite un-

27

mistakably by various time-references—as in *Inferno* xxi—but never says expressly, that the times of his descent into Hell and his emergence from it with Virgil correspond closely with the times of Christ's death and resurrection. The correspondence is deliberately contrived and yet never referred to as a correspondence; much less is there any hint of Paul's doctrine of the soul's mystical unity with Christ—'buried with him, . . . risen with him' (*Col.* ii. 12). It is as if in this strangely veiled yet unmistakable fashion Dante would set forth his way of salvation as being—not by any plan or prior knowledge of his own, but inevitably and by the nature of things—in the very context of the passion and resurrection of Christ. He entered Hell in the dusk of Good Friday; he comes forth when Christ rose, in the hour of wonder and expectancy before dawn, Venus blazing in the whitening east and strange stars shining in the south.

It is possible that Dante had heard of the Southern Cross from Marco Polo, the great Venetian traveller, his contemporary, and as possible that he invented the four stars for his purpose. In any case they represent here the four cardinal virtues, prudence, courage, justice and temperance, specifically the virtues of the active life, of the social and civil order of humanity, that is, of the Empire, the virtues possible to paganism, in contrast with the three 'theological' virtues, faith, hope and love, which belong specifically to the Christian dispensation. Since the fall and the expulsion of the first parents from Eden humanity in general has been 'denied the sight' of them; in comparison with this clear shining, once known to unfallen man, the world is ignorant of the divine order of its life, and the object of all Purgatory, the end for which the penitents are set to climb, is the reversal of the fall, the recovery of the primal virtues, the re-entering of Eden.

Dante's Cato is a visionary and unearthly figure, hardly a realized personality, which appears and vanishes we are not told whence or whither. As a pagan, an enemy of Julius Caesar, and a suicide, he might have been found in one part or another of Hell; but in the medieval mind he had become the legendary ideal of pagan virtue, the hero and martyr of liberty. Dante writes of him in various passages elsewhere: 'O most sacred breast of Cato, who shall presume to speak of thee? Assuredly there can be no greater speech about thee than to be silent. . . . We read of Cato that he thought of himself as born, not for himself, but for his country and for all the world. . . . That he might kindle the love of liberty in the world he showed of what worth it was, for he chose to go forth from life free rather than remain in it without liberty (*Convito* and *De Monarchia*). It would be mere misapprehension to judge of Cato's repudiation of his wife Marcia here otherwise than symbolically; his relations with her are conceived as a mere part of his unredeemed earthly life from which he has passed completely to a higher and holier loyalty, that to 'a lady from Heaven', Beatrice, the truth of God, for whose sake he admits Virgil and his charge. It was political liberty for which Cato died in Utica and it is the liberty of the soul that Dante seeks, the liberty which is identical with virtue; for Dante, public liberty and the liberty of the soul are ultimately one.

Cato's harsh challenge to the travellers indicates the severe conditions of the soul's quest: the faithful, and at first lonely, following of the reason, the assurance of an unseen grace beyond reason, the cleared vision for the heavenly ministries he is to meet with, and utter humbleness. Even Virgil needs direction, for reason is not sufficient here, being but the servant and deputy of higher powers.

Dante must follow Virgil across the lonely plain, 'like one who returns to the road he has lost', the first finding of the way in the life of penitence is a solitary and perplexed experience; and there, at the very base of the sloping shore, Virgil, with a kind of ritual solemnity and gentleness, washes Dante's face with the morning dew, dew being a scriptural image of the divine mercy. There too it is reason that girds him with humility, the same reason that had flung the cord of a formal outward discipline into the pit of fraud (*Inf.* xvi); it is a better security. And in place of the rush taken for his girdle another springs at once; for the penitent, by his humbleness, finds always new reasons for it, a humbleness which is not simply lowliness, but rather the meekness of spirit that 'yields to the buffets', submits to chastisement and is fitted for the ascent.

In the first canto of the *Purgatorio*, as in that of the *Inferno*, the symbolism is elaborate and in some respects perplexing. All the more impressive is the intimate imaginative realism of Dante's story: the transport and expansion of his spirit on emerging from the pit into the serene air under the stars which are fading into the dawn—his silence, as of a child rapt with wonder, throughout—the sudden, august apparition of the aged Cato—the suspense of Dante's confidence as he follows Virgil down to the lonely shore—and his acceptance, as of a sacrament, of the bathing of his face and the girding with the rush. The abstract moral symbols are the framework; the whole is a profoundly imagined experience.

PURGATORIO

Già era 'l sole all'orizzonte giunto
  lo cui meridïan cerchio coverchia
  Ierusalèm col suo più alto punto;
e la notte, che opposita a lui cerchia,
  uscìa di Gange fuor con le Bilance,
  che le caggion di man quando soverchia;
sì che le bianche e le vermiglie guance,
  là dov' i' era, della bella Aurora
  per troppa etate divenivan rance.
Noi eravam lunghesso mare ancora,   10
  come gente che pensa a suo cammino,
  che va col cuore e col corpo dimora.
Ed ecco qual, sul presso del mattino,
  per li grossi vapor Marte rosseggia
  giù nel ponente sovra 'l suol marino,
cotal m'apparve, s' io ancor lo veggia,
  un lume per lo mar venir sì ratto,
  che 'l mover suo nessun volar pareggia.
Dal qual com' io un poco ebbi ritratto
  l'occhio per domandar lo duca mio,   20
  rividil più lucente e maggior fatto.
Poi d'ogne lato ad esso m'apparìo
  un, non sapea che, bianco, e di sotto
  a poco a poco un altro a lui uscìo.
Lo mio maestro ancor non fece motto,
  mentre che i primi bianchi apparser ali:
  allor che ben conobbe il galeotto,

CANTO II

The ship of souls; the angel pilot; Casella's song;
Cato's rebuke

ALREADY the sun had reached the horizon whose
meridian circle covers Jerusalem with its highest
point, and night, circling opposite to it, was issuing
from the Ganges with the Scales, which fall from
her hand when she exceeds the day, so that, there
where I was, the white and rosy cheeks of fair
Aurora, with her increasing age, were turning
orange.[1] We were still beside the sea, like those
that ponder on their road, who go on in heart and
in body linger; and lo, as on the approach of
morning Mars glows ruddy through the thick vapours
low in the west over the ocean floor, so appeared
to me—may I see it again!—a light coming so
swiftly over the sea that no flight could match its
speed; from which when I had taken my eyes for
a moment to question my Leader I saw it again,
grown brighter and larger. Then on either side of
it appeared to me a whiteness, I knew not what,
and below it, little by little, another came forth.
Still my Master did not say a word till the first
whitenesses appeared as wings; then, when he
clearly discerned the pilot, he cried: 'Bend, bend

33

gridò: 'Fa, fa che le ginocchia cali:
 ecco l'angel di Dio: piega le mani:
 omai vedrai di sì fatti officiali.   30
Vedi che sdegna li argomenti umani,
 sì che remo non vuol nè altro velo
 che l'ali sue tra liti sì lontani.
Vedi come l' ha dritte verso il cielo,
 trattando l'aere con l'etterne penne,
 che non si mutan come mortal pelo.'
Poi, come più e più verso noi venne
 l' uccel divino, più chiaro appariva;
 per che l'occhio da presso nol sostenne,
ma chinail giuso; e quei sen venne a riva   40
 con un vasello snelletto e leggiero,
 tanto che l'acqua nulla ne 'nghiottiva.
Da poppa stava il celestial nocchiero,
 tal che parea beato per iscripto;
 e più di cento spirti entro sediero.
'*In exitu Israel de Aegypto*'
 cantavan tutti insieme ad una voce
 con quanto di quel salmo è poscia scripto.
Poi fece il segno lor di santa croce;
 ond'ei si gittar tutti in su la piaggia,   50
 ed el sen gì, come venne, veloce.
La turba che rimase lì selvaggia
 parea del loco, rimirando intorno
 come colui che nove cose assaggia.
Da tutte parti saettava il giorno
 lo sol, ch'avea con le saette conte
 di mezzo il ciel cacciato Capricorno,
quando la nova gente alzò la fronte
 ver noi, dicendo a noi: 'Se voi sapete,
 mostratene la via di gire al monte.'   60
E Virgilio rispuose: 'Voi credete
 forse che siamo esperti d'esto loco;
 ma noi siam peregrin come voi siete.
Dianzi venimmo, innanzi a voi un poco,
 per altra via, che fu sì aspra e forte,
 che lo salire omai ne parrà gioco.'

thy knees, behold the angel of God, clasp thy hands; such ministers shalt thou see henceforth. See how he scorns human instruments and seeks no oar nor other sail than his wings between shores so distant; see how he has them raised toward the sky, fanning the air with the eternal pinions which do not change like mortal plumage.'

echoes Daedalus + Dante doc. & Ulysses

forcing the open sea

Then, as the divine bird came towards us more and more, he appeared brighter, so that my eyes could not bear him close and I cast them down, and he came on to the shore with a vessel so swift and light that the water took in nothing of it. On the poop stood the heavenly steersman, such that blessedness seemed written upon him, and more than a thousand spirits sat within. *In exitu Israel de Aegypto*[2] they sang all together with one voice, with all that is written after of that psalm; then he made over them the sign of Holy Cross, at which they all flung themselves on the beach, and he went swiftly as he came.

The crowd that remained there seemed strange to the place, gazing about like those that make trial of things new. On all sides the sun was shooting forth the day and with his keen arrows had chased Capricorn from mid-heaven,[3] when the new people raised their faces toward us, saying to us: 'If you know, show us the way to go to the mountain.'

And Virgil answered: 'You think, perhaps, we are acquainted with this place, but we are strangers like yourselves; we came but now, a little while before you, by another road which was so rough and hard that now the climb will seem to us a pastime.'

35

L'anime che si fuor di me accorte,
   per lo spirar, ch' i' era ancora vivo,
   maravigliando diventaro smorte.
E come a messagger che porta ulivo   70
   tragge la gente per udir novelle,
   e di calcar nessun si mostra schivo,
così al viso mio s'affisar quelle
   anime fortunate tutte quante,
   quasi oblïando d'ire a farsi belle.
Io vidi una di lor trarresi avante
   per abbracciarmi, con sì grande affetto,
   che mosse me a fare il simigliante.
Oi ombre vane, fuor che nell'aspetto!
   Tre volte dietro a lei le mani avvinsi,   80
   e tante mi tornai con esse al petto.
Di maraviglia, credo, mi dipinsi;
   per che l'ombra sorrise e si ritrasse,
   e io, seguendo lei, oltre mi pinsi.
Soavemente disse ch' io posasse:
   allor conobbi chi era, e pregai
   che, per parlarmi, un poco s'arrestasse.
Rispuosemi: 'Così com' io t'amai
   nel mortal corpo, così t'amo sciolta:
   però m'arresto; ma tu perchè vai?'   90
'Casella mio, per tornar altra volta
   là dov' io son, fo io questo vïaggio;'
   diss' io 'ma a te com'è tanta ora tolta?'
Ed elli a me: 'Nessun m'è fatto oltraggio,
   se quei che leva quando e cui li piace,
   più volte m' ha negato esto passaggio;
chè di giusto voler lo suo si face:
   veramente da tre mesi elli ha tolto
   chi ha voluto intrar, con tutta pace.
Ond' io, ch'era ora alla marina volto   100
   dove l'acqua di Tevero s' insala,
   benignamente fu' da lui ricolto.
A quella foce ha elli or dritta l'ala,
   però che sempre quivi si ricoglie
   quale verso Acheronte non si cala.'

The souls, who had perceived from my breathing
that I was still in life, turned pale with wonder,
and as to a messenger who bears an olive-branch[4]
the people crowd to hear the news and no one
heeds the crush, so every one of these fortunate
souls fixed his eyes on my face, as if forgetting to
go and make them fair. I saw one of them come
forward with so much affection to embrace me that
it moved me to do the same. O empty shades,
except in semblance! Three times I clasped my
hands behind him and as often brought them back
to my breast. Wonder, I think, was painted in my
looks, at which the shade smiled and drew back
and I, following him, pressed forward. Gently he
bade me stand; then I knew who it was and begged
him that he would stay a little and talk with me.

He answered me: 'Even as I loved thee in my
mortal flesh, so do I love thee freed; therefore I
stay. But thou, why art thou on this journey?'

'My Casella,[5] to return another time where I am
I take this road; but from thee how has so much
time been taken?'

And he said to me: 'No wrong is done me if he
who takes up whom and when he will has many
times denied me this passage, for of a righteous
will his own is framed; nevertheless, for three
months he has taken with all peace whoever would
embark.[6] I, therefore, who had now turned to the
shore where Tiber's waters become salt, was kindly
gathered in by him. To that river-mouth he has
now set his wing, for there the souls are always
gathering that sink not down to Acheron.'

37

E io: 'Se nuova legge non ti toglie
   memoria o uso all'amoroso canto
   che mi solea quetar tutte mie voglie,
di ciò ti piaccia consolare alquanto
   l'anima mia, che, con la mia persona   110
   venendo qui, è affannata tanto!'
'*Amor che ne la mente mi ragiona*'
   cominciò elli allor sì dolcemente,
   che la dolcezza ancor dentro mi sona.
Lo mio maestro e io e quella gente
   ch'eran con lui parevan sì contenti,
   come a nessun toccasse altro la mente.
Noi eravam tutti fissi e attenti
   alle sue note; ed ecco il veglio onesto
   gridando: 'Che è ciò, spiriti lenti?   120
qual negligenza, quale stare è questo?
   Correte al monte a spogliarvi lo scoglio
   ch'esser non lascia a voi Dio manifesto.'
Come quando, cogliendo biada o loglio,
   li colombi adunati alla pastura,
   queti, sanza mostrar l'usato orgoglio,
se cosa appare ond'elli abbian paura,
   subitamente lasciano star l'esca,
   perch'assaliti son da maggior cura;
così vid' io quella masnada fresca   130
   lasciar lo canto, e gire inver la costa,
   com' uom che va, nè sa dove rïesca:
nè la nostra partita fu men tosta.

And I: 'If a new law does not take from thee memory or practice of the songs of love which used to quiet all my longings, may it please thee to refresh my soul with them for a while, which is so spent coming here with my body.'

Love that discourses to me in my mind[7] he began then, so sweetly that the sweetness sounds within me still. My Master and I and these people who were with him seemed as content as if nothing else touched the mind of any. We were all rapt and attentive to his notes, when lo, the venerable old man, crying: 'What is this, laggard spirits? What negligence, what delay is this? Haste to the mountain to strip you of the slough that allows not God to be manifest to you.'

As when doves collected at their feeding, picking up wheat or tares, quiet, without their usual show of pride, if something appears that frightens them suddenly leave their food lying, because they are assailed with a greater care; so I saw that new troop leave the song and go towards the slope, like those who go they know not where; nor was our departure in less haste.

See Inf. Canto II where D+F are comp. to descending doves

39

1. The sun passes from the hemisphere whose centre is Jerusalem to that of Purgatory, the two hemispheres being regarded as having a common horizon; midnight is passing over the Ganges with the constellation of the Scales, which night loses in winter when it becomes longer than day; it is dawn in Purgatory.

2. 'When Israel went out of Egypt' (*Ps.* cxiv. 1).

3. The constellation fading from the zenith.

4. Sign of good news.

5. A Florentine musician of Dante's day who died before 1300.

6. In the Papal Jubliee Year, from Christmas of 1299, plenary indulgence was granted to pilgrims.

7. An early poem of Dante's.

NOTE

The elaborately astronomical way of telling the time with which the canto opens is more than a piece of medieval pedantry; it is an introduction to Dante's first representation of the redeemed life, showing the world surrounded by the heavens and marking the newness, the strangeness, the separation from old conditions 'there where I was', with the sun, the light of God, rising on it. The mood of wonder still holds as in the first canto, with the approach of the angel in the gathering dawn, first the mysterious light in the distance, then his near splendour, his power, his swiftness, his silence; and the newness of life for the redeemed shows in their eagerness and their bewilderment.

The general contrast between Hell and Purgatory is wrought out in many correspondences. The ship of souls coming over the ocean is plainly meant to contrast with the ferry on Acheron (*Inf.* iii), the shining angel-pilot with Charon, 'with eyes of burning coal', the chanting of the psalm of redemption by the redeemed with the howling blasphemies of Charon's passengers; and as the monsters in Hell are the embodiments of the sins, holding the souls there captive, so the angels are the agents of grace, working out the souls' deliverance. This angel brings the boat with no aid from the souls in it, 'scorning human instruments' and using only his own wings; souls do not save themselves, they are saved by grace. We are reminded here of the other silent angel at the gate of Dis (*Inf.* ix).

In a letter to Can Grande Dante gave the mystical interpretation of these first words of the psalm, 'When Israel went out of Egypt', as 'the departure of the sanctified soul from the bondage of this corruption to the liberty of eternal glory'. 'The psalm had been from the sixth century in use in the Western Church in the last offices for the dying and in the burial of the dead' (*E. H. Plumptre*), and the song of the mourners is continued as the song of the redeemed; what was in the old life a longing of faith is here a fulfilled deliverance. 'All that is written after of that psalm' is occupied with God's liberation of His people, and the angel as it were completes and verifies it with 'the sign of Holy Cross'. All through Purgatory its disciplines are accompanied with the prayers and praises of the Church, the old liturgies used now with a new depth and integrity of meaning. The Tiber mouth from which the boat has sailed is, of course, the port of Rome; the souls come from the bosom of the Church and are still singing its songs when they land in Purgatory. We shall find more of the Church's fellowship in the next canto.

We are reminded again that Virgil does not know his way in Purgatory as he did in Hell, for he cannot direct the new-comers. For reason itself the way of the soul's penitence and aspiration is a continual revelation and discovery, to be known only by the following of it in the light of the sun and in the fellowship of the redeemed.

The insubstantial nature of the visible forms of these disembodied spirits, which here takes Dante by surprise, is not maintained with entire consistency throughout the poem, but the general idea seems to be that the soul's 'airy shape' is 'more substantial in proportion to its proximity to the centre of the universe (which is also the centre of sin) and more ethereal as it rises above the earth's surface' (*C. H. Grandgent*).

Practically nothing is known of Casella except what is here indicated, that he was a composer of Florence who set some of Dante's verse to music and that he died some time before the supposed date of the vision. Knowing the fact, Dante realizes that Casella's passage to Purgatory has been, for some reason, delayed, and he learns that it was granted in the plenary indulgence given to pilgrims in the Jubilee year by Pope Boniface. That Dante should attach such spiritual authority to the act of such a man as Pope Boniface, as he is known to us in the *Inferno* (xix and xxvii), is a singular evidence of the place held by the Church and the Papacy in his mind.

The meeting of Dante and Casella, with its eager intimacy and its culmination in the song and the company's absorption in it, is the first of many incidents which give a peculiarly human quality to the *Purgatorio* in comparison with the *Inferno* and the *Paradiso*; it has much more of the character of the life we live and know.

Dante's 'song of love' which is sung by Casella must not be taken in the obvious, romantic sense suggested to us by the language of the canto. Whatever it meant originally, it was expounded by Dante himself in the *Convito* as the praise of the Lady Philosophy, following a convention which had precedents in the *Book of Proverbs*, the *Book of Wisdom* and Boethius's *Consolation of Philosophy*. It recalls, therefore, the period of his intense and laborious absorption in the study of scholastic speculation. Not only Dante and the other pilgrims but Virgil himself is seized and held by the song 'as if nothing else touched the mind of any', until they are recalled to their business by Cato's rebuke. The incident tells of Dante's delight, which is otherwise known to us, in music and in the philosophy of which he sang; but it tells too that life is more than speculation, that reason itself may forget its function, that the psalm of redemption means more than this song of love, that God becomes manifest to the soul not by its listening to a song, but by its climbing of a mountain.

PURGATORIO

Avvegna che la subitana fuga
   dispergesse color per la campagna,
   rivolti al monte ove ragion ne fruga,
i' mi ristrinsi alla fida compagna:
   e come sare' io sanza lui corso?
   chi m'avrìa tratto su per la montagna?
El mi parea da sè stesso rimorso:
   o dignitosa coscïenza e netta,
   come t'è picciol fallo amaro morso!
Quando li piedi suoi lasciar la fretta,   10
   che l'onestade ad ogn'atto dismaga,
   la mente mia, che prima era ristretta,
lo 'ntento rallargò, sì come vaga,
   e diedi 'l viso mio incontro al poggio
   che 'nverso il ciel più alto si dislaga.
Lo sol, che dietro fiammeggiava roggio,
   rotto m'era dinanzi, alla figura
   ch'avea in me de' suoi raggi l'appoggio.
Io mi volsi da lato con paura
   d'essere abbandonato, quand' io vidi   20
   solo dinanzi a me la terra oscura;
e 'l mio conforto 'Perchè pur diffidi?'
   a dir mi cominciò tutto rivolto:
   'non credi tu me teco e ch' io ti guidi?
Vespero è già colà dov'è sepolto
   lo corpo dentro al quale io facea ombra:
   Napoli l' ha, e da Brandizio è tolto.
Ora, se innanzi a me nulla s'aombra,
   non ti maravigliar più che de' cieli
   che l' uno all'altro raggio non ingombra.   30

44

CANTO III

Dante's shadow; the Contumacious; Manfred

W H I L E the sudden flight scattered them through the plain, turned to the mountain where reason searches us, I drew close to my faithful comrade. And how should I have sped without him? Who would have brought me up the mountain? He seemed to me smitten with self-reproach. O pure and noble conscience, how bitter a sting to thee is a little fault!

When his feet ceased from the haste that mars the dignity of every action, my mind, till then restrained, took in its eagerness a wider range and I set my face to the hill that rises highest heavenward from the sea. The sun, which was flaming red behind, was broken before me in the shape it made by its rays resting on me. I turned to my side, fearing that I was abandoned when I saw the ground darkened before me only; and my comfort, turning quite round, began to speak to me: 'Why art thou still distrustful? Believest thou not that I am with thee and guide thee? It is evening now in the place where the body is buried within which I cast a shadow; Naples holds it and it was taken from Brindisi.[1] If there is now no shadow before me do not marvel more than at the heavens, that one does not obstruct a ray from another.[2] The

A sofferir tormenti e caldi e geli
   simili corpi la Virtù dispone
   che, come fa, non vuol ch'a noi si sveli.
Matto è chi spera che nostra ragione
   possa trascorrer la infinita via
   che tiene una sustanza in tre persone.
State contenti, umana gente, al *quia*;
   chè se possuto aveste veder tutto,
   mestier non era parturir Maria;
e disïar vedeste sanza frutto   40
   tai che sarebbe lor disio quetato,
   ch'etternalmente è dato lor per lutto:
io dico d'Aristotile e di Plato
   e di molt'altri'; e qui chinò la fronte,
   e più non disse, e rimase turbato.
Noi divenimmo intanto a piè del monte:
   quivi trovammo la roccia sì erta,
   che 'ndarno vi sarìen le gambe pronte.
Tra Lerice e Turbìa, la più diserta,
   la più rotta ruina è una scala,   50
   verso di quella, agevole e aperta.
'Or chi sa da qual man la costa cala'
   disse 'l maestro mio, fermando il passo,
   'sì che possa salir chi va sanz'ala?'
E mentre ch'e' tenendo il viso basso
   essaminava del cammin la mente,
   e io mirava suso intorno al sasso,
da man sinistra m'apparì una gente
   d'anime, che movìeno i piè ver noi,
   e non parea, sì venìan lente.   60
'Leva,' diss' io 'maestro, li occhi tuoi:
   ecco di qua chi ne darà consiglio,
   se tu da te medesmo aver nol puoi.'
Guardò allora, e con libero piglio
   rispuose: 'Andiamo in là, ch'ei vegnon piano;
   e tu ferma la spene, dolce figlio.'
Ancora era quel popol di lontano,
   i' dico dopo i nostri mille passi,
   quanto un buon gittator trarrìa con mano,

Power fits such bodies as these to suffer torments
of heat and frost which wills not that the way of its
working should be revealed to us. Foolish is he
who hopes that our reason can trace the infinite
ways taken by one Substance in three Persons.
Rest content, race of men, with the *quia*;[3] for if
you had been able to see all there was no need for
Mary to give birth, and you have seen the fruitless
desire of men such that their desire would have
been set at rest which is given them for an eternal
grief—I speak of Aristotle and of Plato and of many
others.' And here he bent down his brow and said
no more and remained disquieted.

We came meanwhile to the foot of the mountain.
There we found the cliff so steep that the nimblest
legs would have been useless on it; the wildest and
most broken scree between Lerici and Turbia,[4]
compared with it, is an easy and open stairway.

'Now who knows on which hand the hill slopes,'
said my Master, staying his steps, 'so that one
going without wings may climb?'

And while he held his face down and pon-
dered in his mind on the way and I was gazing
up round the rock, there appeared to me on the left
a company of souls who were moving their steps
towards us and not seeming to approach, they came
so slowly.

'Lift thine eyes, Master,' I said 'see there those
who will give us counsel, if thou canst not find it
in thyself.'

He looked then and with an air of relief replied:
'Let us go that way, for they come slowly, and
thou, dear son, be steadfast in thy hope.'

These people were still at a distance—I mean
after we had gone a thousand paces—as far as a

quando si strinser tutti ai duri massi   70
     dell'alta ripa, e stetter fermi e stretti
     com'a guardar, chi va dubbiando, stassi.
'O ben finiti, o già spiriti eletti,'
     Virgilio incominciò 'per quella pace
     ch' i' credo che per voi tutti s'aspetti,
ditene dove la montagna giace
     sì che possibil sia l'andare in suso;
     chè perder tempo a chi più sa più spiace.'
Come le pecorelle escon del chiuso
     a una, a due, a tre, e l'altre stanno   80
     timidette atterrando l'occhio e 'l muso;
e ciò che fa la prima, e l'altre fanno,
     addossandosi a lei, s'ella s'arresta,
     semplici e quete, e lo 'mperchè non sanno;
sì vid' io muovere a venir la testa
     di quella mandra fortunata allotta,
     pudica in faccia e nell'andare onesta.
Come color dinanzi vider rotta
     la luce in terra dal mio destro canto,
     sì che l'ombra era da me alla grotta,   90
restaro, e trasser sè in dietro alquanto,
     e tutti li altri che venìeno appresso,
     non sappiendo il perchè, fenno altrettanto.
'Sanza vostra domanda io vi confesso
     che questo è corpo uman che voi vedete;
     per che il lume del sole in terra è fesso.
Non vi maravigliate; ma credete
     che non sanza virtù che da ciel vegna
     cerchi di soverchiar questa parete.'
Così 'l maestro; e quella gente degna   100
     'Tornate,' disse 'intrate innanzi dunque',
     coi dossi delle man faccendo insegna.
E un di loro incominciò: 'Chiunque
     tu se', così andando volgi il viso:
     pon mente se di là mi vedesti unque.'
Io mi volsi ver lui e guardail fiso:
     biondo era e bello e di gentile aspetto,
     ma l'un de' cigli un colpo avea diviso.

good slinger's hand would carry, when they all
pressed up to the solid walls of the lofty bank and
stood still and close together, as men stop to look
who are in doubt.

'O ye who have made a good end, spirits already
elect,' Virgil began 'by that peace which, I believe,
awaits you all, tell us where the mountain slopes
so that it is possible to go up; for loss of time most
grieves him that knows best.'

As the sheep come forth from the fold by one
and two and three and the rest stand timid, bending
eyes and muzzle to the ground, and what the first
does the rest do, pressing up behind it if it stops,
simple and quiet, and do not know why; so I saw
start then to come forward the leaders of that
fortunate flock, modest in looks and dignified in
bearing. As soon as those in front saw the light
broken on the ground on my right side so that
the shadow lay from me to the cliff they stopped
and drew back a space, and all the rest that came
behind, not knowing why, did the same.

'Without your asking I declare to you that this
is a human body you see, by which the sun's light
is divided on the ground. Do not marvel, but
believe that not without power which comes from
Heaven he seeks to scale this wall.' Thus the
Master; and that well-deserving company said:
'Turn back then and go on before us', signalling
to us with the back of their hands.

And one of them began: 'Whoever thou art, turn
thy face as thou goest; consider if ever thou hast
seen me yonder.'

I turned to him and looked at him attentively.
He was fair-haired and beautiful and of noble

Quand' i' mi fui umilmente disdetto
   d'averlo visto mai, el disse: 'Or vedi';   110
   e mostrommi una piaga a sommo 'l petto.
Poi sorridendo disse: 'Io son Manfredi,
   nepote di Costanza imperadrice;
   ond' io ti priego che quando tu riedi,
vadi a mia bella figlia, genitrice
   dell'onor di Cicilia e d'Aragona,
   e dichi il vero a lei, s'altro si dice.
Poscia ch' io ebbi rotta la persona
   di due punte mortali, io mi rendei,
   piangendo, a quei che volontier perdona.   120
Orribil furon li peccati miei;
   ma la bontà infinita ha sì gran braccia,
   che prende ciò che si rivolge a lei.
Se 'l pastor di Cosenza, che alla caccia
   di me fu messo per Clemente allora,
   avesse in Dio ben letta questa faccia,
l'ossa del corpo mio sarìeno ancora
   in co del ponte presso a Benevento,
   sotto la guardia della grave mora.
Or le bagna la pioggia e move il vento   130
   di fuor dal regno, quasi lungo il Verde,
   dov'e' le trasmutò a lume spento.
Per lor maladizion sì non si perde
   che non possa tornar l'etterno amore,
   mentre che la speranza ha fior del verde.
Vero è che quale in contumacia more
   di Santa Chiesa, ancor ch'al fin si penta,
   star li convien da questa ripa in fore,
per ogni tempo ch'elli è stato, trenta,
   in sua presunzïon, se tal decreto   140
   più corto per buon prieghi non diventa.
Vedi oggimai se tu mi puoi far lieto,
   revelando alla mia buona Costanza
   come m' hai visto, e anche esto divieto;
chè qui per quei di là molto s'avanza.'

presence, but a blow had cloven one of his eye-
brows. When I had humbly disclaimed ever to have
seen him, 'Look now!' he said, and showed me a
wound high on his breast; then said, smiling: 'I
am Manfred, grandson of the Empress Constance.[5]
Therefore I beg of thee that when thou returnest
thou go to my fair daughter, mother of the pride
of Sicily and of Aragon,[6] and tell her the truth if
another tale is told. After I had my body cleft by
two mortal strokes I gave myself up with tears to
Him who freely pardons; horrible were my sins,
but the infinite goodness has arms so wide that it
receives whoever turns to it. If Cosenza's pastor,
who was sent then by Clement to hunt me down,
had rightly read that page in God,[7] my body's
bones would still be at the bridge-head by Bene-
vento beneath the shelter of the heavy cairn. Now
the rain washes them and the wind drives them,
beyond the Kingdom, near Verde's banks, where
he carried them with lights extinguished. By their
curse none is so lost that the eternal love cannot
return while hope keeps any of it green. It is true
that one who dies in contumacy of Holy Church,
even if he repent at the last, must stay thirty years on
this bank outside for every year he has spent in his
presumption, if that sentence is not made shorter
by holy prayers. See now if thou canst gladden me
by making known to my good Constance how thou
hast seen me, as well as this exclusion; for much is
gained here through those yonder.'

1. Virgil died at Brindisi and Augustus removed his body to Naples.

2. The heavens were supposed to consist of concentric and transparent spheres containing the planets and the fixed stars.

3. Medieval Latin for *that*—the fact, without the reason.

4. The east and west limits of the Italian Riviera.

5. Natural son of Frederick II (*Inf.* x); King of Sicily and leader of the Ghibellines; excommunicated as an enemy of the Church, defeated and killed in battle against the French and Papal forces at Benevento in 1266; his body was afterwards disinterred and cast out of the Church's lands by order of Pope Clement IV.

6. Constance, mother of the Kings of Sicily and Aragon.

7. 'Him that cometh unto me I will in no wise cast out' (*John* vi. 37).

NOTE

The poets, having arrived in Purgatory on the east side, have the sun behind them when Dante 'sets his face to the hill', and when they go to meet the crowd of souls on their left his shadow falls on his right, so that, with the low morning sun, it 'lay from me to the cliff'. Dante is habitually careful in such points of verisimilitude.

Here for the first time, only now being in the sunshine, he is conscious of his shadow and perplexed by the absence of Virgil's, and the penitents, in their turn, are amazed at his. Such passages illustrate the dualism of flesh and spirit which has an important place in the *Purgatorio*, the flesh imposing its own limited standards of reality on the soul, obstructing the light of the sun and setting the pull of gravity against the soul's aspiration. It is a dualism which is not to be resolved in theory, only in experience.

Here as before we have Virgil's acknowledged insufficiency along with Dante's ardent loyalty to him. Virgil himself declares the limitations of reason and is at first completely at a loss, finding no guidance by 'pondering in his mind on the way', until he is directed by the penitents. In this need penitence is wiser than reason, and reason is then most reasonable when it looks beyond itself. The soul's life is experience, a given thing —a *quia*, in the language of scholasticism—to be known only in living, in the last resort as unsearchable as God. But Virgil is not only reason, he is the Empire, reason realized, the ordered, social, moral life of men, and just here, where Virgil comes short and knows his limits, Dante says of him: 'How should I have sped without him? Who would have brought me up the mountain?'

The sheep-like, little-experienced flock of souls which they meet is described with convincing intimacy by the poet who had watched the sheep in their pens as he passed on many a hillside. They are still timid and uncertain of their way, 'as if subdued to the new mystery' (*E. G. Parodi*), each of them ready to follow his neighbour, 'not knowing why'; but they are saved souls, moving always to the right, the way of the sun, though it is very slowly, and they stop in sudden perplexity when they see Virgil and Dante coming the other way. These souls on the lowest slopes of Purgatory have been contumacious to the Church in their earthly life and have died under its ban; they have been deprived of its appointed fellowship and discipline and are poorer for the loss and slower to enter on their effectual purgation. It is only in fellowship, such fellowship as the Church means, that their salvation can be made good, and they must first learn their lessons in it.

But, with all his profound and fundamental reverence for the Church, Dante maintains throughout that the soul's destiny lies in the soul itself, not in any ecclesiastical pronouncement on it. Here he 'would clearly show the difference of God's judgement from that of man. The first soul in Hell was the canonized pope-hermit, whom the world extolled as a perfect type of Christian renunciation and who died in the odour of sanctity (*Inf.* iii); the first soul of the repentant is the king who died excommunicate and whose name was tainted with suspicion of incest and parricide' (*E. G. Gardner*).

Manfred, who died in Dante's infancy, was, in his lifetime and in popular legend after his early death, the typical hero of the Ghibelline cause in Italy; grandson of the great Empress and son of the greater Emperor, handsome, accomplished, wanton, worldly, regardless of the Church and its claims and unscrupulous, but gallant, courteous, debonair, a good soldier and a good prince, idolized by his troops and his subjects. What ground Dante had for his account of Manfred's last-hour repentance we do not know; but he would know many of Manfred's contemporaries and doubtless some of his friends, whose reports would inform him of much that is now lost to us, and he presents us here with a singularly winning and memorable figure, as if from some medieval romance. Manfred will not detain him on his journey but bids him speak as he goes; he smiles as he shows his wounds and speaks without rancour of the Church's old rancour against him; and now, with the humbleness of a saint and the tenderness of a father, he asks Dante to procure for him his daughter's prayers, which may have been restrained by the thought that he was in Hell. For that fellowship which is the Church has no barrier in death, but is one fellowship still.

PURGATORIO

QUANDO per dilettanze o ver. per doglie
   che alcuna virtù nostra comprenda
   l'anima bene ad essa si raccoglie,
par ch'a nulla potenza più intenda;
   e questo è contra quello error che crede
   ch' un'anima sovr'altra in noi s'accenda.
E però, quando s'ode cosa o vede
   che tegna forte a sè l'anima volta,
   vassene il tempo e l' uom non se n'avvede;
ch'altra potenza è quella che l'ascolta,   10
   e altra è quella c' ha l'anima intera:
   questa è quasi legata, e quella è sciolta.
Di ciò ebb' io esperïenza vera,
   udendo quello spirto e ammirando;
   chè ben cinquanta gradi salito era
lo sole, e io non m'era accorto, quando
   venimmo ove quell'anime ad una
   gridaro a noi: 'Qui è vostro dimando.'
Maggiore aperta molte volte impruna
   con una forcatella di sue spine   20
   l'uom della villa quando l'uva imbruna,
che non era la calla onde salìne
   lo duca mio, ed io appresso, soli,
   come da noi la schiera si partìne.
Vassi in Sanleo e discendesi in Noli,
   montasi su Bismantova in cacume
   con esso i piè; ma qui convien ch'om voli;
dico con l'ale snelle e con le piume
   del gran disio, di retro a quel condotto
   che speranza mi dava e facea lume.   30

CANTO IV

The ascent; the sun's course; Belacqua; the Lethargic

WHEN by pleasures or pains which one of our faculties receives the soul concentrates wholly on that, it seems to give heed to no other of its powers, and this is contrary to the error which maintains that one soul is kindled above another in us;[1] and therefore when a thing is heard or seen that keeps the soul strongly bent on it the time passes and one is not aware, for the faculty that listens for it is one and that which holds the entire soul another, this as it were bound, the other free.[2] Of this I had actual experience, hearing that spirit and marvelling, for the sun had climbed full fifty degrees[3] and I had not noted it, when we came to where these souls cried to us all together: 'Here is what you want.'

A larger opening many a time the peasant hedges up with a forkful of his thorns when the grapes are darkening than was the passage by which my Leader, and I after him, climbed by ourselves when the troop parted from us. One goes to San Leo and one descends to Noli and mounts to the summit of Bismantova with feet alone, but here there was need to fly—with the swift wings and plumage, I mean, of great desire, following that guidance which gave me hope and made light for me. We

57

Noi salivam per entro il sasso rotto,
  e d'ogni lato ne stringea lo stremo,
  e piedi e man volea il suol di sotto.
Poi che noi fummo in su l'orlo supremo
  dell'alta ripa, alla scoperta piaggia,
  'Maestro mio,' diss' io 'che via faremo?'
Ed elli a me: 'Nessun tuo passo caggia:
  pur su al monte dietro a me acquista,
  fin che n'appaia alcuna scorta saggia.'
Lo sommo er'alto che vincea la vista,   40
  e la costa superba più assai
  che da mezzo quadrante a centro lista.
Io era lasso, quando cominciai:
  'O dolce padre, volgiti, e rimira
  com' io rimango sol, se non restai.'
'Figliuol mio,' disse 'infin quivi ti tira',
  additandomi un balzo poco in sue
  che da quel lato il poggio tutto gira.
Sì mi spronaron le parole sue,
  ch' i' mi sforzai carpando appresso lui,   50
  tanto che il cinghio sotto i piè mi fue.
A seder ci ponemmo ivi ambedui
  volti a levante ond'eravam saliti,
  che suole a riguardar giovare altrui.
Li occhi prima drizzai ai bassi liti;
  poscia li alzai al sole, ed ammirava
  che da sinistra n'eravam feriti.
Ben s'avvide il poeta ch' ïo stava
  stupido tutto al carro della luce,
  ove tra noi e Aquilone intrava.   60
Ond'elli a me: 'Se Castore e Polluce
  fossero in compagnia di quello specchio
  che su e giù del suo lume conduce,
tu vedresti il Zodïaco rubecchio
  ancora all'Orse più stretto rotare,
  se non uscisse fuor del cammin vecchio.
Come ciò sia, se 'l vuoi poter pensare,
  dentro raccolto, imagina Sïòn
  con questo monte in su la terra stare

climbed within the cloven rock, and the surface on each side pressed close on us and the ground beneath required both hands and feet.

When we were at the upper edge of the high bank, on the open hillside, 'My Master,' I said 'which way shall we take?'

And he said to me: 'Do not fall back a step; still make thy way up the mountain behind me till some wise guide appear for us.'

The summit was so high that it went beyond sight and the slope was far steeper than the line from mid-quadrant to centre. I was weary when I began: 'O sweet father, turn and see how I am left alone unless thou stay.'

'My son,' he said 'drag thyself up as far as there', pointing me to a level a little above, which went all round the hill on that side. His words so spurred me that I forced myself, clambering after him, till the ledge was beneath my feet. There we both sat down, facing the east whence we had climbed, for often it helps us to look that way.[4] First I bent my eyes on the shores below, then lifted them to the sun and marvelled that we were struck by it on the left.[5]

The Poet noted well that I was all amazed at the chariot of the light where it was passing between us and the north, so that he said to me: 'If Castor and Pollux were in company with that mirror which brings its light upwards and downwards thou shouldst see the glowing zodiac wheel still closer to the Bears, unless it left its ancient track.[6] If thou wouldst conceive how this may be, concentrate thy mind and picture Sion and this mountain so placed on the earth that they have one horizon

sì, ch'amendue hanno un solo orizzòn   70
  e diversi emisperi; onde la strada
  che mal non seppe carreggiar Fetòn
vedrai come a costui convien che vada
  dall' un, quando a colui dall'altro fianco,
  se lo 'ntelletto tuo ben chiaro bada.'
'Certo, maestro mio,' diss' io 'unquanco
  non vid' io chiaro sì com' io discerno
  là dove mio ingegno parea manco,
che 'l mezzo cerchio del moto superno,
  che si chiama Equatore in alcun'arte,   80
  e che sempre riman tra 'l sole e 'l verno,
per la ragion che di', quinci si parte
  verso settentrïon, quando li Ebrei
  vedevan lui verso la calda parte.
Ma se a te piace, volontier saprei
  quanto avemo ad andar; chè 'l poggio sale
  più che salir non posson li occhi miei.'
Ed elli a me: 'Questa montagna è tale,
  che sempre al cominciar di sotto è grave;
  e quant' uom più va su, e men fa male.   90
Però, quand'ella ti parrà soave
  tanto, che su andar ti fia leggero
  com'a seconda giù andar per nave,
allor sarai al fin d'esto sentero:
  quivi di riposar l'affanno aspetta.
  Più non rispondo, e questo so per vero.'
E com'elli ebbe sua parola detta,
  una voce di presso sonò: 'Forse
  che di sedere in pria avrai distretta!'
Al suon di lei ciascun di noi si torse,   100
  e vedemmo a mancina un gran petrone,
  del qual nè io nè ei prima s'accorse.
Là ci traemmo; ed ivi eran persone
  che si stavano all'ombra dietro al sasso
  come l' uom per negghienza a star si pone.
E un di lor, che mi sembiava lasso,
  sedeva e abbracciava le ginocchia,
  tenendo il viso giù tra esse basso.

in common and different hemispheres; then thou shalt see how the highway on which Phaeton, to his hurt, failed to drive must needs pass this mountain on the one side and that on the other, if thou give thy mind to it carefully.'[7]

'Truly, my Master,' I said 'never did I see so clearly as I now discern, where my wit seemed lacking, that the mid-circle of the celestial motion, which in a certain science is called the Equator and which lies always between the sun and winter, is, for the reason thou namest, as far northward from here as the Hebrews saw it toward the torrid parts.[8] But, if it please thee, I would fain learn how far we have to go, for the hill rises farther than my eyes can climb.'

And he said to me: 'This mountain is such that it is always hard at the start below and the higher one goes it is less toilsome; therefore when it will seem to thee so pleasant that going up will be as easy for thee as going downstream in a boat, then thou shalt be at the end of this path; there look to rest thy weariness. I have no more to answer, and this I know for truth.'

And as soon as he had spoken these words a voice sounded close by: 'Perhaps before that thou wilt have need of a seat.'

At the sound of it both of us turned round, and we saw on our left a great boulder which neither he nor I had noticed before. We went over to it, and there were people there resting in the shade behind the rock as men settle to rest through indolence, and one of them, who seemed to me weary, sat clasping his knees and holding his face low down between them.

'O dolce segnor mio,' diss' io 'adocchia
  colui che mostra sè più negligente   110
  che se pigrizia fosse sua serocchia.'
Allor si volse a noi e puose mente,
  movendo il viso pur su per la coscia,
  e disse: 'Or va tu su, che se' valente!'
Conobbi allor chi era, e quella angoscia
  che m'avacciava un poco ancor la lena,
  non m' impedì l'andare a lui; e poscia
ch'a lui fu' giunto, alzò la testa a pena,
  dicendo: 'Hai ben veduto come il sole
  dall'omero sinistro il carro mena?'   120
Li atti suoi pigri e le corte parole
  mosson le labbra mie un poco a riso;
  poi cominciai: 'Belacqua, a me non dole
di te omai; ma dimmi, perchè assiso
  quiritta se'? attendi tu iscorta,
  o pur lo modo usato t' ha' ripriso?'
Ed elli: 'O frate, l'andar su che porta?
  chè non mi lascerebbe ire a' martiri
  l'angel di Dio che siede in su la porta.
Prima convien che tanto il ciel m'aggiri   130
  di fuor da essa, quanto fece in vita,
  perch' io indugiai al fine i buon sospiri,
se orazïone in prima non m'aita
  che surga su di cuor che in grazia viva:
  l'altra che val, che 'n ciel non è udita?'
E già il poeta innanzi mi saliva,
  e dicea: 'Vienne omai: vedi ch'è tocco
  meridïan dal sole ed alla riva
cuopre la notte già col piè Morrocco.'

'O my dear Lord,' I said 'cast thine eye on him there who shows himself more indolent than if sloth were his sister.'

Then he turned and took note of us, just moving his face over his thigh, and said: 'Go thou up then who art sturdy.'

I knew then who it was, and the fatigue which still quickened my breath a little did not hinder my going to him; and when I reached him he scarcely raised his head, saying: 'Hast thou quite made out how the sun drives his car past thy left shoulder?'

His lazy movements and curt speech moved my lips a little to a smile, then I began: 'Belacqua,[9] I am not grieved for thee henceforth. But tell me, why art thou seated here? Dost thou wait for escort, or hast thou only resumed the old ways?'

And he said: 'O brother, what is the use of going up, for God's angel that sits in the gateway would not let me pass to the torments?[10] The heavens must first wheel about me, waiting outside, as long as in my lifetime, because I put off good sighs to the last, unless prayer first helps me which rises from a heart that lives in grace. What avails the other that is not heard in Heaven?'

And now the Poet was climbing before me and saying: 'Come now; see, the meridian is touched by the sun and already on the shore night sets its foot on Morocco.'[11]

PURGATORIO

1. The theory of plurality of souls was ascribed to Plato.

2. When a sight or sound occupies the soul, the faculty that listens for the time is out of action, 'free'.

3. About 9.20 a.m.

4. Revelation is from the east. 'The glory of the God of Israel came from the way of the east' (*Ezek.* xliii. 2).

5. Looking east in the southern hemisphere they had the sun north, and left, of them.

6. The sun, 'mirror' of the divine light, directs its course in summer north, and in winter south, of the equator; if it were now in conjunction with the Twins—if it were summer—its 'glow' in the Zodiac would be still farther north.

7. Jerusalem (Sion) and Purgatory being antipodal to each other on the northern and southern hemispheres, the sun's apparent course passes between them.

8. The sun's course is always on the other side of the celestial Equator from winter; it was seen by Dante as far north from Purgatory as it was seen south from Jerusalem by the ancient Hebrews.

9. Said to have been a musical instrument maker of Florence with whom Dante was familiar.

10. Cp. *Purg.* ix.

11. When it was noon in Purgatory it would be dusk at Morocco on the Atlantic.

NOTE

Dante was a child of the Scholastics, learned and absorbed in their tremendous attempt to construct by an intellectual process a consistent scheme of the universe of seen and unseen realities. It was, broadly, a process of deducing the actual system of things from first principles, philosophical and theological, and from Scripture and Aristotle. But what Bagehot said of Shakespeare was as true of Dante, that he had 'an experiencing nature', and it is notably characteristic of him that the current doctrines of psychology and astronomy, of the strange working of the soul and its faculties and of the sun's course through the sky, are alike verified in personal experience. How true to life was the forgetfulness of time of which he speaks appears in various passages of his first biography, by Boccaccio: 'If some thought that had pleased him well should come upon him when in company, howsoever he should be questioned about aught he would answer his questioner never a word until he had either accepted or rejected this his imagination. And many times this chanced to him as he sat at table, or was journeying with companions, or elsewhere, too, when questioned' (*P. H. Wicksteed, The Early Lives of Dante*).

He makes his first ascent in Purgatory to a place 'out on the open hillside' and higher still where he has a greater sky and a wider prospect, and there his new orientation to the sun is emphasized and elaborated and he has a new sense of the vast order of the heavens encompassing and enlightening the life of men. It is in this context that Virgil is twice named in his loftiest character as 'the Poet'.

It was the same 'experiencing nature' that watched and curiously noted the operation of his own faculties, that saw in passing the thrifty farmer protect his vineyard by stopping a gap in his hedge, and that set down with such ease and certainty the sluggish ways and mocking wit of his old friend. It is with something almost of self-banter with regard to his own astronomical expansions that he drops suddenly from them to the business in hand: 'But, if it please thee, I would fain learn how far we have to go', and then reports Belacqua: 'Hast thou quite made out how the sun drives his car past thy left shoulder?', for the business in hand is more urgent than all else.

The figure of Belacqua is in extreme contrast with that of Manfred; but he too has been negligent of grace, not in contumacy but in sloth, and having delayed his repentance must delay his purgation.

In another way Belacqua, hugging his knees and scarcely lifting his head, is contrasted with Dante himself, panting from the climb, eager to know all that may be known, called away in haste by his Master. But it belongs to the genial atmosphere of Purgatory, the prevalence in it of grace, that there breaks through Dante's gravity a smile at Belacqua's 'old ways' and that he tells of Belacqua's longing, beneath all his lethargy and indifference and banter, for what the fellowship of the saints on earth may do to liberate his soul.

It is partly to emphasize the disabling indolence of Belacqua and his company that the steepness and length of the ascent are so insisted on in the same canto. Twice we are told that the summit is out of sight and Dante is urged, beyond his conscious strength, to keep climbing after Virgil, and that although Virgil knows only that the way is upward and himself looks for better guidance. The man who goes farthest, it has been said, is the man who does not know where he is going. Meantime Dante has Virgil's assurance on the steep and incalculable way, 'always hard at the start below', that 'the higher one goes it is less toilsome.' The common physical experience gives its own reality to support the moral experience.

PURGATORIO

Io era già da quell'ombre partito,
  e seguitava l'orme del mio duca,
  quando di retro a me, drizzando il dito,
una gridò: 'Ve' che non par che luca
  lo raggio da sinistra a quel di sotto,
  e come vivo par che si conduca!'
Li occhi rivolsi al suon di questo motto,
  e vidile guardar per maraviglia
  pur me, pur me, e 'l lume ch'era rotto.
'Perchè l'animo tuo tanto s' impiglia'   10
  disse 'l maestro 'che l'andare allenti?
  che ti fa ciò che quivi si pispiglia?
Vien dietro a me, e lascia dir le genti:
  sta come torre ferma, che non crolla
  già mai la cima per soffiar de' venti;
chè sempre l' uomo in cui pensier rampolla
  sovra pensier, da sè dilunga il segno,
  perchè la foga l' un dell'altro insolla.'
Che potea io ridir, se non 'Io vegno'?
  Dissilo, alquanto del color consperso   20
  che fa l'uom di perdon tal volta degno.
E 'ntanto per la costa di traverso
  venivan genti innanzi a noi un poco,
  cantando 'Miserere' a verso a verso.
Quando s'accorser ch' i' non dava loco
  per lo mio corpo al trapassar de' raggi,
  mutar lor canto in un 'Oh!' lungo e roco;
e due di loro, in forma di messaggi,
  corsero incontr'a noi e dimandarne:
  'Di vostra condizion fatene saggi.'   30

CANTO V

*The Penitents of the last hour; Jacopo del
Cassero; Buonconte da Montefeltro; La Pia*

I HAD already parted from those shades and was
following in the steps of my Leader when one
behind me, pointing his finger, cried: 'See, the
rays do not seem to shine on the left of him below[1]
and he seems to bear himself like one alive.'

I turned my eyes at the sound of these words
and saw that they kept looking in amazement at
me and at the light that was broken.

'Why is thy mind so entangled' said the Master
'that thou slackenest thy pace? What is it to thee
what they whisper there? Come after me and let
the people talk. Stand like a firm tower that never
shakes its top for blast of wind; for always the
man in whom thought springs up over thought sets
his mark farther off, for the one thought saps the
force of the other.'

What could I answer but 'I come'? I said it,
suffused somewhat with the colour that sometimes
makes a man deserving of pardon.

And meanwhile people were coming across the
slope a little in front of us, singing the *Miserere*
line by line.[2] When they perceived that I did not
give passage to the rays through my body they
changed their song to an 'Oh!' long-drawn and
hoarse, and two of them as messengers ran to meet
us and asked us: 'Let us know of your condition.'

(cb. Joyce)

69

E 'l mio maestro: 'Voi potete andarne
 e ritrarre a color che vi mandaro
 che 'l corpo di costui è vera carne.
Se per veder la sua ombra restaro,
 com' io avviso, assai è lor risposto:
 faccianli onore, ed esser può lor caro.'
Vapori accesi non vid' io sì tosto
 di prima notte mai fender sereno,
 nè, sol calando, nuvole d'agosto,
che color non tornasser suso in meno;   40
 e, giunti là, con li altri a noi dier volta
 come schiera che scorre sanza freno.
'Questa gente che preme a noi è molta,
 e vegnonti a pregar,' disse il poeta:
 'però pur va ed in andando ascolta.'
'O anima che vai per esser lieta
 con quelle membra con le quai nascesti,'
 venìan gridando 'un poco il passo queta.
Guarda s'alcun di noi unqua vedesti,
 sì che di lui di là novella porti: 50
 deh, perchè vai? deh, perchè non t'arresti?
Noi fummo tutti già per forza morti,
 e peccatori infino all' ultima ora:
 quivi lume del ciel ne fece accorti,
sì che, pentendo e perdonando, fora
 di vita uscimmo a Dio pacificati,
 che del disio di sè veder n'accora.'
E io: 'Perchè ne' vostri visi guati,
 non riconosco alcun; ma s'a voi piace
 cosa ch' io possa, spiriti ben nati,   60
voi dite, e io farò per quella pace
 che dietro a' piedi di sì fatta guida
 di mondo in mondo cercar mi si face.'
E uno incominciò: 'Ciascun si fida
 del beneficio tuo sanza giurarlo,
 pur che 'l voler nonpossa non ricida.
Ond' io, che solo innanzi alli altri parlo,
 ti priego, se mai vedi quel paese
 che siede tra Romagna e quel di Carlo,

66

And my Master said: 'You may go back and report to those who sent you that this man's body is true flesh; if they stopped for seeing his shadow, as I suppose, they have sufficient answer. Let them do him honour and it may profit them.'

Never saw I kindled vapours cleave the clear sky at nightfall or sunset clouds in August³ so swiftly as these returned above and, when they reached the rest, wheeled back with them to us like a troop running with loose rein.

'These people that press on us are many and they come to petition thee,' said the Poet 'but go right on and listen as thou goest.'

'O soul that goest for thy bliss with those members with which thou wast born,' they came crying 'stay thy steps for a little; look if thou hast ever seen any of us, that thou mayst carry news of him yonder. Ah, why dost thou go on? Why dost thou not stop? We were all slain some time by violence and were sinners up to the last hour.——Then light from Heaven gave us understanding, so that, repenting and forgiving, we came forth from life at peace with God, who with desire to see Him pierces our heart.'

And I replied: 'However I gaze in your faces I do not recognize any; but if in anything I can please you, spirits born for bliss, by that peace which makes me seek it from world to world in the steps of such a guide, I will do it.'

And one began: 'Each of us trusts in thy good offices without thine oath, provided lack of power do not thwart the will; therefore, speaking alone before the rest, I beg of thee, if ever thou see the land that lies between Romagna and that of Charles,

che tu mi sia de' tuoi prieghi cortese   70
    in Fano, sì che ben per me s'adori
    pur ch' i' possa purgar le gravi offese.
Quindi fu' io; ma li profondi fori
    ond' uscì 'l sangue in sul quale io sedea,
    fatti mi fuoro in grembo alli Antenori,
là dov' io più sicuro esser credea:
    quel da Esti il fè far, che m'avea in ira
    assai più là che dritto non volea.
Ma s' io fosse fuggito inver la Mira,
    quando fu' sovragiunto ad Orïaco,   80
    ancor sarei di là ove si spira.
Corsi al palude, e le cannucce e 'l braco
    m' impigliar sì, ch' i' caddi; e lì vid' io
    delle mie vene farsi in terra laco.'
Poi disse un altro: 'Deh, se quel disio
    si compia che ti tragge all'alto monte,
    con buona pïetate aiuta il mio!
Io fui da Montefeltro, io son Bonconte:
    Giovanna o altri non ha di me cura;
    per ch' io vo tra costor con bassa fronte.'   90
E io a lui: 'Qual forza o qual ventura
    ti travïò sì fuor di Campaldino,
    che non si seppe mai tua sepultura?'
'Oh!' rispuos'elli 'a piè del Casentino
    traversa un'acqua c' ha nome l'Archiano,
    che sovra l'Ermo nasce in Apennino.
Là 've 'l vocabol suo diventa vano,
    arriva' io forato nella gola,
    fuggendo a piede e 'nsanguinando il piano.
Quivi perdei la vista e la parola;   100
    nel nome di Maria fini', e quivi
    caddi e rimase la mia carne sola.
Io dirò vero e tu 'l ridì tra' vivi:
    l'angel di Dio mi prese, e quel d' inferno
    gridava: "O tu del ciel, perchè mi privi?
Tu te ne porti di costui l'etterno
    per una lacrimetta che 'l mi toglie;
    ma io farò dell'altro altro governo!"

that thou do me the courtesy to beg them in Fano that good prayers be made for me, only that I may purge away my grievous sins.[4] From thence I sprang, but the deep wounds from which poured the blood in which I had my life were given me in the midst of the sons of Antenor, where I thought to be most secure. He of Este had it done, who was incensed against me far more than justice warranted; but had I made my flight towards La Mira when I was overtaken at Oriaco I should still be yonder where men breathe. I ran to the marsh, and the reeds and the mire so entangled me that I fell, and there I saw form on the ground a pool from my veins.'

Then another spoke: 'Pray, so may that desire be satisfied which draws thee to the high mountain, do thou with gracious pity help mine. I was of Montefeltro; I am Buonconte.[5] Neither Giovanna nor any other has care for me, so that I go among these with downcast brow.'

And I said to him: 'What force or what chance took thee so far from Campaldino that thy burial-place was never known?'

'Ah,' he replied 'at the foot of the Casentino a stream crosses called the Archiano which rises above the Hermitage in the Apennines. To the place where its name is lost I came, wounded in the throat, flying on foot, and bloodying the plain. There I lost sight and speech. I ended on the name of Mary and there fell and only my flesh remained. I will tell the truth and do thou tell it again among the living. God's angel took me, and he from Hell cried: "O thou from Heaven, why dost thou rob me? Thou carriest off with thee this man's eternal part for a little tear that takes him from me. But with the other I will deal in other fashion."

Ben sai come nell'aere si raccoglie
   quell'umido vapor che in acqua riede,   110
   tosto che sale dove 'l freddo il coglie.
Giunse quel mal voler che pur mal chiede
   con lo 'ntelletto, e mosse il fummo e 'l vento
   per la virtù che sua natura diede.
Indi la valle, come 'l dì fu spento,
   da Pratomagno al gran giogo coperse
   di nebbia; e 'l ciel di sopra fece intento,
sì che 'l pregno aere in acqua si converse:
   la pioggia cadde ed a' fossati venne
   di lei ciò che la terra non sofferse;   120
e come ai rivi grandi si convenne,
   ver lo fiume real tanto veloce
   si ruinò, che nulla la ritenne.
Lo corpo mio gelato in su la foce
   trovò l'Archian rubesto; e quel sospinse
   nell'Arno, e sciolse al mio petto la croce
ch' i' fe' di me quando 'l dolor mi vinse:
   voltommi per le ripe e per lo fondo;
   poi di sua preda mi coperse e cinse.'
'Deh, quando tu sarai tornato al mondo,   130
   e riposato della lunga via,'
   seguitò il terzo spirito al secondo
'ricorditi di me che son la Pia:
   Siena mi fè; disfecemi Maremma:
   salsi colui che 'nnanellata pria
disposando m'avea con la sua gemma.'

'Thou knowest well how there ga
the moist vapour which changes to v
soon as it rises where the cold conden.
evil will which seeks only evil he joi
intellect and by the power his nature ε
stirred the mists and the winds;[6] then, whe.
was spent, he covered the valley from Pratoma
to the great range with cloud and so charged t.
sky overhead that the pregnant air was turned to
water. The rain fell and that which the ground
refused came to the gullies and gathering in great
torrents poured headlong to the royal river[7] with
such speed that nothing stayed its course. The
raging Archiano found my frozen body near its
mouth and swept it into the Arno and loosed on
my breast the cross I made of myself when pain
overcame me. It rolled me along the banks and
over the bottom, then covered and swathed me with
its spoils.'

'Pray, when thou hast returned to the world and
art rested from the long way,' the third spirit
followed on the second 'do thou remember me,
who am La Pia.[8] Siena gave me birth, Maremma
death. He knows of it who, first plighting troth,
wedded me with his gem.'

1. They are now facing the hill westward, with the sun on their right.

2. *Ps.* li sung responsively; 'Have mercy upon me, O God.'

3. Meteors and summer lightning were both ascribed to 'kindled vapours'.

4. Jacopo del Cassero, a noble of Fano, between Romagna and the Kingdom of Naples, quarrelled, when Governor of Bologna, with the Marquis of Este, Lord of Ferrara, who had him murdered between Venice and Padua in 1298. The Paduans are called 'the sons of Antenor' because Antenor, the betrayer of Troy, was said to have founded Padua, and perhaps to suggest that they were implicated in the murder.

5. Buonconte, son of Count Guido da Montefeltro (*Inf.* xxvii), led the Ghibellines when they were routed by the Florentine Guelfs at Campaldino in 1289 and died on the field. Giovanna was his wife.

6. Evil spirits were supposed to raise storms; 'according to the course of this world, according to the prince of the power of the air' (*Eph.* ii. 2).

7. The Arno; a river reaching the sea was called 'royal'.

8. La Pia's story is obscure, but she is supposed to have belonged to a leading family of Siena and to have been imprisoned by her husband in the Maremma and murdered by his orders in 1295, that he might marry again.

NOTE

Dante's main subject in this part of the *Purgatorio* is the soul's loss and disablement by delay in repentance, and the canto begins with his own momentary distraction from the way of penitence and a rebuke from Virgil which seems disproportioned to his fault. Here in Purgatory Virgil shows a new strictness and urgency as the soul's calling and course become more plain, and already Dante had noted of him, 'How bitter a sting to thee is a little fault!' Dante could not but be a conspicuous figure in any company and he could not but be conscious of the fact; he knew the entanglement of mind and motive that comes from preoccupation with men's looks and talk. Virgil has only a short answer to the wonder of the souls at Dante's shadow; if they are to speak to him he must 'listen as he goes', for it is only a practising pentitent that has any help for penitents.

These 'sinners'—that is, impenitent,—'up to the last hour' have an eagerness and speed which are in sharp and intentional contrast with the lethargy of Belacqua's company. It is as if in their lifetime they had been of the kind that could not stop in their worldly course till, of a sudden, they were 'given understanding' under the challenge of despair, so that each, like Browning's Guido, might 'see, one instant, and be saved'. Their words and behaviour show 'a union of devoutness and distress, of patient resignation and restless longing, plainly answering to the special condition of those who had come to their present state of expectancy and prayer from the raging storm of the passions, issuing bloody from the midst of personal revenges, bitter party strifes, hatreds fatal to family peace, overwhelmed in the whirlwind of violence of which they seem still to feel the final outrage' (*L. Rocca, L.D.*).

Each of the three representatives of the company here had

died forlorn and lonely and their deaths were matter of public note and recent memory: Cassero, hunted down by hired bravos in the reedy bog,—Buonconte, unhorsed and flying alone from the battle, caught in the great storm among the hills and falling helpless in the dark beside the raging Archiano, —and La Pia, meeting her death, we do not know how, in the dreary, malarious jungle of the Maremma. Into their last loneliness and agony Dante's brooding, questing imagination follows each of them and conceives what may have been the issue for their souls.

In the battle of Campaldino, fought in the hill-country of the upper Arno, Dante himself, in his twenty-fourth year, took part among the Florentines, and he would know well the record and reputation of the Ghibelline leader in the field against them and the current reports of his flight and disappearance in the storm of the same evening. Like Manfred in the last canto, Buonconte is the saved son of a lost father—for there is no heredity in destiny—and his story is set in deliberate and significant contrast with that of his father, Count Guido of Montefeltro, which was told at length by Guido himself in the bolgia of the false counsellors (*Inf.* xxvii). He, 'the Fox', had thought to secure himself for eternity by the Franciscan cord and the Pope's absolution and a sham repentance, and at the last the 'black cherub' had snatched him from the hands of St Francis. Buonconte, with none of his father's prudent reckonings and with no priestly shriving nor anything else but 'light from Heaven', his arms crossed on his breast, the name of Mary on his lips, and 'a little tear', is claimed and held by God's angel from the devil who works his will on the mere 'other part' of him. Every circumstance of desolation and terror is employed to show that no earthly conditions can ever avail to determine for good or for evil the issues of life, and the devil's fury wreaked on the helpless flesh is only the demonstration of his futility.

The pathetic reticence, the courtesy and gentleness of La Pia's lines make her a very touching figure. 'Her words are so delicate that they seem to be rather sighed than said, and they accompany as with music the utterance of that poor and gentle name' (*B. Croce*). Writing probably within twenty years of her

death, Dante may have had reasons not known to us for putting
La Pia among the penitents of the last hour.

All three appeal to Dante for the help of his prayers or for
the prayers of their friends, prayers, that is, for their admission
to active purgation. They have, as it were, lost their earthly
years; now their chief care is to make good the loss.

PURGATORIO

QUANDO si parte il gioco della zara,
   colui che perde si riman dolente,
   repetendo le volte, e tristo impara:
con l'altro se ne va tutta la gente;
   qual va dinanzi, e qual di dietro il prende,
   e qual da lato li si reca a mente:
el non s'arresta, e questo e quello intende;
   a cui porge la man più non fa pressa;
   e così dalla calca si difende.
Tal era io in quella turba spessa,   10
   volgendo a loro, e qua e là, la faccia,
   e promettendo mi sciogliea da essa.
Quiv'era l'Aretin che dalle braccia
   fiere di Ghin di Tacco ebbe la morte,
   e l'altro ch' annegò correndo in caccia.
Quivi pregava con le mani sporte
   Federigo Novello, e quel da Pisa
   che fè parer lo buon Marzucco forte.
Vidi Conte Orso e l'anima divisa
   dal corpo suo per astio e per inveggia,   20
   com'e' dicea, non per colpa commisa;
Pier dalla Broccia dico, e qui proveggia,
   mentr'è di qua, la donna di Brabante,
   sì che però non sia di peggior greggia.
Come libero fui da tutte quante
   quell'ombre che pregar pur ch'altri prieghi,
   sì che s'avacci lor divenir sante,
io cominciai: 'El par che tu mi nieghi,
   o luce mia, espresso in alcun testo
   che decreto del cielo orazion pieghi;   30

CANTO VI

The power of intercession; Sordello; the disorders
of Italy and Florence

WHEN the game of hazard breaks up the loser is left disconsolate, going over his throws again, and sadly learns his lesson; with the other all the people go off; one goes in front, one seizes him from behind, another at his side recalls himself to his memory; he does not stop, but listens to this one and that one; each to whom he reaches his hand presses on him no longer and so he saves himself from the throng. Such was I in that dense crowd, turning my face to them this way and that, and by promising I got free from them. There was the Aretine who met his death at the fierce hands of Ghino di Tacco, and the other who was drowned flying in the rout; there Federico Novello was beseeching with outstretched hands, and he of Pisa who made the good Marzucco show his fortitude. I saw Count Orso, and the soul severed from its body through spite and envy, so it said, and not for crime committed—Pierre de la Brosse, I mean; and let the Lady of Brabant look to it, while she is here, that she be not of a worse flock for this.[1]

As soon as I was free of all those shades, whose one prayer was that others pray so that they might come sooner to their holiness, I began: 'It seems to me, O my light, that thou deniest expressly in one passage that prayer bends the decree of heaven,[2]

e questa gente prega pur di questo:
    sarebbe dunque loro speme vana,
    o non m'è 'l detto tuo ben manifesto?'
Ed elli a me: 'La mia scrittura è piana;
    e la speranza di costor non falla,
    se ben si guarda con la mente sana;
chè cima di giudicio non s'avvalla
    perchè foco d'amor compia in un punto
    ciò che de' sodisfar chi qui si stalla;
e là dov' io fermai cotesto punto,   40
    non s'ammendava, per pregar, difetto,
    perchè 'l priego da Dio era disgiunto.
Veramente a così alto sospetto
    non ti fermar, se quella nol ti dice
    che lume fia tra 'l vero e lo 'ntelletto:
non so se 'ntendi; io dico di Beatrice:
    tu la vedrai di sopra, in su la vetta
    di questo monte, ridere e felice.'
E io: 'Segnore, andiamo a maggior fretta,
    chè già non m'affatico come dianzi,   50
    e vedi omai che 'l poggio l'ombra getta.'
'Noi anderem con questo giorno innanzi'
    rispuose 'quanto più potremo omai;
    ma 'l fatto è d'altra forma che non stanzi.
Prima che sie là su, tornar vedrai
    colui che già si cuopre della costa,
    sì che' suoi raggi tu romper non fai.
Ma vedi là un'anima che posta
    sola soletta inverso noi riguarda:
    quella ne 'nsegnerà la via più tosta.'   60
Venimmo a lei: o anima lombarda,
    come ti stavi altera e disdegnosa
    e nel mover delli occhi onesta e tarda!
Ella non ci dicea alcuna cosa,
    ma lasciavane gir, solo sguardando
    a guisa di leon quando si posa.
Pur Virgilio si trasse a lei, pregando
    che ne mostrasse la miglior salita;
    e quella non rispuose al suo dimando,

and for this alone these people pray. Will their hope, then, be vain, or are thy words not rightly clear to me?'

And he said to me: 'My writing is plain and the hope of these souls is not mistaken, if thou consider well with sound judgement; for the height of justice is not lowered because the fire of love fulfils in a moment the satisfaction due from each who sojourns here, and in the place where I set down that point defect was not made good by prayer because the prayer had no access to God. Nevertheless, in so deep a question do not take thy stand unless she tell thee of it who shall be light between the truth and the intellect,—I know not if thou understandest, I speak of Beatrice; thou shalt see her above on the summit of this mountain, smiling and in bliss.'

And I said: 'My Lord, let us make more haste, for now I do not weary as before, and see how the hill now casts its shadow.'

'We will go forward with this day's light' he replied 'as much farther as now we may, but the fact is quite other than thou thinkest; before thou art there above thou shalt see him return that is now hidden by the slope so that thou dost not break his beams. But see there a soul seated by himself apart who is looking towards us; he will point out to us the speediest way.'

We came to him. O Lombard soul, how lofty and disdainful was thy bearing and what dignity in the slow moving of thine eyes! He said nothing to us and was letting us pass, only watching us like a couching lion; but Virgil went up to him, asking him to show us the best ascent, and he did not

ma di nostro paese e della vita   70
    c' inchiese; e 'l dolce duca incominciava:
    'Mantova . . .', e l'ombra, tutta in sè romita,
surse ver lui del loco ove pria stava,
    dicendo: 'O Mantovano, io son Sordello
    della tua terra!'; e l' un l'altro abbracciava.
Ahi serva Italia, di dolore ostello,
    nave sanza nocchiere in gran tempesta,
    non donna di provincie, ma bordello!
Quell'anima gentil fu così presta,
    sol per lo dolce suon della sua terra,   80
    di fare al cittadin suo quivi festa;
e ora in te non stanno sanza guerra
    li vivi tuoi, e l' un l' altro si rode
    di quei ch' un muro ed una fossa serra.
Cerca, misera, intorno dalle prode
    le tue marine, e poi ti guarda in seno,
    s'alcuna parte in te di pace gode.
Che val perchè ti racconciasse il freno
    Iustinïano se la sella è vota?
    Sanz'esso fora la vergogna meno.   90
Ahi gente che dovresti esser devota,
    e lasciar seder Cesare in la sella,
    se bene intendi ciò che Dio ti nota,
guarda come esta fiera è fatta fella
    per non esser corretta dalli sproni,
    poi che ponesti mano alla predella.
O Alberto tedesco ch'abbandoni
    costei ch'è fatta indomita e selvaggia,
    e dovresti inforcar li suoi arcioni,
giusto giudicio dalle stelle caggia   100
    sovra 'l tuo sangue, e sia novo e aperto,
    tal che 'l tuo successor temenza n'aggia!
Ch'avete tu e 'l tuo padre sofferto,
    per cupidigia di costà distretti,
    che 'l giardin dello 'mperio sia diserto.
Vieni a veder Montecchi e Cappelletti,
    Monaldi e Filippeschi, uom sanza cura:
    color già tristi, e questi con sospetti!

reply to his question but enquired of our country and condition. And the gentle Leader began: 'Mantua—'; and the shade, who had been all rapt within himself, sprang towards him from the place where he was, saying: 'O Mantuan, I am Sordello of thy city.'³ And the one embraced the other.

Ah, Italy enslaved, hostel of misery, ship without pilot in great tempest, no princess among the provinces but a brothel! So eager was that noble soul, only for the dear name of his city, to give welcome there to its citizen, and now in thee thy living are never free from war and of those whom one wall and moat shut in one gnaws at the other. Search, wretched one, round the shores of thy seas, then look within thy bosom, if any part of thee rejoice in peace. What avails that Justinian refitted the reins on thee if the saddle is empty?⁴ Without that the shame were less.

Ah, ye that should be devout⁵ and let Caesar sit in the saddle if you gave good heed to God's direction to you, see how this beast has turned vicious for lack of correction by the spurs since you laid hold of the bridle.

O German Albert,⁶ who abandonest her that is become untamed and savage and shouldst bestride her saddle-bow, just judgement from the stars fall upon thy blood and be it so strange and manifest that thy successor may have fear of it! For thou and thy father, held back yonder by greed, have suffered the garden of the Empire to be desolate. Come and see Montagues and Capulets, Monaldi and Filippeschi,⁷ those already wretched and these in dread, thou that hast no care. Come, pitiless,

Vien, crudel, vieni, e vedi la pressura
   de' tuoi gentili, e cura lor magagne;   110
   e vedrai Santafior com'è secura!
Vieni a veder la tua Roma che piagne
   vedova sola, e dì e notte chiama:
   'Cesare mio, perchè non m'accompagne?'
Vieni a veder la gente quanto s'ama!
   e se nulla di noi pietà ti move,
   a vergognar ti vien della tua fama.
E se licito m'è, o sommo Giove
   che fosti in terra per noi crucifisso,
   son li giusti occhi tuoi rivolti altrove?   120
O è preparazion che nell'abisso
   del tuo consiglio fai per alcun bene
   in tutto dell'accorger nostro scisso?
Chè le città d' Italia tutte piene
   son di tiranni, e un Marcel diventa
   ogni villan che parteggiando viene.
Fiorenza mia, ben puoi esser contenta
   di questa digression che non ti tocca,
   mercè del popol tuo che sì argomenta.
Molti han giustizia in cuore, e tardi scocca   130
   per non venir sanza consiglio all'arco;
   ma il popol tuo l'ha in sommo della bocca.
Molti rifiutan lo comune incarco;
   ma il popol tuo sollicito risponde
   sanza chiamare, e grida: 'I' mi sobbarco!'
Or ti fa lieta, chè tu hai ben onde:
   tu ricca, tu con pace, e tu con senno!
   S' io dico ver, l'effetto nol nasconde.
Atene e Lacedemona, che fenno
   l'antiche leggi e furon sì civili,   140
   fecero al viver bene un picciol cenno
verso di te che fai tanto sottili
   provedimenti, ch'a mezzo novembre
   non giugne quel che tu d'ottobre fili.
Quante volte, del tempo che rimembre,
   legge, moneta, officio e costume
   hai tu mutato e rinovate membre!

come and see the distress of thy nobles and heal their hurts, and thou shalt see how safe is Santafiora.[8] Come and see thy Rome, that weeps, widowed and solitary, and cries night and day: 'Caesar, my Lord, why dost thou deny me thy companionship?' Come and see thy people, how they love one another, and, if no pity for us move thee, come for shame of thy repute.

And if it be lawful for me, O Jove[9] supreme who wast crucified on earth for us, are Thy just eyes turned elsewhere, or is it preparation Thou makest in the abyss of Thy counsel for some good quite cut off from our perception? For all the cities of Italy are full of tyrants and every clown that plays the partisan becomes a Marcellus.[10]

My Florence, thou mayst well be at ease with this digression, which does not touch thee, thanks to thy people who are so resourceful. Many have justice at heart, and the arrow is slow to be loosed, for it does not come without consideration to the bow; but thy people have it on the tip of the tongue. Many refuse the common burden; but thy people are eager with their answer without being asked, and cry: 'I take it on.' Count thyself happy then for thou hast good cause, being rich and at peace and wise! If I speak truth the facts do not hide it. Athens and Sparta, which made the ancient laws and were so well ordered, gave little hint of right living beside thee, who makest provisions so fine that the threads thou spinnest in October do not last to mid-November. How many times within thy memory hast thou changed laws, money, offices, customs, and renewed thy members![11] And if thou

E se ben ti ricordi e vedi lume,
   vedrai te somigliante a quella inferma
   che non può trovar posa in su le piume,   150
ma con dar volta suo dolore scherma.

rightly recall thyself to thy sight, thou wilt see thyself like the sick woman that can find no rest on her bed of down but with turning seeks to ease her pain.

1. All six died by violence in Dante's time. An Aretine judge, having condemned a relative of Ghino, nobleman and highwayman, was stabbed by Ghino in open court; 'the other' was drowned in the Arno, perhaps after Campaldino; Novello, of the Conti Guidi, died in battle; 'he of Pisa' was a murdered youth whose father Marzucco, noble turned monk, forgave the murderers; Count Orso was killed by his cousin because of a feud between their fathers, sons of Count Albert (*Inf.* xxxii); de la Brosse, Chamberlain of Philip III of France, was hanged on a false charge, as Dante believed, brought by the Queen, Mary of Brabant.

2. Palinurus, whose body was left unburied, was excluded from the world of the dead and was told by the Sibyl: 'Give up thy hope of bending the decrees of the gods by prayer.'

3. Born near Mantua early in the 13th century; wrote Provençal verse.

4. The Emperor Justinian codified Roman law in the 6th century; now there is no one to enforce it.

5. The clergy, whose interference in civil affairs was a chief source of disorder in Italy; 'God's direction' is: 'Render unto Caesar the things which are Caesar's; and unto God the things that are God's' (*Matt.* xxii. 21).

6. The Emperor Albert of Saxony, like his father the Emperor Rudolph, never came to Italy; his oldest son died in 1307 and he himself was murdered by his nephew in 1308; his successor was Henry VII.

7. Rival families in Verona and Orvieto.

8. The great Ghibelline family of the Aldobrandeschi, Counts of Santafiora, had recently lost much of its land to Siena.

9. It is suggested that Dante supposed *Jove* and *Jehovah* to be the same word.

10. Roman consul and leading opponent of Caesar, who called him 'the talker'; the typical demagogue against the Empire.

11. Reference to the exile and recall of the citizens by the rival parties.

NOTE

The penitents of the last hour are clamorous for the help of
one who has played the game better than they and a part of
whose privilege is intercession, and the question is raised in
Dante's mind of the real, operative force of intercession,
apparently denied by Virgil in his words about Palinurus.
How should his prayers be effectual for these souls? Virgil's
reply describes, on the one hand, intercession as 'the fire of
love', the energy of spiritual fellowship, which 'fulfils in a
moment' the slow work of years in the soul, and he explains,
on the other hand, that the prayer of Palinurus 'had no access
to God', being the prayer of a pagan regarded as beyond the
range of grace. The positive meaning is that intercession is
grace in action, grace current and effectual between living souls;
it is that currency of grace which constitutes the fellowship of
the saints. For the negative, the pagan exclusion from grace,
this is one of various passages which show how heavily it
weighed on Dante's mind, and Virgil's reference of it to
Beatrice shows Dante's refusal, made plain also elsewhere, to
'take his stand in so deep a question'. The whole matter of
prayer, and in particular of intercession, with its inevitable
limitations, is a mystery of grace which only Beatrice can make
finally clear.

At the sound of Beatrice's name, the first mention of it in
the course of his journey, Dante is eager to be at the summit
of the mountain and thinks to reach it that day. It is the
illusion of an impassioned faith, the foreshortening of prophecy,
and he is to learn that the way of sanctification is longer than
he has thought, with its alternation of light and darkness,
striving and rest.

Much scholarly labour has been spent on the problem of the
relation between Dante's Sordello and the Sordello of history

and it is still in some respects obscure. 'The real Sordello was one of those roving Italians who, in the thirteenth century, helped to maintain the waning glory of Provençal verse. . . . He lived the restless and sometimes scandalous life of a handsome adventurer and clever poet at various courts in Lombardy and Piedmont, then in France and Spain, and found at last a mighty protector in the Count of Provence' (*C. H. Grandgent*). Later, in the service of Charles of Anjou in the Kingdom of Naples, he became a man of wealth and dignity, and died in old age, probably in Dante's boyhood, leaving behind him some forty poems in Provençal. So much is to be gathered from the imperfect records of the time, and we are bound to suppose that much more was known to Dante, especially about Sordello's later years in Italy, to justify the singular impressiveness of the figure, rightly called 'michelangelesque' (*F. Novati, L.D.*), which the poets meet with—'seated by himself apart', 'lofty and disdainful', with 'slow-moving eyes', 'watching us like a couching lion'—and to explain his place among the penitents of the last hour. His function in the following canto as the guide of the poets to the Valley of the Princes is plainly due to his most famous poem, a lament for a Provençal baron in which he advised the chief rulers of Europe to eat of his hero's heart so as to gain something of his nobleness and courage.

It is here, as it were in the company and succession of the two poets, the great first singer of the ancient Empire and the recent Italian censor of the rulers of his time, that Dante—now in his own person as narrator and poet and teacher, 'keeping watch for the good of the world' (*De Monarchia*),—takes up the same prophetic task. 'His invective is a historical picture in which, by means of a profound analysis, the political condition of Italy in 1300 lives again in all its aspects: the Papacy usurping the civil power, the Empire now heedless of its fairest part, the people in the cities divided by faction, the feudal Ghibelline nobility falling rapidly into ruin, the communal Guelf democracy grasping at the conquest of government, stand out in vivid delineation, and in the background, as it were a mirror of the rest of Italy, Florence, smitten by its haughty citizen with irony so effective and words so powerful that the reader is drawn on and dominated, without leisure to

examine the terms of judgement and feeling himself constrained
to admiration' (*Casini-Barbi*). There is the bitterness of the
rejected lover in Dante's ironical praise of 'my Florence'. Three
times he speaks to it of 'thy people'; for Florence is far more
and other to him than its passing and perverse generation and
in his heart is 'my Florence' still.

PURGATORIO

POSCIA che l'accoglienze oneste e liete
   furo iterate tre e quattro volte,
   Sordel si trasse, e disse: 'Voi, chi siete?'
'Anzi che a questo monte fosser volte
   l'anime degne di salire a Dio,
   fur l'ossa mie per Ottavian sepolte.
Io son Virgilio; e per null'altro rio
   lo ciel perdei che per non aver fè.'
   Così rispuose allora il duca mio.
Qual è colui che cosa innanzi a sè   10
   subita vede ond' e' si maraviglia,
   che crede e non, dicendo 'Ella è . . . non è . . .',
tal parve quelli; e poi chinò le ciglia,
   e umilmente ritornò ver lui,
   e abbracciòl là 've 'l minor s'appiglia.
'O gloria de' Latin' disse 'per cui
   mostrò ciò che potea la lingua nostra,
   o pregio etterno del loco ond' io fui,
qual merito o qual grazia mi ti mostra?
   S' io son d' udir le tue parole degno,   20
   dimmi se vien d' inferno, e di qual chiostra.'
'Per tutt' i cerchi del dolente regno'
   rispuose lui 'son io di qua venuto:
   virtù del ciel mi mosse, e con lei vegno.
Non per far, ma per non fare ho perduto
   a veder l'alto sol che tu disiri
   e che fu tardi per me conosciuto.
Luogo è là giù non tristo da martìri,
   ma di tenebre solo, ove i lamenti
   non suonan come guai, ma son sospiri.   30

CANTO VII

The greetings of Virgil and Sordello; the Valley of the Princes

AFTER the dignified and joyful greetings had been repeated a third and a fourth time Sordello drew back and said: 'But who are you?'

'Before the souls worthy to ascend to God had turned to this mountain my bones were buried by Octavian;[1] I am Virgil, and for no other fault I lost Heaven but lack of faith.' Thus then replied my Leader.

Like one that sees before him of a sudden a thing he marvels at, who believes and believes not, saying: 'It is, it is not,' such seemed the other; then bent his head and humbly approached him again and embraced him, clasping where the inferior does. 'O glory of the Latins,' he said 'through whom our tongue showed forth its power, O eternal honour of the place from which I come, what deserving or what favour shows thee to me? If I am worthy to hear thy words, tell me if thou comest from Hell, and from what cloister.'

'Through all the circles of the woeful kingdom' he answered him 'I have come hither. Power from Heaven moved me and by its help I come. Not for doing, but for not doing, I have lost the sight of the Sun above for which thou longest and which was known by me too late.[2] There is a place below, sad not with torments but only with darkness, where the laments have no sound of wailing but

95

Quivi sto io coi pargoli innocenti
   dai denti morsi della morte avante
   che fosser dall'umana colpa essenti;
quivi sto io con quei che le tre sante
   virtù non si vestiro, e sanza vizio
   conobber l'altre e seguir tutte quante.
Ma se tu sai e puoi, alcuno indizio
   dà noi per che venir possiam più tosto
   là dove purgatorio ha dritto inizio.'
Rispuose: 'Loco certo non c'è posto;   40
   licito m'è andar suso ed intorno;
   per quanto ir posso, a guida mi t'accosto.
Ma vedi già come dichina il giorno,
   e andar su di notte non si puote;
   però è bon pensar di bel soggiorno.
Anime sono a destra qua remote:
   se mi consenti, io ti merrò ad esse,
   e non sanza diletto ti fier note.'
'Com'è ciò?' fu risposto. 'Chi volesse
   salir di notte, fora elli impedito   50
   d'altrui, o non sarrìa chè non potesse?'
E 'l buon Sordello in terra fregò 'l dito,
   dicendo: 'Vedi, sola questa riga
   non varcheresti dopo il sol partito:
non però ch'altra cosa desse briga
   che la notturna tenebra ad ir suso:
   quella col non poder la voglia intriga.
Ben si porìa con lei tornare in giuso
   e passeggiar la costa intorno errando,
   mentre che l'orizzonte il dì tien chiuso.'   60
Allora il mio segnor, quasi ammirando,
   'Menane' disse 'dunque là 've dici
   ch'aver si può diletto dimorando.'
Poco allungati c'eravam di lici,
   quand' io m'accorsi che 'l monte era scemo,
   a guisa che i vallon li sceman quici.
'Colà' disse quell'ombra 'n'anderemo
   dove la costa face di sè grembo;
   e quivi il novo giorno attenderemo.'

are sighs; there I abide with the little innocents seized by the fangs of death before they were cleared of human guilt,[3] there I abide with those who were not clothed with the three holy virtues but without sin knew the others and followed them every one.[4] But if thou knowest and canst, give us some direction by which we may come more quickly where the true Purgatory begins.'

He answered: 'No fixed place is set for us. I am allowed to go up and round, and as far as I may I shall accompany thee as guide. But see now how the day declines and to go up by night is not possible, so it is well to think of a good resting-place. There are souls on the right here apart; if thou permit me I shall bring thee to them and not without delight they will be known to thee.'

'How is that?' he replied 'he that should wish to climb by night, would he be hindered by another or would he not climb because he could not?'

And the good Sordello drew his finger on the ground, saying: 'See, not even this line shouldst thou cross after the sun is gone, not that anything else hinders the going up but the darkness of night; that baffles the will with helplessness. One might indeed return downward in the dark and go wandering round the hillside while the horizon holds the day shut off.'

Then my Lord, as if wondering, said: 'Lead us, then, where thou sayest we may have pleasure while we stay.'

We had gone a little way on from there when I observed that the mountain-side was hollowed out, as valleys make hollows in the mountains here. 'We will go over there' that shade said 'where the slope makes a lap of itself, and wait there for the new day.'

Tra erto e piano era un sentiero sghembo,   70
   che ne condusse in fianco della lacca,
   là dove più ch'a mezzo muore il lembo.
Oro e argento fine, cocco e biacca,
   indico legno lucido e sereno,
   fresco smeraldo in l'ora che si fiacca,
dall'erba e dalli fior dentr'a quel seno
   posti ciascun sarìa di color vinto,
   come dal suo maggiore è vinto il meno.
Non avea pur natura ivi dipinto,
   ma di soavità di mille odori   80
   vi facea uno incognito e indistinto.
'Salve, Regina' in sul verde e 'n su' fiori
   quindi seder cantando anime vidi,
   che per la valle non parean di fori.
'Prima che 'l poco sole omai s'annidi'
   cominciò il Mantovan che ci avea volti,
   'tra costor non vogliate ch' io vi guidi.
Di questo balzo meglio li atti e' volti
   conoscerete voi di tutti quanti,
   che nella lama giù tra essi accolti.   90
Colui che più siede alto e fa sembianti
   d'aver negletto ciò che far dovea,
   e che non move bocca alli altrui canti,
Rodolfo imperador fu, che potea
   sanar le piaghe c' hanno Italia morta,
   sì che tardi per altro si ricrea.
L'altro che nella vista lui conforta,
   resse la terra dove l'acqua nasce
   che Molta in Albia, e Albia in mar ne porta:
Ottacchero ebbe nome, e nelle fasce   100
   fu meglio assai che Vincislao suo figlio
   barbuto, cui lussuria e ozio pasce.
E quel Nasetto, che stretto a consiglio
   par con colui c' ha sì benigno aspetto,
   morì fuggendo e disfiorando il giglio:
guardate là come si batte il petto!
   L'altro vedete c' ha fatto alla guancia
   della sua palma, sospirando, letto.

There was a winding path, now steep, now level, which brought us to the side of the dell at the point where the bounding ridge falls off to less than half. Gold and finé silver, cochineal and white lead, indigo bright and clear, emerald when it is newly split, every colour would be surpassed by the grass and the flowers growing in that bottom, as the less by the greater. Nor had nature only painted there, but of the sweetness of a thousand odours there it made one, blended and unknown to men. From there I saw, seated on the green turf and the flowers and singing 'Salve Regina',[5] souls that on account of the valley were not seen from outside.

'Before the sun, now shortly sinking, goes to his nest' began the Mantuan who had directed us 'do not ask me to lead you among them there; from this bank you will make out better the movements and features of each than if received among them on the level below. He that sits highest and has the look of having been heedless of his duty and does not move his lips with the singing of the rest, was Rudolph, the Emperor,[6] who might have healed the wounds that have slain Italy, so that it is now too late for another to restore her. The other, who looks as if he comforted him, ruled the land where the waters spring that the Moldau carries to the Elbe and the Elbe to the sea; his name was Ottocar, and in swaddling-bands he was of far more worth than Wenceslaus his son, a bearded man, who battens on wantonness and ease.[7] And he with the small nose, who seems in close counsel with him that is so gracious in his looks, died in flight and deflowering the lily; look there how he beats his breast![8] See the other, who couches

Padre e suocero son del mal di Francia:
   sanno la vita sua viziata e lorda,   110
   e quindi viene il duol che sì li lancia.
Quel che par sì membruto e che s'accorda,
   cantando, con colui dal maschio naso,
   d'ogni valor portò cinta la corda;
e se re dopo lui fosse rimaso
   lo giovanetto che retro a lui siede,
   ben andava il valor di vaso in vaso,
che non si puote dir dell'altre rede;
   Iacomo e Federigo hanno i reami;
   del retaggio miglior nessun possiede.   120
Rade volte risurge per li rami
   l'umana probitate; e questo vole
   quei che la dà, perchè da lui si chiami.
Anche al Nasuto vanno mie parole
   non men ch'all'altro, Pier, che con lui canta,
   onde Puglia e Proenza già si dole.
Tant'è del seme suo minor la pianta,
   quanto più che Beatrice e Margherita,
   Costanza di marito ancor si vanta.
Vedete il re della semplice vita   130
   seder là solo, Arrigo d' Inghilterra:
   questi ha ne' rami suoi migliore uscita.
Quel che più basso tra costor s'atterra,
   guardando in suso, è Guiglielmo Marchese,
   per cui e Alessandria e la sua guerra
fa pianger Monferrato e Canavese.'

his cheek on his hand and sighs. They are the father and the father-in-law of the pest of France;[9] they know his foul and vicious life and from this comes the grief that so pierces them. He that seems so sturdy and sings in time with him of the manly nose wore for his girdle the cord of every virtue,[10] and if the youth who sits behind him had reigned longer after him then indeed his virtue had passed from vessel to vessel, which none can say of the other heirs; James and Frederick have the realms, none holds the better heritage. Rarely does human worth rise through the branches, and this He wills who gives it, that it may be sought from Him. My words concern also the great-nosed one, not less than the other, Peter, who sings with him, so that Apulia and Provence are now in grief; as much is the plant poorer than its seed as Constance yet boasts of her husband more than Beatrice and Margaret of theirs.[11] See the king of the simple life sitting there alone, Henry of England; he has better issue in his branches.[12] He that sits on the ground lowest among them, looking up, is the Marquis William, because of whom Alessandria and its war have brought grief on Monferrato and the Canavese.'[13]

1. Virgil was buried by Augustus in 19 B.C.

2. Christ was known to Virgil only from His visit to Limbo (*Inf.* iv).

3. By baptism.

4. The three 'theological' virtues and the four 'cardinal'.

5. 'Hail, Queen,' a hymn for the last service of the day.

6. Count of Hapsburg, founder of the Austrian imperial line, father of 'German Albert' (Canto vi), reigned from 1272 to 1292

7. Ottocar of Bohemia; his son Wenceslaus was reigning in 1300.

8. Philip III of France, second son of St Louis, suffered a great defeat in 1295, disgracing the fleur-de-lis.

9. Philip IV of France, who transferred the Papacy to Avignon in 1309; often denounced, but never named, by Dante; cp. *Inf.* xix.

10. Peter of Aragon, who defeated and succeeded Charles of Anjou in Sicily; 'Righteousness shall be the girdle of his loins, and faithfulness the girdle of his reins' (*Isa.* xi. 5). With him is Charles of Anjou, brother of St Louis and King of Naples and Sicily, chief champion of the Guelf cause in Italy; defeated and killed Manfred and Beneventum in 1266 (Canto iii).

11. Charles's son is as inferior to him as he (husband first of Beatrice, then of Margaret) is to Peter (husband of Constance).

12. Henry III, father of Edward I.

13. Marquis of Montferrat in North Italy, great Ghibelline leader; Alessandria rose against him and he was captured and imprisoned in an iron cage till his death in 1292; the outrage led to a war of revenge.

NOTE

The life of Purgatory is the Christian life, life under the dispensations of grace and under some of the limitations of the earth; and in approaching a scene so expressly Christian as the Valley of the Princes, where the atmosphere is all of penitence and prayer and spiritual aspiration, it is as it were inevitable that the relations should be defined between Virgil and Sordello, the pagan and the Christian poet. Sordello embraces the greater poet, 'clasping where the inferior does', and yet *here* Virgil must seek Sordello's guidance and learn from him with astonishment the laws of the ascent as something quite strange to him. The daily sunshine is, in symbol, the light of God's face, the only light by which the mountain can be climbed; the interruption of it 'baffles the will with helplessness' and the dark after the daylight belongs to the soul's proof and discipline, requiring it to 'wait for the new day'. It is still 'as if wondering' that Virgil follows Sordello's leading along the hillside to the valley, and throughout the scene there Virgil is silent, except for his few words—these also perplexed—about the three stars, described in the next canto, with which Dante is absorbed. The comparison of pagan and Christian experience is suggested again in Virgil's reference to Limbo, 'where the laments have no sound of wailing but are sighs' and 'without hope they live in desire', in contrast with this scene in the valley, where the sighs of the penitent rulers all turn into prayer and their desire and hope are one. Dante is as sure of the supreme value of the Christian life as he is troubled and burdened by the thought, from which he could not escape, of the pagans who 'without blame' were excluded from it and of the 'little innocents' who had died too soon.

This fourth class of the late-repentant consists of rulers whose preoccupation with their earthly ambitions had long distracted them from greater things. Their old splendour and exclusiveness, which still partly engage them, are represented by the brightness, the fragrance and the seclusion of their flowery valley; but now

> 'The glories of their blood and state
> Are shadows, not substantial things,'

and their deepest longing, always gaining more mastery in them, is uttered in the Church's evening hymn of prayer: 'Hail, Queen, Mother of Mercy, our life, our joy, our hope, hail! We cry to thee, exiled children of Eve. We sigh to thee, groaning and weeping in this vale of tears. . . . Pray for us that we be made worthy of the promises of Christ.'

We cannot tell the reasons for Dante's choice of the eight rulers who are named here as penitents; but the charity of his final judgement of them certainly does not refer either to the character of their rule or to the various party interests which they favoured. All died in Dante's youth and all—except Henry of England, who 'sits alone',—were in one way or another involved in the fierce, entangled and often sordid political struggles of the time. Among them are two pairs of old enemies, now reconciled, the Emperor Rudolph with King Ottocar, 'who by his looks appears to comfort him', and Peter of Aragon with his once fierce and powerful foe, Charles of Anjou, with whom he now 'sings in time'.

Near the end of the canto Dante enlarges on the idea that the 'worth' of a man lies not in his birth but in himself. It is a part of the lesson which these princes, once wholly preoccupied with place and power and valuing themselves on these, are now learning, so that they may be fit for the true Purgatory, the lesson that a king is but a human soul.

In the last lines we are reminded that for all the degeneracy and the warring ambitions of their rulers it is the people that must pay in tears.

PURGATORIO

Era già l'ora che volge il disio
ai navicanti e 'ntenerisce il core
lo dì c' han detto ai dolci amici addio,
e che lo novo peregrin d'amore
punge, s'e' ode squilla di lontano
che paia il giorno pianger che si more,
quand' io incominciai a render vano
l'udire e a mirare una dell'alme
surta che l'ascoltar chiedea con mano.
Ella giunse e levò ambo le palme,   10
ficcando li occhi verso l'orïente,
come dicesse a Dio: 'D'altro non calme.'
'*Te lucis ante*' sì devotamente
le uscìo di bocca e con sì dolci note
che fece me a me uscir di mente;
e l'altre poi dolcemente e devote
seguitar lei per tutto l' inno intero,
avendo li occhi alle superne rote.
Aguzza qui, lettor, ben li occhi al vero,
chè 'l velo è ora ben tanto sottile,   20
certo, che 'l trapassar dentro è leggero.
Io vidi quello essercito gentile
tacito poscia riguardare in sue
quasi aspettando, palido e umile;
e vidi uscir dell'alto e scender giue
due angeli con due spade affocate,
tronche e private delle punte sue.
Verdi come fogliette pur mo nate
erano in veste, che da verdi penne
percosse traean dietro e ventilate.   30

CANTO VIII

The guardian angels; Nino Visconti; the three
stars; the serpent; Conrad Malaspina

It was now the hour that turns back the longing [*homeward*]
of seafarers and melts their heart the day they
have bidden dear friends farewell and pierces the
new traveller with love if he hears in the distance
the bell that seems to mourn the dying day, when
I began to cease hearing his words and to gaze at
one of the souls that had risen and was signing
with his hand to be heard. He joined his palms and
lifted them together, fixing his eyes on the east as
if he said to God: 'For naught else I care.' *'Te lucis*
ante'[1] came from his lips with such devoutness and
with notes so sweet that it drew me out of myself,
and then the rest joined him sweetly and devoutly
through the whole hymn, keeping their eyes on the
celestial wheels.

[*prayer against evil dreams (unconscious sin)*]

Here, reader, sharpen well thine eyes to the
truth, for now, surely, the veil is so fine that to
pass within is easy.

I saw the noble host silent then, looking up as if
in expectancy, pallid and lowly, and I saw come
forth from above and descend two angels with
flaming swords broken short and without their
points. They wore garments green as new-born
leaves, which they trailed behind them, beaten and
fanned by their green wings; one came and took

107

L'un poco sovra noi a star si venne,
 e l'altro scese in l'opposita sponda,
 sì che la gente in mezzo si contenne.
Ben discernea in lor la testa bionda;
 ma nella faccia l'occhio si smarrìa,
 come virtù ch'a troppo si confonda.
'Ambo vegnon del grembo di Maria'
 disse Sordello 'a guardia 'della valle,
 per lo serpente che verrà vie via.'
Ond' io, che non sapeva per qual calle,   40
 mi volsi intorno, e stretto m'accostai,
 tutto gelato, alle fidate spalle.
E Sordello anco: 'Or avvalliamo omai
 tra le grandi ombre, e parleremo ad esse:
 grazïoso fia lor vedervi assai.'
Solo tre passi credo ch' i' scendesse,
 e fui di sotto, e vidi un che mirava
 pur me, come conoscer mi volesse.
Temp'era già che l'aere s'annerava,
 ma non sì che tra li occhi suoi e' miei   50
 non dichiarisse ciò che pria serrava.
Ver me si fece, e io ver lui mi fei:
 Giudice Nin gentil, quanto mi piacque
 quando ti vidi non esser tra' rei!
Nullo bel salutar tra noi si tacque;
 poi dimandò: 'Quant'è che tu venisti
 al piè del monte per le lontane acque?'
'Oh!' diss' io lui 'per entro i luoghi tristi
 venni stamane, e sono in prima vita,
 ancor che l'altra, sì andando, acquisti.'   60
E come fu la mia risposta udita,
 Sordello ed elli in dietro si raccolse
 come gente di subito smarrita.
L' uno a Virgilio e l'altro a un si volse
 che sedea lì, gridando: 'Su, Currado!
 vieni a veder che Dio per grazia volse.'
Poi, volto a me: 'Per quel singular grado
 che tu dei a colui che sì nasconde
 lo suo primo perchè che non li è guado,

his stand a little above us and the other alighted on the opposite bank, so that the company was held between. I plainly discerned their flaxen hair, but in their faces my eyes were dazzled, as a faculty is confounded by excess.

'Both come from Mary's bosom' said Sordello 'to guard the valley, because of the serpents which will come presently.'

I, therefore, not knowing by what path, turned round, all chilled, and pressed close to the trusty shoulders.

And Sordello continued: 'Let us go down now into the valley among the great shades and we shall speak to them; it will give them much pleasure to see you.'

Only three paces, I suppose, I descended, and was below, and I saw one who kept looking at me as if he would recognize me. It was now the time when the air was already darkening, yet not so that it did not make plain between his eyes and mine what it had shut off before. He made towards me and I towards him. Noble Judge Nino,[2] what joy it was to me when I saw thee not to be among the guilty! No fair greeting was unspoken between us; then he asked: 'How long is it since thou camest to the foot of the mountain over the distant waters?'

'Oh,' I said to him 'by way of the woeful regions I came this morning, and I am in the first life, though by going thus I gain the other.'

And when they heard my answer Sordello and he drew back, like men suddenly bewildered. The one turned to Virgil, and the other to one who was seated there, calling: 'Rise, Conrad, come and see what God by His grace has willed'; then, turning to me: 'By that especial gratitude thou owest to Him who hides so deep His primal purpose that

quando sarai di là dalle larghe onde,   70
  dì a Giovanna mia che per me chiami
  là dove alli 'nnocenti si risponde.
Non credo che la sua madre più m'ami
  poscia che trasmutò le bianche bende,
  le quai convien che, misera, ancor brami.
Per lei assai di lieve si comprende
  quanto in femmina foco d'amor dura,
  se l'occhio o 'l tatto spesso non l'accende.
Non le farà sì bella sepultura
  la vipera che 'l Melanese accampa,   80
  com'avrìa fatto il gallo di Gallura.'
Così dicea, segnato della stampa,
  nel suo aspetto, di quel dritto zelo
  che misuratamente in core avvampa.
Li occhi miei ghiotti andavan pur al cielo,
  pur là dove le stelle son più tarde,
  sì come rota più presso allo stelo.
E 'l duca mio: 'Figliuol, che là su guarde?'
  E io a lui: 'A quelle tre facelle
  di che 'l polo di qua tutto quanto arde.'   90
Ond'elli a me: 'Le quattro chiare stelle
  che vedevi staman son di là basse,
  e queste son salite ov'eran quelle.'
Com'ei parlava, e Sordello a sè il trasse
  dicendo: 'Vedi là 'l nostro avversaro';
  e drizzò il dito perchè là guardasse.
Da quella parte onde non ha riparo
  la picciola vallea, era una biscia,
  forse qual diede ad Eva il cibo amaro.
Tra l'erba e' fior venìa la mala striscia,   100
  volgendo ad ora ad or la testa, e 'l dosso
  leccando come bestia che si liscia.
Io non vidi, e però dicer non posso,
  come mosser li astor celestïali;
  ma vidi bene e l'uno e l'altro mosso.
Sentendo fender l'aere alle verdi ali,
  fuggì 'l serpente, e li angeli dier volta,
  suso alle poste rivolando iguali.

there is no fathoming of it, when thou art beyond
the breadth of waters tell my Giovanna to plead for
me there where answer is given to the innocent. I
do not think her mother loves me longer since she
changed the white veil³ which, in her wretchedness,
she must yet long for. By her it is easy indeed to
know how long love's fire endures in woman if
sight and touch do not often kindle it. The viper
which leads the Milanese afield will not make her
so fair a tomb as the cock of Gallura would have
done.' He spoke thus, his face bearing the stamp
of that righteous zeal which burns in due measure
in the heart.

My greedy eyes kept going to the sky just where
the stars are slowest as in a wheel nearest the axle,
and my Leader asked me: 'Son, what art thou
gazing at up there?'

And I answered him: 'At those three torches
with which the pole here is all aflame.'

And he said to me: 'The four bright stars thou
sawest this morning are low down yonder and these
are risen where those were.'

As he spoke, Sordello drew him to himself,
saying: 'See there our adversary', and pointed his
finger for him to look that way. At that part where
the little valley has no rampart was a snake, such,
perhaps, as gave to Eve the bitter food; through
the grass and flowers came the vile streak, turning
its head from time to time and licking its back like
a beast that sleeks itself. I did not see and therefore
cannot tell how the heavenly falcons set out, but
I saw plainly both the one and the other in motion;
hearing the green wings cleave the air the serpent
fled, and the angels wheeled round, flying back
abreast up to their posts.

111

L'ombra che s'era al Giudice raccolta
   quando chiamò, per tutto quello assalto   110
   punto non fu da me guardare sciolta.
'Se la lucerna che ti mena in alto
   truovi nel tuo arbitrio tanta cera,
   quant'è mestiere infino al sommo smalto,'
cominciò ella 'se novella vera
   di Val di Magra o di parte vicina
   sai, dillo a me, che già grande là era.
Fui chiamato Currado Malaspina;
   non son l'antico, ma di lui discesi:
   a' miei portai l'amor che qui raffina.'   120
'Oh!' diss' io lui 'per li vostri paesi
   già mai non fui; ma dove si dimora
   per tutta Europa ch'ei non sien palesi?
La fama che la vostra casa onora
   grida i segnori e grida la contrada,
   sì che ne sa chi non vi fu ancora;
e io vi giuro, s' io di sopra vada,
   che vostra gente onrata non si sfregia
   del pregio della borsa e della spada.
Uso e natura sì la privilegia   130
   che, perchè il capo reo il mondo torca,
   sola va dritta e 'l mal cammin dispregia.'
Ed elli: 'Or va; chè 'l sol non si ricorca
   sette volte nel letto che 'l Montone
   con tutti e quattro i piè cuopre ed inforca,
che cotesta cortese oppinïone
   ti fia chiavata in mezzo della testa
   con maggior chiovi che d'altrui sermone,
se corso di giudicio non s'arresta.'

The shade that had drawn close to the judge when he called had not for an instant, all through that assault, removed his gaze from me. 'So may the lantern that leads thee on high' he began 'find in thy will so much wax as is needful up to the enamelled summit, if thou hast true tidings of Valdimagra or of the parts near it, tell it to me; for there I once was great. I was called Conrad Malaspina,[4] not the old Conrad but descended from him. To my own I bore the love which here is purified.'

'Oh,' I said to him 'I never passed through your lands; but where in all Europe do men dwell that they are not renowned? The fame which honours your house proclaims alike the lords and the country, so that he knows of them who never was there, and I swear to you,[5] as I hope to go above, that your honoured race does not despoil itself of the glory of the purse and of the sword. It is so privileged by nature and by custom that, however the guilty head[6] turn the world awry, it alone goes straight and scorns the evil path.'

And he said: 'It is true; for the sun shall not return seven times to rest in the bed which the Ram covers and bestrides with all four feet[7] before this courteous opinion shall be nailed within thy brain by stronger nails than men's talk, if the course of judgement be not stayed.'

1. A hymn sung at evening prayer.

2. Nino Visconti, grandson of Count Ugolino of Pisa (*Inf.* xxxiii), Judge of Gallura in Sardinia, where he hanged Fra Gomito for barratry (*Inf.* xxii); died in 1296; in 1300 his widow married a Visconti of Milan, whose arms were a viper and Nino's a cock; her second husband was driven from Milan, died, and left her in poverty. Nino's daughter Giovanna was a child of nine in 1300.

3. Widow's weeds.

4. The Malaspini were a distinguished Ghibelline family with estates on the coast of Tuscany.

5. The honorific *you.*

6. The Papacy.

7. The sun is now in the constellation of the Ram. Seven years shall not pass.

NOTE

Of the four classes of the late-repentant,—the contumacious, the lethargic, the headlong, and the preoccupied,—the last, once busy and over-busy in earthly policies, are now represented in the hour of thoughtfulness and recollection, which 'turns back the longing' of the soul to its home and which is described in the opening lines of the canto with singular and moving beauty. The ancient evening hymn *Te lucis ante*, familiar in the English version, 'Before the ending of the day,' which they sing after the *Salve Regina*, is a prayer to the 'Creator of things' for His 'guardian care' against 'dreams and phantoms of the night' and for His 'restraint of our enemy' that he may not 'defile us in the flesh', and it was recommended by Aquinas as an antidote against bad dreams. It is immediately after his account of the singing of the hymn that Dante appeals to his reader to penetrate to the truth under the veil of his lines, and there is recalled to our mind the quite similar appeal in the ninth canto of the *Inferno* at the gate of Dis. There, on the threshold of the true Hell of wilful sin, he was defied by the devils and almost driven to despair and was rescued by 'one sent from Heaven'—by a direct demonstration of grace—from a disablement which lay beyond the range of reason and conscience; and here, near the threshold of the true Purgatory of active cleansing, is another angelic deliverance from evil in a region not under control of the will, the region of dream, and Dante finds as little help in Virgil in the one case as in the other. 'Sin has retreated to its last stronghold' (*J. S. Carroll*). For there are hidden springs of good and evil in the soul—in the unconscious, we should now say—which are, or seem to be, quite beyond our understanding and control and with regard to which, Dante would teach us, the soul's one resource is to wait for God.

The two angels 'come from Mary's bosom', and the serpent was 'such, perhaps, as gave to Eve the bitter food'; for the medievals often associated the powers and working of good and evil, respectively, with the Virgin and Eve, sometimes playing with the reversal of the name *Eva* in Gabriel's first word *Ave* to Mary in Nazareth. Salvation, in these souls, is now working out the reversal of the Fall. The blunted swords of the angels are sufficient to put the serpent to flight, but do not kill it, and their wings and floating garments are green, the colour of hope.

The four stars (Canto i), for the virtues of the active life have now sunk out of sight and in their place appear the three stars which stand for the specifically Christian virtues of the life of contemplation. In the climbing of the mountain by day the soul is practised in the contacts and energies of daily life, and in the intervals of rest and contemplation and in good dreams the soul may

> 'Transcend its wonted themes
> And into glory peep.'

But the time when the active energies are relaxed has its own perils; the serpent winds through the grass and flowers, reaching the imagination through the beauty and delight of life, and it is banished by the sound of the green wings, by present grace and the sure hope that belongs to it.

Of the two rulers with whom Dante converses Nino Visconti was an active and ardent Guelf and Conrad Malaspina belonged to a great Ghibelline family, so little does a man's ultimate worth depend on his party attachments. Nino, who died in 1296, was a visitor to Florence on various occasions during Dante's early life and Dante hails him as an old friend. Six years after the date of the vision, but before this passage was written, Dante was received in his exile as a guest of the Malaspini, and here we have his acknowledgement of their kindness. ' "The old Conrad", brother-in-law of Manfred, had lived in the age which seemed to the Poet to have fulfilled the ideals of chivalric manhood; but the young Conrad boasted himself a branch of that tree, and for not having degenerated from its ancient virtues and for constancy in them this man in his reply will praise the Malaspini who are yet alive' (*E. Dona-doni, L.D.*). Dante can give them no higher praise than to say that they still maintain in their house 'the glory of the purse and of the sword'; for liberality in the use of wealth and prowess in arms were reckoned the highest virtues of the nobility.

In his first reference to the Valley of the Princes Sordello had said to Virgil: 'I shall bring thee to them and not without delight they will be known to thee'; and Virgil's reply was: 'Lead us where thou sayest we may have pleasure while we stay.' In this canto Sordello says to the other two: 'Let us go down now into the valley among the great shades and we shall speak to them; it will give them much pleasure to see you.' It is Dante's way by this reiteration to acknowledge the keen delight he had shared with other poets from time to time in meeting with some of the more cultivated rulers of Italy when he was 'received among them' in their courts, places of refuge from the turbulence and sordidness of the time. Is that company of those who 'once were great' and are now 'looking up as if in expectancy, pallid and lowly', and touched in the gathering dusk with a gentle melancholy and longing as of men at sea hearing across the water their home vesper-bell, a reminiscence of some of Dante's quieter and more intimate hours with his friend Nino and with his hosts in Valdimagra when he learned of the deep nostalgia of the soul that is sometimes found in the splendour of a palace and in the intervals of affairs of state?

PURGATORIO

LA concubina di Titone antico
  già s' imbiancava al balco d'orïente,
  fuor delle braccia del suo dolce amico;
di gemme la sua fronte era lucente,
  poste in figura del freddo animale
  che con la coda percuote la gente;
e la notte de' passi con che sale
  fatti avea due nel loco ov'eravamo,
  e 'l terzo già chinava in giuso l'ale;
quand' io, che meco avea di quel d'Adamo,   10
  vinto dal sonno, in su l'erba inchinai
  là 've già tutti e cinque sedavamo.
Nell'ora che comincia i tristi lai
  la rondinella presso alla mattina,
  forse a memoria de' suo' primi guai,
e che la mente nostra, peregrina
  più dalla carne e men da' pensier presa,
  alle sue visïon quasi è divina,
in sogno mi parea veder sospesa
  un'aguglia nel ciel, con penne d'oro,   20
  con l'ali aperte ed a calare intesa;
ed esser mi parea là dove foro
  abbandonati i suoi da Ganimede,
  quando fu ratto al sommo consistoro.
Fra me pensava: 'Forse questa fiede
  pur qui per uso, e forse d'altro loco
  disdegna di portarne suso in piede.'
Poi mi parea che, poi rotata un poco,
  terribil come folgor discendesse,
  e me rapisse suso infino al foco.   30

CANTO IX

The dream of the eagle; St Lucy; the gate of
Purgatory

THE mistress of old Tithonus, come forth from
her fond lover's arms, was already showing white
on the balcony of the east, her forehead gleaming
with gems set in the form of the cold beast that
strikes men with its tail, and night, in the place
where we were, had made two of her climbing
steps and already the third was folding its wings,[1]
when I, who had with me something of Adam,[2]
lay down, overcome with sleep, on the grass where
all five of us were already seated.

At the hour near morning when the swallow
begins her plaintive songs, in remembrance,
perhaps, of her ancient woes,[3] and when our mind,
more a pilgrim from the flesh and less held by
thoughts, is in its visions almost prophetic, I seemed
to see in a dream an eagle poised in the sky, with
feathers of gold, with open wings, and prepared to
swoop. And I seemed to be in the place where his
own people were left behind by Ganymede when
he was caught up to the supreme conclave;[4] and
I thought within myself,—perhaps it is used to
strike only here and disdains, perhaps, to carry off
any in its claws from elsewhere. Then it seemed
to me that, after wheeling a while, it descended,
terrible as lightning, and caught me up as far as

119

Ivi parea che ella e io ardesse;
   e sì lo 'ncendio imaginato cosse
   che convenne che 'l sonno si rompesse.
Non altrimenti Achille si riscosse,
   li occhi svegliati rivolgendo in giro
   e non sappiendo là dove si fosse,
quando la madre da Chirone a Schiro
   trafuggò lui dormendo in le sue braccia,
   là onde poi li Greci il dipartiro;
che mi scoss' io, sì come dalla faccia   40
   mi fuggì 'l sonno, e diventa' ismorto,
   come fa l'uom che, spaventato, agghiaccia.
Da lato m'era solo il mio conforto,
   e 'l sole er'alto già più che due ore,
   e 'l viso m'era alla marina torto.
'Non aver tema' disse il mio segnore;
   'fatti sicur, chè noi semo a buon punto:
   non stringer, ma rallarga ogni vigore.
Tu se' omai al purgatorio giunto:
   vedi là il balzo che 'l chiude dintorno;   50
   vedi l'entrata là 've par disgiunto.
Dianzi, nell'alba che procede al giorno,
   quando l'anima tua dentro dormìa
   sovra li fiori ond'è là giù adorno,
venne una donna, e disse: "I' son Lucia:
   lasciatemi pigliar costui che dorme;
   sì l'agevolerò per la sua via."
Sordel rimase e l'altre gentil forme:
   ella ti tolse, e come il dì fu chiaro,
   sen venne suso; e io per le sue orme.   60
Qui ti posò, ma pria mi dimostraro
   li occhi suoi belli quella intrata aperta;
   poi ella e 'l sonno ad una se n'andaro.'
A guisa d'uom che 'n dubbio si raccerta,
   e che muta in conforto sua paura,
   poi che la verità li è discoperta,
mi cambia' io; e come sanza cura
   vide me 'l duca mio, su per lo balzo
   si mosse, ed io di retro inver l'altura.

the fire;[5] there it seemed that it and I burned together, and the imagined fire so scorched that perforce my sleep was broken.

Even as Achilles started up, turning his awakened eyes about him and not knowing where he was, when his mother carried him off sleeping in her arms from Chiron to Scyros, whence later the Greeks took him away,[6] so I started, as soon as sleep left my eyes, and turned pale, like one that is chilled with fear. Beside me was my comfort alone, and the sun was already more than two hours high, and my face was turned to the sea.

'Have no fear,' said my Lord 'take confidence, for it is well with us, do not relax but put out all thy strength. Now thou art come to Purgatory. See there the rampart that encloses it about; see the entrance there, where it appears cleft. A little while ago, in the early dawn before day when thy soul was asleep within thee on the flowers that adorn the place below, a lady came, and she said: "I am Lucy.[7] Let me take this man that is sleeping, so I shall speed him on his way." Sordello remained with the other noble souls and she took thee up and as soon as it was clear day went on upwards, and I in her steps. Here she laid thee down; but first her fair eyes showed me that open entrance, then she and sleep together went away.'

Like one who in doubt is reassured and whose fear is turned to confidence when the truth is revealed to him, so I was changed, and as soon as my Leader saw me free from care he moved up by the rampart, and I behind him, towards the height.

Lettor, tu vedi ben com' io innalzo   70
  la mia matera, e però con più arte
  non ti maravigliar s' io la rincalzo.
Noi ci appressammo, ed eravamo in parte,
  che là, dove pareami prima rotto
  pur come un fesso che muro diparte,
vidi una porta, e tre gradi di sotto
  per gire ad essa, di color diversi,
  e un portier ch'ancor non facea motto.
E come l'occhio più e più v'apersi,
  vidil seder sovra 'l grado soprano,   80
  tal nella faccia ch' io non lo soffersi;
e una spada nuda avea in mano,
  che reflettea i raggi sì ver noi,
  ch' io dirizzava spesso il viso in vano.
'Dite costinci: che volete voi?'
  cominciò elli a dire: 'ov'è la scorta?
  guardate che 'l venir su non vi noi.'
'Donna del ciel, di queste cose accorta,'
  rispuose il mio maestro a lui 'pur dianzi
  ne disse: "Andate là: quivi è la porta." '   90
'Ed ella i passi vostri in bene avanzi,'
  ricominciò il cortese portinaio:
  'venite dunque a' nostri gradi innanzi.'
Là ne venimmo; e lo scaglion primaio
  bianco marmo era sì pulito e terso
  ch' io mi specchiai in esso qual io paio.
Era il secondo tinto più che perso,
  d'una petrina ruvida ed arsiccia,
  crepata per lo lungo e per traverso.
Lo terzo, che di sopra s'ammassiccia,   100
  porfido mi parea sì fiammeggiante,
  come sangue che fuor di vena spiccia.
Sovra questo tenea ambo le piante
  l'angel di Dio, sedendo in su la soglia,
  che mi sembiava pietra di diamante.
Per li tre gradi su di buona voglia
  mi trasse il duca mio, dicendo: 'Chiedi
  umilemente che 'l serrame scioglia.'

Thou seest well, reader, that I rise to a higher theme; do not wonder, therefore, if I sustain it with greater art.

We drew near and came to a point from which, where at first there appeared to me merely a gap like a fissure that breaks a wall, I saw a gate, and three steps leading to it from below of different colours, and a warder, who as yet spoke not a word. And as I looked at him more intently I saw that he was seated on the uppermost step, and his face was so bright that I could not bear it, and in his hand he had a naked sword, which so reflected the rays on us that I turned my eyes often upon it in vain.

'Say from there, what would you?' he began. 'Where is the escort? Look that the ascent be not to your hurt.'

'A lady from Heaven with knowledge of these things' my Master answered him 'said to us but now: "Go that way, there is the gate."'

'And may she speed your steps in good!' the courteous warder continued; 'Come forward, then, to our stairs.'

We came on then, and the first step was white marble so smooth and clear that I mirrored myself in it in my true likeness; the second was darkest purple, of rugged and burnt stone split through its length and breadth; the third, resting its mass above, seemed to me porphyry flaming red like blood that spurts from a vein; on this the angel of God rested both his feet, sitting on the threshold which seemed to me of adamant. By the three steps my Leader drew me up with goodwill, saying: 'Ask him humbly to withdraw the bolt.'

123

Divoto mi gittai a' santi piedi:
   misericordia chiesi che m'aprisse,   110
   ma pria nel petto tre fiate mi diedi.
Sette *P* nella fronte mi descrisse
   col punton della spada, e 'Fa che lavi,
   quando se' dentro, queste piaghe' disse.
Cenere o terra che secca si cavi
   d' un color fora col suo vestimento;
   e di sotto da quel trasse due chiavi.
L' una era d'oro e l'altra era d'argento:
   pria con la bianca e poscia con la gialla
   fece alla porta sì ch' i' fu' contento.   120
'Quandunque l'una d'este chiavi falla,
   che non si volga dritta per la toppa,'
   diss'elli a noi 'non s'apre questa calla.
Più cara è l'una; ma l'altra vuol troppa
   d'arte e d' ingegno avanti che diserri,
   perch'ella è quella che nodo digroppa.
Da Pier le tegno; e dissemi ch' i' erri
   anzi ad aprir ch'a tenerla serrata,
   pur che la gente a' piedi mi s'atterri.'
Poi pinse l'uscio alla porta sacrata,   130
   dicendo: 'Intrate; ma facciovi accorti
   che di fuor torna chi 'n dietro si guata.'
E quando fuor ne' cardini distorti
   li spigoli di quella regge sacra,
   che di metallo son sonanti e forti,
non rugghiò sì nè si mostrò sì acra
   Tarpea, come tolto le fu il buono
   Metello, per che poi rimase macra.
Io mi rivolsi attento al primo tuono,
   e '*Te Deum laudamus*' mi parea   140
   udire in voce mista al dolce suono.
Tale imagine a punto mi rendea
   ciò ch' io udiva, qual prender si sòle
   quando a cantar con organi si stea;
ch'or sì or non s' intendon le parole.

Devoutly I threw myself at the holy feet. I asked him of his mercy that he would open to me, but first I smote three times upon my breast.

Seven *P*'s he traced on my brow with the point of the sword and said: 'When thou art within, see thou wash away these wounds.' *(see Manfred in Canto III)*

peccatum = sin ? sins

Ashes, or earth that is dug dry, would be of one colour with his vesture and from beneath it he drew two keys, the one of gold and the other of silver, and he applied first the white and then the yellow to the door so that I was satisfied.

'Whenever one of these keys fails so that it does not turn rightly in the lock' he said to us 'this passage does not open; the one is more precious, but the other requires much skill and wisdom before it will unlock, for it is this that looses the knot. I hold them from Peter and he bade me err rather in opening than in keeping locked, if only the souls prostrate themselves at my feet.' Then he pushed open the door in the hallowed gateway, saying: 'Enter; but I bid you know that he that looks back returns outside.'

And when the pivots of that sacred portal, which were of heavy and resounding metal, turned on the hinges, the Tarpeian roared not so loud nor showed itself so stubborn when the good Metellus was taken from it so that then it was left bare.[8]

I turned away, intent on the first note, and '*Te Deum laudamus*' I seemed to hear in voices mingled with the sweet sound; what I heard gave me the same impression we sometimes get when people are singing with an organ and the words are now distinguished, now lost.

see Augustine on words + music

1. Aurora, dawn, was Tithonus's wife, and Dante makes the moon-dawn his mistress; the moon is near rising in conjunction with the Scorpion, in the third hour of night, about 9 p.m.

2. The body.

3. Philomela, outraged by her sister Procne's husband, was changed to a swallow.

4. Ganymede, when hunting, was caught up by Jove's eagle and became cup-bearer to the gods.

5. A supposed sphere of fire between the earth and the moon.

6. Achilles was brought up by Chiron, the Centaur (*Inf.* xii), carried off and concealed by his mother in Scyros to save him from the Trojan War, discovered by Ulysses and killed in the war.

7. St Lucy (*Inf.* ii).

8. When Caesar took possession of Rome he seized the public treasure kept in a temple on the Tarpeian Rock, Metellus the Tribune making vain resistance.

NOTE

Dante's first dream on Purgatory has the absorbing emotional
reality with the strangeness and unsubstantialness of a dream.
It only *seems*—the word is used four times in these few lines—
and yet it is a true seeming; for Dante held by the ancient
tradition that dreams may be of deep spiritual significance.
'We have a continual experience of our immortality in the
divination of our dreams, and these would not be possible
unless something in us were immortal' (*Convito*).

He had fallen asleep in the valley of the negligent princes, his
mind heavy with thoughts of 'the world awry', the actual Empire
in its failure and decay, and it was in the hour when the swallow
begins her plaintive songs, recalling woeful memories, that in
his dream he was rapt heavenward by the eagle, 'poised in the
sky, with feathers of gold', the symbol of Empire in its
divine idea, a forecast of the heavenly eagle of divine justice
in the *Paradiso*. Ganymede, whose story comes into Dante's
dreaming mind, was a prince of the Trojan, Imperial
race, 'caught up to the supreme conclave'. The terrible
lightning swoop of the eagle and the scorching fire that
broke Dante's sleep indicate the overwhelming character of
such an idea of perfected humanity for a mind used to the
harsh realities of the world. His dream is a flash of prophetic
vision of the Empire of God's intention, of an ordered life for
the world in which 'men should live, on this threshing-floor
of mortality, in freedom and in peace' (*De Monarchia*).

Then, with the mention of Achilles, he comes back from his
dream-rapture to his own weakness and uncertainty and fear,
and to 'his comfort'. As Achilles, the Greek, was carried in his
unconsciousness to the place from which he would set out as
an enemy of Troy—of the Empire—so Dante has been brought
by a power beyond himself to the place of his own committal,

to the threshold of that purgation by which alone a disordered humanity can ever become a divine order, and his vision of the end has prepared him for the beginning. St Lucy— enlightening grace—has brought him to the point of final committal at the gate of the true Purgatory. Hers is a service beyond the power of Virgil, who could only follow 'in her steps' and bid Dante be obedient; reason can never take the place of vision, but reason bids the soul not be disobedient to its heavenly vision. It is with Virgil that St Lucy leaves her instructions for Dante and still, as at the beginning of the journey, reason is but the vicegerent of grace. Virgil, poet of Empire as he is, knows nothing of Dante's dream; that is an inspiration from a height beyond him.

The entire symbolism of the gate represents ideally—and we are here concerned with ideals—the Church's admission of a penitent to the way of salvation. It is in the fellowship and discipline of the Church that men are fitted for the Empire, for the life of citizens, and in preparing men for their earthly citizenship the Church is preparing them too for 'that Rome', beyond the world, 'of which Christ is Roman' (*Purg*. xxxii).

For the elaborate symbolism of the scene at the gateway Dante offers the reader what almost amounts to an apology, explaining that his 'higher theme' demands a 'greater art'. The warder, at first stern, then gracious, is the ideal priesthood; clothed in the colour of ashes, for the true priest is himself a penitent, armed with 'the sword of the Spirit, which is the Word of God' and which flashes back on the penitent the sun's beams, the light of God's law, requiring that the soul approach with due warrant of enlightening grace and with due prostration in penitence, bearing the two keys of the gate, the golden key of divine authority for pardon and the silver key of understanding for the guiding of the penitent and for loosing the knot, the entanglement of sin. There is an obvious and deliberate contrast between the angelic warder and Minos, the infernal judge (*Inf*. v), the contrast between good conscience and bad, repentance and remorse, assurance and despair.

According to the Church's teaching, the sacrament of Penance has three parts,—contrition of the heart, confession by the lips, and satisfaction by works,—and these are symbolized by the three steps to the gate. The first, of white marble, reflects the penitent 'in his true likeness', representing his self-knowledge and sincerity of *Contrition*; the second, of dark, burnt stone, split both ways across, tells of the anguish of his *Confession*, the 'broken and contrite heart'; the third, of glowing porphyry, the colour of blood, that is, of love, his ardour to give *Satisfaction*, to amend for his sin by the exercises of love. The adamant threshold on which the angel-warder is seated with his feet resting on the 'flaming red' step, is the sure foundation of the Church's authority, by which he holds the keys and opens the door; 'Thou art Peter, and upon this rock I will build my church, . . . and I will give unto thee the keys of the kingdom of heaven' (*Matt.* xvi. 18-19). The seven *P's—peccato*, sin—marked with the sword in the penitent's brow are signs of the conviction of sin, the new sense that sin is a 'wound', which is wrought in him by the sword of the Word, and they indicate the seven kinds of sinfulness from which he must be purged on the seven terraces of the mountain. Penitence is not finished, only begun, at the gate.

This multiplication of symbols is apt to be tedious and irksome to us and needs Dante's apology; but it is doubtful if the same would be felt by his first readers, for whom the imagery and ordinances of the Church were as natural and inevitable as the courses of the stars and seasons so that any mere hint of them would carry its immediate sense and more than the sense of the words.

The gate swings hard on its hinges, which are rusty with little use, so seldom is an entrance sought. In comparing the door of Purgatory with that of the ancient temple where victorious Caesar took possession of the Roman treasure, does Dante mean that the founding of the Empire was not so great or so hard a thing to do as the saving of a soul?

When he enters, a great *Te Deum* breaks forth from all the souls on the mountain because another has come to join their fellowship of repentance and redemption; they sing: 'Help Thy servants, whom Thou hast redeemed with Thy precious blood. Make them to be numbered with Thy saints in glory everlasting.'

Poi fummo dentro al soglio della porta
 che 'l malo amor dell'anime disusa,
 perchè fa parer dritta la via torta,
sonando la senti' esser richiusa;
 e s' io avesse li occhi volti ad essa,
 qual fora stata al fallo degna scusa?
Noi salivam per una pietra fessa,
 che si moveva d'una e d'altra parte,
 sì come l'onda che fugge e s'appressa.
'Qui si convene usare un poco d'arte'   10
 cominciò 'l duca mio 'in accostarsi
 or quinci or quindi al lato che si parte.'
E questo fece i nostri passi scarsi,
 tanto che pria lo scemo della luna
 rigiunse al letto suo per ricorcarsi,
che noi fossimo fuor di quella cruna:
 ma quando fummo liberi e aperti
 su, dove il monte in dietro si rauna,
ïo stancato ed amendue incerti
 di nostra via, restammo in su un piano 20
 solingo più che strade per diserti.
Dalla sua sponda, ove confina il vano,
 al piè dell'alta ripa che pur sale,
 misurrebbe in tre volte un corpo umano;
e quanto l'occhio mio potea trar d'ale,
 or dal sinistro e or dal destro fianco,
 questa cornice mi parea cotale.
Là su non eran mossi i piè nostri anco,
 quand' io conobbi quella ripa intorno
 che, dritta, di salita aveva manco, 30

CANTO X

*The First Terrace; the sculptured wall; examples
of humility; the purgation of pride*

WHEN we were within the threshold of the gate
which the soul's perverse love disuses, making the
crooked way seem straight, by the resounding I
heard it closed again; and if I had turned my eyes
to it what excuse would have served for the fault?

We were climbing through a cleft in the rock
which kept bending one way and the other like a
wave that comes and goes, when my Leader began:
'Here there is need to use some skill in keeping
close to this side or that where it turns away'; and
this made our steps so scant that the waning moon
had regained its bed to sink to rest before we were
forth from that needle's eye.[1] But when we were
free and out in the open above, where the moun-
tain draws back, I weary and both uncertain of
our way, we stopped on a level place more solitary
than a desert track. From its edge bordering on the
void to the foot of the lofty bank which rises sheer
would measure three times a man's body, and as
far as my eye could make its flight, now on the
left hand, now on the right, the terrace there seemed
to me the same. Our feet had not yet moved on it
when I perceived that the encircling bank, which
was perpendicular and impossible to climb, was of

131

esser di marmo candido e adorno
   d' intagli sì che non pur Policleto,
   ma la natura lì avrebbe scorno.
L'angel che venne in terra col decreto
   della molt'anni lacrimata pace,
   ch'aperse il ciel del suo lungo divieto,
dinanzi a noi pareva sì verace
   quivi intagliato in un atto soave,
   che non sembiava imagine che tace.
Giurato si sarìa ch'el dicesse 'Ave!';   40
   perchè iv'era imaginata quella
   ch'ad aprir l'alto amor volse la chiave;
e avea in atto impressa esta favella
   'Ecce ancilla Dei', proprïamente
   come figura in cera si suggella.
'Non tener pur ad un loco la mente'
   disse 'l dolce maestro, che m'avea
   da quella parte onde il cuore ha la gente.
Per ch' i' mi mossi col viso, e vedea
   di retro da Maria, da quella costa   50
   onde m'era colui che mi movea,
un'altra storia nella roccia imposta;
   per ch' io varcai Virgilio, e fe'mi presso,
   acciò che fosse alli occhi miei disposta.
Era intagliato lì nel marmo stesso
   lo carro e' buoi traendo l'arca santa,
   per che si teme officio non commesso.
Dinanzi parea gente; e tutta quanta,
   partita in sette cori, a' due mie' sensi
   faceva dir l'un 'No', l'altro 'Sì, canta.'   60
Similemente al fummo delli 'ncensi
   che v'era imaginato, li occhi e 'l naso
   e al sì e al no discordi fensi.
Lì precedeva al benedetto vaso,
   trescando alzato, l'umile salmista,
   e più e men che re era in quel caso.
Di contra, effigïata ad una vista
   d'un gran palazzo, Micòl ammirava
   sì come donna dispettosa e trista.

white marble and adorned with carvings such that
not only Polycletus[2] but nature would be put to
shame there.

The angel who came to earth with the decree of
the many-years-wept-for peace that opened heaven
from its long interdict appeared before us so truly
graven there in a gracious attitude that it did not
seem a silent image. One would have sworn he
said: '*Ave*', for she was imaged there who turned
the key to open the supreme love, and in her
bearing she had this word imprinted: '*Ecce ancilla
Dei*' as clearly as a figure is stamped in wax.[3]

'Do not keep thy mind only on one part', said
the kind Master, who had me on that side of him
where the heart lies, so that I turned my face and
saw beyond Mary, on the same side as he that
prompted me, another story set on the rock; I
went past Virgil, therefore, and drew near to it that
I might have it before my eyes. There, carved in
the same marble, were the cart and oxen drawing
the sacred ark on account of which men fear an
office not committed to them.[4] In front people
appeared and the whole company, divided into
seven choirs, made two of my senses say, the one:
'No', the other: 'Yes, they sing'; in the same way,
at the smoke of the incense that was imaged there,
eyes and nose were in contradiction, with *yes* and
no. There the humble psalmist went before the
blessed vessel girt up and dancing, and that time
he was both more and less than king; opposite,
figured at the window of a great palace, Michal
looked on, like a woman vexed and scornful.

I' mossi i piè del loco dov' io stava, 70
 per avvisar da presso un'altra storia,
 che di dietro a Micòl mi biancheggiava.
Quiv'era storïata l'alta gloria
 del roman principato il cui valore
 mosse Gregorio alla sua gran vittoria—
i' dico di Traiano imperadore;
 e una vedovella li era al freno,
 di lacrime atteggiata e di dolore.
Intorno a lui parea calcato e pieno
 di cavalieri, e l'aguglie nell'oro 80
 sovr'essi in vista al vento si movieno.
La miserella intra tutti costoro
 parea dicer: 'Segnor, fammi vendetta
 di mio figliuol ch'è morto, ond' io m'accoro.'
Ed elli a lei rispondere: 'Or aspetta
 tanto ch' i' torni.' E quella: 'Segnor mio,'
 come persona in cui dolor s'affretta,
'se tu non torni?' Ed ei: 'Chi fia dov' io
 la ti farà.' Ed ella: 'L'altrui bene
 a te che fia, se 'l tuo metti in oblio?' 90
Ond'elli: 'Or ti conforta; ch'ei convene
 ch' i' solva il mio dovere anzi ch' i' mova:
 giustizia vuole e pietà mi ritene.'
Colui che mai non vide cosa nova
 produsse esto visibile parlare,
 novello a noi perchè qui non si trova.
Mentr' io mi dilettava di guardare
 l' imagini di tante umilitadi,
 e per lo fabbro loro a veder care,
'Ecco di qua, ma fanno i passi radi,' 100
 mormorava il poeta 'molte genti:
 questi ne 'nvïeranno alli altri gradi.'
Li occhi miei ch'a mirare eran intenti,
 per veder novitadi ond'e' son vaghi,
 volgendosi ver lui non furon lenti.
Non vo' però, lettor, che tu ti smaghi
 di buon proponimento per udire
 come Dio vuol che 'l debito si paghi.

CANTO X

I moved my feet from where I was to examine close at hand another story which I saw gleaming white beyond Michal. Depicted there was the glorious deed of the Roman prince whose worth moved Gregory to his great victory,—I mean the Emperor Trajan;[5] and a poor widow was at his bridle in a posture of grief and in tears. The place about him seemed trampled and thronged with knights and the eagles on the gold above them moved visibly in the wind. The poor woman among all these seemed to say: 'Lord, avenge me for my son that is dead, for whom I am stricken'; and he to answer her: 'Wait now till I return'; and she: 'My Lord,' like one whose grief is urgent, 'if thou return not?'; and he: 'He that is in my place will do it for thee'; and she: 'What shall another's goodness avail thee if thou art forgetful of thine own?'; he therefore: 'Now take comfort, for I must fulfil my duty before I go; justice requires it and compassion bids me stay.' He for whose sight nothing was ever new wrought this visible speech, new to us because it is not found here.

While I was taking delight in gazing at the images of so great humilities, dear to sight, too, for their Craftsman's sake, 'See on this side many people,' the Poet murmured 'but coming with slow steps; they will direct us to the other stairs.' My eyes, which were looking intently, were not slow in turning to him, being eager for new sights.

But I would not have thee, reader, fall away from good resolve for hearing how God wills that the debt be paid; do not dwell on the form of the

Non attender la forma del martire:
   pensa la succession; pensa ch'al peggio,   110
   oltre la gran sentenza non può ire.
Io cominciai: 'Maestro, quel ch' io veggio
   muovere a noi non mi sembian persone,
   e non so che, sì nel veder vaneggio.'
Ed elli a me: 'La grave condizione
   di lor tormento a terra li rannicchia,
   sì che i miei occhi pria n'ebber tencione.
Ma guarda fiso là, e disviticchia
   col viso quel che vien sotto a quei sassi:
   già scorger puoi come ciascun si picchia.'   120
O superbi cristian, miseri lassi,
   che, della vista della mente infermi,
   fidanza avete ne' retrosi passi,
non v'accorgete voi che noi siam vermi
   nati a formar l'angelica farfalla,
   che vola alla giustizia sanza schermi?
Di che l'animo vostro in alto galla,
   poi siete quasi entomata in difetto,
   sì come vermo in cui formazion falla?
Come per sostentar solaio o tetto,   130
   per mensola tal volta una figura
   si vede giugner le ginocchia al petto,
la qual fa del non ver vera rancura
   nascere 'n chi la vede; così fatti
   vid' io color, quando puosi ben cura.
Vero è che più e meno eran contratti
   secondo ch'avìen più e meno a dosso;
   e qual più pazïenza avea nelli atti
piangendo parea dicer: 'Più non posso.'

torment, think of what follows, think that at worst it cannot go beyond the great Judgement.

'Master,' I began, 'that which I see coming to us does not seem to me persons, and I know not what they are, so confused is my sight.'

And he answered me: 'The grievous nature of their torment doubles them to the ground, so that my eyes at first were in debate about them, but look closely there and disentangle that which comes beneath these stones; already thou mayst discern how each beats his breast.'

O vainglorious Christians, weary wretches who are sick in the mind's vision and put your trust in backward steps, do you not perceive that we are worms born to form the angelic butterfly that soars to judgement without defence? Why does your mind float so high, since you are as it were imperfect insects, like the worm that is undeveloped?

As, for corbel to support ceiling or roof, a figure is sometimes seen joining the knees to the breast which begets from its unreality real distress in him that sees it, in such a posture I saw these when I looked carefully. They were indeed bent down more and less as they had more and less on their back, and he that had most patience in his looks seemed by his weeping to say: 'I can no more.'

PURGATORIO

1. About 9.30 a.m.
2. The ancient Greek sculptor.
3. 'Behold, the handmaid of the Lord" (*Matt.* xxviii. 38).
4. David's bringing of the ark to Jerusalem; Uzzah's presumption in touching it; David's dance and his wife Michal's scorn (2 *Sam.* vi).
5. For his justice and by the intercession of St Gregory Trajan was delivered from Limbo and raised to Paradise; cp. *Par.* xx.

NOTE

With this canto we enter on the essential Purgatory, the active purgation of the soul. As the penalties of Hell represent the last issues of unrepented sin, the penances of Purgatory mean the soul's repentant consciousness of its sinfulness, which is a continual hindrance to be overcome by the prevailing powers of grace. That consciousness and the aspiration which goes with it are continually strengthened by examples brought to the mind of the penitents both of the opposite virtue and of their own sin. 'Whereas in the *Inferno* sin was considered in its manifold effects, in the *Purgatorio* it is regarded in its causes, and all referred to disordered love. . . . Since every agent acts from some love, it is clear that man's first business in life is to set love in order; and indeed the whole moral basis of Dante's *Purgatorio* rests upon a line ascribed to Saint Francis of Assisi: "Set love in order, Thou that lovest me" ' (*E. G. Gardner*). Delivered from its old sinful practices and repentant, and increasingly repentant, of them, the soul must still be delivered from what remains of sinful temper by the practice of the opposite virtue. The mountain is a school of souls, a place of ordered discipline in which they suffer according to their special type of sinfulness, and here on the first terrace they are purged of pride.

Dante's climb from the gate through 'a cleft in the rock', his first endeavour after his full committal to the way of penitence, is hard and slow and wavering, and when he comes forth with Virgil 'from that needle's eye' he is first of all impressed with the emptiness of the terrace, it is 'more solitary than a desert track'. The obvious reference is to the peculiar difficulty and rarity of repentance from pride, with a recollection besides of the words of Christ: 'Strait is the gate, and narrow is the way, which leadeth unto life, and few there be that find it.'

Then the gleaming reliefs on the marble wall hold his eyes; for the first note in repentance is positive and before all else comes the absorption of the soul in good, here in these 'great humilities'.

The Virgin, here as on all the terraces, is the first example of the virtue; every virtue is essentially a part of the operation of grace, and it is expressly as the receiver and the medium of redemptive grace that the Virgin is represented here. The significance of the scene is gathered in 'the words of the choice and the words of the acceptance, the words of exaltation and of humility' (*M. Chini, L.D.*),—'Hail' and 'Behold the hand-maid of the Lord'.

The other two scenes on the wall are taken, according to Dante's plan in the terraces, from Scripture and from secular history. They show David as psalmist and worshipper, 'both more and less than king', and Trajan, the Emperor whose most 'glorious deed' was a deed of justice and mercy and whose salvation was the 'great victory' gained for him by the prayers of the Church's head; so, by the lowliness of kings, religion and civil justice are both secured and Church and Empire stand in their true alliance.

The account of this terrace occupies also the two following cantos, and it will be convenient to postpone to the end of the twelfth our consideration both of the purgation of pride and of Dante's conception of art in relation to the art of his time in Italy.

PURGATORIO

'O PADRE nostro, che ne' cieli stai,
   non circunscritto, ma per più amore
   ch'ai primi effetti di là su tu hai,
laudato sia 'l tuo nome e 'l tuo valore
   da ogni creatura, com'è degno
   di render grazie al tuo dolce vapore.
Vegna ver noi la pace del tuo regno,
   chè noi ad essa non potem da noi,
   s'ella non vien, con tutto nostro ingegno.
Come del suo voler li angeli tuoi   10
   fan sacrificio a te, cantando osanna,
   così facciano li uomini de' suoi.
Dà oggi a noi la cotidiana manna,
   sanza la qual per questo aspro diserto
   a retro va chi più di gir s'affanna.
E come noi lo mal ch'avem sofferto
   perdoniamo a ciascuno, e tu perdona
   benigno, e non guardar lo nostro merto.
Nostra virtù che di leggìer s'adona,
   non spermentar con l'antico avversaro,   20
   ma libera da lui che sì la sprona.
Quest'ultima preghiera, signor caro,
   già non si fa per noi, chè non bisogna,
   ma per color che dietro a noi restaro.'
Così a sè e noi buona ramogna
   quell'ombre orando, andavan sotto il pondo,
   simile a quel che tal volta si sogna,
disparmente angosciate tutte a tondo
   e lasse su per la prima cornice,
   purgando la caligine del mondo.   30

CANTO XI

*The Lord's Prayer; examples of pride; Omberto
Aldobrandeschi; Oderisi; Provenzan Salvani*

'OUR Father which art in heaven, not circum-
scribed but by the greater love Thou hast for Thy
first works on high.[1]

'Praised be Thy name and power by every
creature as it is meet to give thanks for Thy sweet
effluence;[2]

'May the peace of Thy kingdom come to us, for
we cannot reach it of ourselves, if it come not,
with all our striving;

'As Thine angels make sacrifice to Thee of their
will, singing hosannas, so let men make of theirs;

'Give us this day the daily manna, without which
he goes backward through this harsh wilderness
who most labours to advance;

'And as we forgive everyone the wrong we have
suffered, do Thou also forgive in loving-kindness,
and look not on our deserving;

'Our strength that yields so lightly put not to
proof with the old adversary, but deliver us from
him who so goads it. This last petition, dear Lord,
we make not now for ourselves, for there is no
need, but for them that remain behind us.'

Thus beseeching good speed for themselves and
for us those shades went beneath their burden,
such as one sometimes dreams of, all, unequally
distressed, making their weary round on the first
terrace, purging away the fog of the world. If good

143

Se di là sempre ben per noi si dice,
   di qua che dire e far per lor si puote
   da quei ch' hanno al voler buona radice?
Ben si de' loro atar lavar le note
   che portar quinci, sì che, mondi e lievi,
   possano uscire alle stellate rote.
'Deh, se giustizia e pietà vi disgrievi
   tosto, sì che possiate muover l'ala,
   che secondo il disio vostro vi lievi,
mostrate da qual mano inver la scala   40
   si va più corto; e se c'è più d'un varco,
   quel ne 'nsegnate che men erto cala;
chè questi che vien meco, per lo 'ncarco
   della carne d'Adamo onde si veste,
   al montar su, contra sua voglia, è parco.'
Le lor parole, che rendero a queste
   che dette avea colui cu' io seguiva,
   non fur da cui venisser manifeste;
ma fu detto: 'A man destra per la riva
   con noi venite, e troverete il passo   50
   possibile a salir persona viva.
E s' io non fossi impedito dal sasso
   che la cervice mia superba doma,
   onde portar convienmi il viso basso,
cotesti, ch'ancor vive e non si noma,
   guardere' io, per veder s' i' 'l conosco,
   e per farlo pietoso a questa soma.
Io fui latino e nato d' un gran tosco:
   Guiglielmo Aldobrandesco fu mio padre;
   non so se 'l nome suo già mai fu vosco.   60
L'antico sangue e l'opere leggiadre
   di miei maggior mi fer sì arrogante
   che, non pensando alla comune madre,
ogn' uomo ebbi in despetto tanto avante,
   ch' io ne mori'; come, i Sanesi sanno
   e sallo in Campagnatico ogni fante.
Io sono Omberto; e non pur a me danno
   superbia fè, chè tutt' i miei consorti
   ha ella tratti seco nel malanno.

words are always being spoken for us there, what can be said and done for them here by those that have their will rooted in good? Well may we help them to wash away the stains they carried hence, so that pure and light they may go forth to the starry wheels.

'Pray, so may justice and mercy soon disburden you that you may spread the wing that lifts you according to your desire, show us on which hand is the shortest way to the stair and if there is more than one passage let us know which is the less steep; for he that comes with me, for the burden of Adam's flesh with which he is clothed, is, in spite of his goodwill, slow at climbing.'

It was not plain from whom came their words that replied to those spoken by him I followed, but they were: 'Come with us along the bank on the right and you will find the opening where it is possible for a living man to climb; and were I not hindered by the stone which subdues my proud neck so that I must hold my face down I would look at this man who still lives and who is not named, to see if I know him and to move his pity for this load. I was Italian, and born of a great Tuscan. Guglielmo Aldobrandesco was my father,[3] —I know not if his name was ever heard among you. The ancient blood and gallant deeds of my ancestors made me so arrogant that, forgetful of our common mother, I carried my scorn of every man so far that I died for it,—how, the Sienese know and every child in Campagnatico. I am Omberto, and not on me alone has pride wrought ill but all my kinsfolk it has dragged with it into

145

E qui convien ch' io questo peso porti   70
   per lei, tanto che a Dio si sodisfaccia,
   poi ch' io nol fe' tra' vivi, qui tra' morti.'
Ascoltando chinai in giù la faccia;
   e un di lor, non questi che parlava,
   si torse sotto il peso che li 'mpaccia,
e videmi e conobbemi e chiamava,
   tenendo li occhi con fatica fisi
   a me che tutto chin con loro andava.
'Oh!' diss' io lui 'non se' tu Oderisi,
   l'onor d'Agobbio e l'onor di quell'arte   80
   ch'alluminar chiamata è in Parisi?'
'Frate,' diss'elli 'più ridon le carte
   che pennelleggia Franco bolognese:
   l'onore è tutto or suo, e mio in parte.
Ben non sare' io stato sì cortese
   mentre ch' io vissi, per lo gran disio
   dell'eccellenza ove mio core intese.
Di tal superbia qui si paga il fio;
   e ancor non sarei qui, se non fosse
   che, possendo peccar, mi volsi a Dio.   90
Oh vana gloria dell'umane posse!
   com poco verde in su la cima dura,
   se non è giunta dall'etati grosse!
Credette Cimabue nella pintura
   tener lo campo, e ora ha Giotto il grido,
   sì che la fama di colui è scura:
così ha tolto l'uno all'altro Guido
   la gloria della lingua; e forse è nato
   chi l'uno e l'altro caccerà del nido.
Non è il mondan romore altro ch' un fiato   100
   di vento, ch'or vien quinci e or vien quindi,
   e muta nome perchè muta lato.
Che voce avrai tu più, se vecchia scindi
   da te la carne, che se fossi morto
   anzi che tu lasciassi il 'pappo' e 'l 'dindi',
pria che passin mill'anni? ch'è più corto
   spazio all'etterno, ch' un muover di ciglia
   al cerchio che più tardi in cielo è torto.

calamity, and here I must bear this load for it until God be satisfied, here among the dead since I did it not among the living.'

Listening, I bent down my face, and one of them, not he that was speaking, twisted himself under the weight that cumbered him and saw me and knew me and called, laboriously keeping his eyes fixed on me, who went quite bent along with them.

'Oh,' I said to him 'art thou not Oderisi, the honour of Gubbio and of that art which they call in Paris illuminating?'[4]

'Brother,' he said 'the pages smile brighter from the brush of Franco of Bologna; he has now all the honour, of which part is mine. Truly, I should not have been so courteous while I lived, for the great desire to excel on which my heart was set; for such pride we here pay the fee, and I should not yet be here were it not that, having power to sin, I turned to God. O empty glory of human powers, how briefly lasts the green on its top, unless it is followed by an age of dulness! In painting Cimabue thought to hold the field and now Giotto has the cry, so that the other's fame is dim;[5] so has the one Guido taken from the other the glory of our tongue,[6] and he, perhaps, is born that shall chase the one and the other from the nest. The world's noise is but a breath of wind which comes now this way and now that and changes name because it changes quarter. What more fame shalt thou have if thou put off thy flesh when it is old than if thou hadst died before giving up *pappo* and *dindi*,[7] when a thousand years are past, which is a shorter space to eternity than the twinkling of an eye to the slowest-turning circle in the heavens?[8]

Colui che del cammin sì poco piglia
    dinanzi a me, Toscana sonò tutta;   110
    e ora a pena in Siena sen pispiglia,
ond'era sire quando fu distrutta
    la rabbia fiorentina, che superba
    fu a quel tempo sì com'ora è putta.
La vostra nominanza è color d'erba,
    che viene e va, e quei la discolora
    per cui ella esce della terra acerba.'
E io a lui: 'Tuo vero dir m' incora
    bona umiltà, e gran tumor m'appiani:
    ma chi è quei di cui tu parlavi ora?'   120
'Quelli è' rispuose 'Provenzan Salvani;
    ed è qui perchè fu presuntüoso
    a recar Siena tutta alle sue mani.
Ito è così, e va sanza riposo,
    poi che morì: cotal moneta rende
    a sodisfar chi è di là troppo oso.'
E io: 'Se quello spirito ch'attende,
    pria che si penta, l'orlo della vita,
    qua giù dimora e qua su non ascende,
se buona orazïon lui non aita,   130
    prima che passi tempo quanto visse,
    come fu la venuta a lui largita?'
'Quando vivea più glorïoso' disse
    'liberamente nel Campo di Siena,
    ogni vergogna diposta, s'affisse;
e lì, per trar l'amico suo di pena
    che sostenea nella prigion di Carlo,
    si condusse a tremar per ogni vena.
Più non dirò, e scuro so che parlo;
    ma poco tempo andrà che' tuoi vicini   140
    faranno sì che tu potrai chiosarlo.
Quest'opera li tolse quei confini.'

Of him who makes so little headway in front of me all Tuscany resounded, and now there is hardly a whisper of him in Siena, where he was Lord when the mad rabble of Florence was destroyed, at that time as proud as now it is prostitute. Your renown is the colour of grass which comes and goes, and that withers it by which it springs green from the ground.'

And I said to him: 'Thy true speech fills my heart with good humbleness and abates a great swelling in me. But who is he of whom thou didst speak now?'

'That' he replied 'is Provenzan Salvani,[9] and he is here because in his presumption he thought to bring all Siena into his hands; he has gone thus, and goes without rest, since he died. Such coin he pays in quittance who is too daring yonder.'

And I said: 'If the spirit that awaits the verge of life before repenting stays there below and does not ascend here, unless good prayers help him, till as much time pass as he lived, how was it granted him to come here?'

'When he was living most gloriously' he said 'he freely took his stand in the market-place of Siena, putting aside all shame, and there, to deliver his friend from the pains he suffered in the prison of Charles, he brought himself to tremble in every vein.[10] I will not say more, and I know I speak darkly; but little time will pass till thy townsmen act so that thou canst make thy comment on it. This deed released him from those bounds.'

1. The first creations were the heavens and the angels.

2. Wisdom 'is a breath of the power of God and a clear effluence from the glory of the Almighty' (*Wisd.* vii. 25).

3. The Aldobrandeschi were Counts of Santafiora, near Siena; in 1259 their power was destroyed by the Sienese and Omberto was murdered in their castle of Campagnatico.

4. Oderisi (d. 1299) is said to have been the master of Franco of Bologna in miniature painting. Paris was the chief centre for illuminated manuscripts.

5. Cimabue and Giotto his pupil were both living in 1300.

6. Guido Guinicelli of Bologna (Canto xxvi) and Guido Cavalcanti of Florence, Dante's friend (*Inf.* x).

7. Childish words for *bread* and *money*.

8. The sphere of the fixed stars was believed to move eastward one degree in a century; the whole circuit would take 36,000 years.

9. Head of the Sienese government at the time of Montaperti (1260), when Florence was defeated by the Ghibellines; in the subsequent council he advised the destruction of Florence (*Inf.* x).

10. He begged for his friend's ransom.

NOTE

It is apt to strike us as a singular lapse that Dante should exchange the sublime simplicity of the Lord's Prayer for the scholastic and homiletic elaboration of it with which the canto begins, even if allowance be made for the fact that such paraphrasing of Scripture was a common practice of the time and would hardly seem out of place to his contemporaries. Here, at any rate, it gives him opportunity to stress in each petition of the penitents of pride the element of total dependence on the grace of God.

In the ascription of praise with which the prayer begins the divine love, power, and wisdom ('effluence') are named, the supreme attributes which, taken together, are a plain reference, in Dante's manner, to the Holy Trinity, as in the inscription over the gate of Hell (*Inf.* iii); the three words, *amore, valore, vapore,* form the first triple rhyme in the canto, as if to say that 'Our Father' means here the whole fulness of God.

The three penitents named in the canto are typical examples of prevalent forms of pride, Omberto Aldobrandesco of the arrogance of birth, Oderisi of the vainglory of artistry, Provenzan Salvani of the presumption of power.

When he speaks of renown being 'the colour of grass', 'Oderisi does not say "our renown" but "your renown". In the world where he is purged before ascending to God, the world he has left no longer moves him; he sees it as might an inhabitant of another sphere, without passions or illusions, with calm compassion; and that calm, in the midst of sufferings desired and loved as the necessary condition of the infinite good that is to follow them, forms the chief feature of the state of the souls in that intermediate region. A single word suffices to mark the separation between two ways of life so clearly connected and so different' (*Lamennais*, quoted by *De Sanctis*).

Dante's conversation with Oderisi, whom he seems to have known, shows his vivid and understanding interest in the pictorial arts of his time. He distinguishes between the 'smiling' art of the illuminated missals and breviaries, best practised in Paris,—the art of Oderisi and his pupil Franco of Bologna—and the more imposing and popular 'painting' in tempera and fresco on panels and church walls—the art of Cimabue and his pupil Giotto—in which Italy was giving its great lead to the world; and these he links up with his own art of poetry—the art of Guinicelli and Cavalcante and of an unnamed poet who is to follow them. In each case he notes the succession of their masters and shows how, in all the arts, the true artist serves an end beyond himself in which his work has its place and value and in which he must be content to be surpassed.

Oderisi's words, Dante says, 'abate a great swelling' in him, and this is only one of the indications, here and elsewhere, of Dante's own consciousness of pride. He stoops with the penitents, in that degree identifying himself with their penance, and he implies, by the words he puts into Oderisi's mouth, that in the succession of poets he is himself the one who perhaps 'shall chase the one and the other Guido from the nest', eclipsing their fame as Giotto his master's. Such a reference to himself, made in the very place where pride is purged, implies a kind of irony against himself; the hint of his own pre-eminence is followed by the sharpest comment of all on 'the world's noise' and by his acknowledgment that Oderisi's words 'fill his heart with good humbleness'. The passage, most characteristic of Dante, is at once the expression and the rebuke of his own pride.

Then, in connection with Provenzan's honourable self-humiliation, there is given to Dante one of the obscure prophecies of his exile which occur in the poem, forecasting the time when he wrote these lines, the time when, in his own words, he should 'go as a pilgrim, almost a beggar, showing against my will the wounds of fortune for which the blame is many a time imputed unjustly to the wounded man himself'

(*Convito*). It was through the long purgation of his pride, in which he too was made 'to tremble in every vein', that Dante 'could make his comment' on Provenzan's humiliation in Siena and in Purgatory. In spirit he is already one of these penitents, bearing his own load.

PURGATORIO

Di pari, come buoi che vanno a giogo,
    m'andava io con quell'anima carca,
    fin che 'l sofferse il dolce pedagogo;
ma quando disse: 'Lascia loro e varca;
    chè qui è buon con la vela e coi remi,
    quantunque può, ciascun pinger sua barca';
dritto sì come andar vuolsi rife' mi
    con la persona, avvegna che i pensieri
    mi rimanessero e chinati e scemi.
Io m'era mosso, e seguìa volentieri   10
    del mio maestro i passi, ed amendue
    già mostravam com'eravam leggieri;
ed el mi disse: 'Volgi li occhi in giùe:
    buon ti sarà, per tranquillar la via,
    veder lo letto delle piante tue.'
Come, perchè di lor memoria sia,
    sovra i sepolti le tombe terragne
    portan segnato quel ch'elli eran pria,
onde lì molte volte si ripiagne
    per la puntura della rimembranza,   20
    che solo a' pii dà delle calcagne;
sì vid' io lì, ma di miglior sembianza
    secondo l'artificio, figurato
    quanto per via di fuor del monte avanza.
Vedea colui che fu nobil creato
    più ch'altra creatura, giù dal cielo
    folgoreggiando scender da un lato.
Vedea Brïareo, fitto dal telo
    celestïal, giacer dall'altra parte,
    grave alla terra per lo mortal gelo.   30

CANTO XII

*The figured pavement; the proud brought low;
the angel of humility*

SIDE by side with that burdened soul, as oxen go in a yoke, I went on as long as the gentle schoolmaster[1] allowed; but when he said: 'Leave them and pass on, for here it is well that with sail and oar and with all his force each drive his bark', I raised my body erect again as one should walk, though my thoughts remained bowed down and shrunk.

I had set out and was following eagerly in my Master's steps and both of us were showing now how light of foot we were, when he said to me: 'Turn down thine eyes; it will be well for thee to beguile the way by seeing the bed beneath thy feet.'

As over the buried dead, that there may be remembrance of them, the pavement tombs bear designs of what they were before, for which tears are often shed there at the prick of memory that spurs only the pitiful; so I saw figured there, but by the craftsmanship of better likeness, the whole breadth of the roadway that projects from the mountain.

I saw him that was created nobler than any other creature fall as lightning from heaven, on the one side;[2]

I saw Briareus on the other side, pierced by the heavenly shaft, lying heavy on the ground in the chill of death;

155

Vedea Timbreo, vedea Pallade e Marte,
   armati ancora, intorno al padre loro,
   mirar le membra de' Giganti sparte.

Vedea Nembròt a piè del gran lavoro
   quasi smarrito, e riguardar le genti
   che 'n Sennaàr con lui superbi foro.

O Niobè, con che occhi dolenti
   vedea io te segnata in su la strada,
   tra sette e sette tuoi figliuoli spenti!

O Saùl, come su la propria spada   **40**
   quivi parevi morto in Gelboè,
   che poi non sentì pioggia nè rugiada!

O folle Aragne, sì vedea io te
   già mezza ragna, trista in su li stracci
   dell'opera che mal per te si fè.

O Roboam, già non par che minacci
   quivi 'l tuo segno; ma pien di spavento
   nel porta un carro, sanza ch'altri il cacci.

Mostrava ancor lo duro pavimento
   come Almeon a sua madre fè caro   **50**
   parer lo sventurato adornamento.

Mostrava come i figli si gettaro
   sovra Sennacherìb dentro dal tempio,
   e come morto lui quivi lasciaro.

Mostrava la ruina e 'l crudo scempio
   che fè Tamiri, quando disse a Ciro:
   'Sangue sitisti, e io di sangue t'empio.'

Mostrava come in rotta si fuggiro
   li Assiri, poi che fu morto Oloferne,
   e anche le reliquie del martiro.   **60**

Vedea Troia in cenere e in caverne:
   o Ilïòn, come te basso e vile
   mostrava il segno che lì si discerne!

Qual di pennel fu maestro o di stile
   che ritraesse l'ombre e' tratti ch' ivi
   mirar farìeno uno ingegno sottile?

Morti li morti e i vivi parean vivi:
   non vide mei di me chi vide il vero,
   quant' io calcai fin che chinato givi.

I saw Thymbraeus, I saw Pallas and Mars, still armed, about their father, gazing on the giants' scattered limbs;

I saw Nimrod at the foot of his mighty work, as [Tower of Babel] if bewildered, and he was looking at the peoples in Shinar that shared his pride.

O Niobe, I saw thee traced on the roadway, with what tearful eyes, between thy seven and seven children slain!

O Saul, how thou appearedst there dead on thine own sword in Gilboa, which never after felt rain or dew!

O mad Arachne, so did I see thee already half spider, wretched on the shreds of the web thou wroughtest to thy hurt!

O Rehoboam, thine image here does not seem now to threaten, but a chariot bears it off full of terror when no one gives chase!

It showed too, that hard pavement, how Alcmaeon made the luckless ornament seem costly to his mother;

It showed how his sons fell upon Sennacherib within the temple, and how they left him there dead;

It showed the destruction and the cruel butchery that Tomyris wrought when she said to Cyrus: 'Thou didst thirst for blood and with blood I fill thee';

It showed how the Assyrians fled in rout after Holofernes was slain, and also the remains of that slaughter.

I saw Troy in ashes and in heaps; O Ilion,[3] how abased and vile the design showed thee that we saw there!

What master of brush or chisel could have portrayed the shapes and outlines there, which would have filled with wonder a discerning mind? The dead seemed dead and the living living. He saw no better than I who saw the truth of all that which I trod upon while I went stooping. Wax

Or superbite, e via col viso altero,   70
    figliuoli d' Eva, e non chinate il volto
    sì che veggiate il vostro mal sentero!
Più era già per noi del monte volto
    e del cammin del sole assai più speso
    che non stimava l'animo non sciolto,
quando colui che sempre innanzi atteso
    andava, cominciò: 'Drizza la testa;
    non è più tempo di gir sì sospeso.
Vedi colà un angel che s'appresta
    per venir verso noi; vedi che torna   80
    dal servigio del dì l'ancella sesta.
Di reverenza il viso e li atti adorna,
    sì che i diletti lo 'nviarci in suso;
    pensa che questo dì mai non raggiorna!'
Io era ben del suo ammonir uso
    pur di non perder tempo, sì che 'n quella
    matera non potea parlarmi chiuso.
A noi venìa la creatura bella,
    bianco vestito e nella faccia quale
    par tremolando mattutina stella.   90
Le braccia aperse, e indi aperse l'ale;
    disse: 'Venite: qui son presso i gradi,
    e agevole-mente omai si sale.
A questo invito vegnon molto radi:
    o gente umana, per volar su nata,
    perchè a poco vento così cadi?'
Menocci ove la roccia era tagliata:
    quivi mi battè l'ali per la fronte,
    poi mi promise sicura l'andata.
Come a man destra, per salire al monte   100
    dove siede la chiesa che soggioga
    la ben guidata sopra Rubaconte,
si rompe del montar l'ardita foga
    per le scalee che si fero ad etade
    ch'era sicuro il quaderno e la doga;
così s'allenta la ripa che cade
    quivi ben ratta dall'altro girone;
    ma quinci e quindi l'alta pietra rade.

proud now and go your way with lofty looks, sons
of Eve, and bend not down your face to see your
evil path!

More of the mountain was now encircled by us
and much more of the sun's track was sped than
my mind, not being free, had reckoned, when he
who was always looking ahead as he went began:
'Lift up thy head!⁴ There is no more time to go
thus absorbed. See there an angel who hastes to
meet us. See how the sixth handmaid returns from
the service of the day.⁵ Let thy looks and bearing
be graced with reverence, that it may please him
to direct us upwards. Remember that to-day never
dawns again.'

I was well accustomed to his admonitions never
to lose time, so that in that matter his speech could
not be dark to me.

Towards us came the fair creature, clothed in
white, and in his face he seemed like a trembling
star at dawn. He opened his arms, then spread his
wings and said: 'Come; the steps are at hand here
and henceforth the climb is easy. To this bidding
they are very few that come. O race of men, born
to fly upward, why do you fall back so for a little
wind?'

He brought us where the rock was cleft, there
smote on my forehead with his wings, then
promised me safe journeying. As on the right hand
in climbing the hill where the church stands above
Rubaconte that dominates the well-guided city the
bold scarp of the ascent is broken by the stairs
which were made in an age when the records
and measures were safe,⁶ so the bank that falls
there very steeply from the other circle is made
easier, but the lofty rock presses close on the one

Noi volgendo ivi le nostre persone,
  '*Beati pauperes spiritu!*' voci   110
  cantaron sì che nol dirìa sermone.
Ahi quanto son diverse quelle foci
  dall' infernali; chè quivi per canti
  s'entra, e là giù per lamenti feroci.
Già montavam su per li scaglion santi,
  ed esser mi parea troppo più leve
  che per lo pian non mi parea davanti.
Ond' io: 'Maestro, dì, qual cosa greve
  levata s'è da me, che nulla quasi
  per me fatica, andando, si riceve?'   120
Rispuose: 'Quando i *P* che son rimasi
  ancor nel volto tuo presso che stinti,
  saranno come l'un del tutto rasi,
fier li tuoi piè dal buon voler sì vinti
  che non pur non fatica sentiranno,
  ma fia diletto loro esser sospinti.'
Allor fec' io come color che vanno
  con cosa in capo non da lor saputa,
  se non che cenni altrui sospecciar fanno;
per che la mano ad accertar s'aiuta,   130
  e cerca e truova e quello officio adempie
  che non si può fornir per la veduta;
e con le dita della destra scempie
  trovai pur sei le lettere che 'ncise
  quel dalle chiavi a me sovra le tempie:
a che guardando il mio duca sorrise.

side and the other. When we were turning our steps there, *'Beati pauperes spiritu'*⁷ was sung in such tones as no words would tell. Ah, how different these passages from those of Hell, for here the entrance is with songs and there with fierce lamentations!

Now we mounted by the sacred stairway, and I seemed to be far lighter than before on the level, so that I said: 'Master, tell me, what weight has been lifted from me that I find almost no labour in going?'

He answered: 'When the *P*'s that are still left on thy brow all but effaced shall be wholly removed, as the one has been, thy feet will be so mastered by goodwill that not only will they feel no labour but it will be their delight to be urged upward.'

Then I did like those going with something on their head unknown to them but that the signs of others make them suspect, so that the hand helps to make sure and searches and finds, doing the office that sight cannot serve, and with the spread fingers of my right hand I found only six of the letters that he with the keys had traced on my temples; and observing this my Leader smiled.

1. 'The law was our schoolmaster, to bring us unto Christ' (*Gal.* iii. 24).

2. 'I beheld Satan as lightning fall from heaven' (*Luke* x. 18); Briareus, one of the giants who fought with the gods (*Inf.* xxxi); Thymbraeus (Apollo), Pallas and Mars, children of Jupiter; Nimrod, builder of the Tower of Babel (*Inf.* xxxi); Niobe having boasted against Latona, mother of Apollo and Diana, of her 14 children, they were all killed and she turned to stone; Saul's death and David's curse on Gilboa (1 *Sam.* xxxi. 1–4, 2 *Sam.* i. 21); Arachne having challenged Minerva in weaving, Minerva destroyed her web and changed her to a spider; Rehoboam, King of Israel (1 *Kings* xii. 12–18); Alcmaeon avenged his father on his mother Eriphyle, who had betrayed her husband for the bribe of a necklace; Sennacherib of Assyria, oppressor of Jerusalem, killed by his own sons (2 *Kings* xix. 21–28, 37); Queen Tamyris, whose son was killed by Cyrus of Persia, captured and beheaded Cyrus and plunged his head in a basin of blood; Holofernes of Assyria, beheaded by Judith, who left the headless body in his tent.

3. The citadel of Troy.

4. 'Look up, and lift up your heads; for your redemption draweth nigh' (*Luke* xxi. 28).

5. Past noon on Easter Monday.

6. Steps led up to the ancient church of San Miniato which dominates Florence from the south side of the Arno; the bridge there was called Rubaconte from the Governor sixty years earlier. When Dante wrote there were recent scandals in which the city records and the bushel measure had been tampered with.

7. 'Blessed are the poor in spirit' (*Matt.* v. 3).

NOTE

We are now in a position to consider the purgation of pride and its correspondence with the disciplines that follow.

It may be assumed that the penitents' first sight on their arrival on the terrace of pride is, like Dante's own, the sight of the 'great humilities' on the marble wall, which remain in their mind when they are bent under their loads and cannot see them. The first motive in the purgation of a sin is not warning or rebuke but the sense of the opposite grace, and their first lesson is to see how God exalts the humble; *then* they are shown how He casts down the proud. The memorial of these presumptuous spirits figured on the terrace is a truer record 'of what they were before' than the carved pavements familiar in churches and cloisters, with effigies, titles, and coats of arms, are of those they commemorate; this, he says, was, 'by the craftsmanship, of better likeness'.

Dante sums up these representative sinners by pride in a kind of acrostic. The group of four stanzas beginning *I saw* has, in Italian, *V* for the initial letter of each stanza; the next group has *O*; and the third, beginning *It showed*, has *M*. Then a single stanza, on the destruction of Troy, has the same three initials for its three lines, spelling together: *V* (equivalent to *U*) *O M*, the root of *uomo*, man. The folly and futility of pride is that man, the son of Eve, exalts himself against God and against his fellows. The examples of pride, thirteen to three of humility, all ending in death and disaster, are taken alternately from classical and Scriptural story, as if from all history; and then, as it were, they are summed up in Troy,— the original of Rome, of the civil order of humanity,—whose pride was its ruin. Dante, while he wrote, may very well have had in mind these lines of *Ecclesiasticus*: 'The beginning of pride is when a man departeth from God and his heart is

163

turned away from his maker. For pride is the beginning of all sin. . . . For this cause the Lord brought upon them strange calamities and overthrew them utterly. . . . The Lord hath cast down the thrones of proud princes . . . and hath made their memorial to cease from the earth. Pride was not made for men, nor furious anger for them that are born of a woman.'

The acrostic does, of course, strike us as childish and many of Dante's commentators are unwilling to admit that he was capable of it either here or in the similar passage in *Paradiso* xix. But, after all, the device is there and is even more childish if it does not mean anything. There was a good deal of what we should reckon literary childishness in the Middle Ages and something of it even in Dante.

Pride is the first sin to be purged. The sins of pride, envy, and anger, the sins of the spirit, are deeper than the sins of the flesh, avarice, gluttony, and lust, and 'pride is the root-sin and primeval curse of man, the special cause of his fall' (*E. Moore*). There is no deliverance of the soul, it cannot go farther, unless it is first delivered from its pride.

These penitents of pride 'have to become as little children and learn their Paternoster once again' (*E. H. Plumptre*), and they repeat it as they go, acknowledging their insufficiency and need and ill-deserving. Being within the gate and secured by grace they are safe from temptation and they use the petition for deliverance from 'the old adversary' on behalf of those who are still in danger, men in the earthly life and, it may be, those on the lower slopes of the mountain, outside the gate. The interchange of intercession is itself a discipline in humbleness, a mutual acknowledgment of need.

The angel of humility, his face 'like a trembling star at dawn', removes by a stroke of his wing the first mark of sinfulness from Dante's brow and pronounces on him the first beatitude; for under the dispensation of grace no sin is ever merely removed, it is always replaced by its opposite, by a blessing out of the Gospel, and the redemption of the proud is in their lowliness.

Dante does not know that the wound of pride has been healed on his brow till he is told of it by Virgil, so natural and unconscious in the humbled soul is its new humbleness, like the shining of Moses' face. Then, too, he discovers that by the healing of the one *P* the other six are 'all but effaced'. Deliverance from pride makes every other sin more healable 'and henceforth the climb is easy'.

So analysed the allegorical scheme is ingenious, but merely ingenious; in Dante's lines it is a report of experience and discovery and wonder. Strangely personal and touching in its blend of affection and irony and desire is his recollection of the familiar ascent to the ancient church of San Miniato with its great view over Florence, recalling to him in his exile the humbler, better days of his city.

The general scheme or programme is the same on each of the seven terraces of the mountain from the gate upward. In the first place examples of the virtue opposite to their sin, beginning in each case with the Virgin, are brought by some fitting means before the mind of the penitents; then their penance, accompanied with one of the offices of the Church, is described and opportunity is given for Dante to converse with some of the penitents; then notable examples of the sin are recalled; lastly an angel appears who removes with his wing one of the seven *P*'s from Dante's brow, pronounces a beatitude relevant to the particular purgation of the terrace, and shows the passage to the terrace above. It is a scheme which gives a sustained impression of order and consistency, as it were of moral inevitableness, to the whole discipline of the mountain.

Dante's comments on the reliefs on the marble wall and the designs on the pavement are of singular interest in relation to the great artistic revival of his time in Italy. Polycletus meant for Dante and his contemporaries the sculpture of antiquity at its greatest, and these reliefs, he said, would have put Polycletus to shame, having a new life in them that antiquity had not known. They would even have excelled 'nature' herself, and this not in mere vague hyperbole; for art in its perfection is for him more than nature, no mere reduplication of nature's facts but a thing having its own vitality and order. It is a 'visible speech'; its still forms represent and report the moving currents of life; it seizes and stirs the mind, sending it beyond the forms of the art itself and making it imaginatively aware of much that no 'silent image' can expressly tell. How absorbed

Dante was, not only in the subjects of these sculptures but in their workmanship, in the wonder of what art can do, is shown in his multiplication of such expressions as *design, outline, image, carving, figure*, in his account of them, more than the matter in itself requires, and in his repeated exclamations at their craftsmanship. These forms were indeed God's workmanship, such as 'is not found here'; but no language could describe more intimately than this language of Dante's the new art of his day and country, in particular the work of some of the Pisan and Florentine sculptors and the paintings of Giotto. His words about the 'imaged' Virgin, that 'she had in her bearing this word imprinted, "*Ecce ancilla Dei*" ', might have been used with perfect propriety of the same subject, in which only the figure of the Virgin remains, on the marble pulpit in the Duomo of Siena. It was carved in Dante's childhood and was probably familiar to him, and it is tempting and not unreasonable to suppose that he may have had this most tenderly conceived and realized form in mind when he wrote these lines. At any rate he was well aware of the new vitality which was just then pouring into Italy from the Gothic sculptors of northern Europe, breaking through the static and hieratic formalism of the Byzantine tradition in Italy and giving to the work of Nicholas and John of Pisa and of Giotto an emotional and dramatic realism and a sense of the significant in form and movement which had never been known before. The 'sweet new style' of the group of poets of which Dante was the chief was, in its inwardness and sincerity, the literary counterpart of the new Gothic vitality in the pictorial arts. Giotto was not only Dante's townsman and friend, he was also his spiritual kinsman; and as Giotto was the first to paint great pictures, so was Dante the first to write great verse, in the common tongue and in terms of the common life of men.

PURGATORIO

No I eravamo al sommo della scala,
    dove secondamente si risega
    lo monte che salendo altrui dismala:
ivi così una cornice lega
    dintorno il poggio, come la primaia,
    se non che l'arco suo più tosto piega.
Ombra non li è nè segno che si paia;
    parsi la ripa e parsi la via schietta
    col livido color della petraia.
'Se qui per dimandar gente s'aspetta'   10
    ragionava il poeta 'io temo forse
    che troppo avrà d' indugio nostra eletta.'
Poi fisamente al sole li occhi porse;
    fece del destro lato a muover centro,
    e la sinistra parte di sè torse.
'O dolce lume a cui fidanza i' entro
    per lo novo cammin, tu ne conduci'
    dicea 'come condur si vuol quinc'entro.
Tu scaldi il mondo, tu sovr'esso luci:
    s'altra ragione in contrario non pronta,   20
    esser dien sempre li tuoi raggi duci.'
Quanto di qua per un migliaio si conta,
    tanto di là eravam noi già iti,
    con poco tempo, per la voglia pronta;
e verso noi volar furon sentiti,
    non però visti, spiriti parlando
    alla mensa d'amor cortesi inviti.
La prima voce che passò volando
    'Vinum non habent' altamente disse,
    e dietro a noi l'andò reïterando;   30

CANTO XIII

The Second Terrace; examples of kindness; the purgation of envy; Sapia

WE were at the top of the stair where a second time the mountain is cut away that heals men as they climb; there a terrace girds the hill about like the first, except that its arc takes a sharper curve. No shade is there nor is any carving to be seen. We saw the bank and the bare road, with the livid colour of the stone.

'If we wait here to enquire of people,' the Poet observed 'I fear our choice may perhaps be delayed too long.' Then he set his eyes steadily on the sun, made of his right side a centre for his movement, and brought round his left. 'O sweet light by trust in which I enter on this new road,' he said 'do thou guide us with the guidance that is needful in this place. Thou givest warmth to the world, thou sheddest light upon it. Unless other reason urge the contrary thy beams must always be our guide.'

We had already gone as far there as here we should reckon a mile—in a short time, for our will was eager—when flying towards us spirits were heard, but not seen, uttering courteous biddings to the table of love. The first voice that flew by called loudly: '*Vinum non habent*'[1] and passed on repeating it behind us; and before it was quite out of

169

e prima che del tutto non si udisse
    per allungarsi, un'altra 'I' sono Oreste'
    passò gridando, e anco non s'affisse.
'Oh!' diss' io 'padre, che voci son queste?'
    E com' io domandai, ecco la terza
    dicendo: 'Amate da cui male aveste.'
E 'l buon maestro: 'Questo cinghio sferza
    la colpa della invidia, e però sono
    tratte d'amor le corde della ferza.
Lo fren vuol esser del contrario sono: 40
    credo che l' udirai, per mio avviso,
    prima che giunghi al passo del perdono.
Ma ficca 'l viso per l'aere ben fiso,
    e vedrai gente innanzi a noi sedersi,
    e ciascuno è lungo la grotta assiso.'
Allora più che prima li occhi apersi;
    guarda'mi innanzi, e vidi ombre con manti
    al color della pietra non diversi.
E poi che fummo un poco più avanti,
    udìa gridar: 'Maria, ora per noi!;   50
    gridar 'Michele', e 'Pietro', e 'Tutti santi'.
Non credo che per terra vada ancoi
    omo sì duro, che non fosse punto
    per compassion di quel ch' i' vidi poi;
chè, quando fui sì presso di lor giunto,
    che li atti loro a me venivan certi,
    per li occhi fui di greve dolor munto.
Di vil ciliccio mi parean coperti,
    e l' un sofferìa l'altro con la spalla,
    e tutti dalla ripa eran sofferti: 60
così li ciechi a cui la roba falla
    stanno a' perdoni a chieder lor bisogna,
    e l' uno il capo sopra l'altro avvalla,
perchè 'n altrui pietà tosto si pogna,
    non pur per lo sonar delle parole,
    ma per la vista che non meno agogna.
E come alli orbi non approda il sole,
    così all'ombre quivi, ond' io parlo ora,
    luce del ciel di sè largir non vole;

hearing in the distance another passed, crying: 'I am Orestes',[2] and it too did not stay. 'O Father,' I said 'what voices are these?' And as I asked there was a third, saying: 'Love them from whom you have suffered wrong.'[3]

And the good Master said: 'This circle scourges the sin of envy, therefore the cords of the scourge are drawn from love. The curb must be of contrary sound; I think thou wilt hear it, if I can judge, before reaching the pass of pardon. But direct thy sight steadily through the air and thou wilt see people before us, all of them seated along the cliff.'

Then, opening my eyes wider than before, I looked in front of me and saw shades with cloaks not differing in colour from the stone, and when we were a little farther on I heard cries of 'Mary, pray for us', then 'Michael' and 'Peter' and 'All saints'.[4]

I do not think there walks on earth today a man so hard that he would not have been pierced with pity at what I saw then, for when I had come so near them that their actions became plain to me great grief was wrung from my eyes. They appeared to me to be covered with coarse hair-cloth and the one supported the other with his shoulder and all were supported by the bank. Just so the blind who are destitute take their place at pardons[5] to beg for their needs and one sinks his head on another so that the people may be quickly moved to pity not only by the sound of their words but by their looks which plead no less; and as the sun does not profit the blind, so to the shades in the place I speak of heaven's light denies its bounty, for an

ch'a tutti un fil di ferro i cigli fora　　　　　　70
　　e cuce sì, come a sparvier selvaggio
　　si fa, però che queto non dimora.
A me pareva andando fare oltraggio,
　　veggendo altrui, non essendo veduto:
　　per ch' io mi volsi al mio consiglio saggio.
Ben sapev'ei che volea dir lo muto;
　　e però non attese mia dimanda,
　　ma disse: 'Parla, e sie breve ed arguto.'
Virgilio mi venìa da quella banda
　　della cornice onde cader si pote,　　　　　80
　　perchè da nulla sponda s' inghirlanda;
dall'altra parte m'eran le divote
　　ombre, che per l'orribile costura
　　premevan sì che bagnavan le gote.
Volsimi a loro e 'O gente sicura'
　　incominciai 'di veder l'alto lume
　　che 'l disio vostro solo ha in sua cura,
se tosto grazia resolva le schiume
　　di vostra coscïenza sì che chiaro
　　per essa scenda della mente il fiume,　　90
ditemi, chè mi fia grazioso e caro,
　　s'anima è qui tra voi che sia latina;
　　e forse lei sarà buon s' i' l'apparo.'
'O frate mio, ciascuna è cittadina
　　d' una vera città; ma tu vuo' dire
　　che vivesse in Italia peregrina.'
Questo mi parve per risposta udire
　　più innanzi alquanto che là dov' io stava,
　　ond' io mi feci ancor più là sentire.
Tra l'altre vidi un'ombra ch'aspettava　　100
　　in vista; e se volesse alcun dir 'Come?',
　　lo mento a guisa d'orbo in su levava.
'Spirto' diss' io 'che per salir ti dome,
　　se tu se' quelli che mi rispondesti,
　　fammiti conto o per luogo o per nome.'
'Io fui Sanese' rispuose 'e con questi
　　altri rimondo qui la vita ria,
　　lacrimando a colui che sè ne presti.

iron wire pierces all their eyelids and stitches them up, as is done to an untamed falcon when it will not be still.

It seemed to me as I went that I did outrage, seeing others without being seen, so that I turned to my wise counsel. Well he knew what the dumb would say and therefore did not wait for my question, but said: 'Speak, and be brief and to the point.'

Virgil was coming with me on that side of the terrace where one might fall over, for there was no parapet surrounding it, and on the other side of me were the devout shades who were forcing through the horrible seam the tears that bathed their cheeks. I turned to them and began: 'O people assured of seeing the light on high which alone is the object of your desire, so may grace soon clear the scum of your conscience and the stream of memory flow down through it pure, tell me, for I shall hold the kindness dear, if there is any soul here among you that is Italian, and perhaps it will be well for him if I know of it.'

'O my brother, we are every one citizens of one true city;⁶ but thou wouldst say, any that lived in Italy a pilgrim.' This I seemed to hear for answer a little distance on from where I was, so I made myself heard still farther that way. Among the rest I saw a shade that looked expectant, and if any would ask how, it was lifting up its chin in the manner of the blind.

'Spirit' I said 'who subduest thyself to mount, if it be thou that answered me make thyself known to me either by place or name.'

'I was of Siena,' it replied 'and with these others I cleanse here my sinful life, weeping to Him that

Savia non fui, avvegna che Sapia
 fossi chiamata, e fui delli altrui danni   110
 più lieta assai che di ventura mia.
E perchè tu non creda ch' io t' inganni,
 odi s' i' fui, com' io ti dico, folle,
 già discendendo l'arco di miei anni.
Eran li cittadin miei presso a Colle
 in campo giunti co' loro avversari,
 e io pregava Iddio di quel ch'e' volle.
Rotti fuor quivi e volti nelli amari
 passi di fuga; e veggendo la caccia,
 letizia presi a tutte altre dispari,   120
tanto ch' io volsi in su l'ardita faccia,
 gridando a Dio: "Omai più non ti temo!",
 come fè il merlo per poca bonaccia.
Pace volli con Dio in su lo stremo
 della mia vita; ed ancor non sarebbe
 lo mio dover per penitenza scemo,
se ciò non fosse ch'a memoria m'ebbe
 Pier Pettinaio in sue sante orazioni,
 a cui di me per caritate increbbe.
Ma tu chi se' che nostre condizioni   130
 vai dimandando, e porti li occhi sciolti,
 sì com' io credo, e spirando ragioni?'
'Li occhi' diss' io 'mi fieno ancor qui tolti,
 ma picciol tempo, chè poca è l'offesa
 fatta per esser con invidia volti.
Troppa è più la paura ond'è sospesa
 l'anima mia del tormento di sotto,
 che già lo 'ncarco di là giù mi pesa.'
Ed ella a me: 'Chi t' ha dunque condotto
 qua su tra noi, se giù ritornar credi?'   140
 E io: 'Costui ch'è meco e non fa motto.
E vivo sono; e però mi richiedi,
 spirito eletto, se tu vuo' ch' i' mova
 di là per te ancor li mortai piedi.'
'Oh, questa è a udir sì cosa nova'
 rispuose 'che gran segno è che Dio t'ami;
 però col priego tuo talor mi giova.

He grant Himself to us. Sapient I was not though
I was called Sapia,[7] and I rejoiced far more at
others' hurt than at my own good fortune; and
lest thou think I deceive thee hear if I was not,
as I tell thee, mad when the arc of my years was
already descending.[8] My townsmen were near Colle
and had joined battle with their enemies, and I
prayed God for that which He had willed; there
they were routed and turned back in the bitter
steps of flight, and seeing the chase I was filled
with gladness beyond all bounds, so that I turned
upward my bold face, crying to God: "Now I fear
Thee no more", as the blackbird did for a little
sunshine.[9] I sought peace with God at the very
end of my life, and my debt would not yet be
lessened by penitence had it not been that Peter
the comb-seller, who of his charity was grieved
for me, had me in remembrance in his devout
petitions.[10] But who art thou that goest asking of
our condition and hast, as I think, thine eyes free
and speakest with breath?'

'My eyes' I said 'will yet be taken from me here,
but only for a little, for they have little offended
with looks of envy; far greater is the fear, which
holds my soul in suspense, of the torment below, so
that already the load down there is heavy upon me.'

And she said to me: 'Who then has led thee up
here among us, if thou thinkest to return below?'

And I: 'He that is with me here and does not
speak; and I am alive, and therefore ask of me,
elect spirit, if thou wouldst have me yet move for
thee yonder my mortal feet.'

'Ah,' she replied 'this is so strange a thing to
hear that it is a great token that God loves thee.
Help me sometimes, therefore, with thy prayers.

E cheggioti per quel che tu più brami,
  se mai calchi la terra di Toscana,
  che a' miei propinqui tu ben mi rinfami.   150
Tu li vedrai tra quella gente vana
  che spera in Talamone, e perderagli
  più di speranza ch'a trovar la Diana;
ma più vi perderanno li ammiragli.'

And I entreat thee by what thou cravest most that
if ever thou tread the soil of Tuscany thou restore
my name among my kindred. Thou wilt see them
among that vain people which hopes in Talamone
and which will lose more hopes in it than in the
finding of the Diana,—but more still will the
admirals lose there.'[11]

1. At the marriage in Cana 'the mother of Jesus saith unto him, They have no wine' (*John* ii. 3).

2. When Orestes was condemned to death, his friend Pylades pretended to be he to save his life.

3. 'Love your enemies' (*Matt.* v. 44).

4. Chanting the Litany of the Saints.

5. Church services at which indulgences are granted.

6. 'Ye are no more strangers and foreigners, but fellow-citizens with the saints' (*Eph.* ii. 9).

7. A noble lady of Siena at the time of the Florentine defeat of the Sienese Ghibellines under Provenzan Salvani (Canto xi) in 1269.

8. Past the 35th year, 'the middle of the pathway of our life' (*Inf.* i).

9. The last days of January are known in Italy as 'blackbird's days' and the blackbird is said to sing these words in winter sunshine.

10. This Peter became a hermit and his grave in Siena was honoured as that of a saint.

11. Talamone, a small and malarious port of which Siena failed to make a harbour to rival Pisa and Genoa; the Diana, a supposed underground stream below Siena in the search for which the city had been at much expense; 'the admirals' in charge of the port would lose their lives.

NOTE

When they emerge from the stair on the second terrace Dante is bewildered by its contrast with the first; here are no shades and no splendour of sculpture, only 'the bank and the bare road'. There is a certain greatness in pride; envy is a kind of meanness. Dante himself confesses to little envy, but to much pride.

'The livid colour of the stone' is the traditional colour of envy (*livore*), especially in its aspect of rancour and grudging, and for the envious their envy colours all the world they live in. They wear cloaks which make them hardly distinguishable from the rock, in sign of their humble and bitter consciousness of their sin. Their offence has been the looking with an evil eye on men and on men's good (*invidia*, from *vedere*, to see); now they are blinded, like untamed falcons, for the cure of their old restlessness and spleen, and are learning to long with tears for the bounty of the sun that is meantime denied them. They have looked meanly, ungraciously, at men; now, sitting like beggars at a church door, they ask for grace from God and from the saints and from men on earth and practise fellowship together, 'one supporting another with his shoulder'. They have risen above the bitter local jealousies of the time on earth and are now not even Italians, but 'every one citizens of one true city'; their citizenship is in heaven.

By the curiously deliberate account of Virgil's first movement on the terrace, which is described with a kind of military precision, and by the accumulated effect of the words *guide*, *guidance*, *guides* in his short speech, our attention is drawn to the fact that here especially, in the place of the purgation of envy, Virgil commits himself to the guidance of the sun, which gives its warmth and light to the world and which God, in rebuke of our human grudging, 'maketh to rise on the evil and

179

on the good'. The sun is the image and embodiment of God's bounty; it is only reasonable to be guided by it on this 'new road'.

These once envious souls hear, in their blindness, flying voices, perhaps of angels, telling of kindness; Mary's consideration for a neighbour's need, Pylades's offer of his life for his friend, Christ's charge to men to love their enemies.

Not much is known with certainty about Sapia, but she is believed to have been one of the Guelf exiles from Ghibelline Siena, living after her husband's death in her castle near the city, and the aunt of Provenzan Salvani (Canto xi), the Ghibelline leader commanding the Sienese at Colle, where he lost both the battle and his life in the great rout. Dante imagines her watching the battle, 'seeing the chase' and rejoicing in the defeat of her townsmen and the death of her nephew. The scene of Salvani doing penance for his pride in the terrace below, in conjunction with Sapia's account of herself in this canto, reminds us of the fierce rancours which divided and wasted many of the families and communities of the time in Italy. The two kinsfolk had been enemies; now both are under the reconciling discipline of grace and belong, as far as they have gone in that discipline, to the one fellowship of the saints.

The only cure of envy is kindness, so 'the cords of the scourge are drawn from love', and Sapia, once a great lady and once rejoicing in others' harm, now acknowledges her indebtedness for her early admission to Purgatory to the charity of a comb-seller's prayers.

Her last words, about the 'vain people' of Siena, are in the same ironical strain as those of Griffolino, the alchemist, in the last of the Malebolge (*Inf.* xxix); they are in reality Dante's own typically Florentine gibe at the envious and foolish ambitions, as Florence reckoned them, of the rival city in the hills of Tuscany.

PURGATORIO

'CHI è costui che 'l nostro monte cerchia
  prima che morte li abbia dato il volo,
  e apre li occhi a sua voglia e coverchia?'
'Non so chi sia, ma so che non è solo:
  domandal tu che più li t'avvicini,
  e dolcemente, sì che parli, acco'lo.'
Così due spirti, l'uno all'altro chini,
  ragionavan di me ivi a man dritta;
  poi fer li visi, per dirmi, supini,
e disse l' uno: 'O anima che fitta   10
  nel corpo ancora inver lo ciel ten vai,
  per carità ne consola e ne ditta
onde vieni e chi se'; chè tu ne fai
  tanto maravigliar della tua grazia,
  quanto vuol cosa che non fu più mai.'
E io: 'Per mezza Toscana si spazia
  un fiumicel che nasce in Falterona,
  e cento miglia di corso nol sazia.
Di sovr'esso rech' io questa persona:
  dirvi ch' i' sia, sarìa parlare indarno,   20
  chè 'l nome mio ancor molto non sona.'
'Se ben lo 'ntendimento tuo accarno
  con lo 'ntelletto' allora mi rispose
  quei che diceva pria 'tu parli d'Arno.'
E l'altro disse lui: 'Perchè nascose
  questi il vocabol di quella rivera,
  pur com' uom fa dell'orribili cose?'
E l'ombra che di ciò domandata era
  si sdebitò così: 'Non so; ma degno
  ben è che 'l nome di tal valle pera;   30

CANTO XIV

*Guido del Duca; the Arno; the degeneracy of
Romagna; examples of envy*

'Who is this that makes the circuit of our moun-
tain before death has given him flight, and opens
and shuts his eyes at his pleasure?'

'I know not who he is, but I know he is not
alone. Question him, since thou art nearer, and greet
him kindly that he may speak.'

Thus two spirits,[1] leaning towards each other,
talked of me there on my right, then bent
back their faces to speak to me, and one said: 'O
soul still held in the body who makest thy way
heavenward, gratify us of thy charity and tell us
whence thou comest and who thou art; for thou
makest us marvel as much at the grace given thee
as a thing must that never was before.'

And I: 'Through mid-Tuscany winds a stream
that rises in Falterona[2] and a hundred miles of
course do not suffice for it; from its bank I bring
this form. To tell you who I am would be to speak
in vain, for my name as yet makes little sound.'

'If I have the wit rightly to catch thy meaning,'
he that had spoken first then answered me 'thou
speakest of the Arno.'

And the other said to him: 'Why did he conceal
that river's name, just as one does with something
horrible?'

And the shade that was questioned delivered
himself thus: 'I know not, but it is fitting indeed
that the name of such a valley perish; for from its

chè dal principio suo, ov'è sì pregno
   l'alpestro monte ond'è tronco Peloro,
   che 'n pochi luoghi passa oltra quel segno,
infin là 've si rende per ristoro
   di quel che 'l ciel della marina asciuga,
   ond' hanno i fiumi ciò che va con loro,
virtù così per nimica si fuga
   da tutti come biscia, o per sventura
   del luogo, o per mal uso che li fruga:
ond' hanno sì mutata lor natura   40
   li abitator della misera valle,
   che par che Circe li avesse in pastura.
Tra brutti porci, più degni di galle
   che d'altro cibo fatto in uman uso,
   dirizza prima il suo povero calle.
Botoli trova poi, venendo giuso,
   ringhiosi più che non chiede lor possa,
   e da lor disdegnosa torce il muso.
Vassi caggendo, e quant'ella più 'ngrossa,
   tanto più trova di can farsi lupi   50
   la maladetta e sventurata fossa.
Discesa poi per più pelaghi cupi,
   trova le volpi sì piene di froda,
   che non temono ingegno che le occupi.
Nè lascerò di dir perch'altri m'oda;
   e buon sarà costui, s'ancor s'ammenta
   di ciò che vero spirto mi disnoda.
Io veggio tuo nepote che diventa
   cacciator di quei lupi in su la riva
   del fiero fiume, e tutti li sgomenta.   60
Vende la carne loro essendo viva;
   poscia li ancide come antica belva:
   molti di vita e sè di pregio priva.
Sanguinoso esce della trista selva;
   lasciala tal che di qui a mille anni
   nello stato primaio non si rinselva.'
Com'all'annunzio di dogliosi danni
   si turba il viso di colui ch'ascolta,
   da qual che parte il periglio l'assanni,

source, where the rugged mountain-chain from
which Pelorus[3] is broken off so teems with waters
that in few places it is surpassed, down to where
it gives itself up to restore what the sky draws
from the sea so that the rivers may be supplied in
their course, virtue is fled from as an enemy by
all as if it were a snake, either from some mischief
in the place or from bad custom goading them,
and the dwellers in that wretched valley have so
changed their nature that it seems as if Circe had
them at pasture. Among filthy hogs,[4] fitter for
acorns than for any food màde for men, it first
directs its feeble course; then, coming lower, it
finds curs[5] that snarl more than their power
warrants, and in scorn turns its snout from them;
it goes on falling and the more it swells the more
does the accursed and ill-starred ditch find the
dogs turned to wolves;[6] then, after descending
through many a hollow gorge, it finds foxes[7] so
full of guile that they have no fear that any trap
can take them. Nor will I refrain from speech
becanse another hears me, and it will be well for
him if he yet bear in mind what a true inspiration
unfolds for me. I see thy grandson,[8] who becomes
hunter of those wolves on the bank of the savage
stream and puts them all in terror; he sells their
flesh still living, then slaughters them like old
cattle; many he robs of life, and himself of honour;
he comes forth bloody from the wretched wood
and leaves it in such a case that in a thousand
years from now it will not re-forest itself as it
was before.'

As at the announcement of grievous ills the face
of one listening is troubled, from whatever quarter

così vid' io l'altr'anima, che volta   70
   stava a udir, turbarsi e farsi trista,
   poi ch'ebbe la parola a sè raccolta.
Lo dir dell'una e dell'altra la vista
   mi fer voglioso di saper lor nomi,
   e dimanda ne fei con prieghi mista;
per che lo spirto che di pria parlòmi
   ricominciò: 'Tu vuo' ch' io mi diduca
   nel fare a te ciò che tu far non vuo'mi.
Ma da che Dio in te vuol che traluca
   tanto sua grazia, non ti sarò scarso;   80
   però sappi ch' io son Guido del Duca.
Fu il sangue mio d' invidia sì rïarso,
   che se veduto avesse uom farsi lieto,
   visto m'avresti di livore sparso.
Di mia semente cotal paglia mieto:
   o gente umana, perchè poni 'l core
   là 'v'è mestier di consorte divieto?
Questi è Rinier; questi è 'l pregio e l'onore
   della casa da Calboli, ove nullo
   fatto s'è reda poi del suo valore.   90
E non pur lo suo sangue è fatto brullo,
   tra 'l Po e 'l monte e la marina e 'l Reno,
   del ben richesto al vero e al trastullo;
chè dentro a questi termini è ripieno
   di venenosi sterpi, sì che tardi
   per coltivare omai verrebber meno.
Ov'è il buon Lizio e Arrigo Manardi?
   Pier Traversaro e Guido di Carpigna?
   Oh Romagnuoli tornati in bastardi!
Quando in Bologna un Fabbro si ralligna?   100
   quando in Faenza un Bernardin di Fosco,
   verga gentil di picciola gramigna?
Non ti maravigliar s' io piango, Tosco,
   quando rimembro con Guido da Prata
   Ugolin d'Azzo che vivetter nosco,
Federigo Tignoso e sua brigata,
   la casa Traversara e li Anastagi
   (e l'una gente e l'altra è diretata),

the danger assail him, so I saw the other soul, which had turned to hear, become troubled and downcast when it had taken in these words.

The speech of the one and the other's look made me eager to know their names and with much entreaty I questioned them; so the spirit that spoke to me before began again: 'Thou wilt have me consent to do for thee what thou wilt not for me; but since God wills that His grace should so shine forth in thee, I will not be grudging with thee; know, therefore, that I am Guido del Duca. So inflamed with envy was my blood that if I had seen a man make merry thou hadst seen me suffused with livid colour. Of my sowing I reap such straw. O race of men, why do you set your hearts where must needs be exclusion of partnership?

'This is Rinier, this is the boast and honour of the house of Calboli, where none since has made himself heir to his worth. And not his blood alone, between the Po and the mountains and from the Reno to the sea,[9] is stripped of the virtues that belong to earnest and to sport; for within these bounds the land is so filled with poisonous shoots that now it would take long tillage to destroy them. Where is the good Lizio,[10] and Arrigo Mainardi, Pier Traversaro and Guido di Carpigna? O Romagnoles, turned to bastards! When does a Fabbro take root again in Bologna? When in Faenza a Bernardin di Fosco, noble scion of a lowly plant? Do not marvel, Tuscan, if I weep when I remember Guido da Prata and Ugolin d'Azzo, who lived among us, Federico Tignoso and his company, the Traversaro house and the Anastagi—the one family and the other now without an heir—the ladies and the

le donne e' cavalier, li affanni e li agi
  che ne 'nvogliava amore e cortesia   110
  là dove i cuor son fatti sì malvagi.
O Brettinoro, chè non fuggi via,
  poi che gita se n'è la tua famiglia
  e molta gente per non esser ria?
Ben fa Bagnacaval che non rifiglia;
  e mal fa Castrocaro, e peggio Conio,
  che di figliar tai conti più s' impiglia.
Ben faranno i Pagan, da che 'l demonio
  lor sen girà; ma non però che puro
  già mai rimagna d'essi testimonio.   120
O Ugolin de' Fantolin, sicuro
  è il nome tuo, da che più non s'aspetta
  chi far lo possa, tralignando, oscuro.
Ma va via, Tosco, omai; ch'or mi diletta
  troppo di pianger più che di parlare,
  sì m' ha nostra ragion la mente stretta.'
Noi sapavam che quell'anime care
  ci sentivano andar; però, tacendo,
  facean noi del cammin confidare.
Poi fummo fatti soli procedendo,   130
  folgore parve, quando l'aere fende,
  voce che giunse di contra dicendo:
'Anciderammi qualunque m'apprende';
  e fuggì come tuon che si dilegua,
  se subito la nuvola scoscende.
Come da lei l'udir nostro ebbe triegua,
  ed ecco l'altra con sì gran fracasso,
  che somigliò tonar che tosto segua:
'Io sono Aglauro che divenni sasso':
  ed allor, per ristrignermi al poeta,   140
  in destro feci e non innanzi il passo.
Già era l'aura d'ogne parte queta;
  ed el mi disse: 'Quel fu il duro camo
  che dovrìa l'uom tener dentro a sua meta.
Ma voi prendete l'esca, sì che l'amo
  dell'antico avversaro a sè vi tira;
  e però poco val freno o richiamo.

knights, the toils and the sports to which we were moved by love and courtesy where hearts have grown so wicked. O Bertinoro,[11] why dost thou not make away with thyself, when thy family, with many others, has gone to escape corruption? Bagnacavallo does well that breeds no more, and Castrocaro ill, and Conio worse that still troubles to breed such counts. The Pagani will do well when their Devil[12] takes himself off, yet not so that a clean record shall ever be left of them. O Ugolin de' Fantolini, thy name is safe, since no more are looked for who might blacken it by degeneracy. But now, Tuscan, go on thy way, for now my pleasure is far more to weep than talk, our converse has so wrung my heart.'

We knew that those dear spirits heard us go; their silence, therefore, made us confident of the way. When we passed on by ourselves, a voice like lightning when it cleaves the air encountered us, saying: 'Everyone that findeth me shall slay me',[13] and fled, like thunder that dies away when the cloud bursts suddenly. As soon as our ears had respite from it, lo, another with such uproar that it was like a thunder-clap that follows quickly: 'I am Aglauros that turned to stone';[14] and then, to draw close to the Poet, I made a step to the right, not forward.

The air was now quiet on every side and he said to me: 'That was the hard bit which should hold a man within his bounds; but you take the bait, so that the hook of the old adversary draws you to him, and then little avails curb or lure. The

Chiamavi 'l cielo e 'ntorno vi si gira,
   mostrandovi le sue bellezze etterne,
   e l'occhio vostro pur a terra mira;   150
onde vi batte chi tutto discerne.'

heavens call you and wheel about you, showing you their eternal beauties, and your eyes gaze only on the earth; therefore He smites you who sees all.'

1. Guido del Duca, a Ghibelline of the first half of the 13th century, and Rinier da Calboli, a Guelf of the second half, both of Romagna.

2. A height in the Apennines.

3. A height in Sicily supposed to have been once a part of the Apennines.

4. The people of the Casentino.

5. The people of Arezzo, where the Arno, flowing south-east, turns north-west.

6. The people of Florence.

7. The people of Pisa, where at one time was the mouth of the Arno.

8. Fulcieri da Calboli, Rinier's grandson, Governor of Florence in 1302 and 1312; he treated the White Guelfs there with great cruelty.

9. In Romagna.

10. The names following are those of well-known men and families of Romagna in the later 12th and the 13th centuries.

11. Bertinoro (Guido's own birthplace) and the others named are small towns in Romagna.

12. Mainardo Pagano, known as 'the Devil' for his cunning, a leading Ghibelline who sometimes fought for the Guelfs; described in *Inf.* xxvii as 'the Young Lion in the White Lair that changes party from summer to winter'.

13. Cain's words after the murder of Abel (*Gen.* iv. 14).

14. Aglauros, a princess of Athens, petrified by Mercury, her sister's lover, for her jealousy.

NOTE

The two souls from Romagna were 'leaning towards each other' and talking of Dante without seeming to realize that he overheard them as they had overheard him talking to Sapia; then 'they bent back their faces to speak to him'. These realistic particulars are reminders to us of their penal blindness, their condition as penitents of envy. Sapia, speaking for all of them, had said: 'We are every one citizens of one true city', and it is in that spirit, of one lifted above the rivalries and jealousies of the time in Italy and being delivered from his own old grudges, that Guido del Duca utters his great lamentation over the corruptions and confusions which plagued the life of Tuscany and Romagna, the parts best known to Dante, the places of his first and last years. The Arno, the chief river of Tuscany, springing from the teeming mountain height, created by the bounty and harmony and interchange of earth and sea and sky, sinks from stage to stage,—'coming lower', 'it goes on falling', 'descending through many a hollow gorge',—as it were defiled and degraded more and more by the creatures on its banks. There is a curious correspondence between these stages of degeneracy on the Arno with the descending scale of sins in Hell,—incontinence, violence, fraud,—from the mere brutish foulness of the hogs of the Casentino, the feeble, snarling malice of the curs of Arezzo, the fierce rapacity of the wolves of Florence, to the mean cunning of the foxes of Pisa. In the lines about Fulcieri da Calboli's cruelties in Florence Dante dealt with events later than 1300 but fresh and bitter in his memory when he wrote. For the greater shame of Tuscany this account of it comes from a man of Romagna, to whom Dante, as if ashamed to show himself a Florentine, refuses to disclose himself.

Then, with a deeper and more intimate note, Guido mourns

193

over his native Romagna, recalling its nobler memories. These names of men and families and places can mean little, individually, to us now. For Dante 'they were, as the Border legends were to Scott, full of life, associated with memories of romantic scenes and stories which he had heard from eye-witnesses' (*E. H. Plumptre*). Guido's recital is a lament for an age of high romance which is past and yet near enough for passionate remembrance, the age he had himself belonged to, about a century before Dante's. 'Boast, honour, worth, earnest and sport, love and courtesy, form a single series of conceptions intimately connected together in the ideal of the high society of the Middle Ages and in the repertory of the poetry which, in and through that high society, flourished first in Provence, then in Italy' (*F. Torraca*).

It is Guido, once parched with envy and private grudging, who now weeps for his country and proves that he is moved, not with the bitterness of a partisan, but with the grief of a lover, and in the whole account of the two blinded penitents Dante is at pains to note their gentleness and courtesy and their distress on account of public wrongs. The word *charity*, suggesting love in its aspect of breadth and generosity of spirit, is used four times in the three cantos concerned with the purgation of envy, and nowhere else in the *Purgatorio*. 'Charity adds to love a certain perfection of love' (*Aquinas*, quoted by *C. E. Norton*). 'In the Tuscan as in the Romagnole passage, but especially in the former, these features are plain: the lofty gaze of the eagle both on the land and on its history, and the perfect fusion of a wrath and a love which are no longer distinguishable; so wrathful, in Dante as Christian and as citizen, is love, and so pitiful is wrath' (*E. Pistelli, L.D.*).

There is an illustration of Dante's studied order and symmetry in the fact that Guido's accounts of Tuscany and Romagna occupy exactly the same number of lines—31–66 and 88–123—each passage being divisible into three equal portions; and it can hardly be by chance that the three parts of the Romagna passage end respectively with the words *bastards*, *wicked* and *dark*, as if to sum up in final terms the degeneracy of his land and people.

The voices of envy—envy in souls abandoned to it and in

the agony of self-defeat—break on the ear like successive thunder-claps, in warning of what envy can come to in its mastery. Cain's envy of his brother made him a stranger to his kind and terrified of them, and Aglauros's envy of her sister turned her to stone, destroying the natural affections and hardening the whole nature; and in fear of a sin he shared Dante 'drew close to the Poet'.

PURGATORIO

QUANTO tra l'ultimar dell'ora terza
e 'l principio del dì par della spera
che sempre a guisa di fanciullo scherza,
tanto pareva già inver la sera
essere al sol del suo corso rimaso;
vespero là, e qui mezza notte era.
E i raggi ne ferìen per mezzo 'l naso,
perchè per noi girato era sì 'l monte
che già dritti andavamo inver l'occaso,
quand' io senti' a me gravar la fronte   10
allo splendore assai più che di prima,
e stupor m'eran le cose non conte;
ond' io levai le mani inver la cima
delle mie ciglia, e fecimi 'l solecchio,
che del soverchio visibile lima.
Come quando dall'acqua o dallo specchio
salta lo raggio all'opposita parte,
salendo su per lo modo parecchio
a quel che scende, e tanto si diparte
dal cader della pietra in igual tratta,   20
sì come mostra esperïenza ed arte;
così mi parve da luce rifratta
quivi dinanzi a me esser percosso;
per che a fuggir la mia vista fu ratta.
'Che è quel, dolce padre, a che non possò
schermar lo viso tanto che mi vaglia'
diss' io 'e pare inver noi esser mosso?'

CANTO XV

*The angel of mercy; spiritual partnership; the
Third Terrace; visions of gentleness* (anger)

As much as between the ending of the third hour
and the beginning of the day appears of the circle
which is always playing like a child, so much
appeared now to be left of the sun's course towards
nightfall; it was evening there and here *Italy* midnight.
And the beams were striking us full in the face,
for the mountain was so far encircled by us that
we were going straight towards the west,[1] when I
felt my brow weighed down by the splendour far
more than before and the causes being unknown
left me dazed. I raised my hand, therefore, above
my eyebrows and made for myself the shade that
tempers excess of light. As when from water or
mirror the beam leaps the opposite way, rising at
the same angle as it descends, and at an equal
length departs as much from the fall of the stone,
as is shown by science and experiment, so it seemed
to me I was struck by light reflected there before
me, so that my sight was quick to flee.

‘What is that, gentle Father,’ I said ‘from which
I cannot rightly screen my eyes and which seems
to be moving towards us?’

'Non ti maravigliar s'ancor t'abbaglia
  la famiglia del cielo' a me rispose:
  'messo è che viene ad invitar ch'om saglia.   30
Tosto sarà ch'a veder queste cose
  non ti fia grave, ma fieti diletto
  quanto natura a sentir ti dispose.'
Poi giunti fummo all'angel benedetto,
  con lieta voce disse: 'Intrate quinci
  ad un scaleo vie men che li altri eretto.'
Noi montavam, già partiti di linci,
  e *'Beati misericordes!'* fue
  cantato retro, e 'Godi tu che vinci!'
Lo mio maestro e io soli amendue   40
  suso andavamo; e io pensai, andando,
  prode acquistar nelle parole sue;
e dirizza'mi a lui sì dimandando:
  'Che volse dir lo spirto di Romagna,
  e "divieto" e "consorte" menzionando?'
Per ch'elli a me: 'Di sua maggior magagna
  conosce il danno; e però non s'ammiri
  se ne riprende perchè men si piagna.
Perchè s'appuntano i vostri disiri
  dove per compagnia parte si scema,   50
  invidia move il mantaco a' sospiri.
Ma se l'amor della spera suprema
  torcesse in suso il disiderio vostro,
  non vi sarebbe al petto quella tema;
chè, per quanti si dice più lì "nostro,"
  tanto possiede più di ben ciascuno,
  e più di caritate arde in quel chiostro.'
'Io son d'esser contento più digiuno'
  diss'io 'che se mi fosse pria taciuto,
  e più di dubbio nella mente aduno.   60
Com'esser puote ch' un ben distributo
  in più posseditor faccia più ricchi
  di sè che se da pochi è posseduto?'
Ed elli a me: 'Però che tu rificchi
  la mente pur alle cose terrene,
  di vera luce tenebre dispicchi.

'Do not marvel' he answered me 'if the household of heaven still dazzle thee; it is a messenger who comes to invite to the ascent; soon the seeing of these will not be hard for thee, but as great delight as nature has fitted thee to feel.'

When we had reached the blessed angel he said with a glad voice: 'Enter here', at a stairway far less steep than the others. We were mounting, having already passed on from there, when *'Beati misericordes'*² was sung behind us and 'Rejoice, thou that overcomest.'

My Master and I went up by ourselves, and I thought as I went to gain profit from his words and I turned to him and asked: 'What did the spirit from Romagna mean when he spoke of *exclusion* and *partnership*?'

Then he said to me: 'He knows the cost of his own worst fault and therefore it is little wonder if he utter reproach against it that there may be less to mourn for. It is because your desires are fixed where the part is lessened by sharing that envy blows the bellows to your sighs; but if the love of the highest sphere bent upward your longing, that fear would not be in your breast. For there, the more they are who say *ours*, the more of good does each possess and the more of charity burns in that cloister.'

'I am more hungry for satisfaction' I said 'than if I had been silent before and my mind is more filled with perplexity. How can it be that a good distributed among a greater number of possessors makes them richer in it than if it were possessed by few?'

And he to me: 'Because thou still settest thy mind on earthly things thou gatherest darkness

Quello infinito ed ineffabil bene
  che là su è, così corre ad amore
  com'a lucido corpo raggio vene.
Tanto si dà quanto trova d'ardore;   70
  sì che, quantunque carità si stende,
  cresce sovr'essa l'etterno valore.
E quanta gente più là su s'intende,
  più v'è da bene amare, e più vi s'ama,
  e come specchio l'uno all'altro rende.
E se la mia ragion non ti disfama,
  vedrai Beatrice, ed ella pienamente
  ti torrà questa e ciascun'altra brama.
Procaccia pur che tosto sieno spente,
  come son già le due, le cinque piaghe,   80
  che si richiudon per esser dolente.'
Com' io voleva dicer: 'Tu m'appaghe',
  vidimi giunto in su l'altro girone,
  sì che tacer mi fer le luci vaghe.
Ivi mi parve in una visïone
  estatica di subito esser tratto,
  e vedere in un tempio più persone;
e una donna, in su l'entrar, con atto
  dolce di madre dicer: 'Figliuol mio,
  perchè hai tu così verso noi fatto?   90
Ecco, dolenti, lo tuo padre e io
  ti cercavamo.' E come qui si tacque,
  ciò che pareva prima, disparìo.
Indi m'apparve un'altra con quell'acque
  giù per le gote che 'l dolor distilla
  quando di gran dispetto in altrui nacque,
e dir: 'Se tu se' sire della villa
  del cui nome ne' Dei fu tanta lite,
  e onde ogni scïenza disfavilla,
vendica te di quelle braccia ardite   100
  ch'abbracciar nostra figlia, o Pisistrato.'
  E 'l segnor mi parea, benigno e mite,
risponder lei con viso temperato:
  'Che farem noi a chi mal ne disira,
  se quei che ci ama è per noi condannato?'

from the very light. That infinite and unspeakable good which is there above speeds to love as a sunbeam comes to a bright body; so much it gives of itself as it finds of ardour, so that the more charity extends the more does the eternal goodness increase upon it, and the more souls that are enamoured there above the more there are to be rightly loved and the more love there is and like a mirror the one returns it to the other. And if my speech do not relieve thy hunger thou shalt see Beatrice and she will deliver thee wholly from this and every other craving. Strive only that soon may be erased, as the other two are already, the five wounds which are healed by being painful.'

When I was about to say: 'Thou contentest me' I saw that I had reached the next circle, so that my eager eyes held me silent. There I seemed to be rapt of a sudden in an ecstatic vision and to see many people in a temple and a woman at the door with the sweet demeanour of a mother, who said: 'My son, why hast thou thus dealt with us? Behold, thy father and I have sought thee sorrowing.'³ And as here she was silent, that which first appeared vanished. Then appeared to me another woman, with those waters running down her cheeks that grief distils when it springs from great resentment against another, and she said: 'If thou art lord of the city for whose name was such strife among the gods and from which all knowledge shines forth, avenge thee of those daring arms that have embraced our daughter, O Pisistratus.'⁴ And her lord seemed to me to answer her graciously and gently and with tranquil look: 'What shall we do to one that seeks our hurt if we condemn one that loves us?' Then I saw people kindled

Poi vidi genti accese in foco d' ira
  con pietre un giovinetto ancider, forte
  gridando a sè pur: 'Martira, martira!'
E lui vedea chinarsi, per la morte
  che l'aggravava già, inver la terra,   110
  ma delli occhi facea sempre al ciel porte,
orando all'alto Sire, in tanta guerra,
  che perdonasse a' suoi persecutori,
  con quello aspetto che pietà diserra.
Quando l'anima mia tornò di fori
  alle cose che son fuor di lei vere,
  io riconobbi i miei non falsi errori.
Lo duca mio, che mi potea vedere
  far sì com' uom che dal sonno si slega,
  disse: 'Che hai che non ti puoi tenere   120
ma se' venuto più che mezza lega
  velando li occhi e con le gambe avvolte,
  a guisa di cui vino o sonno piega?'
'O dolce padre mio, se tu m'ascolte,
  io ti dirò' diss' io 'ciò che m'apparve
  quando le gambe mi furon sì tolte.'
Ed ei: 'Se tu avessi cento larve
  sovra la faccia, non mi sarìan chiuse
  le tue cogitazion, quantunque parve.
Ciò che vedesti fu perchè non scuse   130
  d'aprir lo core all'acque della pace
  che dall'etterno fonte son diffuse.
Non dimandai "Che hai?" per quel che face
  chi guarda pur con l'occhio che non vede,
  quando disanimato il corpo giace;
ma dimandai per darti forza al piede:
  così frugar conviensi i pigri, lenti
  ad usar lor vigilia quando riede.'
Noi andavam per lo vespero, attenti
  oltre quanto potean li occhi allungarsi   140
  contra i raggi serotini e lucenti.
Ed ecco a poco a poco un fummo farsi
  verso di noi come la notte scuro;
  nè da quello era loco da cansarsi:
questo ne tolse li occhi e l'aere puro.

with the fire of wrath slaying a youth with stones, and they kept crying loudly to each other: 'Kill! kill!'[5] And I saw him sink to the earth, for already death was heavy upon him, but of his eyes he made all the time gateways to heaven, in that great agony praying to the Lord on high to pardon his persecutors, with that look which unlocks compassion.

When my soul returned without to the things that are real outside of it, I recognized my not false errors. My Leader, who could see me act like one that frees himself from sleep, said: 'What ails thee, that thou canst not support thyself but hast come more than half a league with veiled eyes and stumbling feet, like a man overcome with wine or sleep?'

'O my kind Father,' I said 'if thou listen to me I will tell thee what appeared to me when my legs were so taken from me.' And he: 'If thou hadst a hundred masks upon thy face even thy faintest thoughts would not be hid from me. What thou sawest was shown thee that thou mightst not refuse to open thy heart to the waters of peace which are poured from the eternal fountain. I did not ask what ails thee for the reason of one that looks only with an unseeing eye when another's body lies insensible, but I asked in order to give force to thy feet. So must the sluggish be spurred, slow to use their waking hour when it returns.'

We were going on through the evening, looking intently ahead as far as our eyes could reach against the bright late beams, when lo, little by little a smoke approaching us as black as night, nor was there room to escape from it. This took from us our sight and the pure air.

1. The sun is nearly three hours from setting, as long as from its rising to 9 a.m., 'the third hour'; the circle in which it moves, the ecliptic, 'plays' north and south during the year; it is about 3 p.m. there and midnight 'here', in Italy; they have come round from the east towards the north side of Purgatory and are facing the sun westward.

2. 'Blessed are the merciful' (*Matt.* v. 7).

3. Mary to the child Jesus in the Temple (*Luke* ii. 48).

4. Lord of Athens, of which the naming was disputed by the gods; his wife wished him to kill a youth who had kissed their daughter in public.

5. The stoning of Stephen (*Acts* vii. 54–60).

NOTE

The previous canto ended with Virgil's words about the wheeling heavens, God's 'lure' to the soul, and this follows with a reference, in an astronomical passage like that which begins the second canto, to the course of the sun, the image of God's bounty in which Virgil had found guidance for them on their arrival on the terrace of envy. Its beams 'strike them full in the face' when they are about to leave the terrace, and the angel of mercy, chanting his beatitude, adds a glory, bewildering for Dante's eyes, to the sun itself. The incident is made more convincing by the elaborate scientific precision of the account, telling at once of the reality and the wonder of mercy.

We are not told who chants the words 'Rejoice, thou that overcomest', which the stately reserve of the angels of Purgatory makes it unsuitable to ascribe to the angel himself, and it may well be intended for the song of the souls there purging themselves of envy, who can now join in a great congratulation to one who passes up before them.

Cleared now of envy, the second *P* erased from his brow, Dante learns from Virgil something of what that deliverance means. It is the restoration of a fellowship of which envy is the destruction, by the seeking of those things of which there is no private and separating possession, in which the enrichment of each enriches all the rest and the more that are rich the richer is each. It is a fellowship with men which is fellowship with God, the mysterious co-operation of free will and grace, the multiplication of human charity giving wider scope for 'the eternal goodness' to 'increase upon it'. Of Virgil's teaching here the whole of the *Paradiso* is the expansion and fulfilment and what is here his doctrine is there for Beatrice life and experience and Dante is referred to her by Virgil himself.

The third terrace is that for the purgation of sinful anger, the anger which is enmity—for there is another kind—and Dante is 'rapt of a sudden in an ecstatic vision'. Anger is itself a kind of transport, a blinding fog of the mind, a sin, in a sense, of the imagination, and through the imagination comes its cure. Dante had a temperament much subject to anger and he knew its dangers and needed the inward persuasion of great examples of meekness that he might 'open his heart to the waters of peace'; and he had a sensitive and absorbed imagination and needed Virgil's admonition not to be satified with good visions, but to 'use his waking hour when it returns'.

PURGATORIO

Buic d' inferno e di notte privata
   d'ogni pianeta, sotto pover cielo,
   quant'esser può di nuvol tenebrata,
non fece al viso mio sì grosso velo
   come quel fummo ch' ivi ci coperse,
   nè a sentir di così aspro pelo;
chè l'occhio stare aperto non sofferse;
   onde la scorta mia saputa e fida
   mi s'accostò e l'omero m'offerse.
Sì come cieco va dietro a sua guida   10
   per non smarrirsi e per non dar di cozzo
   in cosa che 'l molesti, o forse ancida,
m'andava io per l'aere amaro e sozzo,
   ascoltando il mio duca che diceva
   pur: 'Guarda che da me tu non sia mozzo.'
Io sentìa voci, e ciascuna pareva
   pregar per pace e per misericordia
   l'Agnel di Dio che le peccata leva.
Pur '*Agnus Dei*' eran le loro essordia;
   una parola in tutte era ed un modo,   20
   sì che parea tra esse ogne concordia.
'Quei sono spirti, maestro, ch' i' odo?'
   diss' io. Ed elli a me: 'Tu vero apprendi,
   e d' iracundia van solvendo il nodo.'
'Or tu chi se' che 'l nostro fummo fendi,
   e di noi parli pur come se tue
   partissi ancor lo tempo per calendi?'

CANTO XVI

The purgation of anger; Marco Lombardo; human degeneracy; the Church's misguiding of the world

GLOOM of Hell or night bereft of every planet under a barren sky overcast everywhere with cloud never made a veil to my sight so heavy or of stuff so harsh to the sense as that smoke which covered us there so that it did not let the eye stay open; therefore my wise and trusty escort came close to me and offered me his shoulder. Just as a blind man goes behind his guide that he may not stray or knock against what might injure or perhaps kill him, so I went through the foul and bitter air listening to my Leader, who kept saying: 'See that thou art not cut off from me.' I heard voices and each seemed to pray for peace and mercy to the Lamb of God that takes away sins. Their beginning was always *Agnus Dei*[1] and all had the same words and the same measure so that among them seemed to be complete accord. 'Are these spirits, Master, that I hear?' I said; and he answered me: 'Thou judgest right, and they are now loosing the knot of anger.'

'Who then art thou that cleavest our smoke and speakest of us just as if thou still measuredst time by calends?'[2] Thus one voice spoke. Then my

Così per una voce detto fue;
    onde 'l maestro mio disse: 'Rispondi,
    e domanda se quinci si va sue.'   30
E io: 'O creatura che ti mondi
    per tornar bella a colui che ti fece,
    maraviglia udirai, se mi secondi.'
'Io ti seguiterò quanto mi lece,'
    rispuose 'e se veder fummo non lascia,
    l' udir ci terrà giunti in quella vece.'
Allora incominciai: 'Con quella fascia
    che la morte dissolve men vo suso,
    e venni qui per l' infernale ambascia.
E se Dio m' ha in sua grazia rinchiuso,   40
    tanto che vuol ch' i' veggia la sua corte
    per modo tutto fuor del moderno uso,
non mi celar chi fosti anzi la morte,
    ma dilmi, e dimmi s' i' vo bene al varco;
    e tue parole fien le nostre scorte.'
'Lombardo fui, e fu' chiamato Marco:
    del mondo seppi, e quel valore amai
    al quale ha or ciascun disteso l'arco.
Per montar su dirittamente vai.'
    Così rispuose, e soggiunse: 'I' ti prego   50
    che per me prieghi quando su sarai.'
E io a lui: 'Per fede mi ti lego
    di far ciò che mi chiedi; ma io scoppio
    dentro ad un dubbio, s' io non me ne spiego.
Prima era scempio, e ora è fatto doppio
    nella sentenza tua, che mi fa certo,
    qui e altrove, quello ov' io l'accoppio.
Lo mondo è ben così tutto diserto
    d'ogne virtute, come tu mi sone,
    e di malizia gravido e coverto;   60
ma priego che m'addite la cagione,
    sì ch' i' la veggia e ch' i' la mostri altrui;
    chè nel cielo uno, e un qua giù la pone.'
Alto sospir, che duolo strinse in 'hui!',
    mise fuor prima; e poi cominciò: 'Frate,
    lo mondo è cieco, e tu vien ben da lui.

Master said: 'Answer, and ask if the way up is from here.' And I: 'O creature who cleansest thyself to return fair to Him that made thee, thou shalt hear a marvel if thou bear me company.' 'I will follow thee as far as is allowed me,' he replied 'and if the smoke does not let us see, hearing will keep us together instead.'

Then I began: 'With those swaddling-bands which death unwinds I make my way upward and I came here through the anguish of Hell; and since God has so received me into His grace that He wills that I see His court in a way quite strange to modern use, do not hide from me who thou wast before death, but tell me, and tell me if I am on the right way to the passage, and thy words shall be our escort.'

'I was Lombard and was called Marco.³ I knew the world and loved that worth at which all have now unbent the bow. For mounting up thou goest straight on.' Thus he replied, and added: 'I pray thee that thou pray for me when thou art above.'

And I said to him: 'I pledge my faith to thee to do what thou askest of me. But I am bursting from a doubt within if I do not free myself from it; single before, it is now doubled by thy statement, which confirms to me here that elsewhere with which I couple it.⁴ The world is indeed thus wholly barren of every virtue, as thou declarest to me, and pregnant and overspread with wickedness, but I beg thee to point out to me the cause that I may see it and show it to men, for one places it in the heavens and another here below.'

He first heaved a deep sigh, which grief forced to 'Alas!', then began: 'Brother, the world is blind and indeed thou comest from it. You that are

Voi che vivete ogne cagion recate
    pur suso al cielo, pur come se tutto
    movesse seco di necessitate.
Se così fosse, in voi fora distrutto   70
    libero arbitrio, e non fora giustizia
    per ben letizia, e per male aver lutto.
Lo cielo i vostri movimenti inizia;
    non dico tutti, ma posto ch' i' 'l dica,
    lume v'è dato a bene e a malizia,
e libero voler; che, se fatica
    nelle prime battaglie col ciel dura,
    poi vince tutto, se ben si notrica.
A maggior forza ed a miglior natura
    liberi soggiacete; e quella cria   80
    la mente in voi, che 'l ciel non ha in sua cura.
Però, se 'l mondo presente disvia,
    in voi è la cagione, in voi si cheggia;
    e io te ne sarò or vera spia.
Esce di mano a lui che la vagheggia
    prima che sia, a guisa di fanciulla
    che piangendo e ridendo pargoleggia,
l'anima semplicetta che sa nulla,
    salvo che, mossa da lieto fattore,
    volentier torna a ciò che la trastulla.   90
Di picciol bene in pria sente sapore;
    quivi s' inganna, e dietro ad esso corre,
    se guida o fren non torce suo amore.
Onde convenne legge per fren porre;
    convenne rege aver che discernesse
    dalla vera città almen la torre.
Le leggi son, ma chi pon mano ad esse?
    Nullo, però che 'l pastor che procede,
    ruminar può, ma non ha l' unghie fesse;
per che la gente, che sua guida vede   100
    pur a quel ben fedire ond'ella è ghiotta,
    di quel si pasce, e più oltre non chiede.
Ben puoi veder che la mala condotta
    è la cagion che 'l mondo ha fatto reo,
    e non natura che 'n voi sia corrotta.

living refer every cause up to the heavens alone,
just as if they moved all things with them by
necessity. If it were so, free choice would be
destroyed in you and there would be no justice in
happiness for well-doing and misery for evil. The
heavens initiate your impulses; I do not say all,
but, if I did, light is given on good and evil, and
free will, and if it bear the strain in the first
battlings with the heavens, then, being rightly
nurtured, it conquers all. To a greater power and
to a better nature you, free, are subject, and that
creates the mind in you which the heavens have
not in their charge. Therefore if the present world
goes astray, in you is the cause, in you let it be
sought; and in this I will be to thee now a faithful
scout. From His hand who regards it fondly before
it is, comes forth, like a child that sports, tearful
and smiling, the little simple soul that knows
nothing, but, moved by a joyful Maker, turns
eagerly to what delights it. At first it tastes the
savour of a trifling good; it is beguiled there and
runs after it, if guide or curb do not divert its
love. Therefore there was need for law to be set
as a curb; there was need for a king who should
discern at least the tower of the true city. Laws
there are, but who sets hand to them? None;
because the shepherd who goes before may chew
the cud but has not the hoofs divided;[5] the people,
therefore, who see their leader snatch only at that
good for which they themselves are greedy, feed
on that and ask for nothing more. Thou canst see
plainly that ill-guiding is the cause that has made
the world wicked, and not nature that is corrupt

Soleva Roma, che 'l buon mondo feo,
   due soli aver, che l' una e l'altra strada
   facean vedere, e del mondo e di Deo.
L'un l'altro ha spento; ed è giunta la spada
   col.pasturale, e l' un con l'altro inseme   110
   per viva forza mal convien che vada,
però che, giunti, l' un l'altro non teme:
   se non mi credi, pon mente alla spiga,
   ch'ogn'erba si conosce per lo seme.
In sul paese ch'Adice e Po riga,
   solea valore e cortesia trovarsi,
   prima che Federigo avesse briga:
or può sicuramente indi passarsi
   per qualunque lasciasse per vergogna
   di ragionar coi buoni o d'appressarsi.   120
Ben v'èn tre vecchi ancora in cui rampogna
   l'antica età la nova, e par lor tardo
   che Dio a miglior vita li ripogna:
Currado da Palazzo e 'l buon Gherardo
   e Guido da Castel, che mei si noma,
   francescamente, il semplice Lombardo.
Dì oggimai che la chiesa di Roma,
   per confondere in sè due reggimenti,
   cade nel fango e sè brutta e la soma.'
'O Marco mio,' diss' io 'bene argomenti;   130
   e or discerno perchè dal retaggio
   li figli di Levì furono essenti.
Ma qual Gherardo è quel che tu per saggio
   di' ch'è rimaso della gente spenta,
   in rimprovero del secol selvaggio?'
'O tuo parlar m' inganna, o el mi tenta,'
   rispuose a me 'chè, parlandomi tosco,
   par che del buon Gherardo nulla senta.
Per altro sopranome io nol conosco
   s' io nol togliessi da sua figlia Gaia.   140
   Dio sia con.voi, chè più non vegno vosco.
Vedi l'albor che per lo fummo raia
   già biancheggiare, e me convien partirmi
   —l'angelo è ivi—prima ch' io li paia.'
Così tornò, e più non volle udirmi.

in you. Rome, which made the good world, used to have two suns[6] which made plain the one way and the other, that of the world and that of God. The one has quenched the other and the sword is joined to the crook,[7] and the one together with the other must perforce go ill, since, joined, the one does not fear the other. If thou dost not believe me, consider the ear of corn, for every plant is known by its seed. On the land that is watered by the Adige and the Po valour and courtesy were once to be found, before Frederick met with strife;[8] now it may be safely traversed by anyone who for shame would avoid speaking with the good or coming near them. There are yet indeed three old men in whom the ancient times rebuke the new, and it seems to them long till God remove them to a better life: Currado da Palazzo and the good Gherardo and Guido da Castel, who is better named in the French fashion the guileless Lombard.[9] Tell henceforth that the Church of Rome, by confounding in itself two governments, falls in the mire and befouls both itself and its burden.'

'O my Marco,' I said 'thou reasonest well, and now I perceive why the sons of Levi were debarred from inheritance.[10] But what Gherardo is this who, thou sayest, is left as an example of the extinct race in reproach of the barbarous age?'

'Either thy speech deceives me' he replied 'or it puts me to the test, for, speaking to me in Tuscan, it seems thou knowest nothing of the good Gherardo; I know him by no other surname unless I take it from his daughter Gaia. God be with you, for I come with you no farther. Thou seest the brightness that shines through the smoke already whitening, and I must go—the angel is there—before I am seen by him.'

So he turned back and would not hear me more.

1. From the Litany: 'O Lamb of God that takest away the sins of the world,
   Have mercy upon us.
   O Lamb of God that takest away the sins of the world,
   Grant us thy peace.'

2. The beginning of the month in ancient Rome; the use survived in Italy.

3. Said to have been a witty and accomplished courtier of the time.

4. Marco's judgement of the world confirms that of Guido in the terrace below (Canto xiv) and doubles Dante's perplexity as to the cause of the world's degeneracy.

5. 'Whatsoever parteth the hoof and cheweth the cud, among the beasts, that shall ye eat. The camel and the hare and the coney chew the cud, but divide not the hoof, therefore they are unclean unto you' (*Lev.* xi. 3; *Deut.* xiv. 7). Pope Boniface understands Scripture, but does not distinguish between temporal and spiritual things. 'His doctrine is sound, but his practice or *walk* is corrupt' (*E. Moore*).

6. Emperor and Pope, to guide in earthly and in heavenly things.

7. The Pope seizes political power.

8. The Emperor Frederick II's struggles with the Papacy in the early 13th century were the cause of great disorder in north Italy.

9. Leading Guelfs in Dante's youth, still living in 1300; Guido was called 'guileless' by the French, in contrast with other Lombards, i.e. usurers.

10. 'The Levites shall do the service of the tabernacle. . . . Among the children of Israel they shall have no inheritance' (*Num.* xviii. 23).

NOTE

It is the humiliation and disablement of a resentful and un-disciplined temper that the penitents of the third terrace suffer, and for the time Dante among them, and in that 'foul and bitter air' he dare not separate from his 'wise and trusty escort'; it is only by the leading of his reason that he finds his way into the light again. As on the terraces below, a chant from the Church's services is an operative part of the purgation, here a prayer for mercy and for peace, the fittest for their sin.

Little is now known of Marco Lombardo, but from Dante's earliest commentators we gather that he was 'a poor courtier, one of those shrewd and agreeable familiars of the lords, of lively mind and various culture, apt at giving advice, at forming family ties, at arranging terms of peace, treaties and alliances, and, given time and place, at using their swords, but also—and chiefly so employed—at keeping the prince in good humour by the singing of amorous verses and the telling of good stories, free in speech and in conduct as the times and customs allowed, and prompt with sharp and stinging words' (*A. Zenatti, L.D.*). By the same testimony, Marco was held in general respect for his honourable and generous character,—in fact, as in the poem, a very definite and notable personality. There is a combination of courtesy with directness and restraint in the more personal part of his talk with Dante and a manner of easy authority in his teaching which are in harmony with his reputation and may well be drawn from life. It is not surprising that Dante made one who was so like himself both in temper and con-dition his spokesman on some of the subjects which most exercised his mind.

The doubt with which he 'is bursting'—the expression is a strong one—concerns the cause of the world's degeneracy. Is it in the heavens or in men themselves? Are men merely *made so*, or is it their own doing? It is a question between the inevitableness of nature and the human conscience, in debate then as, in other terms, today, and Dante's answer to it is that of Augustine and Aquinas.

'The heavens initiate your impulses'; they determine the temperament, the bent, the raw material of the man. But the man himself, the soul of him, is not the creature of the heavens but the creature of God, and by his first enlightenment, 'the mind in you, which the heavens have not in their charge,' and by the supreme gift of free will he is able to 'battle with the heavens' and to master his temperament.

In the exquisite passage about 'the little simple soul' Dante recalls a page of his own written years before in the *Convito*: 'Our soul, immediately on entering on the new road of this life never passed before, directs its eyes towards the goal of its supreme good, and therefore, whatever it sees that seems to have some good in it, believes it to be that. And because its knowledge at first is imperfect for lack both of experience and of instruction, trifling good things seem good to it, and these, therefore, it first begins by desiring. Thus we see infants very greatly desiring an apple, then afterwards going on to desire a little bird, then afterwards desiring fine clothes, and then a horse, and then a mistress, and then not great riches, then great riches, then very great; and this happens because in none of these things it finds that which it is seeking and it thinks to find it farther on.'

The soul, by God's making of it, is moved by instincts of desire; it strays in its ignorance, but is fitted, under guidance, for a true social and spiritual order, for a State that is pure righteousness and a Church that is pure worship. Pope and Emperor have been appointed to 'lead the guileless and impressionable souls of men on the right path' (*P. H. Wicksteed*). But the shepherds have betrayed the flock. Emperors have been negligent (Canto vi) and Popes have usurped their power, joining the sword to the crook, and notably Pope Boniface, who claimed authority over all kings and kingdoms. Empire and Church are, in idea, two aspects of the one order of humanity, to be kept distinct and to be kept in unity; for the perfecting of humanity is its perfecting as an order, a moral and spiritual fellowship, a Church and a State.

'Rome'—an ideal and imaginary Rome—'used to have two suns.' This is Dante's reply to the familiar argument for the Papal supremacy, the argument that the sun and moon in the story of creation were, spiritually interpreted, the Papacy and the Empire, the latter with only a reflected light. It is an argument which Dante meets in the *De Monarchia* with the odd reply that the sun and moon were created on the fourth day of creation week and man not till the sixth, so that no need for Church and Empire had yet arisen! Here he maintains instead that Church and Empire are not sun and moon but 'two suns', several creations of God, each holding its commission and authority from Himself,—which is essentially the whole contention of the *De Monarchia*. There is an example of Dante's characteristic and significant repetition of a phrase in *the one* and *the other* occurring four times in the course of a few lines; Church and Empire, that is to say, are not one, they are 'the one and the other'. The issue was for Dante not merely theoretical but practical and urgent.

With medieval ingenuity the Mosaic regulations for food are pressed into the service so as to rank Pope Boniface among the unclean beasts. Being scriptural, the terms of the law must be spiritually interpreted. Chewing the cud—*ruminare*—already meant meditation, and dividing the hoof, by obvious analogy, should mean the making of distinctions, in which the Church under Boniface failed by 'confounding in itself two governments', with its undivided hoofs, moreover, slipping and 'falling in the mire'. That method of handling Scripture made it a very pliable instrument for various purposes and it was used with perfect sincerity and gravity by the ablest men of the time.

At the first signs of the beams of the setting sun whitening through the smoke Marco turns back; for the penitents stay willingly, by constraint of their penitence, in purgation until they are fit to appear before the angel and to receive his beatitude.

PURGATORIO

RICORDITI, lettor, se mai nell'alpe
  ti colse nebbia per la qual vedessi
  non altrimenti che per pelle talpe,
come, quando i vapori umidi e spessi
  a diradar cominciansi, la spera
  del sol debilemente entra per essi;
e fia la tua imagine leggera
  in giugnere a veder com' io rividi
  lo sole in pria, che già nel corcar era.
Sì, pareggiando i miei co' passi fidi   10
  del mio maestro, usci' fuor di tal nube
  ai raggi morti già ne' bassi lidì.
O imaginativa che ne rube
  tal volta sì di fuor, ch'om non s'accorge
  perchè dintorno suonin mille tube,
chi move te, se 'l senso non ti porge?
  Moveti lume che nel ciel s' informa,
  per sè o per voler che giù lo scorge.
Dell'empiezza di lei che mutò forma
  nell' uccel ch'a cantar più si diletta   20
  nell' imagine mia apparve l'orma:
e qui fu la mia mente sì ristretta
  dentro da sè, che di fuor non venìa
  cosa che fosse allor da lei recetta.
Poi piovve dentro all'alta fantasia
  un, crucifisso, dispettoso e fero
  nella sua vista, e cotal si morìa:
intorno ad esso era il grande Assüero,
  Ester sua sposa e 'l giusto Mardoceo,
  che fu al dire ed al far così intero.   30

CANTO XVII

Visions of anger; the angel of peace; disordered
love the principle of sin

RECALL, reader, if ever in the mountains mist
caught thee for which thou couldst not see except
as moles do through the skin,[1] how, when the
moist, dense vapours begin to disperse, the sun's
disk passes feebly through them; and thy imagina-
tion will quickly come to see how, at first, I saw
the sun again, now near its setting. So, measuring
mine with the faithful steps of my Master, I came
forth from such a fog to the beams which were
already dead on the shores below.

O imagination, which so steals us at times from
outward things that we pay no heed though a
thousand trumpets sound about us, who moves
thee if the senses offer thee nothing? A light moves
thee which takes form in the heavens, either of
itself or by a will which directs it downwards. Of
her impious deed who changed her shape into the
bird that most delights to sing[2] the impress appeared
in my imagination, and at this my mind was so
withdrawn within itself that nothing came from
without that was then received by it. Then rained
down within the high fantasy one crucified, scornful
and fierce in his look, and he was dying so;[3] about
him were the great Ahasuerus and Esther his wife
and the just Mordecai, who was in word and deed

E come questa imagine rompeo
    sè per se stessa, a guisa d'una bulla
    cui manca l'acqua sotto qual si feo,
surse in mia visïone una fanciulla
    piangendo forte, e dicea: 'O regina,
    perchè per ira hai voluto esser nulla?
Ancisa t' hai per non perder Lavina:
    or m' hai perduta! Io son essa che lutto,
    madre, alla tua pria ch'all'altrui ruina.'
Come si frange il sonno ove di butto   40
    nova luce percuote il viso chiuso,
    che fratto guizza pria che muoia tutto;
così l' imaginar mio cadde giuso
    tosto che lume il volto mi percosse,
    maggior assai che quel ch'è in nostro uso.
I' mi volgea per veder ov' io fosse,
    quando una voce disse: 'Qui si monta',
    che da ogni altro intento mi rimosse;
e fece la mia voglia tanto pronta
    di riguardar chi era che parlava,   50
    che mai non posa, se non si raffronta.
Ma come al sol che nostra vista grava
    e per soverchio sua figura vela,
    così la mia virtù quivi mancava.
'Questo è divino spirito, che ne la
    via da ir su ne drizza sanza prego,
    e col suo lume sè medesmo cela.
Sì fa con noi come l'uom si fa sego;
    chè quale aspetta prego e l'uopo vede,
    malignamente già si mette al nego.   60
Or accordiamo a tanto invito il piede:
    procacciam di salir pria che s'abbui,
    chè poi non si porìa, se 'l dì non riede.'
Così disse il mio duca, e io con lui
    volgemmo i nostri passi ad una scala;
    e tosto ch' io al primo grado fui,
senti'mi presso quasi un mover d'ala
    e ventarmi nel viso e dir: '*Beati
    pacifici*, che son sanz' ira mala!'

of such integrity. And as this image broke up of itself, like a bubble lacking the water in which it forms, there arose in my vision a girl weeping bitterly, and she said: 'O Queen, why for anger hast thou chosen not to be? Thou hast killed thyself not to lose Lavinia. Now thou hast lost me. It is I who mourn, Mother, for thy destruction before another's.'[4]

As sleep is broken when new light strikes suddenly on the closed eyes and, being broken, wavers before it quite dies away, so my imagination fell from me as soon as a light, far brighter than the light we know, smote on my face. I was turning to see where I was when a voice said: 'Here is the ascent', and drew me away from every other thought; and it made my desire so eager to see who it was that spoke that it never can rest till it is face to face. But as at the sun, which weighs down our sight and veils its form by excess, so my power there came short.

'This is a divine spirit who directs us to the way upward without our asking and hides himself with his own light; he does with us as a man with himself, for he that waits for the asking and sees the need turns his mind already to a harsh refusal. Now let us make our steps answer to such a bidding and let us endeavour to ascend before it darkens, for then it is not possible till day returns.' My Leader spoke thus, and together we turned our footsteps to a stairway; and as soon as I was on the first step I felt beside me as it were the motion of a wing fanning my face and I heard the words: '*Beati pacifici*[5] who are without sinful anger.'

Già eran sovra noi tanto levati   70
  li ultimi raggi che la notte segue,
  che le stelle apparivan da più lati.
'O virtù mia, perchè sì ti dilegue?'
  fra me stesso dicea, chè mi sentiva
  la possa delle gambe posta in triegue.
Noi eravam dove piu non saliva
  la scala su, ed eravamo affissi,
  pur come nave ch'alla piaggia arriva.
E io attesi un poco s' io udissi
  alcuna cosa nel novo girone;   80
  poi mi volsi al maestro mio, e dissi:
'Dolce mio padre, dì, quale offensione
  si purga qui nel giro dove semo?
  Se i piè si stanno, non stea tuo sermone.'
Ed elli a me: 'L'amor del bene scemo
  del suo dover quiritta si ristora;
  qui si ribatte il mal tardato remo.
Ma perchè più aperto intendi ancora,
  volgi la mente a me, e prenderai
  alcun buon frutto di nostra dimora.'   90
'Nè creator nè creatura mai,'
  cominciò el 'figliuol, fu sanza amore,
  o naturale o d'animo; e tu 'l sai.
Lo naturale è sempre sanza errore,
  ma l'altro puote errar per malo obietto
  o per troppo o per poco di vigore.
Mentre ch'elli è nel primo ben diretto,
  e ne' secondi sè stesso misura,
  esser non può cagion di mal diletto;
ma quando al mal si torce, o con più cura   100
  o con men che non dee corre nel bene,
  contra 'l fattore adovra sua fattura.
Quinci comprender puoi ch'esser convene
  amor sementa in voi d'ogni virtute
  e d'ogne operazion che merta pene.
Or, perchè mai non può dalla salute
  amor del suo subietto volger viso,
  dall'odio proprio son le cose tute;

Already the last rays before nightfall were lifted
so high above us that the stars were showing on
many sides. 'O my strength, why dost thou so melt
away?' I said within myself, for I felt the power
of my legs suspended. We were where the stair
went no higher and were stopped just like a ship
that comes to shore; and I listened for a little if I
could hear anything in the new circle, then turned
to my Master and said: 'My kind Father, tell me,
what offence is purged in this circle where we are?
If our feet are stayed, do not stay thy speech.'

And he said to me: 'The love of good which
comes short of its duty is here restored, here the
too slack oar is plied anew; but, that thou mayst
understand yet more clearly, turn thy mind to me
and thou shalt pluck some good fruit from our
delay.'

'Neither Creator nor creature, my son, was ever
without love, either natural or of the mind,' he
began 'and this thou knowest; the natural is
always without error, but the other may err through
a wrong object or through excess or defect of
vigour. While it is directed on the primal good
and on the secondary keeps right measure[6] it
cannot be the cause of sinful pleasure; but when it is
warped to evil, or with more or with less concern
than is due[7] pursues its good, against the Creator
works His creature. From this thou canst under-
stand that love must be the seed in you of every
virtue and of every action deserving punishment.
Now since love can never turn its face from the
welfare of its subject[8] all things are secure from

225

e perchè intender non si può diviso,
   e per sè stante, alcuno esser dal primo,   110
   da quello odiare ogni effetto è deciso.
Resta, se dividendo bene stimo,
   che 'l mal che s'ama è del prossimo; ed esso
   amor nasce in tre modi in vostro limo.
É chi per esser suo vicin soppresso
   spera eccellenza, e sol per questo brama
   ch'el sia di sua grandezza in basso messo;
è chi podere, grazia, onore e fama
   teme di perder perch'altri sormonti,
   onde s'attrista sì che 'l contrario ama;   120
ed è chi per ingiuria par ch'aonti,
   sì che si fa della vendetta ghiotto,
   e tal convien che il male altrui impronti.
Questo triforme amor qua giù di sotto
   si piange: or vo' che tu dell'altro intende
   che corre al ben con ordine corrotto.
Ciascun confusamente un bene apprende
   nel qual si queti l'animo, e disira;
   per che di giugner lui ciascun contende.
Se lento amore in lui veder vi tira,   130
   o a lui acquistar, questa cornice,
   dopo giusto penter, ve ne martira.
Altro ben è che non fa l'uom felice;
   non è felicità, non è la bona
   essenza, d'ogni ben frutto e radice.
L'amor ch'ad esso troppo s'abbandona,
   di sovr'a noi si piange per tre cerchi;
   ma come tripartito si ragiona,
tacciolo, acciò che tu per te ne cerchi.'

self-hatred, and since no being can be conceived
as severed from the First One and self-existing
every creature is cut off from hatred of Him.[9] It
follows, if I distinguish rightly, that the evil that
is loved is a neighbour's, and this love springs up
in three ways in your clay.[10] There is he that hopes
to excel by the abasement of his neighbour and
for that sole reason longs that from his greatness
he may be brought low; there is he that fears
to lose power, favour, honour, and fame because
another surpasses, by which he is so aggrieved
that he loves the contrary; and there is he that
feels himself so disgraced by insult that he becomes
greedy of vengeance, and such a one must needs
contrive another's harm. These three forms of love
are wept for there below.

'Now I would have thee give thought to the
other, which pursues its good in faulty measure.
Everyone confusedly apprehends a good in which
the mind may be at rest and desires it, so that each
strives to reach it, and if the love is sluggish that
draws you to see it or gain it, this terrace, after due
repentance, torments you for that.[11] Other good
there is which does not make men happy; it is not
happiness, it is not the Good Essence, the fruit
and root of every good.[12] The love which abandons
itself to that[13] is wept for above us in three circles,
but how it is described as threefold I do not say,
that thou mayst search it out for thyself.'

1. The mole's eyes were supposed to be covered with a membrane.

2. Procne, sister of Philomena, avenged her husband Tereus's unfaithfulness by killing their son Itys and serving his body as food to Tereus; pursued by Tereus, she was turned into a nightingale.

3. Haman, chief counsellor of Ahasuerus of Persia, executed for his plot against the Jews at the instance of Esther the Queen, whose cousin, Mordecai the Jew, was put in Haman's place (*Esth.* v–viii).

4. When Aeneas came to Italy and fought the King of Latium the Princess Lavinia, betrothed to Turnus, was given by her father in marriage to Aeneas and her mother committed suicide in resentment and in grief for the false report of Turnus's death.

5. 'Blessed are the peacemakers' (*Matt.* v. 9).

6. On God and on earthly things.

7. Less than due concern for the things of God or more for material things.

8. 'Subject' in the scholastic sense; the person loving.

9. The creature, not self-existing but dependent on God, cannot hate Him.

10. In pride, envy and anger; Cantos x to xvii.

11. For spiritual sloth; Canto xviii.

12. God, who alone 'is good by His essence' (*Aquinas*).

13. To material and physical attractions; Cantos xix to xxi.

NOTE

It is not surprising that one whose imaginative experience was so large and so intense as Dante's should ask himself, without finding any sufficient answer, how the imagination is prompted, how it finds and handles its material, what relation there is between its world and the worlds of sense and of spirit. He is persuaded that visions can be heavenly inspirations and it is as if he meant to suggest the mysterious access of the vision to the mind by the variety of his expressions about those here; the vision of Procne *appeared*, that of Haman *rained down*, that of Lavinia *arose*—that is all he can say of them.

Procne's crime was 'impious' in the old Roman sense of the word, an outrage on the primary human ties and obligations; Haman's rage was directed against the sacred race of the Jews; Amata's suicide was committed in passionate 'refusal of the fated wedlock' of her daughter Lavinia with the father of the Roman people—in the language of Dante's public letter to the Emperor Henry VII. That fury of resentful anger is set forth by these instances as essentially destructive of all human order, all that is meant for men by creation and by providence.

The description of each vision stresses the folly and futility of such anger. Procne, after her crime, turned into a mere singing-bird; Haman, 'scornful and fierce in his look', 'was dying so' and the image of him 'broke up like a bubble'; and Amata died 'not to lose Lavinia' and lost her, choosing 'not to be'. All their rages passed, leaving only evil memories.

The angel of peace directs the Poets upward 'without their asking', with that positive and anticipating grace which is the soul's deliverance from the bitterness and futility of anger.

Sordello told them the previous evening (Canto vii) that the coming of night, the loss of the sun, 'baffles the will with helplessness', and they are stopped at the head of the stair, where we have a discourse from Virgil on the moral plan of Purgatory corresponding to his account of the circles of Hell (*Inf*. xi).

Much ingenuity has been employed in attempts to establish some kind of agreement between the ethical systems of Hell and Purgatory and the difficulties have only seemed to make it clearer that Dante did not intend any such agreement. The plan of Hell is taken in the main from pagan sources, chiefly Aristotle and Cicero; that of Purgatory from Christian tradition. In Hell *sins* are punished, the soul's committal by its own acts to evil; in Purgatory *sinfulness* is purged by the committal of the soul, with its conscious weakness and faults of temper, to the healing grace of God. In the *Inferno* Dante was free to make his own plan; in the *Purgatorio* the canon of sinfulness was provided for him by the Church's long tradition of the Seven Deadly Sins. The different intentions of the *Inferno* and the *Purgatorio* admitted and called for different ethical schemes.

It remained for Dante, accepting the traditional scheme, to order and rationalize it and for this he makes use of the principle of love, of which more is to be heard in the next canto. Love, in the sense of desire and endeavour after good or supposed good of any kind, is the cause of all virtue and of all sin. The perverted love of evil, that is of evil for others, takes form in the sins of the spirit, pride, envy, and anger, purged on the three lower terraces; 'the love of good' —of God, that is—'which comes short of its duty', defines the sin of spiritual sloth, partly of the spirit, partly of the flesh, which is purged on this fourth terrace; and the excessive love of earthly things, things good in themselves but 'not happiness, not the Good Essence', issues in the sins of the flesh, avarice, gluttony, and lust, purged on the three terraces above.

However abstract and unreal for us is all such formal partitioning of the various aspects of human nature and life, it proves in its whole setting a persistent and believing search for principle and order in human experience and in the divine dealing with men which was deeply characteristic of the best minds of Dante's time, and not least of his greatest master Aquinas and of Dante himself. It belongs to his greatness that in his whole work he brought the imagination and the intellect into one field and laboured with all the resources available to him to reconcile them.

PURGATORIO

POSTO avea fine al suo ragionamento
l'alto dottore, ed attento guardava
nella mia vista s' io parea contento;
e io, cui nova sete ancor frugava,
di fuor tacea, e dentro dicea: 'Forse
lo troppo dimandar ch' io fo li grava.'
Ma quel padre verace, che s'accorse
del timido voler che non s'apriva,
parlando, di parlare ardir mi porse.
Ond' io: 'Maestro, il mio veder s'avviva   10
sì nel tuo lume, ch' io discerno chiaro
quanto la tua ragion porti o descriva.
Però ti prego, dolce padre caro,
che mi dimostri amore, a cui reduci
ogni buono operare e 'l suo contraro.'
'Drizza' disse 'ver me l'agute luci
dello 'ntelletto, e fieti manifesto
l'error dei ciechi che si fanno duci.
L'animo, ch'è creato ad amar presto,
ad ogni cosa è mobile che piace,   20
tosto che dal piacere in atto è desto.
Vostra apprensiva da esser verace
tragge intenzione, e dentro a voi la spiega,
sì che l'animo ad essa volger face;
e se, rivolto, inver di lei si piega,
quel piegare è amor, quell'è natura
che per piacer di novo in voi si lega.
Poi, come 'l foco movesi in altura
per la sua forma ch'è nata a salire
là dove più in sua matera dura,   30

232

CANTO XVIII

The exposition of love; the Fourth Terrace; the purgation of sloth; examples of zeal and sloth

THE lofty Teacher had made an end of his discourse and looked intently in my face to see if I was satisfied; and I, whom a new thirst was urging still, kept silence without and said within myself: 'Perhaps I trouble him with too much questioning.' But that true father, who was aware of the timid desire that did not declare itself, spoke and gave me courage to speak; I said therefore: 'Master, my sight is so quickened in thy light that I discern clearly all that thy words set forth and explain; I pray therefore, dear and gentle Father, that thou expound love to me, to which thou reducest every good action and its opposite.'

'Direct on me the keen eyes of thy understanding' he said 'and the error will be manifest to thee of the blind who make themselves guides. The mind, created quick to love, is readily moved towards everything that pleases, as soon as by the pleasure it is roused to action. Your perception takes from outward reality an impression and unfolds it within you, so that it makes the mind turn to it; and if the mind, so turned, inclines to it, that inclination is love, that is nature, which by pleasure is bound on you afresh.[1] Then, as fire moves upward by its form, being born to mount where it most abides

233

così l'animo preso entra in disire,
  ch'è moto spiritale, e mai non posa
  fin che la cosa amata il fa gioire.
Or ti puote apparer quant'è nascosa
  la veritate alla gente ch'avvera
  ciascun amore in sè laudabil cosa,
però che forse appar la sua matera
  sempre esser buona; ma non ciascun segno
  è buono, ancor che buona sia la cera.'
'Le tue parole e 'l mio seguace ingegno'   40
  rispuos' io lui 'm' hanno amor discoverto,
  ma ciò m' ha fatto di dubbiar più pregno;
chè s'amore è di fuori a noi offerto,
  e l'anima non va con altro piede,
  se dritta o torta va, non è suo merto.'
Ed elli a me: 'Quanto ragion qui vede
  dir ti poss' io; da indi in là t'aspetta
  pur a Beatrice, ch'è opra di fede.
Ogni forma sustanzïal, che setta
  è da matera ed è con lei unita,   50
  specifica virtù ha in sè colletta,
la qual sanza operar non è sentita,
  nè si dimostra mai che per effetto,
  come per verdi fronde in pianta vita.
Però, là onde vegna lo intelletto
  delle prime notizie, omo non sape,
  e de' primi appetibili l'affetto,
che sono in voi, sì come studio in ape
  di far lo mele; e questa prima voglia
  merto di lode o di biasmo non cape.   60
Or perchè a questa ogn'altra si raccoglia,
  innata v'è la virtù che consiglia,
  e dell'assenso de' tener la soglia.
Quest'è il principio là onde si piglia
  ragion di meritare in voi, secondo
  che buoni e rei amori accoglie e viglia.
Color che ragionando andaro al fondo
  s'accorser d'esta innata libertate;
  però moralità lasciaro al mondo.

in its matter, so the mind thus seized enters into desire, which is a spiritual movement, and never rests till the thing loved makes it rejoice. Now may be plain to thee how hidden is the truth for those who maintain that every love is in itself praiseworthy, perhaps because its matter always seems good; but not every stamp is good, even if it be good wax.'[2]

'Thy words and my following wit' I answered him 'have revealed the nature of love to me, but that has made me more full of perplexity; for if love is offered to us from without and if the soul moves with no other feet, it has no merit whether it goes straight or crooked.'

And he said to me: 'As far as reason sees here I can tell thee; beyond that wait only for Beatrice, for it is matter of faith. Every substantial form,[3] being both distinct from matter and united with it, holds within itself a specific virtue, which is not perceived except in operation nor is ever demonstrated but by its effect, as life in a plant by green leaves. Therefore, whence come the knowledge of primary ideas and the bent to the primary objects of desire, no man knows; they are in you just as in bees zeal to make honey and this primal will admits no deserving of praise or blame. Now in order that to this will every other may be conformed[4] there is innate in you the faculty which counsels and which ought to hold the threshold of assent. This is the principle in which is found the reason of desert in you according as it garners and winnows out good and guilty loves. Those who in their reasoning went to the root recognized this innate freedom and therefore left ethics to the world.[5]

Onde, poniam che di necessitate 70
   surga ogni amor che dentro a voi s'accende,
   di ritenerlo è in voi la podestate.
La nobile virtù Beatrice intende
   per lo libero arbitrio, e però guarda
   che l'abbi a mente, s'a parlar ten prende.'
La luna, quasi a mezza notte tarda,
   facea le stelle a noi parer più rade,
   fatta com' un secchion che tutto arda;
e correa contra 'l ciel per quelle strade
   che 'l sole infiamma allor che quel da Roma 80
   tra' Sardi e' Corsi il vede quando cade.
E quell'ombra gentil per cui si noma
   Pietola più che villa mantovana,
   del mio carcar diposta avea la soma;
per ch' io, che la ragione aperta e piana
   sovra le mie quistioni avea ricolta,
   stava com'om che sonnolento vana.
Ma questa sonnolenza mi fu tolta
   subitamente da gente che dopo
   le nostre spalle a noi era già volta. 90
E quale Ismeno già vide ed Asopo
   lungo di sè di notte furia e calca,
   pur che i Teban di Bacco avesser uopo,
cotal per quel giron suo passo falca,
   per quel ch' io vidi di color, venendo,
   cui buon volere e giusto amor cavalca.
Tosto fur sovra noi, perchè correndo
   si movea tutta quella turba magna;
   e due dinanzi gridavan piangendo:
'Maria corse con fretta alla montagna; 100
   e Cesare, per soggiogare Ilerda,
   punse Marsilia e poi corse in Ispagna.'
'Ratto, ratto che 'l tempo non si perda
   per poco amor,' gridavan li altri appresso;
   'chè studio di ben far grazia rinverda.'
'O gente in cui fervore aguto adesso
   ricompie forse negligenza e indugio
   da voi per tepidezza in ben far messo,

Admitting then that every love that is kindled in you arises of necessity, the power to control it is in you; that noble faculty Beatrice means by freewill and therefore see thou have it in mind if she would speak of it to thee.'

The moon, delayed almost to midnight, made the stars appear scarcer to us, being shaped like a bucket that is all on fire, and its course against the sky was on those tracks which the sun inflames when one at Rome sees it set between the Sardinians and the Corsicans;[6] and that noble shade through whom Pietola[7] is more famed than any other Mantuan town had laid down the load with which I burdened him, so that I, having garnered his clear and explicit discourse on my questions, remained like one that rambles drowsily.

But this drowsiness was taken from me suddenly by people who had now come round to us behind our back; and as Ismenus and Asopus saw of old a tumult and throng on their banks at night whenever the Thebans had need of Bacchus,[8] such a throng came bending their way round that circle, whom, by what I saw of them, right will and just love were driving on. Soon they were upon us, for all that great crowd kept running, and two in front cried out with tears: 'Mary went into the hill country with haste',[9] and 'Caesar, to subdue Lerida, thrust at Marseilles and then made speed to Spain.'[10] 'Haste, haste, lest time be lost for little love,' the rest cried behind 'that zeal in well-doing may make grace come green again.'

'O people in whom keen fervour now makes good, perhaps, negligence and delay that you have shown by lukewarmness in well-doing, this man,

questi che vive, e certo i' non vi bugio,
   vuole andar su, pur che il sol ne riluca;   110
   però ne dite ond'è presso il pertugio.'
Parole furon queste del mio duca;
   e un di quelli spirti disse: 'Vieni
   di retro a noi, e troverai la buca.
Noi siam di voglia a muoverci sì pieni,
   che restar non potem; però perdona,
   se villania nostra giustizia tieni.
Io fui abate in San Zeno a Verona
   sotto lo 'mperio del buon Barbarossa,
   di cui dolente ancor Melan ragiona.   120
E tale ha già l'un piè dentro la fossa,
   che tosto piangerà quel monastero,
   e tristo fia d'avere avuta possa;
perchè suo figlio, mal del corpo intero,
   e della mente peggio, e che mal nacque,
   ha posto in loco di suo pastor vero.'
Io non so se più disse o s'ei si tacque,
   tant'era già di là da noi trascorso;
   ma questo intesi, e ritener mi piacque.
E quei che m'era ad ogni uopo soccorso   130
   disse: 'Volgiti qua: vedine due
   venir dando all'accidïa di morso.'
Di retro a tutti dicean: 'Prima fue
   morta la gente a cui il mar s'aperse,
   che vedesse Iordan le rede sue;
e quella che l'affanno non sofferse
   fino alla fine col figlio d'Anchise,
   sè stessa a vita sanza gloria offerse.'
Poi quando fuor da noi tanto divise
   quell'ombre, che veder più non potiersi,   140
   novo pensiero dentro a me si mise,
del qual più altri nacquero e diversi;
   e tanto d' uno in altro vaneggiai,
   che li occhi per vaghezza ricopersi,
e 'l pensamento in sogno trasmutai.   145

who lives—and indeed I do not lie to you—would go up as soon as the sun shines on us again; tell us, then, where the opening is at hand.'

These were my Leader's words, and one of those spirits said: 'Come behind us and thou shalt find the gap. We are so filled with desire to keep moving that we cannot rest; pardon us, then, if thou take our penance for discourtesy. I was Abbot of San Zeno at Verona under the rule of the good Barbarossa, of whom Milan still talks with grief;[11] and there is one that has already a foot in the grave who will soon weep on account of that monastery and will be wretched for having had power there, because his son, defective in body, worse in mind, and basely born, he has put in place of its true shepherd.'[12]

I do not know whether he said more or was silent, he had already run on so far past us, but this I heard and chose to retain.

And he that was my succour in every need said: 'Turn round here; see two of them who come putting a bit on sloth.' Behind all the rest they were saying: 'The people for whom the sea opened were dead before Jordan saw its heirs',[13] and 'Those that did not endure the toil to the end with Anchises' son gave themselves to a life without glory.'[14]

Then when these shades were so far parted from us that they could no longer be seen a new thought arose within me, from which others many and diverse were born; and I rambled so from one to the other that in my wandering my eyes closed and I changed my musing into dream.

See Cantos 9, 27

1. 'Natural love' (Canto xvii), which is instinctive and innocent, is confirmed by attainment and by pleasure in the thing loved; it makes for its object just as fire by its 'form', its essential nature, ascends towards the sphere of fire, 'its matter .

2. The instinct of love is the wax, the particular object the stamp.

3. 'Form', the scholastic term for the underlying, essential being of anything; the 'substantial form' of man is the soul, with specific qualities such as axiomatic truths, natural desires and freewill—that which makes him to *be* a man.

4. That deliberate desire. may conform to the innocence of natural bent.

5. Ethics was traced to Plato and Aristotle.

6. The moon, moving east in its monthly course, is in Sagittarius, where the sun is in November; then, the sunset from Rome is in the line between Corsica and Sardinia. The moon is now gibbous, five nights after full, rising near midnight.

7. The Mantuan village where Virgil was born.

8. Bacchanalian festival, when Bacchus was appealed to for a good vintage.

9. Mary's visit to Elisabeth after the annunciation (*Luke* i. 39).

10. In the Civil War against Pompey.

11. The Emperor Frederick Barbarossa destroyed Milan in 1162.

12. Alberto della Scala, Lord of Verona (d. 1301), made his bastard son, a cripple, Abbot of San Zeno against the law of the Church.

13. The Hebrews who passed the Red Sea did not, for their lack of faith, survive to enter Canaan (*Num*. xiv. 23, etc.).

14. The Trojans, 'weary of the great enterprise' and 'with no craving for renown (*Aeneid* v), whom Aeneas left behind in Sicily.

NOTE

It was natural that Dante should ask Virgil to 'expound love' to him, for two reasons. Love, from romantic passion to the philosophical pursuit of truth and the love of God, was the main subject of the poetry of the group of vernacular poets in Tuscany of whom Dante in his youth was the chief, and it was much discussed among them; and love, in the sense of natural bent and craving, a dominant force in nature and in human nature, was central in the 'Epicurean' teaching of the time, the teaching of 'the blind who make themselves guides' and who 'maintain that every love is in itself praiseworthy'. Against this heresy of the inevitableness of mere obedience to natural inclination, a man following his bent as a stone falls and a flame rises, Dante raises his polemic through the lips of Virgil and asserts that which for him is central in man, 'the faculty which counsels', the liberty of the soul. This unique endowment, given to a creature who is immersed in nature, surrounded by it, in many respects a part of it, Virgil can expound in its operation and in its relation to natural impulse. Of its higher implications, in relation to the will and the grace of God, he cannot speak; that is for Beatrice.

Virgil's discourse here, based mainly on Aquinas, carries on the argument of the last two cantos, and when he speaks of 'the soul created quick to love' he is in effect repeating what Marco Lombardo said in the sixteenth canto of 'the little simple soul that knows nothing, but, moved by a joyful Maker, turns eagerly to what delights it'; but here the argument is broadened and deepened. Dante is no mere special pleader for the orthodoxies. He is absorbed by the interplay and antinomy of necessity and freedom, both of which, he maintains, have their place in the nature of things, of 'natural' love, shared with the stones and the beasts and innocent, and love deliberate,

241

committing the soul to good or to evil. 'Love is the golden net, whereby God draws back to Himself all creatures that He has made, whether inanimate, sensitive or rational, by the tendencies or inclinations He has given them to make them seek the end for which they are ordered and disposed, according to His eternal law. Rational beings alone have Free Will, by which man merits or demerits from the Divine Justice, according as he inclines to good or evil loves. Love's tendency to good is the precious material upon which Free Will acts like the craftsman's hand, to fashion a satyr's mask or a crucifix' (*E. G. Gardner*).

The word used here and commonly translated *sloth* is *accidia*—the *accidie* of Chaucer's Parson—and means originally unconcern. It expresses an idea primarily associated with the life of the monastery and connotes spiritual ennui, a state of aversion and embitterment with regard to worship and all that belongs to the religious life. Here, characteristically, Dante broadens the conception to that of 'lukewarmness in well-doing', 'the love of good which comes short of its duty', love that is not love enough to be effectual. These penitents of *accidia* making good their old negligence and delay are compared for their present zeal with the Bacchanals shouting to their god for a good vintage—as if to say, Christians may well care as much for their souls.

This is the only one of the seven terraces of Purgatory in which there is no prayer or office of the Church, and no reader of Dante will suppose the omission to be accidental. The place in the narrative where we look for prayer, between the 'whip' and the 'bit', is occupied here by the cry of the spirits: 'Haste, haste, lest time be lost for little love, so that zeal in well-doing may make grace come green again'; and their cry explains the omission. Their 'little love' has so far disabled these souls for prayer that until grace blooms again in them they have not the power to pray; that is a part of their penance.

The examples of zeal and of sloth, taken in each case from Scripture and from paganism, correspond, in Dante's manner, with the interests of the Church and the Empire: Mary, the predestined mother of her Lord, and Caesar, the predestined founder of imperial Rome, both eager in their course, and the

Hebrews under Moses and the Trojans under Aeneas alike coming short of their providential calling.

The Abbot of San Zeno who replies to Virgil is hardly even a name to us, and he is obviously introduced as the mouthpiece of Dante's own protest against the appointment of the cripple and degenerate Giuseppe della Scala to the same monastery. We do not know much of the circumstances, but they were recent and Dante knew the della Scala family; the appointment was made in 1292 by the father of Dante's friend and hero Can Grande (*Inf.* i) and there is a restrained vehemence in Dante's line 'This I heard and chose to retain' which indicates something of what he thought of this outrage on the Church and its worship.

PURGATORIO

NELL'ORA che non può 'l calor dïurno
    intepidar più il freddo della luna,
    vinto da terra e talor da Saturno;
quando i geomanti lor Maggior Fortuna
    veggiono in orïente, innanzi a l'alba,
    surger per via che poco le sta bruna;
mi venne in sogno una femmina balba,
    nelli occhi guercia, e sovra i piè distorta,
    con le man monche, e di colore scialba.
Io la mirava; e come 'l sol conforta   10
    le fredde membra che la notte aggrava,
    così lo sguardo mio le facea scorta
la lingua, e poscia tutta la drizzava
    in poco d'ora, e lo smarrito volto,
    com'amor vuol, così le colorava.
Poi ch'ell'avea il parlar così disciolto,
    cominciava a cantar sì, che con pena
    da lei avrei mio intento rivolto.
'Io son,' cantava 'io son dolce serena,
    che i marinari in mezzo mar dismago;   20
    tanto son di piacere a sentir piena!
Io volsi Ulisse del suo cammin vago
    al canto mio; e qual meco si ausà
    rado sen parte, sì tutto l'appago.'
Ancor non era sua bocca richiusa,
    quand'una donna apparve santa e presta
    lunghesso me per far colei confusa.

CANTO XIX

*The dream of the Siren; the angel of zeal; the
Fifth Terrace; the purgation of avarice and
prodigality; Pope Adrian V*

IN the hour when the day's heat, overcome by the
earth and sometimes by Saturn, can no longer
temper the cold of the moon,[1] when the geomancers
see their *Fortuna Major*[2] rise in the east before
dawn by a path which does not long stay dark
for it, there came to me in dream a woman, stam-
mering, cross-eyed, and crooked on her feet, with
maimed hands and of sallow hue. I gazed at her,
and as the sun revives cold limbs benumbed by
the night, so my look gave her a ready tongue and
then in a little time made her quite erect and
coloured her wan features as love desires. When
she had her speech thus set free she began to sing
so that it would have been hard for me to turn
my mind from her. 'I am,' she sang 'I am the
sweet siren who beguile the sailors in mid-sea, so
great delight it is to hear me. I turned Ulysses,[3]
eager on his way, to my song, and he who dwells
with me rarely departs, so wholly I content him.'
Her lips were not yet closed again when a lady
holy and alert appeared beside me to put her to
confusion. 'O Virgil, Virgil, who is this?' she said

'O Virgilio, o Virgilio, chi è questa?'
   fieramente dicea; ed el venìa
   con li occhi fitti pur in quella onesta.   30

L'altra prendea, e dinanzi l'aprìa
   fendendo i drappi, e mostravami 'l ventre:
   quel mi svegliò col puzzo che n'uscìa.

Io mossi li occhi al buon maestro: 'Almen tre
   voci t' ho messe!' dicea. 'Surgi e vieni:
   troviam l'aperta per la qual tu entre.'

Su mi levai, e tutti eran già pieni
   dell'alto dì i giron del sacro monte,
   e andavam col sol novo alle reni.

Seguendo lui, portava la mia fronte   40
   come colui che l' ha di pensier carca,
   che fa di sè un mezzo arco di ponte;

quand' io udi': 'Venite; qui si varca,'
   parlare in modo soave e benigno,
   qual non si sente in questa mortal marca.

Con l'ali aperte che parean di cigno,
   volseci in su colui che sì parlonne
   tra' due pareti del duro macigno.

Mosse le penne poi e ventilonne,
   '*Qui lugent*' affermando esser beati,   50
   ch'avran di consolar l'anime donne.

'Che hai che pur inver la terra guati?'
   la guida mia incominciò a dirmi,
   poco amendue dall'angel sormontati.

E io: 'Con tanta sospeccion fa irmi
   novella visïon ch'a sè mi piega,
   sì ch' io non posso dal pensar partirmi.'

'Vedesti' disse 'quell'antica strega
   che sola sovra noi omai si piagne;
   vedesti come l'uom da lei si slega.   60

Bastiti, e batti a terra le calcagne:
   li occhi rivolgi al logoro che gira
   lo rege etterno con le rote magne.'

Quale il falcon, che prima a' piè si mira,
   indi si volge al grido e si protende
   per lo disio del pasto che là il tira;

with anger. And he came with his eyes fixed on that honourable one; he seized the other and laid her bare in front, tearing her clothes, and showed me her belly. That awoke me with the stench that came from her. I turned my eyes to the good Master. 'Three times at least I have called thee,' he said 'rise and come, let us find the opening by which thou enterest.'

I rose up; and all the circles of the holy mountain were already filled with high day and we went on with the new sun at our back. Following him, I bore my brow like one who has it burdened with thought and makes of himself a half-arch of a bridge, when I heard: 'Come, here is the passage,' spoken in such sweet and gracious tones as are not heard within these mortal bounds. With open wings which seemed a swan's he that spoke to us directed us upward between the two walls of flinty stone, then moved his feathers and fanned us, declaring *qui lugent*[4] to be blessed, for they shall have their souls possessed of consolation.

'What ails thee that thou keepst gazing on the ground?' my Guide began to me when we had both climbed a little above the angel; and I: 'With such misgiving a new vision makes me go, which bends me so to itself that I cannot give up thinking of it.'

'Thou sawest' he said 'that ancient witch who alone is now wept for above us; thou sawest how man is freed from her. Let it suffice thee, and strike thy heels on the ground. Turn thine eyes to the lure which the Eternal King spins with the great wheels.'

Like the falcon which looks first to its feet, then turns to the call and stretches forward through the desire for food that draws it there, such I became,

tal mi fec' io; e tal, quanto si fende
 la roccia per dar via a chi va suso,
 n'andai infin dove 'l cerchiar si prende.

Com' io nel quinto giro fui dischiuso, 70
 vidi gente per esso che piangea,
 giacendo a terra tutta volta in giuso.

'*Adhaesit pavimento anima mea*'
 sentìa dir lor con sì alti sospiri,
 che la parola a pena s' intendea.

'O eletti di Dio, li cui soffriri
 e giustizia e speranza fa men duri,
 drizzate noi verso li altri saliri.'

'Se voi venite dal giacer sicuri,
 e volete trovar la via più tosto, 80
 le vostre destre sien sempre di furi.'

Così pregò il Poeta e sì risposto
 poco dinanzi a noi ne fu; per ch' io
 nel parlare avvisai l'altro nascosto;

e volsi li occhi alli occhi al signor mio:
 ond'elli m'assentì con lieto cenno
 ciò che chiedea la vista del disio.

Poi ch' io potei di me fare a mio senno,
 trassimi sovra quella creatura
 le cui parole pria notar mi fenno, 90

dicendo: 'Spirto in cui pianger matura
 quel sanza 'l quale a Dio tornar non pòssi,
 sosta un poco per me tua maggior cura.

Chi fosti e perchè volti avete i dossi
 al su, mi dì, e se vuo' ch' io t' impetri
 cosa di là ond' io vivendo mossi.'

Ed elli a me: 'Perchè i nostri diretri
 rivolga il cielo a sè, saprai; ma prima
 scias quod ego fui successor Petri.

Intra Sïestri e Chiaveri s'adima 100
 una fiumana bella, e del suo nome
 lo titol del mio sangue fa sua cima.

Un mese e poco più prova' io come
 pesa il gran manto a chi dal fango il guarda,
 che piuma sembran tutte l'altre some.

and such, as far as the rock is cloven to make a way for the ascent, I went on to where the circuit is taken.

When I had come out in the open on the fifth round I saw people along it who were weeping, all lying face downward on the ground. '*Adhaesit pavimento anima mea*'[5] I heard them say with sighs so deep that the words could hardly be distinguished.

'O elect of God, whose sufferings both justice and hope make less hard, direct us to the next stairway.' 'If you come exempt from lying prostrate and would find the way most quickly let your right hand be always on the outside.' Thus the Poet asked and thus came the answer from a little way ahead, so that I made out by his speech the other who was hidden and I turned my eyes on the eyes of my Lord; at which he assented with a glad sign to that which my look of desire had asked. When I was free to act as I wished I drew forward above that soul whose words had first made me note him, saying: 'Spirit in whom weeping ripens that without which can be no return to God, stay awhile for me thy greater care. Who thou wast and why you have your backs turned upward, tell me, and whether thou wilt have me gain aught for thee yonder whence I set out alive.'

And he said to me: 'Why heaven turns our backs to itself thou shalt know, but first *scias quod ego fui successor Petri*.[6] Between Sestri and Chiavari pours down a fair stream and from its name the title of my blood makes its boast.[7] A month and little more I proved how the great mantle weighs on him that keeps it from the mire, so that all other burdens seem a feather. My conversion, alas,

La mia conversïone, ohmè!, fu tarda;
   ma come fatto fui roman pastore,
   così scopersi la vita bugiarda.
Vidi che lì non si quetava il core,
   nè più salir potïesi in quella vita;   110
   per che di questa in me s'accese amore.
Fino a quel punto misera e partita
   da Dio anima fui, del tutto avara:
   or, come vedi, qui ne son punita.
Quel ch'avarizia fa, qui si dichiara
   in purgazion dell'anime converse,
   e nulla pena il monte ha più amara.
Sì come l'occhio nostro non s'aderse
   in alto, fisso alle cose terrene,
   così giustizia qui a terra il merse.   120
Come avarizia spense a ciascun bene
   lo nostro amore, onde operar perdèsi,
   così giustizia qui stretti ne tene,
ne' piedi e nelle man legati e presi;
   e quanto fia piacer del giusto sire,
   tanto staremo immobili e distesi.'
Io m'era inginocchiato e volea dire;
   ma com' io cominciai ed el s'accorse,
   solo ascoltando, del mio reverire,
'Qual cagion' disse 'in giù così ti torse?'   130
   E io a lui: 'Per vostra dignitate
   ma coscïenza dritto mi rimorse.'
'Drizza le gambe, levati su, frate!'
   rispuose. 'Non errar: conservo sono
   teco e con li altri ad una podestate.
Se mai quel santo evangelico sono
   che dice "*Neque nubent*" intendesti,
   ben puoi veder perch' io così ragiono.
Vattene omai: non vo' che più t'arresti;
   chè la tua stanza mio pianger disagia,   140
   col qual maturo ciò che tu dicesti.
Nepote ho io di là c' ha nome Alagia,
   buona da sè, pur che la nostra casa
   non faccia lei per essemplo malvagia;
e questa sola di là m'è rimasa.'   145

was late, but when I was made Roman Shepherd I discovered how lying is life. I saw that there the heart was not at rest; nor was it possible to mount higher in that life, so that love of this was kindled in me. Till that moment I was a soul wretched and separate from God, wholly avaricious. Now, as thou seest, I am here punished for it. What avarice does is here declared for the purging of the converted souls, and the mountain has no bitterer pain. Just as our eyes, fixed on earthly things, did not lift themselves on high, so justice here has sunk them to the earth; as avarice quenched all our love of good so that our labours were vain, so justice here holds us fast, seized and bound in feet and hands, and as long as it shall please the righteous Lord so long shall we stay motionless and outstretched.'

I had kneeled and was about to speak; but as soon as I began and he perceived, merely by listening, that I did him reverence, 'What cause' he said 'has bent thee down thus?' And I said to him: 'Because of your[8] dignity my conscience stung me, standing erect.'

'Straighten thy legs, rise up, brother,' he replied 'do not err; I am a fellow-servant with thee and with the others of one Potentate.[9] If ever thou didst understand that holy gospel word which says "*Neque nubent*",[10] thou mayst well see why I reason thus. Go thy way now. I would not have thee stop longer, for thy stay hinders my weeping with which I ripen that which thou hast spoken of. A niece I have yonder who is named Alagia,[11] good in herself if indeed our house do not by example make her wicked, and she alone is left to me yonder.'

1. The earth was supposed to be naturally cold and both Saturn and the moon to shed cold on it.

2. The 'Greater Fortune', an arrangement of six stars used by diviners in fortune-telling.

3. Medieval version of the classical story.

4. 'Blessed are *they that mourn*' (*Matt.* v. 4).

5. 'My soul cleaveth unto the dust' (*Ps.* cxix. 25).

6. 'Know that I was a successor of Peter.'

7. Pope Adrian V, of the Fieschi family, Counts of Lavagna, the title taken from the river in the Eastern Riviera; he died five weeks after his election, in 1276.

8. Honorific *your*.

9. Cp. *Rev.* xix. 10.

10. '*They neither marry* nor are given in marriage' (*Matt.* xxii. 30).

11. Wife of Moroello Malaspina, the 'thunderbolt' of *Inf.* xxiv and probably Dante's host in 1306 (*Purg.* viii).

NOTE

The dream of the Siren is rather invented than imagined; its allegorical mechanism is cumbrous and its significance in detail is debatable. Like the dream of the eagle in the ninth canto it is a prophetic morning dream, to be interpreted in relation to its fulfilment. Dante has not yet passed from the terrace of the purgation of 'little love', the cowardly or slothful non-committal of the soul to a divine end which is yet known and desired—desired, but not enough—and he is now shown in a momentary drama his danger before the seductions of the flesh and the soul's illusion and disillusion with regard to them. Saturn, believed to be the farthest of the planets from the sun and the coldest, was traditionally associated with spiritual contemplation and ascetic abstinence, as we shall find it to be in the *Paradiso*; it was in the earth's coldest hour, when the day's heat was all spent and when the mysterious Greater Fortune of the geomancers was in the sky before the dawn, that the Siren 'came to him in dream' and then was 'put to confusion'. The conditions for a lesson of warning and of the way of deliverance are fitting and relevant.

The sins of the flesh, the intemperate love of earthly good, in the forms of avarice, gluttony, and lust, are, when first seen by the soul in its innocence, mere figures of perversion and helplessness. In the soul's 'gaze' they are transformed to a beauty which acts like an enchantment and it is only by an enlightenment higher than reason itself, by the apparition and the authority of a good which is not of the earth, that the soul is made to see them in their reality and is shocked with a violence of revulsion which is its deliverance. As the Siren represents the cravings of the flesh, so does the 'lady, holy and alert,' the aspirations of the spirit; only a higher love can 'set love in order' in us. Dante is not convinced through the

initiative and instructions of Virgil, for Virgil in the dream
needs the lady's rebuke and then the real Virgil can hardly
wake him, but by discovery of his own weakness and peril;
and he is fitted to pass from the circle of *accidia*, not by an
access of triumphant zeal for God but by a humbled and
penitent consciousness of his insufficiency. When he wakes the
mountain is 'filled with high day', but, following Virgil, he
'makes of himself a half-arch of a bridge', and even after the
angel of zeal has spoken the beatitude and brushed the fourth
P from his brow he still 'goes with misgiving'. The beatitude
is on 'them that mourn', for the first mark of zeal for God is
penitence and longing and it is to such mourning that consola-
tion is given. The penitents blessed by the angel are penitents
still, mourning that their care for the best does not yet secure
them from over-care for things less than the best, and to know
their danger belongs to their fitness for meeting it.

If the dream is a somewhat laboured invention, the passage
immediately following it—the angel's greeting, Virgil's admoni-
tion and Dante's response—is full of the urge and beauty of
an imagined experience. The splendid imagery of the divine
falconry, with the lure of the wheeling heavens and the falcon
eager to escape from the jesses on its feet and to soar after
its food, recalls the similar but less definite imagery at the end
of the fourteenth canto. Dante's frequent use of the incidents
of hawking shows how familiar it was to him in some of the
Italian courts where he was from time to time a guest.

On the fifth circle avarice is purged, and here, as on the
terrace of anger, the penance seems to represent the sin itself
rather than the reversal of it; the condition of the penitents,
that is to say, expresses their painful consciousness of their
sin. The chant of these prostrate souls, 'My soul cleaveth unto
the dust', which goes on, 'Quicken thou me according to thy
word', is a confession and a prayer, and Adrian says of it:
'What avarice does is here declared for the purging of the
converted souls and the mountain has no bitterer pain'; their
confession is itself their penance and none could be harder.

Adrian is the one pope whom Dante meets in Purgatory—
another he sees later in the crowd of the gluttonous—and it
is wholly characteristic that the saving of the Pope is, as it

were, at the expense of the Papacy: 'when I was made Roman Shepherd I discovered how lying is life.' The words of the penitent Pope 'are lance-thrusts for the corrupt popes' (*F. Romani, L.D.*). That the Pope should have no one left to him on earth whose prayers he values except his niece Alagia, with some doubt of her, adds a last touch of pathos and irony.

The reference to Christ's words, 'In the resurrection they neither marry nor are given in marriage', is an example of the medieval freedom in the application of Scripture. Here it means the dissolution of earthly offices and honours in the heavenly life and in particular of Adrian's old status as the Church's 'spouse'.

PURGATORIO

CONTRA miglior voler voler mal pugna;
   onde contra 'l piacer mio, per piacerli,
   trassi dell'acqua non sazia la spugna.
Mossimi; e 'l duca mio si mosse per li
   luoghi spediti pur lungo la roccia,
   come si va per muro stretto a' merli;
chè la gente che fonde a goccia a goccia
   per li occhi il mal che tutto il mondo occupa,
   dall'altra parte in fuor troppo s'approccia.
Maladetta sie tu, antica lupa,   10
   che più di tutte l'altre bestie hai preda
   per la tua fame sanza fine cupa!
O ciel, nel cui girar par che si creda
   le condizion di qua giù trasmutarsi,
   quando verrà per cui questa disceda?
Noi andavam con passi lenti e scarsi,
   e io attento all'ombre, ch' i' sentìa
   pietosamente piangere e lagnarsi;
e per ventura udi' 'Dolce Maria!'
   dinanzi a noi chiamar così nel pianto   20
   come fa donna che in parturir sia;
e seguitar: 'Povera fosti tanto
   quanto veder si può per quello ospizio
   dove sponesti il tuo portato santo.'
Seguentemente intesi: 'O buon Fabrizio,
   con povertà volesti anzi virtute
   che gran ricchezza posseder con vizio.'

CANTO XX

Examples of generosity; Hugh Capet and the Capetian Dynasty; examples of avarice; the earthquake and the Gloria in excelsis

WILL strives ill with better will; therefore to please him against my pleasure I drew the sponge unfilled from the water. I moved on; and my Leader made his way, keeping to the parts left free alongside the rock as one goes on a wall close to the battlements, for the people who pour from their eyes, drop by drop, the evil that fills all the world came too near the edge on the other side. Accursed be thou, ancient wolf, who hast more prey than all the other beasts for thy hunger which is bottomless! O heavens, by whose wheeling men seem to believe their conditions are changed here below, when will he come before whom she shall flee?

We went on with steps slow and short and I was intent on the shades, hearing their pitiful weeping and lamentation, and by chance I heard one ahead of us call through his tears: 'Sweet Mary!' even as a woman does who is in travail, and going on: 'How poor thou wast may be seen from that hostelry where thou didst lay down thy holy burden.'[1] After that I heard: 'O good Fabricius, thou chosest for thy possessions virtue with poverty rather than great riches with wickedness.'[2]

257

Queste parole m'eran sì piaciute,
   ch' io mi trassi oltre per aver contezza
   di quello spirto onde parean venute.   30
Esso parlava ancor della larghezza
   che fece Niccolò alle pulcelle,
   per condurre ad onor lor giovinezza.
'O anima che tanto ben favelle,
   dimmi chi fosti' dissi 'e perchè sola
   tu queste degne lode rinovelle.
Non fia sanza mercè la tua parola,
   s' io ritorno a compièr lo cammin corto
   di quella vita ch'al termine vola.'
Ed elli: 'Io ti dirò, non per conforto   40
   ch' io attenda di là, ma perchè tanta
   grazia in te luce prima che sie morto.
Io fui radice della mala pianta
   che la terra cristiana tutta aduggia,
   sì che buon frutto rado se ne schianta.
Ma se Doagio, Lilla, Guanto e Bruggia
   potesser, tosto ne sarìa vendetta;
   e io la cheggio a lui che tutto giuggia.
Chiamato fui di là Ugo Ciappetta:
   di me son nati i Filippi e i Luigi   50
   per cui novellamente è Francia retta.
Figliuol fu' io d'un beccaio di Parigi.
   Quando li regi antichi venner meno
   tutti, fuor ch' un renduto in panni bigi,
trova'mi stretto nelle mani il freno
   del governo del regno, e tanta possa
   di nuovo acquisto, e sì d'amici pieno,
ch'alla corona vedova promossa
   la testa di mio figlio fu, dal quale
   cominciar di costor le sacrate ossa.   60
Mentre che la gran dota provenzale
   al sangue mio non tolse la vergogna,
   poco valea, ma pur non facea male.
Lì cominciò con forza e con menzogna
   la sua rapina; e poscia, per ammenda,
   Pontì e Normandia prese e Guascogna.

These words so pleased me that I pressed forward to have knowledge of that spirit from whom they seemed to come, and he went on to tell of the bounty which Nicholas showed to the maidens to guide their youth to honour.[3]

'O soul that speakest of such goodness, tell me who thou wast' I said 'and why thou alone renewest these merited praises. Thy words shall not be without reward if I return to finish the short road of that life which flies to its end.'

And he: 'I will tell thee, not for any comfort I expect from yonder but because so great grace shines in thee before thy death. I was the root of the evil tree which overshadows all Christendom so that good fruit is rarely gathered there; but if Douai, Lille, Ghent, and Bruges had power there would soon be vengeance on it, and this I beg from Him who judges all. I was called Hugh Capet yonder.[4] Of me were born the Philips and Louis by whom of late France is ruled. I was the son of a butcher of Paris. When the ancient kings had failed, all but one, a grey-clad monk, I found firm in my hands the reins of the government of the kingdom and such new-gained power and friends in such abundance that to the widowed crown my son's head was advanced, from whom began their consecrated bones.[5] So long as the great dowry of Provence had not deprived my blood of shame it was of small account but at least did no harm; then with force and fraud began its rapine and after, for amends, it took Ponthieu and Normandy and Gascony;

Carlo venne in Italia e, per ammenda,
   vittima fè di Curradino; e poi
   ripinse al ciel Tommaso, per ammenda.
Tempo vegg' io, non molto dopo ancoi,   70
   che tragge un altro Carlo fuor di Francia,
   per far conoscer meglio e sè e' suoi.
Sanz'arme n'esce e solo con la lancia
   con la qual giostrò Giuda, e quella ponta
   sì ch'a Fiorenza fa scoppiar la pancia.
Quindi non terra, ma peccato e onta
   guadagnerà, per sè tanto più grave,
   quanto più lieve simil danno conta.
L'altro, che già uscì preso di nave,
   veggio vender sua figlia e patteggiarne   80
   come fanno i corsar dell'altre schiave.
O avarizia, che puoi tu più farne,
   poscia c' ha' il mio sangue a te sì tratto,
   che non si cura della propria carne?
Perchè men paia il mal futuro e il fatto,
   veggio in Alagna intrar lo fiordaliso,
   e nel vicario suo Cristo esser catto.
Veggiolo un'altra volta esser deriso;
   veggio rinovellar l'aceto e 'l fele,
   e tra vivi ladroni esser anciso.   90
Veggio il novo Pilato sì crudele,
   che ciò nol sazia, ma sanza decreto
   porta nel Tempio le cupide vele.
O Segnor mio, quando sarò io lieto
   a veder la vendetta che, nascosa,
   fa dolce l' ira tua nel tuo secreto?
Ciò ch' io dicea di quell'unica sposa
   dello Spirito Santo e che ti fece
   verso me volger per alcuna chiosa,
tanto è risposta a tutte nostre prece   100
   quanto 'l dì dura; ma com'el s'annotta,
   contrario suon prendemo in quella vece.
Noi repetiam Pigmalïon allotta,
   cui traditore e ladro e parricida
   fece la voglia sua dell'oro ghiotta;

Charles came into Italy and, for amends, made a victim of Conradin, and then, for amends, drove Thomas back to heaven.[6] I see a time, not long from now, which brings another Charles out of France[7] to make both him and his people better known; he comes forth unarmed and only with the lance with which Judas jousted, and so couches it that he bursts the paunch of Florence; from this he shall gain, not land, but sin and shame, so much the heavier for him the lighter he reckons such disgrace. The other, who once went forth a prisoner from his ship, I see selling his daughter and bargaining over her as pirates do with other slave-women.[8] O avarice, what more canst thou do to us, since thou hast so drawn my blood to thyself that it has no care for its own flesh? That past and future ill may seem less, I see the fleur-de-lis enter Anagni and in His Vicar Christ made captive; I see Him mocked a second time; I see renewed the vinegar and the gall and Him slain between living thieves; I see the new Pilate so ruthless that this does not sate him, but without law he bears into the Temple his greedy sails.[9] O my Lord, when shall I rejoice to see the vengeance which, hid in Thy secret counsel, makes sweet Thy wrath?[10]

'That which I said of that only bride of the Holy Ghost[11] and which made thee turn to me for some comment is, so long as day lasts, the response in all our prayers, but when night falls we take up instead an opposite strain. We recall then Pygmalion, whom ravenous lust for gold made traitor and thief and parricide, and the misery of

e la miseria dell'avaro Mida,
    che seguì alla sua dimanda ingorda,
    per la qual sempre convien che si rida.
Del folle Acàn ciascun poi si ricorda,
    come furò le spoglie, sì che l' ira   110
    di Iosuè qui par ch'ancor lo morda.
Indi accusiam col marito Safira;
    lodiamo i calci ch'ebbe Elïodoro;
    ed in infamia tutto il monte gira
Polinestòr ch'ancise Polidoro:
    ultimamente ci si grida: "Crasso,
    dilci, che 'l sai: di che sapore è l'oro?"
Talor parla l'uno alto e l'altro basso,
    secondo l'affezion ch' a dir ci sprona
    ora a maggiore e ora a minor passo: 120
però al ben che 'l dì ci si ragiona,
    dianzi non era io sol; ma qui da presso
    non alzava la voce altra persona.'
Noi eravam partiti già da esso,
    e brigavam di soverchiar la strada
    tanto quanto al poder n'era permesso,
quand' io senti', come cosa che cada,
    tremar lo monte; onde mi prese un gelo
    qual prender suol colui ch'a morte vada:
certo non si scotea sì forte Delo,   130
    pria che Latona in lei facesse 'l nido
    a parturir li due occhi del cielo.
Poi cominciò da tutte parti un grido
    tal che 'l maestro inverso me si feo,
    dicendo: 'Non dubbiar, mentr' io ti guido.'
'Glorïa in excelsis' tutti 'Deo'
    dicean, per quel ch' io da' vicin compresi,
    onde intender lo grido si poteo.
No' istavamo immobili e sospesi
    come i pastor che prima udir quel canto,   140
    fin che 'l tremar cessò ed el compièsi.
Poi ripigliammo nostro cammin santo,
    guardando l'ombre che giacean per terra,
    tornate già in su l'usato pianto.

the avaricious Midas which followed on his inordinate demand that must always be a thing for laughter; each then remembers the foolish Achan, how he stole the spoils, so that the wrath of Joshua seems to sting him here again; then we accuse Sapphira with her husband; we celebrate the kicks that Heliodorus bore; and in infamy the name of Polymnestor, who slew Polydorus, circles all the mountain; last, the cry is: "Tell us, Crassus, for thou knowest, what is the taste of gold?"[12] Sometimes one speaks loud and another low, according to the ardour that spurs our speech with greater or less force; therefore in talking of goodness, as we do here by day, I was not alone just now, but near this no other soul raised his voice.'

We were already parted from him and were striving to get over the ground as fast as we were able, when I felt the mountain shake like a thing that is falling; at which a chill seized me such as seizes one that goes to his death. Assuredly Delos was not shaken so hard before Latona made her nest there to give birth to the two eyes of heaven.[13] Then began on all sides such a shout that the Master drew close to me, saying: 'Do not fear while I guide thee.' '*Gloria in excelsis Deo*'[14] were the words of all, by what I made out from those near, where the cry could be understood. We stood motionless and in suspense, like the shepherds who first heard that song, until it was ended and the trembling ceased; then we took again our sacred path, looking at the shades that lay on the ground having returned now to

263

Nulla ignoranza mai con tanta guerra
  mi fè disideroso di sapere,
  se la memoria mia in ciò non erra,
quanta parìemi allor, pensando, avere;
  nè per la fretta dimandare er' oso,
  nè per me lì potea cosa vedere: 150
così m'andava timido e pensoso.

their accustomed weeping. Never did ignorance so strive in me making me eager to know, if my memory does not err, than I felt it do then in my thought, nor, for our haste, did I dare ask nor could of myself see anything there. So I went on timid and thoughtful.

1. 'She laid him in a manger; because there was no room for them in the inn' (*Luke* ii. 7).

2. The Roman Consul who refused to betray the Republic for bribes of the enemy.

3. St Nicholas saved three destitute girls from disgrace by providing them with dowries.

4. Founder of the Capetian dynasty of France in the 10th century; its representatives were named Louis or Philip for two and a half centuries. In 1300 its power reached from the Netherlands to Sicily and in 1301-2 the Flemish cities rose and defeated it with great slaughter.

5. 'The ancient kings' were the Carlovingians; the Capetians were consecrated by the Archbishop of Rheims.

6. In the 13th century Provence became by marriage a dependency of France. Charles of Anjou, King of Naples—'he of the manly nose' (*Purg.* vii)—defeated and executed his young rival Conradin, nephew of Manfred (*Purg.* iii), in 1268 and was suspected of poisoning Aquinas in 1274.

7. Charles of Valois, 'Lackland', brother of Philip IV of France, sent by Pope Boniface as peace-maker to Florence in 1301, took possession of the city and admitted the Blacks, who pillaged it and expelled the Whites.

8. Charles II of Anjou, son of Charles I, taken in a naval engagement in 1284, married his daughter in 1305 to the notorious Marquis d'Este of Ferrara, who is said to have paid him liberally.

9. Philip IV of France quarrelled with Boniface over taxation of the clergy and was excommunicated in 1303; two of his emissaries seized Boniface in Anagni, his country-seat, and plundered the palace and Boniface died a month later. In 1307 Philip accused the Order of the Templars of many crimes and tortured many of the members; he had the Order suppressed by his creature Pope Clement V and seized its wealth in 1312.

10. 'The righteous shall rejoice when he seeth the vengeance' (*Ps.* lviii. 10).

11. The Virgin. 'That which is conceived in her is of the Holy Ghost' (*Matt.* i. 20).

12. Pygmalion, brother of Dido, killed her husband Sychaeus for his wealth. Midas's wish was granted that all he touched should become gold. Achan stole the spoil at the capture of Jericho and was stoned by Joshua's orders (*Josh.* vii). Ananias and Sapphira kept back part of their gift to the Church by fraud (*Acts* v. 1-11). Heliodorus, seizing the Temple treasures in Jerusalem, was driven back by an angelic rider whose horse kicked him (2 *Mac.* iii. 25). Polymnestor killed his ward Polydorus for his wealth (*Inf.* xxx). Crassus, Triumvir with Caesar, was killed by the Parthians, who sent his head, with the mouth full of gold, to their king.

13. Delos, formerly a floating island, was fixed by Jove so that Latona's twins, Apollo and Diana, identified with the sun and moon, might be born there.

14. 'Glory to God in the highest' (*Luke* ii. 9).

NOTE

The number of the penitents of avarice, crowding the terrace
to the edge, moves Dante to an outburst against that 'ancient
wolf', and his language recalls directly that of the first canto
of the *Inferno* and confirms the usual interpretation of the wolf
there, whose 'greedy appetite is never satisfied', as the symbol
of covetousness. Here as there the idea of the wolf calls up
the hope of a deliverer; here, 'him before whom she shall flee',
there, 'the hound' that shall drive her 'back to Hell'.

After the Virgin the examples of generosity are Fabricius,
a saint of Roman paganism described in the *Aeneid* as 'powerful
in poverty', and Nicholas, one of the most widely known and
loved saints of the Church, the special protector of travellers
and children, the subject of tales and songs in many lands and
familiar in the north to-day as Santa Claus.

Adrian in the last canto, once 'wholly avaricious', is now
wholly penitent, his mind utterly aloof from the old world of
his ambition. Hugh Capet is of another breed, ardent indeed
in penitence for his grasping ambition three hundred years
ago, calling to Mary 'even as a woman does who is in travail'
and heard by Dante above the rest for his ardour, but ardent
too in his agony of shame and wrath for the records of 'his
blood' before and after the time when he spoke. It is as if his
very sin had been to father such a succession as now plagues
the world.

Dante offers, as was his custom, to 'reward' Capet for
answers to his questions by asking Capet's friends in the
world to pray for him, and Capet replies to him 'not for any com-
fort I expect from yonder'. 'It is as if he said: "My descendants
down there are not people who will trouble to pray for me
and their prayers would be no more acceptable to God than
the fruits of Cain" ' (*F. D'Ovidio*).

267

The story of the Capetian dynasty of France is told as it was known in Dante's day and the inaccuracies of fact here are not, for our purpose, material, except that it should be noted that the widespread suspicion of Charles I of Anjou's foul play against Aquinas, which was accepted by Dante, is now regarded as without foundation.

Capet's great outburst against his posterity is Dante's judgement on the royal house of France. When he wrote France had been ruled for some twenty-seven years by Philip IV, who is never named in the *Divine Comedy* but is many times referred to, always with scorn and reprobation. In *Inferno* xix he is compared by Pope Nicholas III—as 'he that rules France'—with the corrupt Syrian King Antiochus; in *Purgatorio* vii he is spoken of by Sordello as 'the pest of France'; here he is 'the new Pilate'; and we shall hear more of him later and nothing better. For Dante the rising power of France, now predominant in Europe, defying and weakening the Empire, corrupting and enslaving the Church, intriguing and interfering by force and fraud in the affairs of Italy, was the public enemy of divine providence and Philip the personal and perfect embodiment of its arrogance and rapacity and guile. So monstrous in Dante's eyes was Philip's outrage on the Pope in 1303 that he makes Capet describe it prophetically with an astounding comparison of Boniface to Christ in the Passion and use language in telling of it which, as surprisingly, has obvious reminiscences of a poem on the Passion written by Boniface himself. It appears indeed that the comparison may have been suggested by Boniface's own words and bearing in the palace at Anagni, where he is reported to have said when his assailants approached him: 'If I am betrayed like Christ, I am ready to die like Christ', and to have awaited them with the daring and dignity suited to his office. It was not merely Boniface, but the Papacy, that Philip attacked—a profanation in Dante's eyes—and in defying Philip and refusing to yield the independence of the clergy in France to the Crown Boniface was, as Dante would hold, taking for once the high and honourable course. In comparison with Philip and in relation to him, even Boniface was, as it were, transfigured to heroism and martyrdom.

Capet's words about his line are studiously contemptuous; it is an 'evil tree', its 'Philips and Louis' spring from 'a butcher of Paris' and its members are summed up as 'consecrated bones'; its disgrace within two years at the hands of the burghers of the Netherlands is forecast in Capet's prayer; it 'did no harm' only so long as it was feeble; then, gaining strength, it lost shame and each offence—'for amends', making up for lost time—eclipsed the last, up to the culmination in the outrage of Anagni and the pillage of 'the Temple'. From Dante, the homeless exile from Florence, the victim of the lance of Judas in the hands of Charles of Valois, and the impassioned prophet still of the Empire whose cause was lost, we must not ask for a just and measured judgement of contemporary France. That we do not get here, but a flame which is white and smokeless by conviction and by appeal to the righteousness of God.

The fact that Charles of Anjou, who 'made a victim of Conradin' and 'drove Thomas back to heaven', was seen singing among the penitents in the Valley of the Princes (*Purg.* vii) —that is, in the way of salvation—makes it the more strange that Charles's brother St Louis, whose long reign over France ended in Dante's childhood—the noblest of the Capetian line and one of the greatest figures of the 13th century, the friend of Aquinas and the martyr of the last crusade—is not only not named here but is not once referred to in Dante's writings. The omission is such as can hardly be other than deliberate. Was it due to the fact that Louis was canonized by Pope Boniface in 1297 in order to flatter his grandson, Philip IV?

The trembling of the mountain, which leaves us too 'in suspense', belongs to the context of the next canto.

PURGATORIO

La sete natural che mai non sazia
   se non con l'acqua onde la femminetta
   sammaritana dimandò la grazia,
mi travagliava, e pungìemi la fretta
   per la 'mpacciata via dietro al mio duca,
   e condolìemi alla giusta vendetta.
Ed ecco, sì come ne scrive Luca
   che Cristo apparve a' due ch'erano in via,
   già surto fuor della sepulcral buca,
ci apparve un'ombra, e dietro a noi venìa,   10
   dal piè guardando la turba che giace;
   nè ci addemmo di lei, sì parlò pria,
dicendo: 'O frati miei, Dio vi dea pace.'
   Noi ci volgemmo subiti, e Virgilio
   rendè lui 'l cenno ch'a ciò si conface.
Poi cominciò: 'Nel beato concilio
   ti ponga in pace la verace corte
   che me rilega nell'etterno essilio.'
'Come!' diss'elli, e parte andavam forte:
   'se voi siete ombre che Dio su non degni,   20
   chi v' ha per la sua scala tanto scorte?'
E 'l dottor mio: 'Se tu riguardi a' segni
   che questi porta e che l'angel profila,
   ben vedrai che coi buon convien ch'e' regni.
Ma perchè lei che dì e notte fila
   non li avea tratta ancora la conocchia
   che Cloto impone a ciascuno e compila,
l'anima sua, ch'è tua e mia serocchia,
   venendo su, non potea venir sola,
   però ch'al nostro modo non adocchia.   30

CANTO XXI

Statius; the completion of his penance; his greeting of Virgil

THE natural thirst which is never quenched but with the water which the woman of Samaria begged as a boon[1] was tormenting me and our haste was urging me along the encumbered way behind my Leader and I was grieving over the just vengeance; and lo, as Luke writes for us that Christ, new-risen from the sepulchral cave, appeared to the two who were in the way,[2] a shade appeared to us, and he came behind us while we were watching the crowd that lay at our feet, and we were not aware of him till he first spoke and said: 'O my brothers, God give you peace.'

We turned quickly and Virgil answered him with the sign suited to his greeting, then began: 'May the faithful court which holds me in eternal exile bring thee in peace to the assembly of the blest.'

'How,' he said, and meanwhile we went on speedily, 'if you are shades whom God above does not count worthy, who has brought you so far on His stairway?'

And my Teacher said: 'If thou look at the marks which this man bears and which are traced by the angel, thou shalt see plainly that he must reign with the righteous. But since she that spins day and night had not yet drawn off for him the flax which Clotho loads and packs for each. on the distaff,[3] his soul, which is thy sister and mine, could not make the ascent alone, because it does not see in our

271

Ond' io fui tratto fuor dell'ampia gola
   d' inferno per mostrarli, e mosterrolli
   oltre, quanto 'l potrà menar mia scola.
Ma dimmi, se tu sai, perchè tai crolli
   diè dianzi il monte, e perchè tutti ad una
   parver gridare infino a' suoi piè molli.'
Sì mi diè, dimandando, per la cruna
   del mio disio, che pur con la speranza
   si fece la mia sete men digiuna.
Quei cominciò: 'Cosa non è che sanza   40
   ordine senta la religïone
   della montagna, o che sia fuor d'usanza.
Libero è qui da ogni alterazione:
   di quel che 'l ciel da sè in sè riceve
   esser ci puote, e non d'altro, cagione.
Per che non pioggia, non grando, non neve,
   non rugiada, non brina più su cade
   che la scaletta di tre gradi breve:
nuvole spesse non paion nè rade,
   nè coruscar, nè figlia di Taumante,   50
   che di là cangia sovente contrade:
secco vapor non surge più avante
   ch'al sommo de' tre gradi ch' io parlai,
   dov' ha il vicario di Pietro le piante.
Trema forse più giù poco od assai;
   ma per vento che 'n terra si nasconda,
   non so come, qua su non tremò mai.
Tremaci quando alcuna anima monda
   sentesi, sì che surga o che si mova
   per salir su; e tal grido seconda.   60
Della mondizia sol voler fa prova,
   che, tutto libero a mutar convento,
   l'alma sorprende, e di voler le giova.
Prima vuol ben, ma non lascia il talento
   che divina giustizia, contra voglia,
   come fu al peccar, pone al tormento.
E io, che son giaciuto a questa doglia
   cinquecent'anni e più, pur mo sentii
   libera volontà di miglior soglia:

fashion. I, therefore, was drawn forth from the wide throat of Hell for his guidance and I shall guide him as much farther as my school can bring him. But tell us, if thou canst, why the mountain made such quaking just now and why all seemed to shout at once, down to its watery base.'

By his question he so threaded the needle of my desire that with the very hope he made my thirst less parching, and the other began: 'The holy rule of the mountain suffers nothing that is without order or contrary to custom. This place is free from all change. From that which heaven receives from itself to itself[4] there may be occasion of change, and from nothing else, so that neither rain nor hail nor snow nor dew nor hoar-frost falls above the short stairway of three steps. Clouds dense or rare do not appear, nor lightning-flash, nor Thaumas's daughter who often shifts her region yonder,[5] nor does dry vapour[6] rise beyond the highest of the three steps I speak of where Peter's Vicar sets his feet. Lower down, perchance, it trembles much or little, but from the wind that is hid in the earth it has never, I know not how, trembled here above; here it trembles when some soul feels itself pure so that it may rise or set out for the ascent, and that shout follows. Of its purity the will alone gives proof, and the soul, wholly free to change its convent, it takes by surprise and by willing avails for it. It wills indeed before, but the desire consents not which the Divine Justice, against the will, sets to the torment as it was once set to the sin.[7] And I, who have lain in this pain five hundred years and more, felt but now my will free for a better threshold, therefore

però sentisti il tremoto e li pii   70
   spiriti per lo monte render lode
   a quel Segnor che tosto su li 'nvii.'
Così ne disse; e però ch'el si gode
   tanto del ber quant'è grande la sete,
   non saprei dir quant'el mi fece prode.
E 'l savio duca: 'Omai veggio la rete
   chi qui v' impiglia e come si scalappia,
   perchè ci trema, e perchè congaudete.
Ora chi fosti, piacciati ch' io sappia,
   e perchè tanti secoli giaciuto   80
   qui se', nelle parole tue mi cappia.'
'Nel tempo che 'l buon Tito, con l'aiuto
   del sommo rege, vendicò le fora
   ond'uscì 'l sangue per Giuda venduto,
col nome che più dura e più onora
   era io di là' rispuose quello spirto
   'famoso assai, ma non con fede ancora.
Tanto fu dolce mio vocale spirto,
   che, tolosano, a sè mi trasse Roma,
   dove mertai le tempie ornar di mirto.   90
Stazio la gente ancor di là mi noma:
   cantai di Tebe, e poi del grande Achille;
   ma caddi in via con la seconda soma.
Al mio ardor fuor seme le faville,
   che mi scaldar, della divina fiamma
   onde sono allumati più di mille;
dell'Eneïda dico, la qual mamma
   fummi e fummi nutrice poetando:
   sanz'essa non fermai peso di dramma.
E per esser vivuto di là quando   100
   visse Virgilio, assentirei un sole
   più che non deggio al mio uscir di bando.'
Volser Virgilio a me queste parole
   con viso che, tacendo, disse: 'Taci';
   ma non può tutto la virtù che vole;
chè riso e pianto son tanto seguaci
   alla passion di che ciascun si spicca
   che men seguon voler ne' più veraci.

thou didst feel the earthquake and hear the devout spirits through the mountain render praises to the Lord—soon may He send them above!' He spoke thus to us, and since the draught is more enjoyed the greater the thirst I cannot tell how much he profited me.

And the wise Leader said: 'I see now the net which here entangles you and how you are released, why it trembles here and at what you rejoice together. Now be pleased to make me know who thou wast and let me gather from thine own words why thou hast lain here so many centuries.'

'In the time when the good Titus, by help of the King Most High, avenged the wounds from which poured the blood sold by Judas'[8] replied that spirit 'I bore yonder the name that most endures and honours most,[9] famous indeed, but still without faith. So sweet was my spirit of song that Rome drew me, a Toulousan, to itself and there I was worthy to have my brows adorned with myrtle. Men yonder still speak my name, which is Statius;[10] and I sang of Thebes and then of great Achilles, but fell by the way with the second burden. The sparks that kindled the fire in me were from the divine flame from which more than a thousand have been lit—I mean the *Aeneid*, which was in poetry my mother and my nurse; without it I had not weighed a drachm, and to have lived yonder when Virgil lived I would have consented to a sun more than I was due before coming forth from banishment.'

These words turned Virgil to me with a look that said in silence: 'Be silent.' But the power to will cannot do all, for laughter and tears are so close followers on the passions from which they spring that they least follow the will in the most

Io pur sorrisi come l'uom ch'ammicca;
   per che l'ombra si tacque, e riguardommi   110
   nelli occhi ove 'l sembiante più si ficca;
e 'Se tanto labore in bene assommi'
   disse 'perchè la tua faccia testeso
   un lampeggiar di riso dimostrommi?'
Or son io d'una parte e d'altra preso:
   l'una mi fa tacer, l'altra scongiura
   ch' io dica; ond' io sospiro, e sono inteso
dal mio maestro, e 'Non aver paura'
   mi dice 'di parlar; ma parla e digli
   quel ch'e' dimanda con cotanta cura.'   120
Ond' io: 'Forse che tu ti maravigli,
   antico spirto, del rider ch' io fei;
   ma più d'ammirazion vo' che ti pigli.
Questi, che guida in alto li occhi miei,
   è quel Virgilio dal qual tu togliesti
   forza a cantar delli uomini e de' dei.
Se cagion altra al mio rider credesti,
   lasciala per non vera, ed esser credi
   quelle parole che di lui dicesti.'
Già s' inchinava ad abbracciar li piedi   130
   al mio dottor, ma el li disse: 'Frate,
   non far, chè tu se' ombra e ombra vedi.'
Ed ei surgendo: 'Or puoi la quantitate
   comprender dell'amor ch'a te mi scalda,
   quand' io dismento nostra vanitate,
trattando l'ombre come cosa salda.'

truthful. I only smiled, like one that gives a hint; at which the shade was silent and looked into my eyes, where the expression most holds its place, and said: 'So may thy great labour end in good, why did thy face just now show me a gleam of mirth?'

Now I am held on the one side and the other, the one makes me keep silence, the other conjures me to speak, so that I sigh and am understood by my Master, and 'Do not fear to speak', he says to me 'but speak and tell him what he asks so eagerly.'

I therefore: 'Thou wonderest, perhaps, ancient spirit, at my smiling, but I would have greater wonder seize thee. He that directs my eyes on high is that Virgil from whom thou didst take power to sing of men and gods; if thou didst suppose another reason for my smile, put it away as untrue and believe it was those words thou didst speak of him.'

Already he was bending to embrace my Teacher's feet; but he said to him: 'Brother, do not so, for thou art a shade and a shade thou seest.'

And he, rising: 'Now thou canst understand the measure of the love that burns in me for thee, when I forget our emptiness and treat shades as solid things.'

PURGATORIO

1. 'Sir, give me this water' (*John* iv. 15); knowledge of the truth.

2. *Luke* xxiv. 13, ff.

3. Clotho, the first of the Fates, prepares the flax with which Lachesis spins the thread of life.

4. When a soul returns to God.

5. Iris, the rainbow.

6. According to Aristotle, moist vapours cause rain, etc., and dry vapours cause winds and, when enclosed in the earth, earthquakes.

7. *Will*, here, is the soul's fundamental craving for its good; *desire*, its immediate choice, which may be right or, in the earthly life, wrong.

8. Titus, afterwards Emperor, destroyed Jerusalem in A.D. 70; this was regarded as avenging the Crucifixion.

9. The name of poet.

10. Latin poet in latter half of the first century; he left his *Achilleid* unfinished.

NOTE

The salvation of a soul has, in Dante's thought, a significance which is much more than personal; it concerns not only the whole fellowship of the saints but, in some mysterious and fundamental sense, the whole frame of things, the earth and the circling heavens, creation in its divine intention and highest operation. He tells us, with his skill of dramatic narrative, first of the trembling of the mountain, followed, as at a signal, by the *Gloria in excelsis Deo*, and these events come on them without warning or explanation. Something has happened, as it were in the very substance of Purgatory, that is beyond their understanding and seems to be of overwhelming significance. The sense here of a supernatural mystery reminds us inevitably of Virgil's reference to the other earthquake, that of the Crucifixion, in which he said that Hell 'trembled on every side so that I thought the universe felt love' (*Inf.* xii). The comparison with Delos, too, recalls a great—but not greater—cosmic event, the birth of the sun and moon. For the soul's saving is at once the most inward of events, the realized freedom and autonomy of the purged will, and the most profoundly cosmic, the labour and travail of creation bringing forth. 'For the earnest expectation of the creation waiteth for the revealing of the sons of God.'

As the earthquake recalls the death of Christ, so, more explicitly, does the *Gloria* His birth, the Samaritan woman His gift of 'living water', and the meeting with 'the two who were in the way' His resurrection. The soul's deliverance is all set in that context.

Much of the language here is the characteristic language of the Church and it emphasizes the idea of Purgatory as the ideal Church of Christ. '*Gloria in excelsis Deo*' was the Church's morning song; Statius meets the poets with the priestly greeting,

'O my brothers, God give you peace', and Virgil's response to him is the wish that he may be 'brought in peace to the assembly of the blest'; the entrance of the true Purgatory is described as the place 'where Peter's Vicar sets his feet'; and the purged soul is 'wholly free to change its convent'. It is the Church Militant, but assured anew of becoming the Church Triumphant and including even those below the gate, that 'renders praises to the Lord'. The earlier liberation of one soul does not weaken but confirms and enriches the existing fellowship of the saints which is ideally the Church.

The true upper Purgatory is beyond common earthly conditions and subject only to spiritual forces, and these varying conditions of the earthly life are typified by the weather, which by an ancient tradition is under 'the prince of the power of the air', the same power as 'stirred the mists and the winds' of the Casentino and drowned Buonconte in 'the raging Archiano' (*Purg.* v). These higher slopes are raised above the apparently arbitrary malignancy of events and in that serene air, through all their penances, the souls 'know that all things work together for good to them that love God'.

Statius's account of the soul's liberation, which is in fact Dante's version of the teaching of Aquinas, is well paraphrased by Wicksteed: 'The repentant souls, though they wish to gain the term and gather the fruit of their penance, are meanwhile as keen to suffer as once they were to sin; and when their present impulse unites with their ultimate desire and creates the instant will to rise, this in itself is a token and assurance that their purgation is complete, and the whole mountain rings with the praises of the spirits. May they, too, soon be sped upon their way!' (*Temple Dante*). The language here is in effect a forecast of the closing lines of the *Paradiso*, in which we are told of the final unity of the soul's immediate choice and its ultimate craving: 'Now, like a wheel that spins with even motion, my desire and will were impelled by the love that moves the sun and the other stars.'

It is of no great consequence for a reader of Dante that scholars do not support either Dante's estimate of Statius's poetry nor Statius's account of his conversion in the next canto, where it appears to be Dante's own invention. Statius

is here in great measure a fictitious character and he serves
Dante's purpose not only as an illustration of a completed
penance but also as a kind of Christian colleague of Virgil
in what remains of the ascent, able to speak of the redeemed
life, as Virgil cannot, from within.

In the scene between the three poets at the end of the canto
it is not Statius the Christian but Statius the pagan poet and
follower of Virgil that appears, and the whole passage is warm
with affection and reverence and gracious courtesies, its play-
fulness approaching as near as Dante ever does approach to
humour.

The apparent inconsistency between Sordello's and Virgil's
meeting in the sixth canto, when 'the one embraced the other',
and the failure of Statius in his attempt to embrace Virgil here,
can hardly be due to an oversight, but no sufficient explanation
of it has been suggested.

PURGATORIO

GIÀ era l'angel dietro a noi rimaso,
    l'angel che n'avea volti al sesto giro,
    avendomi dal viso un colpo raso;
e quei c' hanno a giustizia lor disiro
    detti n'avea beati, e le sue voci
    con *sitïunt*, sanz'altro, ciò forniro.
E io più lieve che per l'altre foci
    m'andava, sì che sanz'alcun labore
    seguiva in su li spiriti veloci,
quando Virgilio incominciò: 'Amore,   10
    acceso di virtù, sempre altro accese,
    pur che la fiamma sua paresse fore;
onde dall'ora che tra noi discese
    nel limbo dello 'nferno Giovenale,
    che la tua affezion mi fè palese,
mia benvoglienza inverso te fu quale
    più strinse mai di non vista persona,
    sì ch'or mi parran corte queste scale.
Ma dimmi, e come amico mi perdona
    se troppa sicurtà m'allarga il freno,   20
    e come amico omai meco ragiona:
come potè trovar dentro al tuo seno
    loco avarizia, tra cotanto senno
    di quanto per tua cura fosti pieno?'
Queste parole Stazio mover fenno
    un poco a riso pria; poscia rispose:
    'Ogni tuo dir d'amor m'è caro cenno.
Veramente più volte appaion cose
    che danno a dubitar falsa matera
    per le vere cagion che son nascose.   30

CANTO XXII

Statius's indebtedness to Virgil and his conversion; the Sixth Terrace; the purgation of gluttony; examples of temperance

NOW the angel who had directed us to the sixth circle was left behind us, having erased a scar from my face, and he had declared to us that they whose desire is for righteousness are blessed, his words completing this with *sitiunt* and without the rest.[1] And I was going on lighter than at the other passages so that I followed the swift spirits up without any labour, when Virgil began: 'Love kindled by virtue always kindles another, if only its flame appear without; from the hour, therefore, when Juvenal descended among us in the Limbo of Hell and made thy affection known to me[2] my goodwill toward thee was as great as ever held anyone for a person not seen, so that now these stairs will seem short to me. But tell me—and as a friend forgive me if with too much assurance I slacken the rein, and as a friend speak with me now—how could avarice find a place in thy breast along with so much wisdom as by thy zeal thou wast filled with?'

These words first made Statius begin to smile a little, then he replied: 'Every word of thine is a dear token to me of thy love; but in truth things often so appear, because their true cause is hid, that they give false matter for perplexity. Thy

283

La tua dimanda tuo creder m'avvera
 esser ch' i' fossi avaro in l'altra vita,
 forse per quella cerchia dov' io era.
Or sappi ch'avarizia fu partita
 troppo da me, e questa dismisura
 migliaia di lunari hanno punita.
E se non fosse ch' io drizzai mia cura,
 quand' io intesi là dove tu chiame,
 crucciato quasi all'umana natura:
"Per che non reggi tu, o sacra fame   40
 dell'oro, l'appetito de' mortali?"
 voltando sentirei le giostre grame.
Allor m'accorsi che troppo aprir l'ali
 potean le mani a spendere, e pente'mi
 così di quel come delli altri mali.
Quanti risurgeran coi crini scemi
 per ignoranza, che di questa pecca
 toglie 'l penter vivendo e nelli stremi!
E sappie che la colpa che rimbecca
 per dritta opposizione alcun peccato 50
 con esso insieme qui suo verde secca:
però, s' io son tra quella gente stato
 che piange l'avarizia, per purgarmi,
 per lo contrario suo m'è incontrato.'
'Or quando tu cantasti le crude armi
 della doppia tristizia di Iocasta'
 disse 'l cantor de' bucolici carmi,
'per quello che Cliò teco lì tasta,
 non par che ti facesse ancor fedele
 la fede, sanza qual ben far non basta. 60
Se così è, qual sole o quai candele
 ti stenebraron, sì che tu drizzasti
 poscia di retro al pescator le vele?'
Ed elli a lui: 'Tu prima m' inviasti
 verso Parnaso a ber nelle sue grotte,
 e prima appresso Dio m'alluminasti.
Facesti come quei che va di notte,
 che porta il lume dietro e sè non giova,
 ma dopo sè fa le persone dotte,

question makes plain to me thy belief that I was avaricious in the other life, doubtless because of that circle where I was; know then that avarice was too far removed from me, and this excess thousands of moons have punished. And had it not been that I corrected my ways when I understood the lines where, as if enraged at human nature, thou didst cry: "To what, O cursed hunger for gold, dost thou not drive the appetite of mortals?",[3] I should be rolling the weights and know the dismal jousts. Then I learned that our hands can spread their wings too wide in spending and I repented of that as of my other sins. How many will rise again with scant locks[4] through ignorance, which takes away repentance of this sin in life and in the last hour! Know, too, that the fault which runs counter to any sin in direct opposition is here, along with it, withered of its green; therefore if I have been for my purging among these people who weep for avarice it is for the contrary this has befallen me.'

'Now, when thou didst sing the cruel arms of the double woe of Jocasta'[5] said the singer of the *Bucolics* 'it does not appear by the notes which Clio[6] touches with thee there that the faith yet made thee faithful without which well-doing is not enough.[7] If that is so, what sun or what candles[8] dispelled thy darkness so that thereafter thou didst lift thy sails behind the fisherman?'

And the other answered him: 'Thou first directedst me to Parnassus to drink in its caves, and first, after God, enlightenedst me. Thou didst like him that goes by night and carries the light behind him and does not help himself but makes wise

285

quando dicesti: "Secol si rinova;   70
  torna giustizia e primo tempo umano,
  e progenïe scende da ciel nova."
Per te poeta fui, per te cristiano:
  ma perchè veggi mei ciò ch' io disegno,
  a colorar distenderò la mano.
Già era 'l mondo tutto quanto pregno
  della vera credenza, seminata
  per li messaggi dell'etterno regno;
e la parola tua sopra toccata
  si consonava a' nuovi predicanti;   80
  ond' io a visitarli presi usata.
Vennermi poi parendo tanto santi,
  che quando Domizian li perseguette,
  sanza mio lacrimar non fur lor pïanti;
e mentre che di là per me si stette,
  io li sovvenni, e i lor dritti costumi
  fer dispregiare a me tutte altre sette.
E pria ch' io conducessi i Greci a' fiumi
  di Tebe, poetando, ebb' io battesmo;
  ma per paura chiuso cristian fu'mi,   90
lungamente mostrando paganesmo;
  e questa tepidezza il quarto cerchio
  cerchiar mi fè più che 'l quarto centesmo.
Tu dunque che levato hai il coperchio
  che m'ascondeva quanto bene io dico,
  mentre che del salire avem soverchio,
dimmi dov'è Terenzio nostro antico,
  Cecilio e Plauto e Vario, se lo sai:
  dimmi se son dannati, ed in qual vico.'
'Costoro e Persio e io e altri assai'   100
  rispuose il duca mio 'siam con quel greco
  che le Muse lattar più ch'altro mai,
nel primo cinghio del carcere cieco:
  spesse fïate ragioniam del monte
  che sempre ha le nutrici nostre seco.
Euripide v'è nosco e Antifonte,
  Simonide, Agatone e altri piùe
  greci che già di lauro ornar la fronte.

those that follow, when thou saidst: "The age
turns new again; justice comes back and the primal
years of men, and a new race descends from
heaven." Through thee I was poet, through thee
Christian; but, that thou mayst see better what I
outline, I shall set my hand to colour it. Already
the world was everywhere big with the true faith,
sown by the messengers of the eternal kingdom,
and thy words I have just spoken were so in
accord with the new preachers that I formed the
habit of visiting them. They came then to seem to
me so holy that when Domitian persecuted them
their weeping did not lack my tears and while I
remained yonder I succoured them and their
upright ways made me despise all other sects.
Then before I had brought the Greeks to the
rivers of Thebes in my verse I received baptism;
but, for fear, I was a hidden Christian long making
show of paganism, and this lukewarmness made
me circle the fourth circle for more than four
centuries. Thou, then, who hast lifted the veil that
concealed from me the great good I speak of, tell
me, while we still have time on the ascent, where
is our ancient Terence, Cecilius and Plautus and
Varius,⁹ if thou knowest; tell me if they are lost
and in what quarter.'

'These and Persius and I and many others'
replied my Leader 'are with that Greek whom the
Muses suckled more than any other,¹⁰ in the first
circle of the blind prison; very often we talk of
the mountain that has always with it those that
nursed us. Euripides is there with us and
Antiphon, Simonides and Agathon and many
other Greeks who once adorned their brows with

287

Quivi si veggion delle genti tue
　　Antigonè, Deïfilè e Argia,　　　　　　　110
　　e Ismenè sì trista come fue.
Vedeisi quella che mostrò Langìa:
　　evvi la figlia di Tiresia e Teti
　　e con le suore sue Deïdamìa.'
Tacevansi ambedue già li poeti,
　　di novo attenti a riguardar dintorno,
　　liberi dal salire e da' pareti;
e già le quattro ancelle eran del giorno
　　rimase a dietro, e la quinta era al temo,
　　drizzando pur in su l'ardente corno,　　120
quando il mio duca: 'Io credo ch'allo stremo
　　le destre spalle volger ne convegna,
　　girando il monte come far solemo.'
Così l'usanza fu lì nostra insegna,
　　e prendemmo la via con men sospetto
　　per l'assentir di quell'anima degna.
Elli givan dinanzi, ed io soletto
　　di retro, e ascoltava i lor sermoni,
　　ch'a poetar mi davano intelletto.
Ma tosto ruppe le dolci ragioni ·　　　　130
　　un alber che trovammo in mezza strada,
　　con pomi a odorar soavi e boni;
e come abete in alto si digrada
　　di ramo in ramo, così quello in giuso,
　　cred' io perchè persona su non vada.
Dal lato onde 'l cammin nostro era chiuso,
　　cadea dell'alta roccia un liquor chiaro
　　e si spandeva per le foglie suso.
Li due poeti all'alber s'appressaro;
　　e una voce per entro le fronde　　　　140
　　gridò: 'Di questo cibo avrete caro.'
Poi disse: 'Più pensava Maria onde
　　fosser le nozze orrevoli ed intere,
　　ch'alla sua bocca, ch'or per voi risponde.
E le Romane antiche per lor bere
　　contente furon d'acqua; e Danïello
　　dispregiò cibo ed acquistò savere.

laurel. Of thy people[11] are seen there Antigone, Deiphyle and Argia and Ismene, sad still as she was; she that showed Langia is seen there; there is the daughter of Tiresias, and Thetis and Deidamia with her sisters.'

Both the Poets were now silent, intent again on looking about them, being freed from the ascent and the walls, and already the four handmaids of the day were left behind and the fifth was at the shaft, directing still upward its burning horn,[12] when my Leader said: 'I think we must turn our right shoulders to the edge and circle the mountain as we are accustomed.'

Thus use was our instruction there, and we took our way with less uncertainty because of the assent of that elect soul. They went in front and I by myself behind listening to their talk, which gave me understanding in making verse. But soon their pleasant converse was broken by a tree which we found in the middle of the way, with fruits that smelled sweet and good, and as a fir tapers upwards from branch to branch so it did downwards, I think so that no one should climb it. On the side where our way was bounded there fell from the high rock clear water which was dispersed above among the leaves. The two Poets approached the tree and a voice from among the boughs cried: 'You may not eat of this food'; then said: 'Mary had more thought that the marriage-feast should be honourable and complete than for her own mouth which now answers for you,[13] and the Roman women of old were content with water for their drink, and Daniel despised food and gained

Lo secol primo quant'oro fu bello;
  fè savorose con fame le ghiande,
  e nettare con sete ogni ruscello.   150
Mele e locuste furon le vivande
  che nodriro il Batista nel diserto;
  per ch'elli è glorïoso e tanto grande
quanto per l' Evangelio v' è aperto.'

wisdom.[14] The first age was beautiful as gold; it made acorns savoury with hunger and with thirst made nectar of every brook. Honey and locusts were the viands that nourished the Baptist in the desert, for which he is glorious and as great as by the Gospel he is declared to you.'[15]

1. The beatitude is here limited to: 'Blessed are they which *thirst after* righteousness' (*Matt.* v. 6).

2. Juvenal, Latin satirist, contemporary of Statius, whom he outlived and praised in one of his poems.

3. *Aeneid* iii.

4. Cp. 'cropt hair' in *Inf.* vii.

5. Jocasta of Thebes, whose sons, Eteocles and Polynices, fought for the succession to the crown and killed each other.

6. The Muse of history.

7. 'Without faith it is impossible to please him' (*Heb.* xi. 6).

8. Divine or human aid.

9. These four and Persius, ancient Latin poets.

10. Homer: cp. *Inf.* iv.

11. Persons named in Statius's poems.

12. The hours drew the sun's car in turn (*Purg.* xii); it is about 10.30 a.m.

13. 'The mother of Jesus saith unto him, They have no wine' (*John* ii. 3). Mary, as mediator, 'answers' in heaven for the penitents.

14. 'Daniel purposed in his heart that he would not defile himself with the portion of the king's meat, nor with the wine which he drank' (*Dan.* i. 8).

15. 'He shall be great in the sight of the Lord, and shall drink neither wine nor strong drink' (*Luke* i. 15). 'Among those that are born of women there is not a greater prophet than John the Baptist' (*Luke* vii. 28).

NOTE

Statius, by an apparently gratuitous invention of Dante's, is a penitent of prodigality, a less grave offence indeed than avarice, outwardly its opposite and hardly regarded by the world or by the sinner himself as a sin at all, yet essentially another form of that 'cursed hunger for gold' denounced in the *Aeneid*, which 'drives the appetite of mortals' to disaster. It is a species of folly which Dante seems almost to go out of his way to reprobate, and the fact that he notes here, as on the terrace of pride, that when the scar was taken from his brow he 'felt lighter than at the other passages' has suggested to some readers that Dante himself had shared Statius's sin and his deliverance.

'If the account given of himself by Statius is Dante's own invention, rarely has a romance been imagined of such historical verisimilitude or such knowledge of the human heart. The young poet, celebrated, applauded by the crowd, filled with veneration for the *Aeneid*, which he has taken as his model, and for Virgil, reads the lines of the fourth *Eclogue*, which seem to him, as they did to many others, a prophecy of the renewal of the world. He knows that "the new preachers" are announcing something of the kind and the strange similarity arrests his attention and induces him to visit them. Going among them he sees their holy life and is attracted by it; his fellow-feeling moves him to compassion when they are unjustly persecuted and he helps them and their "upright ways" fill him with contempt for the followers of all the other faiths. When, after long reflection, he resolves to receive baptism, the Christians being still hated and persecuted, he, young, admired, famous, rich, has not the courage to expose himself to imprisonment and torture, he has not the force to face martyrdom and he continues for a long time to make a show of paganism in his life and writings' (*F. Torraca*). Although the conversion of Statius is invented, the invention had support in popular legends telling of similar conversions from paganism under the influence of Virgil's words.

The language of the fourth *Eclogue*, some lines of which are freely translated in the canto, is strikingly similar to some of the radiant chapters of *Isaiah*. The poem speaks of a child just born under whom the iron race shall cease and a golden spring up throughout the world, which he shall rule in peace; the earth, then, shall bring forth without tillage; the goats shall of themselves bring home their udders swollen with milk and the herds shall not fear great lions; purple grapes shall hang on the wild brambles and the hard oaks shall distil honey like dew; the serpent shall die and the plants treacherous with poison; see how all things rejoice in the coming age! It is little wonder that the poem, written in the dawn of the Empire and forty years before the birth of Christ, should have been accepted by many generations of Christians as an inspired prophecy in paganism of Christianity and should have been a chief factor in the extraordinary glorification of Virgil in medieval Christendom.

'As little children lisp, and tell of heaven,
   So thoughts beyond their thought to those high bards
      were given.'

Statius's language to Virgil is an outlet for Dante's own reverent affection for his Master; and it is, not less, his statement that reason finds its verification and fulfilment, not in itself, but in faith—as Virgil is verified and fulfilled in Beatrice—and that the Empire, with its own high earthly authority, belongs to an order that reaches beyond the world.

The account of the arrival of the poets on the sixth terrace will be best considered along with the next canto.

PURGATORIO

Mentre che li occhi per la fronda verde
   ficcava ïo sì come far suole
   chi dietro alli uccellin sua vita perde,
lo più che padre mi dicea: 'Figliuole,
   vienne oramai, chè 'l tempo che n'è imposto
   più utilmente compartir si vuole.'
Io volsi 'l viso, e 'l passo non men tosto,
   appresso i savi, che parlavan sìe
   che l'andar mi facean di nullo costo.
Ed ecco piangere e cantar s' udìe   10
   'Labïa mëa, Domine,' per modo
   tal che diletto e doglia parturìe.
'O dolce padre, che è quel ch' i' odo?'
   comincia' io. Ed elli: 'Ombre che vanno
   forse di lor dover solvendo il nodo.'
Sì come i peregrin pensosi fanno,
   giugnendo per cammin gente non nota,
   che si volgono ad essa e non restanno,
così di retro a noi, più tosto mota,
   venendo e trapassando ci ammirava   20
   d'anime turba tacita e devota.
Nelli occhi era ciascuna oscura e cava,
   palida nella faccia, e tanto scema,
   che dall'ossa la pelle s' informava:
non credo che così a buccia strema
   Eresitone fosse fatto secco
   per digiunar, quando più n'ebbe tema.
Io dicea fra me stesso pensando: 'Ecco
   la gente che perdè Ierusalemme,
   quando Maria nel figlio diè di becco!'   30

CANTO XXIII

*The wasted forms of the penitents; Forese Donati;
his warning to the women of Florence*

WHILE I strained my eyes through the green
foliage, as he sometimes does who wastes his life
after the birds,[1] my more than father said to me:
'Son, come on now, for the time appointed us must
be put to better use.'

I turned my face, and my steps not less quickly,
after the sages, who were talking so that they
made the going of no cost to me, and lo, '*Labia
mea, Domine,*'[2] we heard wept and sung in tones
that brought delight and grief.

'O sweet Father, what is that I hear?' I began;
and he: 'Shades, perhaps, that go loosing the knot
of their debt.'

Just as travellers absorbed in thought, when they
overtake strangers on the road, turn to them
without stopping, so, coming behind us with more
speed and passing on, a crowd of souls, silent and
devout, gazed at us with wonder. Each was dark
and hollow in the eyes, pallid in face, and so
wasted that the skin took shape from the bones;
I do not believe that Erysicthon had become so
withered to the very rind by hunger when he had
most fear of it.[3] I said to myself in thought: 'See
the people who lost Jerusalem when Mary preyed
on her child!'[4] The eye-pits were like rings without

297

Parean l'occhiaie anella sanza gemme:
   chi nel viso delli uomini legge 'omo'
   ben avrìa quivi conosciuta l'emme.
Chi crederebbe che l'odor d'un pomo
   sì governasse, generando brama,
   e quel d'un'acqua, non sappiendo como?
Già era in ammirar che sì li affama,
   per la cagione ancor non manifesta
   di lor magrezza e di lor trista squama,
ed ecco del profondo della testa   40
   volse a me li occhi un'ombra e guardò fiso;
   poi gridò forte: 'Qual grazia m'è questa?'
Mai non l'avrei riconosciuto al viso;
   ma nella voce sua mi fu palese
   ciò che l'aspetto in sè avea conquiso.
Questa favilla tutta mi raccese
   mia conoscenza alla cangiata labbia,
   e ravvisai la faccia di Forese.
'Deh, non contendere all'asciutta scabbia
   che mi scolora' pregava 'la pelle,   50
   nè a difetto di carne ch' io abbia;
ma dimmi il ver di te, e chi son quelle
   due anime che là ti fanno scorta:
   non rimaner che tu non mi favelle!'
'La faccia tua, ch' io lagrimai già morta,
   mi dà di pianger mo non minor doglia'
   rispuos' io lui 'veggendola sì torta.
Però mi dì, per Dio, che sì vi sfoglia:
   non mi far dir mentr' io mi maraviglio,
   chè mal può dir chi è pien d'altra voglia.'   60
Ed elli a me: 'Dell'etterno consiglio
   cade vertù nell'acqua e nella pianta
   rimasa dietro ond' io sì m'assottiglio.
Tutta esta gente che piangendo canta
   per seguitar la gola oltre misura,
   in fame e 'n sete qui si rifà santa.
Di bere e di mangiar n'accende cura
   l'odor ch'esce del pomo e dello sprazzo
   che si distende su per sua verdura.

the gem. He that reads *OMO* in men's faces
might easily have made out the *M* there.[5] Who,
not knowing the reason, would believe that the
odour of fruit and of water, by the craving it
caused, would operate so?

I was now wondering what so famished them,
the cause of their leanness and wretched scurf
being still unknown to me, when lo, from the
depth of the head a shade turned his eyes on me
and looked steadily, then cried aloud: 'What a
favour is this to me!' I should never have known
him again by his looks, but in his voice was plain
to me that which was destroyed in his aspect; that
spark rekindled in me all my knowledge of the
changed features and I recognized the face of
Forese.[6]

'Ah,' he begged 'do not set thy mind on the
withered scab that discolours my skin nor on this
lack of flesh in me, but tell me the truth about
thyself and who these two souls are there that give
thee escort. Do not delay to speak to me.'

'Thy face which once I wept for dead' I answered
him 'now gives me no less cause for tears, seeing
it so disfigured; therefore tell me, in God's name,
what so wastes you. Do not make me speak while
I am marvelling, for he can ill speak whose mind
is full of something else.'

And he said to me: 'From the eternal counsel
virtue descends into the water and into the tree
left behind us, by which I am made thus lean;
all these people who weep as they sing, having
followed their appetite beyond measure, regain
here in hunger and thirst their holiness. The
fragrance which comes from the fruit and from
the spray that is dispersed over its verdure kindles

E non pur una volta, questo spazzo   70
  girando, si rinfresca nostra pena:
  io dico pena, e dovrìa dir sollazzo,
chè quella voglia all'arbore ci mena
  che menò Cristo lieto a dire "Elì",
  quando ne liberò con la sua vena.'
E io a lui: 'Forese, da quel dì
  nel qual mutasti mondo a miglior vita,
  cinqu'anni non son volti infino a qui.
Se prima fu la possa in te finita
  di peccar più, che sorvenisse l'ora   80
  del buon dolor ch'a Dio ne rimarita,
come se' tu qua su venuto ancora?
  Io ti credea trovar là giù di sotto
  dove tempo per tempo si ristora.'
Ond'elli a me: 'Sì tosto m' ha condotto
  a ber lo dolce assenzo de' martiri
  la Nella mia con suo pianger dirotto.
Con suoi prieghi devoti e con sospiri
  tratto m' ha della costa ove s'aspetta,
  e liberato m' ha delli altri giri.   90
Tanto è a Dio più cara e più diletta
  la vedovella mia, che molto amai,
  quanto in bene operare è più soletta;
chè la Barbagia di Sardigna assai
  nelle femmine sue più è pudica
  che la Barbagia dov' io la lasciai.
O dolce frate, che vuo' tu ch' io dica?
  Tempo futuro m'è già nel cospetto,
  cui non sarà quest'ora molto antica,
nel qual sarà in pergamo interdetto   100
  alle sfacciate donne fiorentine
  l'andar mostrando con le poppe il petto.
Quai barbare fuor mai, quai saracine,
  cui bisognasse, per farle ir coperte,
  o spiritali o altre discipline?
Ma se le svergognate fosser certe
  di quel che 'l ciel veloce loro ammanna,
  già per urlare avrìen le bocche aperte;

in us the craving to eat and drink, and not once only our pain is renewed as we go round this level; I say pain and ought to say solace, for that will leads us to the tree which led Christ gladly to say *Eli*, when with His own veins He freed us.'[7]

And I said to him: 'Forese, from that day when thou didst exchange the world for a better life not five years have revolved till now, and if the power to sin more ended for thee before the hour arrived of the good grief that weds us again to God, how art thou come up here already? I thought to find thee down below, where time is made good by time.'

Then he said to me: 'It is my Nella that has brought me so soon to drink the sweet wormwood of the torments; by her flood of tears, by her devout prayers and sighs, she has drawn me from the slope where they wait and has set me free from the other circles. So much more precious to God and more beloved is my widow, whom I greatly loved, as she is more alone in well-doing; for the Barbagia of Sardinia is far modester in its women than the Barbagia where I left her.[8] O sweet brother, what wilt thou have me say? A coming time is already before my eyes to which this hour will not be very old when from the pulpit it shall be forbidden to the brazen women of Florence to go showing the breast with the paps. What barbarous women, what Saracens, ever were there that needed, to make them go covered, spiritual disciplines or any other? But had the shameless creatures knowledge of what the swift heavens prepare for them, they would have their mouths open already for howling; for if our foresight here

chè se l'antiveder qui non m' inganna,
 prima fien triste che le guance impeli   110
 colui che mo si consola con nanna.
Deh, frate, or fa che più non mi ti celi!
 vedi che non pur io, ma questa gente
 tutta rimira là dove 'l sol veli.'
Per ch' io a lui: 'Se tu riduci a mente
 qual fosti meco, e qual io teco fui,
 ancor fia grave il memorar presente.
Di quella vita mi volse costui
 che mi va innanzi, l'altr' ier, quando tonda
 vi si mostrò la suora di colui',   120
e 'l sol mostrai. 'Costui per la profonda
 notte menato m' ha di veri morti
 con questa vera carne che 'l seconda.
Indi m' han tratto su li suoi conforti,
 salendo e rigirando la montagna
 che drizza voi che 'l mondo fece torti.
Tanto dice di farmi sua compagna,
 che io sarò là dove fia Beatrice:
 quivi convien che sanza lui rimagna.
Virgilio è questi che così mi dice'   130
 e addita' lo; 'e quest'altro è quell'ombra
 per cu' iscosse dianzi ogni pendice
lo vostro regno, che da sè lo sgombra.'

does not deceive me they shall be sorrowful before he has hair on his cheeks who now is soothed with lullabies.[9] Pray, brother, do not longer hide thy story from me; thou seest that not only I but all these people are gazing where thou veilest the sun.'

On that I said to him: 'If thou bring back to mind what thou wast with me and I with thee, the present memory will be grievous still. He that goes before me turned me from that life some days ago, when the sister of him'—and I pointed to the sun—'showed herself round to you. It is he that has led me through the profound night of the truly dead with this true flesh that follows him; his succours have drawn me up thence, climbing and circling the mountain which straightens you whom the world made crooked. So long he says he will bear me company till I shall be where Beatrice is; there I must be left without him. It is Virgil who speaks thus to me'—and I pointed to him—'and this other is the shade for whom your kingdom shook all its slopes just now, discharging him from itself.'

1. In hawking.

2. 'O Lord, open thou my lips' (*Ps.* li. 15).

3. Eyisicthon, punished with insatiable hunger for offending Ceres, ate his own flesh.

4. Mary, a Jewess, said to have eaten her own child in the siege of Jerusalem.

5. *OMO*—for *homo*, man—supposed to be legible in the eyes, eye-brows and nose.

6. Forese Donati, a friend of Dante in Florence; died in 1296.

7. 'Jesus cried with a loud voice, saying, Eli, Eli, lama sabachthani? that is to say, My God, my God, why hast thou forsaken me?' (*Matt.* xxvii. 46). 'That will', the desire for conformity with God's will.

8. Barbagia, a mountainous part of Sardinia, regarded as uncivilized.

9. Florence suffered various calamities in the years after 1300, culminating in a disastrous defeat in 1315.

NOTE

There is a marked antithesis at the end of the twenty-second canto and at the beginning of the twenty-third between the talk of the two elder poets and the business presently in hand, between their reminiscences of pagan predecessors and heroes, to which Dante listened with delight, and the Christian purgation of the souls. 'Their pleasant converse was broken by a tree which we found in the middle of the way', and 'they were talking so that they made the going of no cost to me, and lo *Labia mea, Domine*, we heard wept and sung' by the penitents; and the talk of the poets is forgotten. There is here nothing of reproach such as there was in Cato's language to the 'laggard spirits' who lingered for Casella's song (*Purg*. ii), but there is the same reminder of the essential priority of the soul's main concern, to 'cast its slough'.

In line with this are the repeated references to haste in the account of this terrace, as if to mark the correction, by a new energy and urgency, of the soul's sluggish surrender to the persuasions of natural appetite. Virgil checks Dante's lingering at the tree—'the time appointed us must be put to better use '—and Dante 'turns his face, and his steps not less quickly, after the sages'; the crowd of souls comes on behind them 'with more speed' and passes on without stopping; in the next canto we are told that Dante and Forese, 'conversing, went on quickly, like a ship driven by a fair wind'; the penitents 'hastened their steps, being light both with leanness and desire'; and Forese parts from Dante like a rider at full gallop, saying that while he stays he is losing time, which is precious there. This cumulative statement of haste means that these souls, once soft and yielding at the bidding of their appetites, are now being braced to hardness and perfected in energy and singleness of purpose.

The tree in the middle of the way is, by the singular plan of its foliage which allows only the fragrance of the fruit and water to reach the penitents and by the voices that come from it, an obvious symbol of abstinence. But the tree and its voices not only set forth abstinence, the denial of appetite; their lesson is positive too. They tell of the end and profit of abstinence, the gain and delight of temperance as it was in the golden age, which 'made acorns savoury with hunger and with thirst made nectar of every brook'; they tell of Mary providing wine for the wedding-feast and of the Baptist's viands of honey and locusts in the desert. It is by the correction of excess and the control of appetite that appetite itself becomes an element in life's excellence and a part of its joy. The condition of the penitents here, as Forese explains it to Dante, is a state of tension between natural appetite and abstinence, the 'bringing of the body under' the soul. The old cravings are continually re-quickened that they may be as often mastered, and by that conflict the soul, agonized and yet choosing to be so,

'Mounts, and that hardly, to eternal life.'

Forese's language about the pains of the penitents—'I say pain and ought to say solace', 'the sweet wormwood of the torments' —recalls that of Von Hügel, no less characteristic of its author: 'Such souls thus taste an ever-increasing bliss and peace within their ever-decreasing pain, whilst those impurities and hardenings are slowly, surely, sufferingly yet serenely, purified, softened and willed away.' Their chant is 'Open thou my lips' —lips once given to gluttony—'and my mouth shall show forth thy praise.'

Little is known of the facts of Dante's friendship with Forese Donati, who belonged to a leading family of Florence and was related to Dante's wife. An incidental mark of their old intimacy is that Dante speaks to Forese of Beatrice by name, without explanation, as he does to no one else. The meeting of the two old friends here recalls an obscure part of Dante's life of which the only memorials left to us are these lines and three pairs of sonnets which were exchanged by the two young Florentines. These are mere bandyings in a competition of abuse, possibly jocular but in that case jests in the worst of taste. Their interest for us here is that in one of his three sonnets Dante banters Forese on his gluttony and in another makes sorry fun of Forese's wife for her never-ending cough and for her husband's neglect of her. How much is to be made of these paltry rhymes as serious biographical material it is hard to say; but they seem to make the tender and beautiful acknowledgment of the goodness of his wife Nella which Dante puts into the mouth of Forese here Dante's deliberate reparation for his old gibes at her and they go to confirm his 'grievous memory' of his former life with Forese as a life that was little creditable to either. The mention of 'that life' leads him to trace in a few stanzas his great experience, in Virgil's charge, from the gloomy wood and threatening beasts to 'where Beatrice is'. Vulgar and worthless as the sonnets are, they serve to illustrate the fundamental realism of Dante's imagination. He starts from experience and, essentially, never leaves it. He follows Virgil through the depths of Hell and up the steeps of Purgatory 'with this true flesh', as a living man, as Dante Alighieri.

PURGATORIO

Nè 'l dir l'andar, nè l'andar lui più lento
   facea; ma, ragionando, andavam forte,
   sì come nave pinta da buon vento;
e l'ombre, che parean cose rimorte,
   per le fosse delli occhi ammirazione
   traean di me, di mio vivere accorte.
E io, continüando al mio sermone,
   dissi: 'Ella sen va su forse più tarda
   che non farebbe, per altrui cagione.
Ma dimmi, se tu sai, dov'è Piccarda;   10
   dimmi s' io veggio da notar persona
   tra questa gente che sì mi riguarda.'
'La mia sorella, che tra bella e bona
   non so qual fosse più, triunfa lieta
   nell'alto Olimpo già di sua corona.'
Sì disse prima; e poi: 'Qui non si vieta
   di nominar ciascun, da ch'è sì munta
   nostra sembianza via per la dïeta.
Questi' e mostrò col dito 'è Bonagiunta,
   Bonagiunta da Lucca; e quella faccia   20
   di là da lui più che l'altre trapunta
ebbe la Santa Chiesa in le sue braccia:
   dal Torso fu, e purga per digiuno
   l'anguille di Bolsena e la vernaccia.'
Molti altri mi nomò ad uno ad uno;
   e del nomar parean tutti contenti,
   sì ch' io però non vidi un atto bruno.
Vidi per fame a voto usar li denti
   Ubaldin dalla Pila e Bonifazio
   che pasturò col rocco molte genti.   30

CANTO XXIV

*Bonagiunta; 'the sweet new style'; the second
tree; examples of gluttony; the angel of temperance*

NEITHER did the talk make the going, nor the
going it, more slow and, conversing, we went on
quickly like a ship driven by a fair wind; and the
shades, that seemed things twice dead, drew in
through the pits of their eyes amazement at me,
perceiving that I was alive. And I, continuing my
talk, said: 'He goes up, perhaps, more slowly than
he would, because of the other. But tell me, if
thou canst, where is Piccarda.[1] Tell me if I see
any person to be noted among these people who
are gazing at me so.'

'My sister, of whom I know not if she was more
fair or good, already triumphs in high Olympus,
rejoicing in her crown.' This he said first, and
then: 'Here it is not forbidden to name any, our
features are so drained away by the fast. He there'
—and he pointed with his finger—'is Bonagiunta,
Bonagiunta of Lucca,[2] and that one beyond him,
the face more seamed than the rest, had Holy
Church in his arms; he is from Tours and purges
by fasting the eels of Bolsena and the Vernaccian.'[3]

Many others he named to me one by one, and
all seemed glad to be named so that I did not see
a dark look on account of it. I saw, for hunger
plying his teeth on vacancy, Ubaldin dalla Pila,
and Bonifazio, who pastured many flocks with his

Vidi messer Marchese, ch'ebbe spazio
  già di bere a Forlì con men secchezza,
  e sì fu tal che non si sentì sazio.
Ma come fa chi guarda e poi si prezza
  più d'un che d'altro, fei a quel da Lucca,
  che più parea di me voler contezza.
El mormorava; e non so che 'Gentucca'
  sentiv' io là, ov'el sentìa la piaga
  della giustizia che sì li pilucca.
'O anima' diss' io 'che par sì vaga   40
  di parlar meco, fa sì ch' io t' intenda,
  e te e me col tuo parlare appaga.'
'Femmina è nata, e non porta ancor benda'
  cominciò el 'che ti farà piacere
  la mia città, come ch' uom la riprenda.
Tu te n'andrai con questo antivedere:
  se nel mio mormorar prendesti errore,
  dichiareranti ancor le cose vere.
Ma dì s' i' veggio qui colui che fore
  trasse le nove rime, cominciando   50
  "Donne ch'avete intelletto d'amore." '
E io a lui: 'I' mi son un che, quando
  Amor mi spira, noto, e a quel modo
  ch'e' ditta dentro vo significando.'
'O frate, issa vegg' io' diss'elli 'il nodo
  che 'l Notaro e Guittone e me ritenne
  di qua dal dolce stil novo ch' i' odo!
Io veggio ben come le vostre penne
  di retro al dittator sen vanno strette,
  che delle nostre certo non avvenne;   60
e qual più a riguardare oltre si mette
  non vede piu dall'uno all'altro stilo.'
  E, quasi contentato, si tacette.
Come li augei che vernan lungo 'l Nilo,
  alcuna volta in aere fanno schiera,
  poi volan più a fretta e vanno in filo;
così tutta la gente che lì era,
  volgendo 'l viso, raffrettò suo passo,
  e per magrezza e per voler leggera.

staff[4]; I saw Messer Marchese, who once had leisure for drinking at Forlì with less drouth, yet was such that he never felt satisfied.[5] But as one looks and then takes more note of one than of another so I did with him of Lucca, who seemed more desirous to know me. He was muttering and something like *Gentucca*[6] I heard at the place where he was feeling the stroke of justice that so consumes them.[7]

'O soul' I said 'that seemst so eager to speak with me, pray let me hear thee plainly and satisfy both thyself and me with thy speech.'

'A woman is born and does not yet wear the wimple'[8] he began 'who shall make my city pleasing to thee, however men revile it; with this presage thou shalt go thy way, and if thou take a wrong sense from my muttering the facts themselves will yet make it clear to thee. But tell me if I see here him that brought forth the new rhymes, beginning with *Ladies that have intelligence of love.*'

And I said to him: 'I am one who, when love breathes in me, take note, and in that manner which he dictates within go on to set it forth.'

'O brother,' he said 'now I see the knot that held back the Notary[9] and Guittone[10] and me short of the sweet new style that I hear; I see well how your pens follow close behind the dictator, which assuredly did not happen with ours, and he that sets himself to examine further sees nothing else between the one style and the other.' And, as if satisfied, he was silent.

As birds that winter along the Nile sometimes make a troop in the air, then fly with more speed and go in file, so all the people that were there, facing round, quickened their steps, being light both with leanness and desire; and as one tired

E come l'om che di trottare è lasso   70
  lascia andar li compagni, e sì passeggia
  fin che si sfoghi l'affollar del casso,
sì lasciò trapassar la santa greggia
  Forese, e dietro meco sen veniva,
  dicendo: 'Quando fia ch' io ti riveggia?'
'Non so' rispuos' io lui 'quant' io mi viva;
  ma già non fia 'l tornar mio tanto tosto
  ch' io non sia col voler prima alla riva;
però che 'l loco u' fui a viver posto
  di giorno in giorno più di ben si spolpa,   80
  e a trista ruina par disposto.'
'Or va;' diss'el 'chè quei che più n' ha colpa
  vegg' io a coda d'una bestia tratto
  inver la valle ove mai non si scolpa.
La bestia ad ogni passo va più ratto,
  crescendo sempre, fin ch'ella il percuote,
  e lascia il corpo vilmente disfatto.
Non hanno molto a volger quelle rote',
  e drizzò li occhi al ciel, 'che ti fia chiaro
  ciò che 'l mio dir più dichiarar non pote.   90
Tu ti rimani omai; chè 'l tempo è caro
  in questo regno, sì ch' io perdo troppo
  venendo teco sì a paro a paro.'
Qual esce alcuna volta di gualoppo
  lo cavalier di schiera che cavalchi,
  e va per farsi onor del primo intoppo,
tal si partì da noi con maggior valchi;
  e io rimasi in via con esso i due
  che fuor del mondo sì gran marescalchi.
E quando innanzi a noi intrato fue,   100
  che li occhi miei si fero a lui seguaci,
  come la mente alle parole sue,
parvermi i rami gravidi e vivaci
  d'un altro pomo, e non molto lontani
  per esser pur allora volto in laci.
Vidi gente sott'esso alzar le mani
  e gridar non so che verso le fronde
  quasi bramosi fantolini e vani,

with running lets his companions go on and then walks till the heaving of his chest is relieved, so Forese let the holy flock pass and came on with me behind, saying: 'How long will it be till I see thee again?'

'I know not' I answered him 'how long I shall live; but truly my return will not be so soon that in desire I shall not be sooner at the shore, for the place where I have been put to live strips itself of good day by day and seems destined to woeful ruin.'

'It is true,' he said 'and I see him who has most blame for it dragged at the tail of a beast towards the valley where there is no absolving; the beast goes faster at every step, still gaining speed, till it dashes him down and leaves the body vilely undone.[11] Not long have those wheels to turn'—and he raised his eyes to the sky—'till that shall be plain to thee which my speech cannot more plainly tell. Do thou remain now, for time is precious in this realm and I lose too much coming thus along with thee.'

As sometimes a horseman comes forth at a gallop from a troop of riders and goes to gain for himself the honour of the first encounter, so he parted from us with greater strides, and I remained on the way with these two who were so great captains of the world.

And when he had passed on ahead of us so that my eyes were left in pursuit of him as my mind of his words, there appeared to me the branches of another tree, loaded and verdant and not far off, for we had just then come round there. I saw people beneath it lifting up their hands and crying I knew not what towards the foliage, like eager

che pregano e 'l pregato non risponde,
  ma, per fare esser ben la voglia acuta,   110
  tien alto lor disio e nol nasconde.
Poi si partì sì come ricreduta;
  e noi venimmo al grande arbore adesso,
  che tanti prieghi e lagrime rifiuta.
'Trapassate oltre sanza farvi presso:
  legno è più su che fu morso da Eva,
  e questa pianta si levò da esso.'
Sì tra le frasche non so chi diceva;
  per che Virgilio e Stazio e io, ristretti,
  oltre andavam dal lato che si leva.   120
'Ricordivi' dicea 'de' maladetti
  nei nuvoli formati, che, satolli,
  Teseo combatter co' doppi petti;
e delli Ebrei ch'al ber si mostrar molli,
  per che no i volle Gedeon compagni,
  quando ver Madïan discese i colli.'
Sì accostati all'un de' due vivagni
  passammo, udendo colpe della gola
  seguite già da miseri guadagni.
Poi, rallargati per la strada sola,   130
  ben mille passi e più ci portar oltre,
  contemplando ciascun sanza parola.
'Che andate pensando sì voi sol tre?'
  subita voce disse; ond' io mi scossi
  come fan bestie spaventate e poltre.
Drizzai la testa per veder chi fossi;
  e già mai non si videro in fornace
  vetri o metalli sì lucenti e rossi,
com' io vidi un che dicea: 'S'a voi piace
  montare in su, qui si conven dar volta;   140
  quinci si va chi vuole andar per pace.'
L'aspetto suo m'avea la vista tolta;
  per ch' io mi volsi dietro a' miei dottori,
  com' uom che va secondo ch'elli ascolta.
E quale, annunziatrice delli albori,
  l'aura di maggio movesi ed olezza,
  tutta impregnata dall'erba e da' fiori;

and thoughtless children who beg and he they beg
of does not answer, but, to make their desire
keener, holds up the thing they want and does not
hide it. Then they went away as if undeceived, and
we came presently to the great tree which refuses
so many prayers and tears. 'Pass on without coming
close; a tree is above that was eaten of by Eve[12]
and this plant was raised from it.' So someone
spoke among the leaves, at which Virgil and Statius
and I, drawing close together, went on at the side
where the cliff rises. 'Remember' he said 'the
accursed creatures, formed in the clouds, who,
when gorged, fought Theseus with their double
breasts,[13] and the Hebrews who at the drinking
showed themselves soft, so that Gideon would not
have them in his company when they went down
the hills against Midian.'[14] Thus keeping close to
the one side of the way we passed on, hearing of
sins of gluttony followed of old by wretched wages;
then, spread out on the lonely road, a thousand
steps and more brought us on, each in meditation
without speech.

'What are you thinking on as you go, you three
by yourselves?' said a sudden voice; at which I
started, as do scared and timid beasts. I raised my
head to see who it was, and never in furnace was
glass or metal seen so glowing red as I saw one
who said: 'If you wish to mount above, here you
must make the turn. This way he goes who would
go for peace.' His aspect had taken my sight from
me, so that I turned after my teachers as one that
goes by his hearing. And as the breeze of May,
herald of the dawn, stirs and gives fragrance, being
all impregnate with the grass and flowers, such a

tal mi senti' un vento dar per mezza
  la fronte, e ben senti' mover la piuma,
  che fè sentir d'ambrosïa l'orezza.   150
E senti' dir: 'Beati cui alluma
  tanto di grazia, che l'amor del gusto
  nel petto lor troppo disir non fuma,
esurïendo sempre quanto è giusto!'

wind I felt strike full on my brow and I plainly
felt the moving of his wing, which made me feel
the odour of ambrosia; and I heard the words:
'Blessed are they whom so much grace illumines
that appetite does not fill their breast with the
fumes of too great desire, hungering always so far
as is just.'[15]

1. Forese Donati's sister (*Par.* iii).

2. Poet, senior contemporary of Dante.

3. Pope Martin IV (1281–5), once Treasurer of Tours Cathedral; he cooked eels in Vernaccian wine.

4. Archbishop of Ravenna in Dante's time, with wide jurisdiction and many courtiers.

5. A noble of Romagna in Dante's time; told that he was always drinking, he said he was always thirsty.

6. A woman's name.

7. At his lips.

8. Worn by married women.

9. Poet in Frederick's court in Sicily; died in 1250.

10. Representative of the philosophical poets of Tuscany; died in 1294.

11. Corso Donati, brother of Forese and Piccarda, chief of the Florentine Blacks

12. The tree of the knowledge of good and evil (*Gen.* ii. 17), in the Earthly Paradise on the summit of Purgatory.

13. The Centaurs, born of a cloud having the form of Juno; being drunk at a wedding they tried to seize the bride and other women and were overcome by Theseus.

14. Gideon refused those that 'bowed down upon their knees to drink water' (*Judges* vii. 6–7).

15. An adaptation of the beatitude, 'Blessed are they which do *hunger* . . . after righteousness' (*Matt.* v. 6), completing the beatitude of the fifth terrace (*Purg.* xxii).

NOTE

The Donati family was well known to Dante not only through his wife's relationship to it and his intimacy with Forese but also for its prominence in the social and political life of Florence.

We have already met with several instances of the division of destiny between father and son—the Emperor Frederick II and Manfred (*Inf.* x and *Purg.* iii), Count Guido da Montefeltro and Buonconte (*Inf.* xxvii and *Purg.* v), and Ubaldin dalla Pila in this terrace of gluttony and his son the Archbishop Ruggieri in the deepest circle of Hell (*Inf.* xxxiii). The same idea of the members of one household finding their several places in eternity soul by soul is set forth here, Forese Donati telling in Purgatory of his sister Piccarda in Paradise and of his brother Corso still on earth and doomed to be 'dragged at the tail of a beast towards the valley where there is no absolving'. The contrast in character and in fate between his sister and brother—the latter not named nor called his brother—is dramatically enforced by the report of them coming from their brother's lips. Of Piccarda little is known beyond what is told us here and in the third canto of the *Paradiso*, but Corso Donati was for years a notable figure in the history of the time. The Donati were an ancient family of Guelf nobles, natural rivals, therefore, of the new rich bourgeoisie of the growing republic. Corso, even by the report of his enemies, was a man of handsome person, fine address and distinguished abilities in peace and war, as well as great personal ambition. In the division of the Blacks and Whites in 1300, foretold by Ciacco (*Inf.* vi), the Blacks were led by the Donati and the Whites, 'the party of the rustics', by the Cerchi, a wealthy trading house of humble origin, and Corso shared the exile which was imposed on the leaders of both parties in that year.

More dangerous to Florence outside than inside the city, he was largely responsible for the scheme by which Charles of Valois, couching 'the lance with which Judas jousted' (*Purg.* xx), entered Florence in 1301 and re-admitted the Blacks, who attacked the Whites, pillaged and burned their houses and drove them out of the city, and it was then that Dante, in his absence from Florence, was declared an exile. Seven years later Corso's restless ambition raised such suspicions that the authorities of the republic condemned him to death and in an attempt to escape he fell from his horse and was killed. Forese's account is, of course, Dante's own comment, made within a few years of the event and well understood by his first readers.

The name of Gentucca 'muttered' by Bonagiunta refers to some incident of Dante's wandering life which is now forgotten. Any idea of an amorous attachment such as has been fancied by romantic readers is not only without evidence but would seem quite unsuitable to the context, while it is possible that Bonagiunta's words about taking 'a wrong sense from my muttering' may be Dante's repudiation of some such contemporary story. Probably the reference is his acknowledgment of the kindness of a lady of Lucca who may, like others, have given hospitality to the homeless exile. He had himself 'reviled' her city by the mouth of a devil—'Every man there is a barrator; there *No* is made *Ay* for cash' (*Inf.* xxi)—and this sounds like amends.

The lines occupied by Dante's conversation with Bonagiunta about the poets and the poetry of the time have been the subject of much discussion. In the first half of the century the love-songs of the Provençal troubadours had wakened echoes in the Sicilian court of Frederick II, where 'the Notary', an official of Frederick's, was a poet of distinction. Later, the same fashion of imitative and artificial verse was practised in Central Italy and Tuscany, where the more scholastic temper of the north turned the use of verse to the semi-philosophical discussion of themes of love. During Dante's youth in Florence there came into note a group of poets whose writings marked a vigorous reaction against the abstractness and artificiality of the current versifying in theme and manner, and of this new vitality Dante's poem, *Ladies that have intelligence of love*, was widely recognized as an outstanding example. This ode in praise of Beatrice, celebrating the spiritual worth which makes her to be 'desired in high heaven', brought to Dante a youthful fame which he recalls twenty-five or more years later, and he tells in a single stanza the secret of that 'sweet new style' which was first practised by himself and others of his group in Florence and which he was to develop later to such mighty results: 'I am one who, when love breathes in me, take note, and in that manner which he dictates within go on to set it forth.' The language has a significant correspondence with that of Wordsworth in the Introduction to *Lyrical Ballads*, the landmark of another historical return of poetry to nature: 'Poetry . . . takes its origin from emotion recollected in tranquillity.' Dante's *love* is Wordsworth's *emotion* and Dante's *taking note* is Wordsworth's *recollection in tranquillity*. 'The principle holds good, whatever significance may be given to the word *love*; whether the poet sings the ardours of an earthly affection, or the ecstasy of a spiritual worship, or the pain and the joy of learning, or the laborious conquests of thought, whether he is a humble popular rhymer or the most accomplished craftsman of allegorical and doctrinal odes' (*V. Rossi, L.D.*). The primary emotional experience, recalled and re-imagined, then freely and faithfully expressed—the veracity, the integrity of the whole process, from the first impulse to the last line on the page: that is Dante's account of his own poetry, of that 'sweet new style' which, in any age, cannot be other than new. For Bonagiunta, the representative of the old school, as for Dante himself, there is no more to be said— 'and, as if satisfied, he was silent.'

The fact that the second tree on the terrace was raised from a shoot of the tree of the forbidden fruit in Eden has led some readers to suppose that the first, described in the twenty-second canto, was in the same relation to the tree of life (*Gen*. ii. 9), and the idea is in harmony with its function of disciplining the penitents by abstinence even from 'fruits that smell sweet and good'. Here, the tree, recalling the divine command, man's disobedience and the fall, has the sterner lesson of warning, the 'bit' on the soul. The comparison of the penitents to 'eager and thoughtless children' recalls Aquinas's characterization of gluttony as a childish sin.

If the two trees offer a somewhat laboured and ineffective piece of symbolism, the angel of temperance makes amends. The eager energy of the penitents of the terrace culminates in the ardour imaged in his form, 'glowing red' so that Dante is, for the moment, blinded by it. Surrounded, as it were, by the air of dawn and shedding fragrance from his wings, he is the very sublimation of appetite, the purification and release of natural feeling till it becomes a kind of spiritual sense. In each line of the stanza in which he tells of the angel's wing clearing the sixth *P* from his brow Dante repeats the word *feel* (*sentire*), and it occurs again in the following line—where *felt* has to be rendered *heard*—announcing the beatitude of the soul in its deliverance by grace from the vile 'fume' of gluttony and drunkenness. The enrichment of the soul's feeling is a part of its well-being and reward and the last word of blessing upon it is of 'hungering always so far as is just'.

PURGATORIO

Ora era onde 'l salir non volea storpio;
   chè 'l sole avea il cerchio di merigge
   lasciato al Tauro e la notte allo Scorpio:
per che, come fa l'uom che non s'affigge
   ma vassi alla via sua, checchè li appaia,
   se di bisogno stimolo il trafigge,
così entrammo noi per la callaia,
   uno innanzi altro prendendo la scala
   che per artezza i salitor dispaia.
E quale il cicognin che leva l'ala   10
   per voglia di volare, e non s'attenta
   d'abbandonar lo nido, e giù la cala;
tal era io con voglia accesa e spenta
   di dimandar, venendo infino all'atto
   che fa colui ch'a dicer s'argomenta.
Non lasciò, per l'andar che fosse ratto,
   lo dolce padre mio, ma disse: 'Scocca
   l'arco del dir, che 'nfino al ferro hai tratto.'
Allor sicuramente apri' la bocca
   e cominciai: 'Come si può far magro   20
   là dove l'uopo di nodrir non tocca?'
'Se t'ammentassi come Meleagro
   si consumò al consumar d'un stizzo,
   non fora' disse 'a te questo sì agro;
e se pensassi come al vostro guizzo
   guizza dentro allo specchio vostra image,
   ciò che par duro ti parrebbe vizzo.

CANTO XXV

The generation of the body and creation of the soul; the Seventh Terrace; the purgation of lust; examples of chastity

It was an hour when the ascent brooked no delay, for the sun had left to the Bull, and night to the Scorpion, the meridian circle;[1] therefore, like him that does not stop but keeps on his way whatever may appear to him, if he is pricked by the goad of necessity, we entered by the gap, one before the other taking the stair which by its narrowness separates the climbers. And as the little stork lifts its wing with desire to fly and does not venture to leave the nest and drops it again, such was I with the desire to question kindled and quenched, going as far as the movement of one that prepares to speak. My gentle Father did not, for all the speed of our going, refrain, but said: 'Loose the bow of thy speech that thou hast drawn to the iron.'

Then, having confidence, I opened my mouth and began: 'How is it possible to become lean where there is no need of nourishment?'

'If thou call to mind how Meleager was consumed in the consuming of a brand'[2] he said 'this will not be so difficult for thee; and if thou consider how with your least movement your image moves within the glass, that which seems hard to

325

Ma perchè dentro a tuo voler t'adage,
  ecco qui Stazio; e io lui chiamo e prego
  che sia or sanator delle tue piage.'   30
'Se la veduta etterna li dislego'
  rispuose Stazio 'là dove tu sie,
  discolpi me non potert' io far nego.'
Poi cominciò: 'Se le parole mie,
  figlio, la mente tua guarda e riceve,
  lume ti fiero al come che tu die.
Sangue perfetto, che mai non si beve
  dall'assetate vene, e si rimane
  quasi alimento che di mensa leve,
prende nel core a tutte membra umane   40
  virtute informativa, come quello
  ch'a farsi quelle per le vene vane.
Ancor digesto, scende ov'è più bello
  tacer che dire; e quindi poscia geme
  sovr'altrui sangue in natural vasello.
Ivi s'accoglie l'uno e l'altro inseme,
  l'un disposto a patire, e l'altro a fare
  per lo perfetto loco onde si preme;
e, giunto lui, comincia ad operare
  coagulando prima, e poi avviva   50
  ciò che per sua matera fè constare.
Anima fatta la virtute attiva
  qual d'una pianta, in tanto differente,
  che questa è in via e quella è già a riva,
tanto ovra poi che già si move e sente,
  come fungo marino; e indi imprende
  ad organar le posse ond'è semente.
Or si spiega, figliuolo, or si distende
  la virtù ch'è dal cor del generante,
  dove natura a tutte membra intende.   60
Ma come d'animal divenga fante,
  non vedi tu ancor: quest'è tal punto,
  che più savio di te fè già errante,
sì che per sua dottrina fè disgiunto
  dall'anima il possibile intelletto,
  perchè da lui non vide organo assunto.

thee will seem easy. But, that thou mayst be set at rest in thy desire, here is Statius, and I call him and beg of him now to be healer of thy wounds.'

'If I unfold to him in thy presence the things seen in the eternal life,' Statius replied 'let it be my excuse that I cannot refuse thee.' Then he began: 'Son, if thy mind heed and receive my words they will enlighten thee how this can be. Perfect blood, which is never drunk by the thirsty veins and is left like food thou removest from the table, takes in the heart informing power for all the bodily members, like that which takes its course through the veins to become these.[3] Further digested, it descends where silence is fitter than speech and thence drops afterwards on another's blood in the natural vessel. There the one mingles with the other, the one fitted to be passive and the other, on account of the perfect place from which it springs, active, and this, so united, begins to operate, first coagulating, then quickening that to which, for its material, it has given consistency.[4] The active force having become a soul, like a plant's but so far different that it is on the way and the other already at the shore, then operates to the point that now it moves and feels, like a sea-fungus, and from that goes on to produce organs for the faculties of which it is the seed.[5] Now, my son, develops and spreads the force that is from the heart of the begetter, where nature makes provision for all the members. But how from animal it becomes a child thou seest not yet; this is the point which once made a wiser than thou to err, so that in his teaching he made the possible intellect separate from the soul, because he did not see an organ

327

Apri alla verità che viene il petto;
   e sappi che, sì tosto come al feto
   l'articular del cerebro è perfetto,
lo motor primo a lui si volge lieto   70
   sovra tant'arte di natura, e spira
   spirito novo di vertù repleto,
che ciò che trova attivo quivi, tira
   in sua sustanzia, e fassi un'alma sola,
   che vive e sente e sè in sè rigira.
E perchè meno ammiri la parola,
   guarda il calor del sol che si fa vino,
   giunto all'omor che della vite cola.
Quando Lachèsis non ha più del lino,
   solvesi dalla carne, ed in virtute   80
   ne porta seco e l'umano e 'l divino:
l'altre potenze tutte quante mute,
   memoria, intelligenza e volontade
   in atto molto più che prima agute.
Sanza restarsi, per sè stessa cade
   mirabilmente all'una delle rive:
   quivi conosce prima le sue strade.
Tosto che loco lì la circunscrive,
   la virtù informativa raggia intorno
   così e quanto nelle membra vive: 90
e come l'aere, quand'è ben pïorno,
   per l'altrui raggio che 'n sè si reflette,
   di diversi color diventa adorno;
così l'aere vicin quivi si mette
   in quella forma che in lui suggella
   virtüalmente l'alma che ristette;
e simigliante poi alla fiammella
   che segue il foco là 'vunque si muta,
   segue lo spirto sua forma novella.
Però che quindi ha poscia sua paruta,   100
   è chiamata ombra; e quindi organa poi
   ciascun sentire infino alla veduta.
Quindi parliamo e quindi ridiam noi;
   quindi facciam le lacrime e' sospiri
   che per lo monte aver sentiti puoi.

appropriated by it.⁶ Open thy breast to the truth
that follows and know that as soon as the articu-
lation of the brain is perfected in the embryo
the First Mover turns to it, rejoicing over such
handiwork of nature, and breathes into it a new
spirit full of power, which draws into its own
substance that which it finds active there and
becomes a single soul that lives and feels and
itself revolves upon itself.⁷ And, that thou mayst
wonder less at my words, consider the sun's heat
which becomes wine when it is joined to the juice
that pours from the vine. When Lachesis has no
more flax⁸ the soul is loosed from the flesh and
carries with it potentially both the human and the
divine faculties—all the others mute, memory,
intelligence and will in action and far keener than
before. Without pausing it falls, marvellously, of
itself, to one of the shores.⁹ There it first comes
to know its course. As soon as space envelops it
there the formative virtue radiates round about, in
form and measure as in the living members; and
as the air, when it is full of rain, becomes adorned
with various colours through another's beams that
are reflected in it, so the neighbouring air sets
itself into that form which the soul that stopped
there stamps upon it by its power, and then, like
the flame that follows the fire wherever it shifts,
its new form follows the spirit. Since it has by
this its semblance henceforth, it is called a shade,
and by this it then makes organs for every sense,
even to sight; by this we speak and by this smile,
by this we shed tears and make the sighs thou
mayst have heard on the mountain. According as

Secondo che ci affiggono i disiri
 e li altri affetti, l'ombra si figura;
 e quest'è la cagion di che tu miri.'
E già venuto all' ultima tortura
 s'era per noi, e volto alla man destra,   110
 ed eravamo attenti ad altra cura.
Quivi la ripa fiamma in fuor balestra,
 e la cornice spira fiato in suso
 che la reflette e via da lei sequestra;
ond' ir ne convenìa dal lato schiuso
 ad uno ad uno; e io temea il foco
 quinci, e quindi temea càder giuso.
Lo duca mio dicea: 'Per questo loco
 si vuol tenere alli occhi stretto il freno,
 però ch'errar potrebbesi per poco.'   120
'*Summae Deus clementïae*' nel seno
 al grande ardore allora udi' cantando,
 che di volger mi fè caler non meno;
e vidi spirti per la fiamma andando;
 per ch' io guardava a loro e a' miei passi
 compartendo la vista a quando a quando.
Appresso il fine ch'a quell' inno fassi,
 gridavano alto: '*Virum non cognosco*';
 indi ricominciavan l' inno bassi.
Finitolo anco, gridavano: 'Al bosco   130
 si tenne Diana, ed Elice caccionne
 che di Venere avea sentito il tosco.'
Indi al cantar tornavano; indi donne
 gridavano e mariti che fuor casti
 come virtute e matrimonio imponne.
E questo modo credo che lor basti
 per tutto il tempo che 'l foco li abbrucia:
 con tal cura conviene e con tai pasti
che la piaga da sezzo si ricucia.

desires and other affections impress us the shade takes form, and this is the cause of that at which thou marvellest.'

And now we had come to the last circuit and had turned to the right and were intent on another care. There the bank shoots forth flames and the edge of the terrace sends a blast upwards which bends them back and keeps them away from it, so that we had to go on the open side, one by one, and I feared the fire on this hand and on that feared to fall below.

My Leader said: 'Along this way the rein must be kept tight on the eyes, for it would be easy to err.'

'*Summae Deus clementiae*'[10] I then heard sung in the heart of the great burning, which made me not less eager to turn, and I saw spirits walking through the flames, so that I kept looking at them and at my steps, dividing my glance from time to time. After that hymn was sung to the end they cried aloud: 'I know not a man',[11] then softly began the hymn again; when it was finished they cried next: 'Diana kept to the woods and drove out Helice, who had felt the poison of Venus';[12] then they returned to the singing, then cried out of wives and husbands who were chaste as virtuous wedlock requires of us; and this fashion lasts with them, I think, all the time the fire burns them. With such treatment and with such fare must the last wound of all be healed.

PURGATORIO

1. At 2 p.m. the sun, in the Ram, had declined from noon and the next constellation, the Bull, was overhead; 'night', the opposite point to the sun, had declined as much from Jerusalem, leaving the Scorpion on the meridian there.

2. Meleager's life was limited by the Fates to the time of the burning of a brand in the fire.

3. Besides the blood in the veins—'veins' including arteries—which forms and nourishes the members, the man's heart produces a more 'perfect blood', the semen, which has a similar 'informing power' in generation.

4. The active 'blood' from the man's heart, along with the passive female blood, forms the embryo.

5. The embryo attains first the vegetative, then the animal, faculties.

6. Averroes taught, in Dante's interpretation of him, that the 'possible intellect' is the mere passive reception of general ideas from without, not an independent faculty of the individual mind.

7. The soul, with its higher faculties, is a direct creation, which absorbs the lower faculties in its own unity.

8. When Lachesis, the second Fate, has spun the thread of life.

9. The mouth of Tiber or the bank of Acheron (*Inf.* iii).

10. *God of highest clemency*, hymn in the Breviary containing a prayer against lust.

11. Mary's reply to Gabriel: 'How shall this be, seeing I know not a man' (*Luke* i. 34).

12. Diana discovered the unchastity of her nymph Helice, seduced by Jupiter.

NOTE

The twenty-fifth canto is chiefly occupied with a long and difficult exposition, but the note of urgency, 'the goad of necessity' that pricks the travellers, is never forgotten. They think as they go and 'the speed of their going' continues while they talk. The discourse of Statius ends abruptly as if there were no time for Dante's response—'And now we had come to the last circuit' and were 'intent on another care'.

But their talk is relevant to their journey. In these upper terraces of Purgatory we are concerned with the purgation of the sins of the flesh and the question naturally arises of the relation of man's spiritual nature to his body and its faculties. What part has the soul in these cravings of the flesh and their satisfaction? In the scholastic fashion of the time Statius expounds the teaching of Aristotle as it was received and expanded by Aquinas and as, further, it was extended by Dante himself. The main outcome of the whole discourse is that the soul is no mere product or accompaniment of the body but a direct and immediate creation of God which appropriates and possesses the body before it is born, absorbing the bodily faculties into itself as *its* faculties and carrying with it after death the same faculties, higher and lower, its own and the body's, as before, though for the lower it must then find new organs. (This last feature is Dante's addition to Aquinas.) Statius's teaching continues that of Virgil in the seventeenth and eighteenth cantos, and although the moral implications are not directly handled here the implied conclusion is that even in these sins of the flesh it is the soul that sins and the soul that is purged and that the agony of these forms wasted with their cravings is the agony of the soul's penitence and purgation, the hard and slow recovery of its self-mastery and freedom. The subject is here regarded objectively, as it were disinterestedly and without concern for the moral interests involved, and therefore the more convincingly: the wonder of physical generation, then the greater wonder of the 'new spirit' breathed into the embryo by the First Mover, the renewal in each human creature of the first creation—'The Lord God breathed into his nostrils the breath of life, and man became a living soul.'

The task of enlightening Dante is given by Virgil to Statius and Virgil may almost be said to suggest his own incompetence for it by offering mere vague analogies to the experience of these shades that turn lean with unsatisfied craving—Meleager and the brand, and the reflected movement in the glass—and then referring the matter to Statius. Averroes, the great Moslem Aristotelian of the twelfth century 'who made the Great Commentary' (*Inf.* iv), had not yet come to hold the bad eminence given to him in the course of the fourteenth century as the typical heretic and enemy of the truth, the negative counterpart of Aquinas, and he was still, for Dante, 'a wiser' than Dante himself and one of the great non-Christian souls in Limbo. But the fact that his teaching about the 'possible intellect', that human reason consists in mere passivity in relation to a superhuman reason, had been expressly controverted by Aquinas seems to show that it is definitely as a Christian that Statius is called on to expound certain doctrines held to be essential to a Christian view of things and held then to need assertion. These doctrines may be reduced to three: first, the direct and independent creation of the individual soul, as against the heresy that the soul comes into being like the body, by mere natural descent; second, the unity of the soul, including in itself both the lower and the higher faculties, as against the view 'that one soul is kindled above another in us' (*Purg.* iv), the vegetative, the animal, the intellectual: and third, the soul's autonomy, as of a creature endowed with memory, intelligence, and will, 'itself revolving upon itself', as against mere passive participation in an impersonal universal mind, a participation which seemed to leave the thinking soul no life and immortality of its own. These were all matters of current and keen debate in the schools and it was under such terms as these that it was sought, especially by Aquinas, to demonstrate and establish the supreme worth and the eternal sacredness of the soul of man. The soul as the unity of the whole man, a being reflective, responsible, immortal; that is the outcome of the whole argument and the subject of the *Divine Comedy*. The discourse of Statius is apt to seem to us dull and unimaginative; for Dante it was vital and fundamental.

The seventh terrace will be considered in the note on the next canto.

PURGATORIO

Mentre che sì per l'orlo, uno innanzi altro,
  ce n'andavamo, e spesso il buon maestro
  diceami: 'Guarda: giovi ch' io ti scaltro'
ferìami il sole in su l'omero destro,
  che già, raggiando, tutto l'occidente
  mutava in bianco aspetto di cilestro;
e io facea con l'ombra più rovente
  parer la fiamma; e pur a tanto indizio
  vidi molt'ombre, andando, poner mente.
Questa fu la cagion che diede inizio   10
  loro a parlar di me; e cominciarsi
  a dir: 'Colui non par corpo fittizio';
poi verso me, quanto potean farsi,
  certi si feron, sempre con riguardo
  di non uscir dove non fosser arsi.
'O tu che vai, non per esser più tardo,
  ma forse reverente, alli altri dopo,
  rispondi a me che 'n sete e 'n foco ardo.
Nè solo a me la tua risposta è uopo;
  chè tutti questi n' hanno maggior sete   20
  che d'acqua fredda Indo o Etïopo.
Dinne com'è che fai di te parete
  al sol, pur come tu non fossi ancora
  di morte intrato dentro dalla rete.'
Sì mi parlava un d'essi; e io mi fora
  già manifesto, s' io non fossi atteso
  ad altra novità ch'apparse allora;
chè per lo mezzo del cammino acceso
  venne gente col viso incontro a questa,
  la qual mi fece a rimirar sospeso.   30

CANTO XXVI

Dante's shadow on the flames; examples of lust;
Guinicelli; Arnaut

WHILE we went thus along the edge one before
the other, the good Master often saying to me:
'Watch, take heed of my warning', the sun was
striking on my right shoulder;[1] for now its beams
were changing the whole face of the west from
azure to white and with my shadow I made
the flame appear more glowing, and even at that
faint sign I saw many of the shades, as they went,
give heed. It was this that first gave occasion for
them to speak of me and they began to say to each
other: 'This man does not seem unreal flesh'; then
some of them came as near to me as they could,
always with care not to come out where they
would not be burned.

'O thou that goest behind the others, not from
tardiness but perhaps from reverence, answer me
who burn with thirst and with the fire; it is not
only I that crave an answer from thee, but all these
are thirstier for it than Indian or Ethiopian for cold
water. Tell us, how it is that thou makest a wall
of thyself to the sun, even as if thou hadst not yet
entered into death's net?'

Thus one of them spoke to me, and now I
would have made myself known if I had not been
intent on another strange thing that appeared then:
for in the middle of the blazing path came people
facing opposite to these, who held me gazing in

337

Lì veggio d'ogne parte farsi presta
  ciascun'ombra e baciarsi una con una
  sanza restar, contente a brieve festa:
così per entro loro schiera bruna
  s'ammusa l'una con l'altra formica,
  forse ad espiar lor via e lor fortuna.
Tosto che parton l'accoglienza amica,
  prima che 'l primo passo lì trascorra,
  sopragridar ciascuna s'affatica:
la nova gente: 'Soddoma e Gomorra';   40
  e l'altra: 'Nella vacca entra Pasife,
  perchè 'l torello a sua lussuria corra.'
Poi come grue ch'alle montagne Rife
  volasser parte e parte inver l'arene,
  queste del gel, quelle del sole schife,
l'una gente sen va, l'altra sen vene;
  e tornan, lacrimando, a' primi canti
  e al gridar che più lor si convene;
e raccostansi a me, come davanti,
  essi medesmi che m'avean pregato,   50
  attenti ad ascoltar ne' lor sembianti.
Io, che due volte avea visto lor grato,
  incominciai: 'O anime sicure
  d'aver, quando che sia, di pace stato,
non son rimase acerbe nè mature
  le membra mie di là, ma son qui meco
  col sangue suo e con le sue giunture.
Quinci su vo per non esser più cieco:
  donna è di sopra che m'acquista grazia
  per che 'l mortal per vostro mondo reco.   60
Ma se la vostra maggior voglia sazia
  tosto divegna, sì che 'l ciel v'alberghi
  ch'è pien d'amore e più ampio si spazia,
ditemi, acciò ch'ancor carte ne verghi,
  chi siete voi, e chi è quella turba
  che se ne va di retro a' vostri terghi.'
Non altrimenti stupido si turba
  lo montanaro, e rimirando ammuta,
  quando rozzo e salvatico s' inurba,

suspense. I see there every shade on either side make haste and kiss another, not stopping, content with brief greeting; so within their dark troop one ant touches muzzle with the other, perhaps to enquire of their way and fortune. As soon as they end the friendly salutation, before taking the first step to pass on, each tries to outcry the rest—the new people: 'Sodom and Gomorrah!'[2] and the others: 'Pasiphae enters the cow that the bull may run to her lust.'[3] Then, like cranes flying, some towards the Riphean Mountains and some towards the sands,[4] these shunning the frost and those the sun, the one crowd goes and the other comes on, and they return with tears to their former chants and to the cry that most befits them. And the same who entreated me come close to me as before, by their looks eager to listen.

I, having twice seen their desire, began: 'O souls secure of gaining, whensoever it be, a state of peace, my members are not left yonder green or ripe but are here with me, with their blood and their joints. I go up hence not to be longer blind. A lady is above who gains grace for me by which I bring my mortal part through your world. But —so may your greatest longing soon be satisfied and that heaven lodge you which is full of love and has the widest reach[5]—tell me, that I may yet note it on my page, who are you and what is that crowd that goes away behind you?'

Not less bewildered and amazed is the mountaineer, gazing about him speechless when rude and rustic he enters the city, than was each shade

339

che ciascun'ombra fece in sua paruta;   70
   ma poi che furon di stupore scarche,
   lo qual nelli alti cuor tosto s'attuta,
'Beato te, che delle nostre marche'
   ricominciò colei che pria m' inchiese
   'per morir meglio esperïenza imbarche!
La gente che non vien con noi offese
   di ciò per che già Cesar, triunfando,
   "Regina" contra sè chiamar s' intese:
però si parton "Soddoma" gridando,
   rimproverando a sè, com' hai udito,   80
   ed aiutan l'arsura vergognando.
Nostro peccato fu ermafrodito;
   ma perchè non servammo umana legge,
   seguendo come bestie l'appetito,
in obbrobrio di noi, per noi si legge,
   quando partinci, il nome di colei
   che s' imbestiò nelle 'mbestiate schegge.
Or sai nostri atti e di che fummo rei:
   se forse a nome vuo' saper chi semo,
   tempo non è di dire, e non saprei.   90
Farotti ben di me volere scemo:
   son Guido Guinizelli; e già mi purgo
   per ben dolermi prima ch'allo stremo.'
Quali nella tristizia di Licurgo
   si fer due figli a riveder la madre,
   tal mi fec' io, ma non a tanto insurgo,
quand' io odo nomar sè stesso il padre
   mio e delli altri miei miglior che mai
   rime d'amore usar dolci e leggiadre;
e sanza udire e dir pensoso andai   100
   lunga fïata rimirando lui,
   nè, per lo foco, in là più m'appressai.
Poi che di riguardar pasciuto fui,
   tutto m'offersi pronto al suo servigio
   con l'affermar che fa credere altrui.
Ed elli a me: 'Tu lasci tal vestigio,
   per quel ch' i' odo, in me e tanto chiaro,
   che Letè nol può torre nè far bigio.

in his looks; but when they were relieved of their amazement, which is quickly subdued in lofty hearts: 'Blessed art thou,' he began again that had questioned me before, 'who, to die better, takest freight of experience from our bounds! The people who do not come with us offended in that for which Caesar in a triumph once heard them call "*Regina*" against him,[6] therefore they go off crying "*Sodom*", as thou hast heard, in self-reproach and by their shame they aid the burning. Our sin was hermaphrodite;[7] but because we observed not human law, following appetite like beasts, we repeat at parting, to our disgrace, her name who made herself a beast in the beast-like timber. Now thou knowest our deeds and of what we were guilty. If, perchance, thou wouldst know who we are by name, there is no time to tell and I should not be able. About myself, indeed, I will satisfy thy wish. I am Guido Guinicelli,[8] and I make my purgation already because of my good sorrowing before the end.'

Such as, in the grief of Lycurgus, the two sons became on seeing their mother again,[9] I became, but with more restraint, when I heard speak his own name the father of me and of others my betters, whoever have used sweet and graceful rhymes of love, and without hearing or speech I went on a long way in thought gazing at him, and did not, for the fire, go nearer him. When I had fed my sight on him I offered myself wholly ready at his service, with the assurance that gains belief.

And he said to me: 'Thou leavest such a trace and so clear in me by that which I hear thee tell as Lethe cannot destroy or dim; but if thy words

Ma se le tue parole or ver giuraro,
    dimmi che è cagion per che dimostri   110
    nel dire e nel guardare avermi caro.'
E io a lui: 'Li dolci detti vostri,
    che, quanto durerà l'uso moderno,
    faranno cari ancora i loro incostri.'
'O frate,' disse 'questi ch' io ti cerno
    col dito', e additò un spirto innanzi,
    'fu miglior fabbro del parlar materno.
Versi d'amore e prose di romanzi
    soverchiò tutti; e lascia dir li stolti
    che quel di Lemosì credon ch'avanzi.   120
A voce più ch'al ver drizzan li volti,
    e così ferman sua oppinïone
    prima ch'arte o ragion per lor s'ascolti.
Così fer molti antichi di Guittone,
    di grido in grido pur lui dando pregio,
    fin che l' ha vinto il ver con più persone.
Or se tu hai sì ampio privilegio,
    che licito ti sia l'andare al chiostro
    nel quale è Cristo abate del collegio,
falli per me un dir d'un paternostro,   130
    quanto bisogna a noi di questo mondo,
    dove poter peccar non è più nostro.'
Poi, forse per dar luogo altrui secondo
    che presso avea, disparve per lo foco,
    come per l'acqua il pesce andando al fondo.
Io mi feci al mostrato innanzi un poco,
    e dissi ch'al suo nome il mio disire
    apparecchiava grazïoso loco.
    cominciò liberamente a dire:
       '*Tan m'abellis vostre cortes deman,*   140
       qu' ieu no me puese ni voill a vos cobrire.
Ieu sui Arnaut, que plor e vau cantan;
    consiros vei la passada folor,
    e vei jausen lo joi qu'esper, denan.
Ara vos prec, per aquella valor
    que vos guida al som de l'escalina,
    sovenha vos a temps de ma dolor!'
Poi s'ascose nel foco che li affina.

have now sworn truth, tell me for what cause thou
showest thyself, by speech and look, to hold me
dear.'

And I to him: 'Those sweet lines of yours,[10]
which so long as the modern use[11] shall last will
make their ink still dear.'

'O brother,' he said 'he there whom I point
out to thee'—and he pointed to a spirit ahead—
'was a better craftsman of the mother tongue;
verses of love and tales of romance, he surpassed
them all, and let the fools talk who think that he
of Limoges excels. They give heed to reputation
more than truth and thus settle their opinion before
listening to art or reason; so did many of old with
Guittone, from cry to cry giving praise to him
only, until with most the truth has prevailed.[12]
Now, if thou hast such ample privilege that it is
permitted thee to go to the cloister in which Christ
is abbot of the brotherhood, do thou say to Him
a Paternoster for me, so far as is needful for us
of this world where the power to sin is no longer
ours.[13]

Then, perhaps to give place to others who were
near him, he disappeared through the fire as
through the water a fish goes to the bottom.

I put myself forward a little towards him that
had been pointed out and said that my desire
offered a place of welcome for his name, and he
readily began to speak:[14] 'So much does your
courteous question please me that I neither can
nor would conceal myself from you. I am Arnaut,
who weep and sing as I go. I see with grief past
follies and see, rejoicing, the day I hope for before
me. Now I beg of you, by that goodness which
guides you to the summit of the stairway, to take
thought in due time for my pain.' Then he hid
himself in the fire that refines them.

1. They were on the west side of Purgatory, going south; the sun was near setting.

2. *Gen.* xix. 4–8, 24–25. They recall the sin of sodomy.

3. Pasiphae, mother of the Minotaur by a bull (*Inf.* xii).

4. Riphean Mountains, imaginary heights in Northern Europe; 'the sands' of Africa.

5. The Empyrean.

6. Caesar was said to have been thus taunted for having criminal relations with the King of Bithynia.

7. Bisexual.

8. Bolognese poet who died in Dante's childhood.

9. Lycurgus's child was killed through Hypsipyle's neglect; condemned to death, she was saved by the arrival of her two sons, who embraced her.

10. The honorific plural.

11. Vernacular poetry.

12. 'He of Limoges' (Giraut de Borneil) and Arnaut Daniel both wrote Provençal verse at the beginning of the 13th century.

13. They have no need of the last petitions; cp. *Purg.* xi.

14. The following lines are in Provençal. Arnaut uses the honorific *you* to Dante.

NOTE

Purification by fire is a familiar image in Scripture: 'He is like a refiner's fire' (*Mal.* iii. 2); 'The trial of your faith, being much more precious than that of gold that perisheth, though it be tried with fire' (1 *Peter* i. 7)—such passages made the purgation by fire the obvious cure of corruption.

The Virgin, the supreme Christian type of chastity, is coupled with Diana, the moon-goddess, the chaste queen of paganism. Then, as if to guard against a false asceticism, the souls are made to cry out also 'of wives and husbands who were chaste as virtuous wedlock requires of us'.

The two classes of sexual sinners are those, the less guilty, that have sinned by excess of natural passion and those that have sinned against nature itself, and both are represented at their very worst: the one by the shaming of Imperial Caesar and the other by the beastliness of Pasiphae whose passion produced the Minotaur, the monster of violence. The word *beast* is used three times by Guinicelli with reference to Pasiphae, as if to mark that 'the subjection of reason to desire' is, in fact, the lowering of man to the brute.

When the souls in the two troops make haste to kiss when they meet, they are fulfilling the injunction which occurs five times in the New Testament to 'greet one another with an holy kiss'; it is only by the practice of the pure affections that the foul are overcome.

The first half of this canto offers an example of the inventiveness with which Dante sometimes approaches an incident of special interest to himself and his readers and gives it verisimilitude. He notes, first, the rays of the sinking sun changing the western sky and striking on his right shoulder as they walk; then his faint, glowing shadow on the flame observed by some of the shades, who begin to talk of him; then one not named

345

who speaks for them all and questions him about it; then the distraction caused by the meeting and greeting of the two troops of souls: after that, Dante's reply to the question he had left unanswered and his own question in return, asking who they are; then the interruption of their reply by their amazement on hearing that he is still in life; then the same speaker's account of the two troops of souls; and then, at last, the speaker's own name: 'I am Guido Guinicelli', the name that was dear to Dante's youth. It comes on the reader in fact, as it came on Dante in fiction, without preparation or apparent device, in the natural sequence of events, and we believe in Dante's absorbed amazement and accept the reality of the talk that follows between the two poets.

The report of his meeting and conversation with Guinicelli and with Arnaut illustrates, like some other passages, Dante's intense self-consciousness as a poet and his deep sense of a fellowship and common understanding among poets of the true succession. We recall his own first meeting with Virgil, near the gloomy wood (*Inf.* i), the reception of him as of their number by the great poets of antiquity, in Limbo (*Inf.* iv), Sordello's amazed greeting of Virgil, in Anti-Purgatory—'O glory of the Latins'—(*Purg.* vii), Statius 'bending to embrace the Teacher's feet', on the fifth terrace of Purgatory (*Purg.* xxi), and Bonagiunta's hailing of Dante as the writer of *Ladies that have intelligence of love* and master of 'the sweet new style', on the sixth terrace (*Purg.* xxiv). The subject of poetry has a great place in Dante's poem, because for him the poet, according to his degree, is a seer and a sage.

When Dante knew that it was Guinicelli who spoke to him he 'went on a long way in thought, gazing at him'. 'How many were his memories of early youth and maturer years! When, hardly eighteen years old, "he saw by himself the art of putting words in rhyme", he certainly searched and studied lovingly the models left by the famous Bolognese' (*F. Torraca*). No other modern poet is so often named or quoted in Dante's writings as Guinicelli and it is always in terms of praise; here he addresses him with the reverential *you*. 'That serene exaltation of spiritual beauty' (*V. Rossi*) and the vital expression of it, which were the chief marks of the 'new rhymes' of Dante's

group in Florence, had been in an important measure antici-
pated by Guinicelli in Bologna and he was 'unique among the
rhymers of the doctrinal school in knowing how to combine
beauty of form with sincerity of inspiration' (*Casini-Barbi*).
His ode beginning:

> 'Within the gentle heart Love shelters him,
> As birds within the green shades of the grove,'

and his sonnet:

> 'Yea, let me praise my Lady whom I love,
> Likening her unto the lily and rose:'

—translated by D. G. Rossetti—show him reaching quite be-
yond the arid theorizing in verse about love which was then
the vogue in north Italy to something far more experienced
and real, which made him 'the father' of younger Florentines
such as 'the other Guido' (Cavalcante) and Dante.

While Dante calls Guinicelli 'the father of me and of others
my betters', he makes Guinicelli point to Arnaut the Provençal
as 'a better craftsman of the mother tongue'. Arnaut was 'the
most minutely ingenious and metrically resourceful, but at the
same time one of the most laborious and tiresome, of the
Provençal versifiers. His words are a mosaic of odd conceits
and rare and difficult forms' (*C. H. Grandgent*). He was admired
by Dante, it appears, chiefly for his *craftsmanship* in the mother
tongue, for his skill in using the common speech for un-
common ends and in making his verses the medium of subtle
and difficult thoughts. Such craftsmanship as Arnaut's pre-
pared an instrument for Guinicelli, who used it to better
purpose and opened the way for Dante, who turned the
mother tongue to uses never before conceived.

What reason Dante had for putting these two poets among
the penitents of lust we do not know, unless it be that among
the writings of both are poems of amatory passion without
measure or restraint or trace of spiritual value. Arnaut is
praised expressly because he surpassed the common 'verses of
love and tales of romance' of his time and country and Guinicelli

347

for 'those sweet lines of his, which so long as the modern use shall last will make their ink still dear.' Was it that their greater work, belonging to the poetic succession which culminated in Dante's praise of Beatrice and his vision of her in Paradise, was for him the sign and proof of their repentance?

PURGATORIO

Sì come quando i primi raggi vibra
    là dove il suo fattor lo sangue sparse,
    cadendo Ibero sotto l'alta Libra,
e l'onde in Gange da nona rïarse,
    sì stava il sole; onde 'l giorno sen giva,
    come l'angel di Dio lieto ci apparse.
Fuor della fiamma stava in su la riva,
    e cantava: '*Beati mundo corde!*'
    in voce assai più che la nostra viva.
Poscia: 'Più non si va, se pria non morde,   10
    anime sante, il foco: intrate in esso,
    ed al cantar di là non siate sorde'
ci disse come noi li fummo presso;
    per ch' io divenni tal, quando lo 'ntesi,
    qual è colui che nella fossa è messo.
In su le man commesse mi protesi,
    guardando il foco e imaginando forte
    umani corpi già veduti accesi.
Volsersi verso me le buone scorte;
    e Virgilio mi disse: 'Figliuol mio,   20
    qui può esser tormento, ma non morte.
Ricorditi, ricorditi! . . . e se io
    sovresso Gerion ti guidai salvo,
    che farò ora presso più a Dio?
Credi per certo che se dentro all'alvo
    di questa fiamma stessi ben mille anni,
    non ti potrebbe far d'un capel calvo.
E se tu forse credi ch' io t' inganni,
    fatti ver lei, e fatti far credenza
    con le tue mani al lembo de' tuoi panni.   30

CANTO XXVII

The angel of chastity; the passage through the fire; the dream of Leah; Virgil's last speech

As when it shoots the first rays where its Maker shed His blood, the Ebro lying under the lofty Scales and the waters of the Ganges scorched by noon, so stood the sun;[1] the day, therefore, was departing when God's glad angel appeared to us. He stood outside the flames on the terrace and sang *'Beati mundo corde'*[2] with a voice far clearer than ours; then: 'There is no way farther, holy souls, unless first the fire's sting is felt; enter into it and be not deaf to the singing beyond' he said to us when we were near him, so that I became, when I heard him, like one that is laid in the grave. I stretched up my clasped hands, gazing at the fire and strongly imagining bodies I once saw burned.

The good escorts turned to me and Virgil said: 'My son, here may be torment, but not death. Remember, remember; and if even on Geryon I brought thee safely, what shall I do now nearer to God? Be well assured that didst thou stay in the heart of this flame a thousand years it could not touch a hair of thy head; and if thou think, perhaps, that I deceive thee, go close to it and try it with thine own hands on the edge of thy garment. Put

351

Pon giù omai, pon giù ogni temenza:
   volgiti in qua; vieni ed entra sicuro!'
   E io pur fermo e contra coscïenza.
Quando mi vide star pur fermo e duro,
   turbato un poco, disse: 'Or vedi, figlio,
   tra Beatrice e te è questo muro.'
Come al nome di Tisbe aperse il ciglio
   Piramo in su la morte, e riguardolla,
   allor che 'l gelso diventò vermiglio;
così, la mia durezza fatta solla,   40
   mi volsi al savio duca, udendo il nome
   che nella mente sempre mi rampolla.
Ond'ei crollò la fronte e disse: 'Come?
   volenci star di qua?'; indi sorrise
   come al fanciul si fa ch'è vinto al pome.
Poi dentro al foco innanzi mi si mise,
   pregando Stazio che venisse retro,
   che pria per lunga strada ci divise.
Sì com fui dentro, in un bogliente vetro
   gittato mi sarei per rinfrescarmi,   50
   tant'era ivi lo 'ncendio sanza metro.
Lo dolce padre mio, per confortarmi,
   pur di Beatrice ragionando andava,
   dicendo: 'Li occhi suoi già veder parmi.'
Guidavaci una voce che cantava
   di là; e noi, attenti pur a lei,
   venimmo fuor là ove si montava.
'Venite, benedicti Patris mei,'
   sonò dentro a un lume che lì era,
   tal, che mi vinse e guardar nol potei.   60
'Lo sol sen va' soggiunse 'e vien la sera:
   non v'arrestate, ma studiate il passo,
   mentre che l'occidente non si annera.'
Dritta salìa la via per entro 'l sasso
   verso tal parte ch' io togliea i raggi
   dinanzi a me del sol ch'era già basso.
E di pochi scaglion levammo i saggi,
   che 'l sol corcar, per l'ombra che si spense,
   sentimmo dietro e io e li miei saggi.

away, henceforth, put away every fear, turn hither, come and enter with confidence.' And I stood still, though against my conscience.

When he saw me remain standing stubborn, being troubled a little he said: 'Look now, my son, between Beatrice and thee is this wall.'

As at the name of Thisbe Pyramus lifted his eyelids at the point of death and gazed at her, at the time when the mulberry became red,[3] so, my stubbornness softened, I turned to the wise Leader, hearing the name that ever springs up in my mind; at which he shook his head and said: 'What, are we to stay on this side?', then smiled as one does at a child that is won with an apple. Then he put himself into the fire before me, asking Statius, who for a long way had been between us, to come behind.

As soon as I was in it I would have cast myself into boiling glass to cool me, so beyond measure was the burning there, and my sweet Father, to comfort me, kept talking of Beatrice as he went, saying: 'I seem to see her eyes already.' Guiding us was a voice that sang beyond, and giving all our heed to it we came forth where the ascent began. '*Venite, benedicti Patris mei*,'[4] sounded within a light that was there, such that it overcame me and I could not look at it. 'The sun departs' it continued 'and evening comes; do not stop, but hasten your steps before the west grows dark.'

The way went straight up through the rock in such a direction that I cut off before me the rays of the sun, which was now low, and we had gained only a few steps when both I and my sages perceived by the disappearance of the shadow that

353

E pria che 'n tutte le sue parti immense   70
  fosse orizzonte fatto d'uno aspetto,
  e notte avesse tutte sue dispense,
ciascun di noi d'un grado fece letto;
  chè la natura del monte ci affranse
  la possa del salir più che il diletto.
Quali si stanno ruminando manse
  le capre, state rapide e proterve
  sovra le cime avante che sien pranse,
tacite all'ombra, mentre che 'l sol ferve,
  guardate dal pastor, che 'n su la verga   80
  poggiato s'è e lor poggiato serve;
e quale il mandrïan che fori alberga,
  lungo il peculio suo queto pernotta,
  guardando perchè fiera non lo sperga;
tali eravam noi tutti e tre allotta,
  io come capra, ed ei come pastori,
  fasciati quinci e quindi d'alta grotta.
Poco parer potea lì del di fori;
  ma, per quel poco, vedea io le stelle
  di lor solere e più chiare e maggiori.   90
Sì ruminando e sì mirando in quelle,
  mi prese il sonno; il sonno che sovente,
  anzi che 'l fatto sia, sa le novelle.
Nell'ora, credo, che dell'orïente
  prima raggiò nel monte Citerea,
  che di foco d'amor par sempre ardente,
giovane e bella in sogno mi parea
  donna vedere andar per una landa
  cogliendo fiori; e cantando dicea:
'Sappia qualunque il mio nome dimanda   100
  ch' i' mi son Lia, e vo movendo intorno
  le belle mani a farmi una ghirlanda.
Per piacermi allo specchio qui m'adorno;
  ma mia suora Rachel mai non si smaga
  dal suo miraglio, e siede tutto giorno.
Ell' è de' suoi belli occhi veder vaga
  com' io dell'adornarmi con le mani;
  lei lo vedere, e me l'ovrare appaga.'

the sun had set behind us; and before the horizon, in all its vast expanse, had takeι one aspect and night held all her domains each of us made his bed of a step, for the nature of the mountain took from us the power rather than the desire of climbing farther.

As goats that have been quick and wanton on the heights before they fed lie mildly chewing the cud, silent in the shade while the sun is burning, watched by the shepherd who leans on his staff and tends them while he leans—and as the herdsman who lodges in the open passes the night beside his quiet flock, watching lest a beast should scatter them; such were we then all three, I like a goat and they like shepherds, shut in on the one side and the other by the high rock. Little outside could be seen there, but by that little I saw the stars both bigger and brighter than their wont.

So ruminating and so gazing at them, sleep seized me—sleep, which often has news before the event. In the hour, I think, when Cytherea,[5] who seems always burning with the fire of love, first shone on the mountain from the east, I seemed to see in a dream a lady young and beautiful going through a meadow gathering flowers and singing: 'Know, whoever asks my name, that I am Leah,[6] and I go plying my fair hands here and there to make me a garland; to please me at the glass I here adorn myself, but my sister Rachel never leaves her mirror and sits all day. She is fain to see her own fair eyes as I to adorn me with my hands. She with seeing, and I with doing am satisfied.'

355

E già per li splendori antelucani,
  che tanto a' pellegrin surgon più grati,   110
  quanto, tornando, albergan men lontani,
le tenebre fuggìan da tutti lati,
  e 'l sonno mio con esse; ond' io leva'mi,
  veggendo i gran maestri già levati.
'Quel dolce pome che per tanti rami
  cercando va la cura de' mortali,
  oggi porrà in pace le tue fami.'
Virgilio inverso me queste cotali
  parole usò; e mai non furo strenne
  che fosser di piacere a queste iguali.   120
Tanto voler sopra voler mi venne
  dell'esser su, ch'ad ogni passo poi
  al volo mi sentìa crescer le penne.
Come la scala tutta sotto noi
  fu corsa e fummo in su 'l grado superno,
  in me ficcò Virgilio li occhi suoi,
e disse: 'Il temporal foco e l'etterno
  veduto hai, figlio; e se' venuto in parte
  dov' io per me più oltre non discerno.
Tratto t' ho qui con ingegno e con arte;   130
  lo tuo piacere omai prendi per duce:
  fuor se' dell'erte vie, fuor se' dell'arte.
Vedi lo sol che in fronte ti riluce;
  vedi l'erbetta, i fiori e li arbuscelli,
  che qui la terra sol da sè produce.
Mentre che vegnan lieti li occhi belli
  che, lacrimando, a te venir mi fenno,
  seder ti puoi e puoi andar tra elli.
Non aspettar mio dir più nè mio cenno:
  libero, dritto e sano è tuo arbitrio,   140
  e fallo fora non fare a suo senno:
per ch' io te sovra te corono e mitrio.'

And now with the splendours before dawn, which rise so much the welcomer to travellers as, returning, they lodge less far from home, the shadows were fleeing on every side and my sleep with them; therefore I rose, seeing the great masters risen already.

'That sweet fruit which the care of mortals goes to seek on so many boughs shall to-day give peace to thy cravings.' Such were Virgil's words to me, and never was there boon to give such pleasure as these. So greatly desire upon desire came to me to be above that with every step I felt then my feathers grow for flight. When all the stair was sped beneath us and we were on the topmost step Virgil fixed his eyes on me and said: 'The temporal fire and the eternal thou hast seen, my son, and art come to a part where of myself I discern no further. I have brought thee here with under-standing and with skill. Take henceforth thy pleasure for guide. Thou hast come forth from the steep and the narrow ways. See the sun that shines on thy brow; see the grass, the flowers and trees which the ground here brings forth of itself alone; till the fair eyes come rejoicing which weeping made me come to thee thou mayst sit or go among them. No longer expect word or sign from me. Free, upright and whole is thy will and it were a fault not to act on its bidding; therefore over thyself I crown and mitre thee.'

1. Near sunrise at Jerusalem, midnight in Spain, noon in India, and near sunset in Purgatory. Cp. beginning of Canto ii.

2. 'Blessed are the pure in heart' (*Matt.* v. 8).

3. Thisbe's lover Pyramus, finding her blood-stained garment and thinking her dead, stabbed himself; she found him dying and killed herself and from their blood the mulberry turned red.

4. 'Come, ye blessed of my Father' (*Matt.* xxv. 34).

5. Venus, called from Cythera, where she rose from the sea.

6. Leah and Rachel, Jacob's wives (*Gen.* xxix. 16 ff.), types of the active and the contemplative life.

NOTE

In the imagery of the terrace of the purgation of lust, just below the Garden of Eden on the summit, Dante's inventiveness was not as free as elsewhere in Purgatory, since the Church's tradition had made of the 'flaming sword which turned every way, to keep the way of the tree of life', in the story of the Fall, a wall of fire completely surrounding Eden. The flames here have to serve, therefore, both for the specific purgation of this terrace and for the final barrier on the way to the place of innocence. That we may take for the reason why Statius, whose purgation is already completed and who does no penance here, must yet pass through the flames, and that is why there are two angels on this terrace, one on either side of the fiery wall.

The twenty-seventh canto, like the second and the fifteenth, begins with an astronomical telling of the time. 'All the heavens, whether visible or not, circle round in the vast spaces of the Poet's imagination' (*M. B. Anderson*). The earth is circled by the sun, and Jerusalem, 'where its Maker shed His blood', Spain and India and Purgatory are one world, all its life in one context of sin and suffering and repentance and attainment through grace.

Then, with the beatitude which is peculiarly fitted for the final purgation, 'Blessed are the pure in heart, for they shall see God', the drama concentrates on Dante himself and the whole canto is lyric and personal. When the angel bids him enter into the fire, 'I became, when I heard him, like one that is laid in the grave.' The note of personal experience is stressed here as on no other of the seven terraces. On their first arrival Dante 'feared the fire on this hand and on that feared to fall below' and he was admonished by Virgil that 'a tight rein must be kept on the eyes'. While they walked Virgil said to him often: 'Watch, take heed of my warning', and, with all his interest in the souls there, Dante 'kept looking at them and at his steps, dividing his glance from time to time'. The canto in its earlier part is full of his terror of the penitential flames, a terror which Virgil's urgency fails to overcome till he names Beatrice, when Dante, like Pyramus, is 'at the point of death', and 'as soon as I was in it I would have cast myself into boiling glass to cool me, so beyond measure was the burning there'. It is not easy to see how Dante could have told us more convincingly of his own peculiar agony of repentance for the sin that is purged here. What may have been the circumstances of his offending we do not know, and it must be remembered that the passage was written by a man of stern and lofty moral judgement, reflecting, near his fiftieth year, on his own early manhood; but the evidence is as plain as he could make it that here, on the terrace of carnal lust, he is a penitent whose repentance and purgation are an agony new to his experience on the mountain and not to be borne except in the strength that comes to him with the thought of Beatrice.

Looking back over the seven terraces of Purgatory, we find that on three of them, and on these only, Dante in some sense shares in the penances borne by the penitents. On the first terrace he stoops with the burdened penitents of pride, and the talk of one of them, he says, 'fills my heart with good humbleness and abates a great swelling in me'; on the next terrace Virgil walks with him 'on that side of the terrace where one might fall over', and Dante fears the torment below 'so that already the load down there is heavy upon me'. On the third terrace he has to grope in the bitter and blinding smoke which is the penalty and purgation of anger; 'therefore my wise and trusty escort came close to me and offered me his shoulder', and he 'kept saying: "See that thou art not cut off from me."' And here on the seventh terrace Virgil repeatedly warns him, then urges him to pass through the fire that purges the penitents of lust. These correspondences, limited to these three penances, are plainly not fortuitous but deliberate and significant. They are an implicit confession of his besetting sins of pride, anger, and lust and of his need for the strength of his reason and conscience against them, and these are precisely the sins, out of all the seven, to which Dante, being the man we know, might be tempted more than another man. It is such a confession as we might expect from Dante, conscious of his own great qualities and of the danger of them, his lofty self-assurance, his 'indignant soul', his impassioned sensibility 'when love breathes in me'. He makes besides a measured admission on the terrace of envy: 'My eyes will yet be taken from me here, but only for a little.' Telling of the penitents he is himself a penitent, and not of sin in general but of his own sinfulness, and his confession strongly emphasizes the autobiographical factor as a fundamental element in the whole poem.

It is only at the name of Beatrice that Dante consents to follow Virgil into the fire. In plain terms, lust is not cured by reason itself, but by a higher love, by the demonstration of ends and gains for the soul which are beyond earthly reason's reach, and Dante was guided in the flames by 'a voice that sang beyond'. It is no longer the mere escape from sin that moves him but more and more the compulsion of heavenly things, and passing out of the fire they discover that the voice is singing the beatitude which is the sum of all the beatitudes: 'Come, ye blessed of my Father, inherit the kingdom prepared for you.'

In the dream of Leah Dante makes use of an old tradition of the Church in which Leah is the Old Testament representative of the active life, the perfecting of which is the express business of Purgatory, and Rachel of the life of contemplation. 'St. Gregory the Great, when the office of the Papacy was forced upon him, bewailed the loss of his Rachel, the quiet life of contemplation in his monastery: "The beauty of the contemplative life I have loved as Rachel, barren indeed but clear-eyed and fair, which, although by its quiet it bears less, yet sees the light more clearly. Leah is wedded to me in the night, the active life namely, fruitful but blear-eyed, seeing less though bringing forth abundantly"' (J. S. Carroll). The distinction and the relation between the active and the contemplative life, between well-doing and the knowledge of God, which will occupy us later, were fundamental in medieval thinking.

The dream of Leah came to Dante 'in the hour when Cytherea first shone on the mountain from the east'. It is an instance of Dante's sensitive relevancy that among the many references to Venus in the *Comedy* it is here only, when he dreams of the perfected earthly life of the soul, that the love-goddess—'burning with the fire of love'—is named in her most virginal character, from the place where she rose new-born from the sea.

It is plain that Leah and Rachel in the dream are a forecast and, so far, a characterization of Matilda and Beatrice in the scenes that follow.

In Virgil's last words to Dante we seem to hear his tones of grave authority and tenderness as he lays down his finished task: 'Therefore over thyself I crown and mitre thee.' The words were doubtless suggested by such passages of the New Testament as 'Ye are a royal priesthood' and 'Christ hath made us kings and priests unto God and his Father'. They recall Dante's own language in the *De Monarchia* about the Empire and the Church: 'Since these regimens are for men's direction to certain ends, if man had continued in the state of innocence in which God created him he would not have needed such directions; regimens of that kind, then, are remedies against the infirmity of sin.' Dante is yet to hear much of Church and Empire in his journey and to see both in their divine idea and fulfilment; but as outward authorities for his discipline and control, he, the purified spirit returning to the place of man's first innocence, is no more subject to them but is now king and priest over himself. He has reached that liberty of which, as Virgil told Cato at the foot of the mountain, he went in search. His will is free because it is upright and whole and to follow it is at once his freedom and his obedience. In passing, in the next canto, from Virgil's guidance to that of the lady of the forest he is passing beyond the urgings and corrections of conscience to the free delight in good.

PURGATORIO

Vago già di cercar dentro e dintorno
    la divina foresta spessa e viva,
    ch'alli occhi temperava il novo giorno,
sanza più aspettar, lasciai la riva,
    prendendo la campagna lento lento
    su per lo suol che d'ogni parte auliva.
Un'aura dolce, sanza mutamento
    avere in sè, mi ferìa per la fronte
    non di più colpo che soave vento;
per cui le fronde, tremolando, pronte   10
    tutte quante piegavano alla parte
    u' la prim'ombra gitta il santo monte;
non però dal loro esser dritto sparte
    tanto che li augelletti per le cime
    lasciasser d'operare ogni lor arte;
ma con piena letizia l'ore prime,
    cantando, ricevìeno intra le foglie,
    che tenevan bordone alle sue rime,
tal qual di ramo in ramo si raccoglie
    per la pineta in su 'l lito di Chiassi,   20
    quand'Eolo Scirocco fuor discioglie.
Già m'avean trasportato i lenti passi
    dentro alla selva antica tanto, ch' io
    non potea rivedere ond' io mi 'ntrassi;
ed ecco più andar mi tolse un rio,
    che 'nver sinistra con sue picciole onde
    piegava l'erba che 'n sua ripa uscìo.
Tutte l'acque che son di qua più monde
    parrìeno avere in sè mistura alcuna
    verso di quella, che nulla nasconde,   30

CANTO XXVIII

*The Earthly Paradise; the fair lady and the
stream; the seeds dispersed on the earth*

EAGER now to search within and about the divine
forest green and dense which tempered to my eyes
the new day, I left the slope without waiting
longer, taking the level very slowly over the ground
which gave fragrance on every side. A sweet air
that was without change was striking on my brow
with the force only of a gentle breeze, by which
the fluttering boughs all bent freely to the part
where the holy mountain throws its first shadow,
yet were not so much swayed from their erect-
ness that the little birds in the tops did not still
practise all their arts, but, singing, they greeted
the morning hours with full gladness among the
leaves, which kept such undertone to their rhymes
as gathers from branch to branch in the pine wood
on the Chiassi shore when Aeolus looses the
Sirocco.[1]

Already my slow steps had brought me so far
within the ancient wood that I could not see the
place where I had entered, and lo, my going farther
was prevented by a stream which with its little
waves bent leftwards the grass that sprang on its
bank. All the waters that are purest here would
seem to have some defilement in them beside that,

avvegna che si mova bruna bruna
   sotto l'ombra perpetüa, che mai
   raggiar non lascia sole ivi nè luna.
Coi piè ristetti e con li occhi passai
   di là dal fiumicello, per mirare
   la gran varïazion di freschi mai;
e là m'apparve, sì com'elli appare
   subitamente cosa che disvia
   per maraviglia tutto altro pensare,
una donna soletta che si gìa   40
   cantando e scegliendo fior da fiore
   ond'era pinta tutta la sua via.
'Deh, bella donna, che a' raggi d'amore
   ti scaldi, s' i' vo' credere a' sembianti
   che soglion esser testimon del core,
vegnati in voglia di trarreti avanti'
   diss' io a lei 'verso questa rivera,
   tanto ch' io possa intender che tu canti.
Tu mi fai rimembrar dove e qual era
   Proserpina nel tempo che perdette   50
   la madre lei, ed ella primavera.'
Come si volge con le piante strette
   a terra ed intra sè donna che balli,
   e piede innanzi piede a pena mette,
volsesi in su i vermigli ed in su i gialli
   fioretti verso me non altrimenti
   che vergine che li occhi onesti avvalli;
e fece i prieghi miei esser contenti,
   sì appressando sè, che 'l dolce sono
   veniva a me co' suoi intendimenti.   60
Tosto che fu là dove l'erbe sono
   bagnate già dall'onde del bel fiume,
   di levar li occhi suoi mi fece dono:
non credo che splendesse tanto lume
   sotto le ciglia a Venere, trafitta
   dal figlio fuor di tutto suo costume.
Ella ridea dall'altra riva dritta,
   trattando più color con le sue mani,
   che l'alta terra sanza seme gitta.

which conceals nothing though it flows quite dark under the perpetual shade which never lets sun or moon shine there.

With feet I stopped and with eyes passed over beyond the streamlet to look at the great variety of fresh-flowering boughs, and there appeared to me there, as appears of a sudden a thing that for wonder drives away every other thought, a lady all alone, who went singing and culling flower from flower with which all her way was painted.

'Pray, fair lady, who warmest thyself in love's beams, if I am to believe the looks which are wont to be testimony of the heart,' I said to her 'may it please thee to come forward to this stream so near that I may hear what thou singest. Thou makest me recall where and what was Proserpine at the time her mother lost her and she the spring.'[2]

As a lady turns in the dance with feet close together on the ground and hardly puts one foot before the other, she turned towards me on the red and yellow flowerets like a virgin that veils her modest eyes and gave satisfaction to my prayer, approaching so that the sweet sound came to me with its meaning. As soon as she was where the grass was just bathed with the waves of the beautiful river she did me the grace to lift her eyes; and I do not believe such light shone from beneath the lids of Venus when, through strange mischance, she was pierced by her son.[3] Erect, she smiled from the other bank, arranging in her hands many colours which the high land puts forth without

Tre passi ci facea il fiume lontani;   70
   ma Ellesponto, là 've passò Serse,
   ancora freno a tutti orgogli umani,
più odio da Leandro non sofferse,
   per mareggiare intra Sesto ed Abido,
   che quel da me perch'allor non s'aperse.
'Voi siete nuovi, e forse perch' io rido'
   cominciò ella 'in questo luogo eletto
   all'umana natura per suo nido,
maravigliando tienvi alcun sospetto;
   ma luce rende il salmo *Delectasti*,   80
   che puote disnebbiar vostro intelletto.
E tu che se' dinanzi e mi pregasti,
   dì s'altro vuoli udir; ch' i' venni presta
   ad ogni tua question tanto che basti.'
'L'acqua' diss' io 'e 'l suon della foresta
   impugnan dentro a me novella fede
   di cosa ch' io udi' contraria a questa.'
Ond'ella: 'Io dicerò come procede
   per sua cagion ciò ch'ammirar ti face,
   e purgherò la nebbia che ti fiede.   90
Lo sommo ben, che solo esso a sè piace,
   fece l'uom buono e a bene, e questo loco
   diede per arra a lui d'etterna pace.
Per sua difalta qui dimorò poco;
   per sua difalta in pianto ed in affanno
   cambiò onesto riso e dolce gioco.
Perchè 'l turbar che sotto da sè fanno
   l'essalazion dell'acqua e della terra,
   che quanto posson dietro al calor vanno,
all'uomo non facesse alcuna guerra,   100
   questo monte salìo verso 'l ciel tanto,
   e libero n'è d' indi ove si serra.
Or perchè in circuito tutto quanto
   l'aere si volge con la prima volta,
   se non li è rotto il cerchio d'alcun canto,
in questa altezza ch'è tutta disciolta
   nell' aere vivo, tal moto percuote,
   e fa sonar la selva perch'è folta;

seed. Three paces the river kept us apart; but
Hellespont where Xerxes passed, a bridle still on
all men's boasts, did not bear more hatred from
Leander for its swelling waters between Sestos
and Abydos than that from me because it did not
open then.[4]

'You are new here' she began 'and, perhaps
because I smile in this place set apart to the human
kind for its nest, some doubt keeps you wondering,
but the psalm *Delectasti*[5] gives light that may
dispel the cloud from your mind. And thou who
art in front and didst make request of me, say if
thou wouldst hear more, for I have come ready
for all thy questions till thou art satisfied.'

'The water' I said 'and the sound of the forest
contend in me with a recent belief in a thing I
have heard contrary to this.'[6]

She said therefore: 'I will tell how that which
makes thee marvel proceeds from its cause and I
will rid thee of the cloud that has fallen on thee.
The Supreme Good who does only His own
pleasure made man good and for good and gave
him this place for earnest of eternal peace; through
his fault he had short stay here, through his fault
he exchanged for tears and toil honest mirth and
sweet sport. In order that the disturbance which
the exhalations of land and sea make of themselves
below, following the heat as far as they may, should
do no injury to man, this mountain rose thus far
towards heaven and stands clear of them from
where it is barred. Now, since all the air revolves
in a circuit with the first circling,[7] unless its
revolution is interrupted at any point, that move-
ment strikes on this height, which is all free in
the living air, and makes the wood, because it is

e la percossa pianta tanto puote,
 che della sua virtute l'aura impregna, 110
 e quella poi, girando, intorno scuote;
e l'altra terra, secondo ch'è degna
 per sè e per suo ciel, concepe e figlia
 di diverse virtù diverse legna.
Non parrebbe di là poi maraviglia,
 udito questo, quando alcuna pianta
 sanza seme palese vi s'appiglia.
E saper dèi che la campagna santa
 dove tu se' d'ogni semenza è piena,
 e frutto ha in sè che di là non si schianta. 120
L'acqua che vedi non surge di vena
 che ristori vapor che gel converta,
 come fiume ch'acquista e perde lena;
ma esce di fontana salda e certa,
 che tanto dal voler di Dio riprende
 quant'ella versa da due parti aperta.
Da questa parte con virtù discende
 che toglie altrui memoria del peccato;
 dall'altra d'ogni ben fatto la rende.
Quinci Letè; così dall'altro lato 130
 Eunoè si chiama; e non adopra
 se quinci e quindi pria non è gustato:
a tutti altri sapori esto è di sopra.
 E avvegna ch'assai possa esser sazia
 la sete tua perch' io più non ti scopra,
darotti un corollario ancor per grazia;
 nè credo che 'l mio dir ti sia men caro,
 se oltre promission teco si spazia.
Quelli ch'anticamente poetaro
 l'età dell'oro e suo stato felice, 140
 forse in Parnaso esto loco sognaro.
Qui fu innocente l'umana radice;
 qui primavera sempre ed ogni frutto;
 nettare è questo di che ciascun dice.'
Io mi rivolsi 'n dietro allora tutto
 a' miei poeti, e vidi che con riso
 udito avean l'ultimo costrutto;
poi alla bella donna torna' il viso.

dense, resound; and the smitten plants have such potency that with their virtue they impregnate the air, which in its circling then scatters it abroad, and the other land,[8] according to its fitness in itself and in its sky, conceives and brings forth from diverse virtues diverse growths. Were this understood it would not then seem a marvel yonder when some plant takes root without visible seed, and thou shouldst know that the holy ground where thou art is full of every seed and has in it fruit that is not plucked yonder.[9] The water thou seest does not spring from a vein which is restored by vapour that cold condenses, like a river that gains and loses force, but issues from a constant and sure fountain which by God's will regains as much as it pours forth, open on either side. On this side it flows down with virtue which takes from men the memory of sin; on the other it restores that of every good deed; here it is called Lethe and on the other side Eunoe and it does not operate here or there unless it is first tasted,—this last surpasses every other sweetness.

'And notwithstanding that thy thirst may be fully satisfied though I reveal no more to thee I will give thee also a corollary as a grace, nor do I think my words will be less welcome to thee if they reach beyond my promise. Those who in old times sang of the age of gold and of its happy state perhaps dreamed on Parnassus of this place; here the human root was innocent, here was lasting spring and every fruit, this is the nectar of which each tells.'

I turned then right round to my poets and saw that they had heard the last sentence with a smile. Then I brought my eyes back to the fair lady.

PURGATORIO

1. Chiassi, modern Classe, on the coast near Ravenna, gets the South-East wind from the Adriatic; Aeolus, king of the winds, kept them shut up in a mountain.

2. Proserpine, seized by Pluto, king of the underworld, when gathering flowers with her mother.

3. Embracing his mother, Cupid wounded her accidentally and she fell violently in love with Adonis.

4. Xerxes of Persia, invading Greece, crossed Hellespont by a bridge of boats; returning after defeat he escaped in a fishing-boat. Leander of Abydos used to swim across to visit Hero of Sestos and was drowned.

5. '*Thou*, Lord, *hast made me glad* through thy work; I will triumph in the works of thy hands' (*Ps.* xcii. 4).

6. Statius's account of the mountain (*Purg.* xxi).

7. The outermost material heaven, the Primum Mobile, communicates its motion, east to west, to the lower heavens and so to the earth's atmosphere.

8. The northern hemisphere.

9. 'The Lord God planted a garden eastward in Eden . . . and out of the ground made the Lord God to grow every tree that is pleasant to the sight and good for food' (*Gen.* ii. 8–9).

NOTE

In the *De Monarchia* Dante says that of the two ends proposed by divine providence for man the first is 'the blessedness of this life, which consists in the exercise of his natural powers and which is figured in the Earthly Paradise'. He has now journeyed from the gloomy wood to the divine forest, from the moral disorder of his own soul and of the world about him to 'the blessedness of this life' and Paradise regained. 'And that Paradise is still uncorrupted nature as it came from its Maker's hand. Over all the rest of the world nature is perverted and waste, hostile to man, at strife with itself; in the bowels of the earth is Hell, and the holy mountain itself, from circle to circle, is all torment. Alone uncontaminated and unharmed, in the middle of the vastness of the ocean, under the unchanging sky, is this lofty summit, this little plateau, an islet, as it were, of purity and peace and happiness, from which it is only natural the soul should be released for its flight to heaven' (*A. Graf, L.D.*). Medieval Christendom held much debate about the locality and present condition of the Garden of Eden and produced many accounts of it, with features, such as the island, the great height, the surpassing natural beauties, which became traditional and of which Dante made use.

The lady seen beyond the stream is the genius of the place, as much a part of it as the flowers she gathers. She is the obvious fulfilment of the dream of Leah, like her singing and gathering flowers, but a fulfilment which is better than the dream. Leah delights in the work of her own hands, with which she adorns herself; the other is made glad through God's work and 'shows forth his loving-kindness in the morning' (*Ps.* xcii. 2), and all her handling of the flowers expresses that gladness. She is busy and her business is the active life of human

373

innocence, of the soul at peace with itself and with the natural world, the soul and the world as they were when 'God saw everything that he had made, and, behold, it was very good'. She is the image of humanity unfallen or restored to Eden; and Dante, an outcast while he writes in a turbulent and disordered world, tells how he looked with a rapt longing across the streamlet at her and at the place which man had lost, and of the memories which crowd upon him of the best that had been imagined by man of beauty and passion and daring for love. His absorbed delight in her is as virginal as is the representation of herself. The lady is not less fair than Proserpine in the meadow when Pluto seized her, or Venus when she was pierced by Cupid's dart, and not less to be desired and dared for than she whom Leander desired and dared for across the Hellespont. The three examples are taken from pagan story, and that deliberately. Dante chooses his comparisons from the imaginations of the natural man at their height, to declare that here is the better reality which they suggest and of which they all come short, and that the soul redeemed and purged burns in its passion for the blessed life with an intenser, whiter flame than any of which these stories tell.

The lady, still anonymous, is a symbol of the active life in its perfection; but it would hardly be possible for Dante to mean so human a figure to be only a symbol, and no question with regard to the *Divine Comedy* has been more debated and with less final agreement than the question of her identity. The only hint given to us is Beatrice's naming of her, incidentally, *Matilda* in the thirty-third canto, and of the many possibilities perhaps that supported by D'Ovidio among others is the best, that she is a German nun, a senior contemporary of Dante, Mechtildis von Hackenborn, who died in 1298 and whose sweet and gentle visions of the Earthly Paradise are in some respects in agreement with Dante's and may well have attracted and influenced him. The question of the earthly identity of the lady here is, after all, of little consequence; she is such as Dante conceives her and her name adds nothing to her.

On the terraces below, after the meeting with Statius, Dante has come behind the other two poets; in the fire on the last terrace and on the stair above it he was between them and had the immediate companionship of Virgil; here it is more than once indicated that he goes in front of the others, having no need of any outward direction, for now 'his pleasure' is his guide.

Nothing in the canto is more characteristic of Dante or of his time than the abrupt change, as it seems to us, from the lyrical beauty of the first part to the didactic and scientific manner of the rest; and in the change he does not fall away from his imaginative purpose but fulfils it. Not only does the formal explanation of the phenomena of the mountain give it an added verisimilitude as something that can bear to be examined and accounted for, but it brings the garden under credible heavenly influences and connects it with the world we know; it tells of the soft, steady wind caused by the moving spheres on the summit which rises clear of the exhalations and disturbances of the earth below, the seeds which float from the garden and are self-sown round the world, and the rivers flowing from a supernatural and unfailing spring. And as the common flora of the lower world springs from the seeds of Eden, so, according to Matilda's 'corollary', the best dreams of all the poets are hints and premonitions of a reality which surpasses them all; and Virgil and Statius smile to find that their dreams are true.

Both the structure of the verse—by which the canto might naturally have ended with line 133—and the curiously deliberate way in which the 'corollary' is added suggest that it was an afterthought. It is as if the Christian poet went out of his way to bring the poets of paganism—'my poets'—into the context of revelation. His last glimpses of Virgil are, here, of his smile, and, in the next canto, of his look of baffled amazement at the approach of revelation.

PURGATORIO

CANTANDO come donna innamorata,
    continüò col fin di sue parole:
    'Beati quorum tecta sunt peccata!'
E come ninfe che si givan sole
    per le salvatiche ombre, disïando,
    qual di veder, qual di fuggir lo sole,
allor si mosse contra il fiume, andando
    su per la riva, e io pari di lei,
    picciol passo con picciol seguitando.
Non eran cento tra' suoi passi e' miei,   10
    quando le ripe igualmente dier volta,
    per modo ch'a levante mi rendei.
Nè ancor fu così nostra via molta,
    quando la donna tutta a me si torse,
    dicendo: 'Frate mio, guarda e ascolta.'
Ed ecco un lustro subito trascorse
    da tutte parti per la gran foresta,
    tal che di balenar mi mise in forse.
Ma perchè 'l balenar, come vien, resta,
    e quel, durando, più e più splendeva,   20
    nel mio pensar dicea: 'Che cosa è questa?'
E una melodia dolce correva
    per l'aere luminoso; onde buon zelo
    mi fè riprender l'ardimento d' Eva,
che là dove ubidìa la terra e 'l cielo,
    femmina sola e pur testè formata,
    non sofferse di star sotto alcun velo;
sotto 'l qual se divota fosse stata,
    avrei quelle ineffabili delizie
    sentite prima e più lunga fïata.   30

CANTO XXIX

The walk by the river; the pageant of revelation

SINGING like a lady enamoured she continued, when she had finished speaking: '*Beati quorum tecta sunt peccata!*'[1] and, like nymphs that used to wander alone through woodland shades, one choosing to see, another to avoid, the sun, she moved then against the stream, going along the bank, and I level with her accompanying the little steps with mine. We had not taken a hundred between us when the banks made an equal bend in such a way that I faced the east again, and we had not gone far that way when the lady turned quite round to me, saying: 'My brother, look and listen.' And lo, a sudden brightness swept through the great forest on all sides, such that it put me in doubt if it was lightning; but since lightning ceases as it comes and that, continuing, shone more and more, I said in my mind: 'What thing is this?' And a sweet melody ran through the shining air; at which good zeal made me blame Eve's boldness, that, where earth and heaven were obedient, a woman, alone and but then formed, she did not bear to stay under any veil,[2] under which had she been submissive I should have tasted those unspeakable delights before and for longer time.

377

Mentr' io m'andava tra tante primizie
   dell'etterno piacer, tutto sospeso
   e disïoso ancora a più letizie,
dinanzi a noi, tal quale un foco acceso
   ci si fè l'aere sotto i verdi rami;
   e 'l dolce suon per canti era già inteso.
O sacrosante Vergini, se fami,
   freddi o vigilie mai per voi soffersi,
   cagion mi sprona ch' io mercè vi chiami.
Or convien che Elicona per me versi,   40
   e Uranìa m'aiuti col suo coro
   forti cose a pensar mettere in versi.
Poco più'oltre, sette alberi d'oro
   falsava nel parere il lungo tratto
   del mezzo ch'era ancor tra noi e loro;
ma quand' i' fui sì presso di lor fatto
   che l'obietto comun, che 'l senso inganna,
   non perdea per distanza alcun suo atto,
la virtù ch'a ragion discorso ammanna,
   sì com'elli eran candelabri apprese,   50
   e nelle voci del cantare 'osanna'.
Di sopra fiammeggiava il bello arnese
   più chiaro assai che luna per sereno
   di mezza notte nel suo mezzo mese.
Io mi rivolsi d'ammirazion pieno
   al buon Virgilio, ed esso mi rispose
   con vista carca di stupor non meno.
Indi rendei l'aspetto all'alte cose
   che si movìeno incontr'a noi sì tardi
   che foran vinte da novelle spose.   60
La donna mi sgridò: 'Perchè pur ardi
   sì nello aspetto delle vive luci,
   e ciò che vien di retro a lor non guardi?'
Genti vid' io allor, come a lor duci,
   venire appresso, vestite di bianco;
   e tal candor di qua già mai non fuci.
L'acqua splendea dal sinistro fianco,
   e rendea me la mia sinistra costa,
   s' io riguardava in lei, come specchio anco.

While I went on among so many first-fruits of eternal happiness, all in suspense and desirous still of other joys, the air before us under the green boughs became like a blazing fire and the sweet sound was now heard as songs.

O most holy virgins,[3] if fastings, cold, or vigils I have ever borne for you, need drives me to ask you for reward; now must Helicon pour forth for me and Urania help me with her choir to put in verse things hard for thought.

A little way on, a false appearance of seven trees of gold was caused by the long space still intervening between us and them; but when I had come so near that the ambiguous shape which deceives the sense did not lose by distance any of its features, the faculty which provides for the discourse of reason[4] made them out as they were, candlesticks, and in the voices of the singing, 'Hosanna'. Above flamed the splendid array, far brighter than the moon in the clear midnight sky in her mid-month. I turned round full of wonder to the good Virgil and he answered me with a look no less charged with amazement; then I turned my face again to the high things, which moved towards us so slowly that they would have been outstripped by new-made brides.

The lady chid me: 'Why art thou so eager only on the sight of the living lights and givest no heed to that which comes behind them?'

I saw people then coming after them as after their leaders, clothed in white, and such whiteness never was here. The water shone on my left and, even like a mirror, gave back to me my left

Quand' io dalla mia riva ebbi tal posta,　　70
　che solo il fiume mi facea distante,
　per veder meglio ai passi diedi sosta,
e vidi le fiammelle andar davante,
　lasciando dietro a sè l'aere dipinto,
　e di tratti pennelli avean sembiante;
sì che lì sopra rimanea distinto
　di sette liste, tutte in quei colori
　onde fa l'arco il Sole e Delia il cinto.
Questi ostendali in dietro eran maggiori
　che la mia vista; e, quanto a mio avviso,　　80
　diece passi distavan quei di fori.
Sotto così bel ciel com' io diviso,
　ventiquattro seniori, a due a due,
　coronati venìen di fiordaliso.
Tutti cantavan: 'Benedicta tue
　nelle figlie d'Adamo, e benedette
　sieno in etterno le bellezze tue!'
Poscia che i fiori e l'altre fresche erbette
　a rimpetto di me dall'altra sponda
　libere fuor da quelle genti elette,　　90
sì come luce luce in ciel seconda,
　vennero appresso lor quattro animali,
　coronati ciascun di verde fronda.
Ognuno era pennuto di sei ali,
　le penne piene d'occhi; e li occhi d'Argo,
　se fosser vivi, sarebber cotali.
A descriver lor forme più non spargo
　rime, lettor; ch'altra spesa mi strigne
　tanto ch'a questa non posso esser largo;
ma leggi Ezechïel, che li dipigne　　100
　come li vide dalla fredda parte
　venir con vento e con nube e con igne;
e quali i troverai nelle sue carte,
　tali eran quivi, salvo ch'alle penne
　Giovanni è meco e da lui si diparte.
Lo spazio dentro a lor quattro contenne
　un carro, in su due rote, triunfale,
　ch'al collo d'un grifon tirato venne.

side when I gazed in it. When I was at a point on my bank where only the river parted me from them, to see better I held my steps and saw the flames move forward, leaving the air behind them painted, and they had the appearance of streaming pennons, so that overhead it remained streaked with seven bands in all those colours of which the sun makes his bow and Delia her girdle.[5] These standards went back beyond my sight and, as well as I could judge, the outermost were ten paces apart. Beneath so fair a sky as I describe four and twenty elders came two and two, crowned with lilies; all sang: 'Blessed art thou among the daughters of Adam and blessed forever be thy beauty!' After the flowers and other fresh herbage opposite to me on the other bank were left clear of those elect people, as light follows light in heaven four living creatures came after them, each crowned with green leaves; every one was plumed with six wings, the plumage full of eyes, and the eyes of Argus,[6] were they alive, would be such. To describe their forms, reader, I do not waste more rhymes, for other outlay so presses on me that I cannot be lavish in this; but read Ezekiel, who depicts them as he saw them come from the cold parts with wind and cloud and fire, and as thou shalt find them on his pages such they were here, except that for the wings John is with me and departs from him.[7] The space between these four contained a triumphal car on two wheels, which came drawn at the neck of a griffin; it

Esso tendeva in su l'una e l'altra ale
  tra la mezzana e le tre e tre liste,   110
  sì ch'a nulla, fendendo, facea male.
Tanto salivan che non eran viste;
  le membra d'oro avea quant'era uccello,
  e bianche l'altre, di vermiglio miste.
Non che Roma di carro così bello
  rallegrasse Affricano, o vero Augusto,
  ma quel del Sol sarìa pover con ello;
quel del Sol che, svïando, fu combusto
  per l'orazion della Terra devota,
  quando fu Giove arcanamente giusto.   120
Tre donne in giro dalla destra rota
  venìan danzando: l'una tanto rossa
  ch'a pena fora dentro al foco nota;
l'altr'era come se le carni e l'ossa
  fossero state di smeraldo fatte;
  la terza parea neve testè mossa;
e or parean dalla bianca tratte,
  or dalla rossa; e dal canto di questa
  l'altre toglìen l'andare e tarde e ratte.
Dalla sinistra quattro facean festa,   130
  in porpora vestite, dietro al modo
  d'una di lor ch'avea tre occhi in testa.
Appresso tutto il pertrattato nodo
  vidi due vecchi in abito dispari,
  ma pari in atto ed onesto e sodo.
L' un si mostrava alcun de' famigliari
  di quel sommo Ipocràte che natura
  alli animali fè ch'ell' ha più cari;
mostrava l'altro la contraria cura
  con una spada lucida e aguta,   140
  tal che di qua dal rio mi fè paura.
Poi vidi quattro in umile paruta;
  e di retro da tutti un vecchio solo
  venir dormendo, con la faccia arguta.
E questi sette col primaio stuolo
  erano abitüati, ma di gigli
  dintorno al capo non facean brolo,

stretched up the one wing and the other between the middle band and the three and three so that it did not harm any by cutting through, and they rose so high that they were lost to sight. It had its members of gold so far as it was a bird and the rest white mingled with red. Not only did Rome not gladden Africanus or Augustus himself with a car so splendid,[8] but that of the sun would be poor beside it—that of the sun, which, straying, was consumed at the devout petition of the earth, when Jove in his secret counsel was just.[9] Three ladies came dancing in a round at the right wheel, one so red that she would hardly have been noted in the fire, another as if the flesh and bones had been of emerald, the third seeming new-fallen snow; and they seemed to be led, now by the white, now by the red, and from this one's song the others took their movement fast and slow. On the left four made festival, clothed in purple, following the measure of one of them that had three eyes in her head. Behind the whole group I have described I saw two old men, different in dress but alike in grave and dignified bearing; the one showed himself of the household of that great Hippocrates whom nature made for the creatures she holds dearest,[10] the other showed the opposite care, with a sword so bright and sharp that on the far side of the river it put me in fear. Then I saw four of humble aspect, and behind all an old man alone come sleeping, with keen visage. And these seven were clad like the foremost file, except that they did not have wreaths

383

anzi di rose e d'altri fior vermigli:
  giurato avrìa poco lontano aspetto
  che tutti ardesser di sopra da' cigli.   150
E quando il carro a me fu a rimpetto,
  un tuon s' udì, e quelle genti degne
  parvero aver l'andar più interdetto,
fermandosi ivi con le prime insegne.

of lilies about their head but of roses and other red flowers; looking from a little distance one would have sworn that all were burning above the eyebrows. And when the car was opposite me a thunder-clap was heard and that noble throng seemed forbidden to go farther and stopped there along with the banners in front.

1. 'Blessed are they whose sins are covered' (*Ps.* xxxii. 1, in the Vulgate).

2. The veil of ignorance, not knowing good and evil; cp. *Gen.* iii. 1–6.

3. The Muses; Mt Helicon, with springs sacred to them; Urania, Muse of astronomy or heavenly things.

4. 'Your perception takes from outward reality an impression and unfolds it within you, so that it makes the mind turn to it' (*Purg.* xviii).

5. Solar and lunar rainbows; Diana, born in Delos, here called Delia.

6. Argus, with a hundred eyes.

7. In *Ezekiel* i. 1–14 they have four wings; in *Revelation* iv. 6–8 they have six.

8. Scipio Africanus and the Emperor Augustus were given public triumphs.

9. When Phaeton misguided the chariot of the sun and endangered the earth Jupiter killed him with a thunderbolt.

10. Greek physician, the father of medicine.

NOTE

The subject of the twenty-ninth canto is the pageant of divine revelation and its keynote is given at once in Matilda's song: 'Blessed are they whose sins are covered.' When she and Dante have turned to the sacred east it is his longing for the perfect life, it is Matilda, that bids him 'look and listen' and, later, 'give heed'; 'and to the single song, liquid, pure, clear, of Matilda answers from the distance a choir of unseen spirits singing Hosanna' (*L. Pietrobono, L.D.*), the greeting to the coming Christ.

At the first splendour and the distant sound Dante recalls 'Eve's boldness' which cost humanity so dear and called for so great a remedy; and to tell of these things, which are 'hard for thought', he asks for the Muses' help, as he has done three times before (*Inf.* ii and xxxii and *Purg.* i) and as he is to do again when he must speak of the divine idea of the Empire in Paradise (*Par.* xviii), for it too is a thing that is 'hard for thought'. It is now, for the last time, that Dante exchanges glances with Virgil, who at the approach of revelation has no help for him, only 'a look charged with amazement'.

With his usual narrative skill Dante tells of the crescendo of sight and sound as the pageant approaches—first the sudden brightness and sweet melody, then the appearance of blazing fire under the green boughs and the sound heard as songs, then, at last, the candlesticks and the Hosanna; and he describes in the formal scholastic way how slowly the soul comes to the right apprehension of the things of God.

The pageant is for some of Dante's readers a lapse from poetry into laborious prose, and most will agree that in some of its imagery there is more of inventiveness than imagination. Yet it is hardly too much to say that 'here beats the heart of the great work' (*L. Rocca, L.D.*); for the heart-beat of the

387

Divine Comedy is Dante's passion for the redemption of human life, and that is what is represented here. 'Against the sad conditions of the Church of his day he would set the primitive simplicity of Christianity, the time when the Church's greed of wealth and craving for earthly power had not yet come to birth and it gathered humbly and devoutly under the shadow of the Gospels, in meditation on the truths revealed to it and in the exercise of the Christian virtues' (*L. Rocca, L.D.*). In setting forth the Church in its ideal as a part of the revelation in which it was born Dante uses the only language possible for him. His representation of revelation must be super-natural, symbolical, august, and drawn in the main from the ancient sacred tradition, the imagery of the Old and New Testaments as it was then interpreted. Some parts of the Hebrew apocalyptic must have been very uncongenial to Dante's keenness and clarity of imagination, and at one point he turns away with a characteristic directness, not to 'waste more rhymes', from the elaborate visions of Ezekiel and bids the reader read for himself. But Dante and his first readers were familiar with allegorical pageantry both sacred and secular in their own cities, and a representation such as we have in these cantos was for them the natural language for such a theme.

The theme is divine revelation as it is embodied in the books of the Old and New Testaments under the prevailing enlighten-ment of the Spirit of God and as it culminates in the Christian Church. The candlesticks, or candlestick with seven lights, taken from passages in *Exodus* and *Revelation*, represent the seven gifts of the Spirit—wisdom and understanding, counsel and might, knowledge and piety and the fear of the Lord, taken from the Vulgate of *Isaiah* xi. 2–3; and the lights, of different colours, stream like long pennons over the whole cortege and make it one. The twenty-four elders (*Rev.* iv. 4) are the writers, or the books, of the Old Testament, as the number was reckoned by St Jerome; and they are clothed in white for faith, crowned with lilies for purity, and they sing in praise of the Virgin, of whom their pages were believed to be full of prophecy. On his first sight of them, the water of Lethe, when he looked into it, gave back to him his left side, the worse part of himself; it is the resurgence of shameful memory in the soul confronted by the truth of God. The four winged creatures about the car are the forms of man, lion, ox, and eagle familiar in medieval art as the symbols of the Evangelists, and they are crowned with green in sign of hope. The triumphal car is the Church, more splendid than any of ancient Rome or that of the sun, for *its* triumph is of the spirit. 'The Chariot of the ideal Church is more glorious than any triumphal car either of State or of that degenerate Church which has swerved so dangerously from its appointed course that the secret judgement of God will soon strike down its charioteers' (*J. S. Carroll*). In *Paradise* xii St Francis and St Dominic are called the wheels of 'the chariot in which Holy Church defended herself', so that we may take the 'two wheels' of the car here to represent the two great monastic orders which sought and served, respectively, love and knowledge. The car is drawn by a griffin, an ancient fabulous creature found both in classical antiquity and in Scripture (*Dan.* vii. 4), which represents not so much Christ as the theological idea of Christ, the mystery of the divine and human natures set forth in the strangeness, as of heaven and earth at once, of the eagle-lion; its vast wings reaching to heaven and engaging and harmonizing with the flames of the candlesticks may have been suggested by the language of the thirty-sixth Psalm:

'Thy mercy, O Lord, is in the heavens,
And thy faithfulness reacheth unto the clouds. . . .
Therefore the children of men put their trust under the
    shadow of thy wings.'

The gold of its upper parts means divinity and the white and red of the rest humanity.

The three ladies dancing on the right of the car are the evangelical virtues, faith, hope, and love, in their symbolical colours, faith and love taking the lead in the dance alternately, but love alone giving the time with her song; and the four on the left the cardinal, or moral, virtues, wisdom or prudence, courage, justice, and temperance, all in purple, the colour of Empire, and led by prudence, who sees every way—but whose 'three eyes in her head' are a lapse on Dante's part which might have been thought impossible. The two old men following the car are Luke, 'the beloved physician'—representing here not the Third Gospel but *The Acts of the Apostles*—and his greater comrade Paul, with 'the sword of the spirit, which is the word of God'. The 'four of humble aspect' are the writers of the General Epistles, and the 'old man alone' who comes 'sleeping, with keen visage', is John as the visionary of *Revelation*. The New Testament writers, 'clad like the foremost file' for their agreement in faith with the Old Testament, are distinguished from the others by the wreaths which make them appear to be 'burning above the eyebrows', for they write under the new law of love. It is an example of the studied order of Dante's imagery that the three groups representing the books of Scripture are crowned in the colours, respectively, of faith, hope, and love.

Dante's vocabulary is always significant and in the whole account of the pageant there is a marked choice of expressions more or less military—*pennons, standards, banners, leaders, file, array,* with *army, squadron, soldiery, colours,* in the thirty-second canto; and the 'triumphal car' would at once suggest to his readers the *carroccio,* the great war-chariot carrying the flag which accompanied the forces of an Italian commune in the field. For this is the Church Militant —not now in its dispersed and suffering members as on the slopes of the mountain, but in its ruling forces—that Dante sees here, the ranked orders of the spirit, whose victory is the world's redemption. In *Paradiso* xxv Beatrice says of Dante that 'the Church Militant has not a son more full of hope', and here, like his spiritual kinsman in England five hundred years later, he hopes

'till hope creates
From its own wreck the thing it contemplates'.

PURGATORIO

QUANDO il settentrïon del primo cielo
  che nè occaso mai seppe nè orto
  nè d'altra nebbia che di colpa velo,
e che faceva lì ciascuno accorto
  di suo dover, come 'l più basso face
  qual temon gira per venire a porto,
fermo s'affisse, la gente verace,
  venuta prima tra 'l grifone ed esso,
  al carro volse sè come a sua pace;
e un di loro, quasi da ciel messo,   10
  '*Veni, sponsa, de Libano*' cantando
  gridò tre volte, e tutti li altri appresso.
Quali i beati al novissimo bando
  surgeran presti ognun di sua caverna,
  la revestita voce alleluiando;
cotali in su la divina basterna
  si levar cento, *ad vocem tanti senis*,
  ministri e messaggier di vita etterna.
Tutti dicean: '*Benedictus qui venis!*'
  e fior gittando di sopra e dintorno,   20
  '*Manibus o date lilïa plenis!*'
Io vidi già nel cominciar del giorno
  la parte orïental tutta rosata,
  e l'altro ciel di bel sereno adorno;
e la faccia del sol nascere ombrata,
  sì che, per temperanza di vapori,
  l'occhio la sostenea lunga fïata:
così dentro una nuvola di fiori
  che dalle mani angeliche saliva
  e ricadeva in giù dentro e di fori,   30

CANTO XXX

Beatrice on the car; the disappearance of Virgil;
Beatrice's rebuke of Dante

WHEN the Wain of the first heaven stood still
that never knew setting or rising or veil of any
mist but of sin and there made each know
his duty as does the Wain below for him that
turns the helm to come to port,[1] the truthful
company that came at first between it and the
Griffin turned to the car as to their peace; and
one of them, like a messenger from heaven, called
three times, singing: *'Veni, sponsa, de Libano'*,[2]
and all the others after him. As the blessed shall
rise at the last trump each eager from his tomb,
the reclad voice singing Hallelujah, there rose up
on the divine chariot at the voice of so great an
elder a hundred ministers and messengers of
eternal life, who all cried: *'Benedictus qui venis'*,[3]
and, throwing flowers up and around, *'Manibus o
date lilia plenis.'*[4] I once saw at the beginning of
the day the eastern parts all rosy and the rest of
the sky clear and beautiful and the sun's face
come forth shaded so that through the tempering
vapours the eye could bear it long; so, within
a cloud of flowers which rose from the angels'
hands and fell again within and without, a lady

393

sovra candido vel cinta d'uliva
   donna m'apparve, sotto verde manto
   vestita di color di fiamma viva.
E lo spirito mio, che già cotanto
   tempo era stato che alla sua presenza
   non era di stupor tremando affranto,
sanza delli occhi aver più conoscenza,
   per occulta virtù che da lei mosse,
   d'antico amor sentì la gran potenza.
Tosto che nella vista mi percosse   40
   l'alta virtù che già m'avea trafitto
   prima ch' io fuor di puerizia fosse,
volsimi alla sinistra col rispitto
   col quale il fantolin corre alla mamma
   quando ha paura o quando elli è afflitto,
per dicere a Virgilio: 'Men che dramma
   di sangue m'è rimaso che non tremi:
   conosco i segni dell'antica fiamma';
ma Virgilio n'avea lasciati scemi
   di sè, Virgilio dolcissimo patre,   50
   Virgilio a cui per mia salute die'mi;
nè quantunque perdeo l'antica matre
   valse alle guance nette di rugiada,
   che, lacrimando, non tornasser atre.
'Dante, perchè Virgilio se ne vada,
   non pianger anco, non piangere ancora;
   chè pianger ti conven per altra spada.'
Quasi ammiraglio che in poppa ed in prora
   viene a veder la gente che ministra
   per li altri legni, e a ben far l' incora;   60
in su la sponda del carro sinistra,
   quando mi volsi al suon del nome mio,
   che di necessità qui si registra,
vidi la donna, che pria m'apparìo
   velata sotto l'angelica festa,
   drizzar li occhi ver me di qua dal rio.
Tutto che 'l vel che le scendea di testa,
   cerchiato delle fronde di Minerva,
   non la lasciasse parer manifesta,

appeared to me, girt with olive over a white veil, clothed under a green mantle with the colour of living flame. And my spirit, which now so long had not been overcome with awe, trembling in her presence,[5] without having more knowledge by the eyes, through hidden virtue that came from her, felt old love's great power. As soon as the lofty virtue smote on my sight which already had pierced me before I was out of my boyhood,[6] I turned to the left with the confidence of a little child that runs to his mother when he is afraid or in distress, to say to Virgil: 'Not a drop of blood is left in me that does not tremble; I know the marks of the ancient flame.'[7] But Virgil had left us bereft of him, Virgil sweetest father, Virgil to whom I gave myself for my salvation, nor did all the ancient mother lost avail my cheeks washed with dew that they should not be stained again with tears.

'Dante, because Virgil leaves thee weep not, weep not yet, for thou must weep for another sword.'

Like an admiral who goes to poop and prow to see the men that serve on the other ships and to hearten them in their work, so on the left side of the car—when I turned at the sound of my name, which is noted here of necessity—I saw the lady who first appeared to me veiled under the angelic festival direct her eyes on me beyond the stream. Although the veil that fell from her head, encircled with Minerva's leaves, did not let her be plainly

regalmente nell'atto ancor proterva   70
  continüò come colui che dice
  e 'l più caldo parlar dietro reserva:
'Guardaci ben! Ben son, ben son Beatrice.
  Come degnasti d'accedere al monte?
  non sapei tu che qui è l'uom felice?'
Li occhi mi cadder giù nel chiaro fonte;
  ma,veggendomi in esso, i trassi all'erba,
  tanta vergogna mi gravò la fronte.
Così la madre al figlio par superba,
  com'ella parve a me; perchè d'amaro   80
  sent' il sapor della pietade acerba.
Ella si tacque; e li angeli cantaro
  di subito *'In te Domine, speravi'*;
  ma oltre *'pedes meos'* non passaro.
Sì come neve tra le vive travi
  per lo dosso d'Italia si congela,
  soffiata e stretta dalli venti schiavi,
poi, liquefatta, in sè stessa trapela,
  pur che la terra che perde ombra spiri,
  sì che par foco fonder la candela;   90
così fui sanza lacrime e sospiri
  anzi 'l cantar di quei che notan sempre
  dietro alle note delli etterni giri;
ma poi ch' i' 'ntesi nelle dolci tempre
  lor compatire a me, più che se detto
  avesser: 'Donna, perchè sì lo stempre?',
lo gel che m'era intorno al cor ristretto
  spirito e acqua fessi, e con angoscia
  della bocca e delli occhi uscì del petto.
Ella, pur ferma in su la detta coscia   100
  del carro stando, alle sustanze pie
  volse le sue parole così poscia:
'Voi vigilate nell'etterno dìe,
  sì che notte nè sonno a voi non fura
  passo che faccia il secol per sue vie;
onde la mia risposta è con più cura
  che m' intenda colui che di là piagne,
  perchè sia colpa e duol d'una misura.

396

seen, royally, still stern in her bearing, she continued like one who while he speaks holds back
his hottest words: 'Look at me well; I am, I am
indeed Beatrice. How durst thou approach the
mountain? Didst thou not know that here man is
happy?'

My eyes fell down to the clear fount, but, seeing
myself in it, I drew them back to the grass, so
great shame weighed on my brow; so does the
mother seem harsh to her child as she seemed to
me, for the savour of stern pity tastes bitter. She
was silent; and at once the angels sang: '*In te,
Domine, speravi*', but did not go beyond '*pedes
meos*'.[8] Even as the snow among the living beams
along the back of Italy freezes, blown and packed
by the Slavonian winds, then, dissolved, drips into
itself if only the land that loses shadow breathes,
so that it seems fire melting a candle;[9] so was I
without tears or sighs before the singing of those
who keep ever in tune with the notes of the eternal
spheres, but when I heard in the sweet harmonies
their compassion on me, more than if they had
said: 'Lady, why dost thou so shame him?', the
ice that was bound about my heart turned to
breath and water and with anguish came forth
from my breast by mouth and eyes.

She, still standing motionless on the same side
of the car, then directed her words to the pitiful
spirits: 'Ye keep watch in the eternal day, so that
neither night nor sleep robs you of a step the
world makes in its course; therefore my answer is
made with more care that he should hear me who
weeps yonder, so that sin and sorrow may be of

Non pur per ovra delle rote magne,
 che drizzan ciascun seme ad alcun fine   110
 secondo che le stelle son compagne,
ma per larghezza di grazie divine,
 che sì alti vapori hanno a lor piova
 che nostre viste là non van vicine,
questi fu tal nella sua vita nova
 virtüalmente, ch'ogni abito destro
 fatto averebbe in lui mirabil prova.
Ma tanto più maligno e più silvestro
 si fa 'l terren col mal seme e non colto,
 quant'elli ha più di buon vigor terrestre.   120
Alcun tempo il sostenni col mio volto;
 mostrando li occhi giovanetti a lui,
 meco il menava in dritta parte volto.
Sì tosto come in su la soglia fui
 di mia seconda etade e mutai vita,
 questi si tolse a me, e diessi altrui.
Quando di carne a spirto era salita
 e bellezza e virtù cresciuta m'era,
 fu' io a lui men cara e men gradita;
e volse i passi suoi per via non vera,   130
 imagini di ben seguendo false,
 che nulla promission rendono intera.
Nè l' impetrare ispirazion mi valse,
 con le quali ed in sogno e altrimenti
 lo rivocai; sì poco a lui ne calse!
Tanto giù cadde, che tutti argomenti
 alla salute sua eran già corti,
 fuor che mostrarli le perdute genti.
Per questo visitai l'uscio de' morti,
 e a colui che l' ha qua su condotto   140
 li preghi miei, piangendo, furon porti.
Alto fato di Dio sarebbe rotto,
 se Letè si passasse e tal vivanda
 fosse gustata sanza alcuno scotto
di pentimento che lagrime spanda.'

one measure. Not only by operation of the great
wheels which direct each seed to some end accord-
ing to the stars in their company, but by largess
of divine graces which rain down from vapours so
high that our sight does not come near them, this
man in his early life was such potentially that
every right disposition would have come to mar-
vellous proof in him; but so much the more
noxious and wild the ground becomes, with bad
seed and untilled, as it has more good strength of
soil. For a time I sustained him with my coun-
tenance. Showing him my youthful eyes I brought
him with me, bound on the right way. As soon as
I was on the threshold of my second age and I
changed life[10] he took himself from me and gave
himself to another. When I had risen from flesh
to spirit and beauty and virtue had increased in
me I was less dear to him and less welcome and
he bent his steps in a way not true, following after
false images of good which fulfil no promise; nor
did it avail me to gain inspirations for him with
which both in dream and in other ways I called
him back, so little did he heed them. He fell so
low that all means for his salvation now came short
except to show him the lost people; for this I
visited the threshold of the dead and to him who
has brought him up here my prayers were offered
with tears. God's high decrees would be broken
if Lethe were passed and such a draught were
tasted without some scot of penitence and shedding
of tears.'

1. 'The Wain'—from Charles Wain's, '*Settentrione*', formed of seven stars—here the seven lights, the gifts of the Spirit, belonging to the Empyrean of God's presence and hid from men by sin; 'the Wain below', the actual constellation of the Great Bear in the heaven of the Fixed Stars. Wisdom

> 'is fairer than the sun
> And above all the constellations of the stars' (*Wisd.* vii. 29).

2. The elder representing the *Song of Solomon* sings: 'Come with me from Lebanon, my spouse' (iv. 8); in the Vulgate the word *veni* occurs three times.

3. 'Blessed art thou that comest'; cp. *Matt.* xxi. 9.

4. 'O give lilies with full hands' (*Aeneid*).

5. Beatrice died in 1290.

6. 'I saw her almost at the end of my ninth year' (*Vita Nuova*).

7. The last words are from the *Aeneid*.

8. 'In thee, O Lord, have I hoped' (Vulgate of *Ps.* xxxi. 1); to the 8th verse, 'Thou hast set *my feet* in a large room.'

9. Snow in the woods on the Apennines is frozen by the north-east wind from Slavonia and melted by the south wind from Africa.

10. Beatrice died in her 25th year, at the end of 'adolescence' and the beginning of 'youth'.

(This canto will be considered along with the next.)

PURGATORIO

"O TU che se' di là dal fiume sacro,'
   volgendo suo parlare a me per punta,
   che pur per taglio m'era paruto acro,
ricominciò, seguendo sanza cunta,
   'dì, dì se questo è vero: a tanta accusa
   tua confession conviene esser congiunta.'
Era la mia virtù tanto confusa
   che la voce si mosse, e pria si spense
   che dalli organi suoi fosse dischiusa.
Poco sofferse; poi disse: 'Che pense?   10
   Rispondi a me; chè le memorie triste
   in te non sono ancor dall'acqua offense.'
Confusione e paura insieme miste
   mi pinsero un tal 'sì' fuor della bocca,
   al quale intender fuor mestier le viste.
Come balestro frange, quando scocca
   da troppa tesa, la sua corda e l'arco,
   e con men foga l'asta il segno tocca,
sì scoppia' io sott'esso grave carco,
   fuori sgorgando lacrime e sospiri,   20
   e la voce allentò per lo suo varco.
Ond'ella a me: 'Per entro i mie' disiri,
   che ti menavano ad amar lo bene
   di là dal qual non è a che s'aspiri,
quai fossi attraversati o quai catene
   trovasti, per che del passare innanzi
   dovessiti così spogliar la spene?
E quali agevolezze o quali avanzi
   nella fronte delli altri si mostraro,
   per che dovessi lor passeggiare anzi?'   30

CANTO XXXI

*Dante's confession; the passage through Lethe;
Beatrice unveiled*

'O THOU that art on that side of the sacred river',
she began again, turning against me the point of
her speech which even with the edge had seemed
sharp to me[1] and continuing without pause, 'say,
say if this is true; to such an accusation thy con-
fession must needs be joined.'

My faculties were so confounded that my voice
began and was spent before it was released from
its organs.

She forbore a little, then said: 'What thinkest
thou? Answer me, for the sad memories are not
yet destroyed in thee by the water.'

Confusion and fear mingled together drove forth
from my mouth a *Yes* such that to hear it there
was need of sight. As a cross-bow shot with too
great strain breaks the cord and bow and the shaft
touches the mark with less force, so I broke down
under that heavy charge, pouring forth tears and
sighs, and my voice failed in its passage. At which
she said to me: 'In the desires for me which were
leading thee in love of the good beyond which
there is nothing to be longed for, what cross-
ditches or chains didst thou meet with for which
thou must thus give up the hope of going forward,
and what attractions and advantages showed in the
aspect of other things for which thou must be at
their service?'

Dopo la tratta d' un sospiro amaro,
   a pena ebbi la voce che rispose,
   e le labbra a fatica la formaro.
Piangendo dissi: 'Le presenti cose
   col falso lor piacer volser miei passi,
   tosto che 'l vostro viso si nascose.'
Ed ella: 'Se tacessi o se negassi
   ciò che confessi, non fora men nota
   la colpa tua: da tal giudice sassi!
Ma quando scoppia della propria gota   40
   l'accusa del peccato, in nostra corte
   rivolge sè contra 'l taglio la rota.
Tuttavia, perchè mo vergogna porte
   del tuo errore, e perchè altra volta,
   udendo le serene, sie più forte,
pon giù il seme del piangere ed ascolta:
   sì udirai come in contraria parte
   mover dovìeti mia carne sepolta.
Mai non t'appresentò natura o arte
   piacer, quanto le belle membra in ch' io   50
   rinchiusa fui, e sono in terra sparte;
e se 'l sommo piacer sì ti fallìo
   per la mia morte, qual cosa mortale
   dovea poi trarre te nel suo disio?
Ben ti dovevi, per lo primo strale
   delle cose fallaci, levar suso
   di retro a me che non era più tale.
Non ti dovea gravar le penne in giuso,
   ad aspettar più colpi, o pargoletta
   o altra vanità con sì breve uso.   60
Novo augelletto due o tre aspetta;
   ma dinanzi dalli occhi di pennuti
   rete si spiega indarno o si saetta.'
Quali i fanciulli, vergognando, muti
   con li occhi a terra stannosi, ascoltando
   e sè riconoscendo e ripentuti,
tal mi stav' io; ed ella disse: 'Quando
   per udir se' dolente, alza la barba,
   e prenderai più doglia riguardando.'

After heaving a bitter sigh I had hardly the voice to answer and the lips shaped it with difficulty; weeping, I said: 'Present things with their false pleasure turned my steps as soon as your² face was hid.'

And she: 'Hadst thou kept silence or denied what thou confessest, thy fault would be not less plain, by such a judge is it known, but when from a man's own cheek breaks forth condemnation of his sin, in our court the wheel turns back against the edge.³ Nevertheless, in order that thou mayst now bear the shame of thy wandering and another time, hearing the Sirens, be stronger, lay aside the sowing of tears and hearken; so shalt thou hear how my buried flesh should have directed thee the other way. Never did nature or art set before thee beauty so great as the fair members in which I was enclosed, and they are crumbled in the dust; and if the highest beauty thus failed thee by my death, what mortal thing should then have drawn thee into desire for it? Truly thou oughtest, at the first shaft of deceptive things, to have risen up after me who was such no longer. No young girl or other vanity of such brief worth should have bent thy wings downward to await more shots. A young chick waits for two or three, but in vain is the net spread or arrow shot in the sight of the full-fledged bird.'

As children ashamed stand dumb with eyes on the ground, listening and acknowledging their fault and repentant, so I stood there, and she said: 'Since by hearing thou art grieved, lift up thy beard and thou shalt have grief by looking.'

Con men di resistenza si dibarba   70
   robusto cerro, o vero al nostral vento
   o vero a quel della terra di Iarba,
ch' io non levai al suo comando il mento;
   e quando per la barba il viso chiese,
   ben conobbi il velen dell'argomento.
E come la mia faccia si distese,
   posarsi quelle prime creature
   da loro aspersïon l'occhio comprese;
e le mie luci, ancor poco sicure,
   vider Beatrice volta in su la fera   80
   ch'è sola una persona in due nature.
Sotto 'l suo velo e oltre la rivera
   vincer parìemi più sè stessa antica,
   vincer che l'altre qui, quand'ella c'era.
Di pentèr sì mi punse ivi l'ortica
   che di tutte altre cose qual mi torse
   più nel suo amor, più mi si fè nemica.
Tanta riconoscenza il cor mi morse,
   ch' io caddi vinto; e quale allora femmi,
   salsi colei che la cagion mi porse.   90
Poi, quando il cor virtù di fuor rendemmi,
   la donna ch' io avea trovata sola
   sopra me vidi, e dicea: 'Tiemmi, tiemmi!'
Tratto m'avea nel fiume infin la gola,
   e tirandosi me dietro sen giva
   sovresso l'acqua lieve come scola.
Quando fui presso alla beata riva,
   'Asperges me' sì dolcemente udissi,
   che nol so rimembrar, non ch' io lo scriva.
La bella donna nelle braccia aprissi;   100
   abbracciommi la testa e mi sommerse
   ove convenne ch' io l'acqua inghiottissi.
Indi mi tolse, e bagnato m'offerse
   dentro alla danza delle quattro belle;
   e ciascuna del braccio mi coperse.
'Noi siam qui ninfe e nel ciel siamo stelle:
   pria che Beatrice discendesse al mondo,
   fummo ordinate a lei per sue ancelle.

With less resistance is uprooted the sturdy oak, whether in the wind from our parts or from the country of Iarbas,[4] than I raised at her command my chin, and when by the beard she demanded my face I noted well the venom of the argument. And when my face was lifted up my sight marked those primal creatures pause in their scattering of flowers, and my eyes, still lacking confidence, saw Beatrice turned toward the beast which is one sole person in two natures. Beneath her veil and beyond the stream, she seemed to me to surpass her former self more than she surpassed the others here when she was with us. The nettle of remorse so stung me there that of all other things that which had most bent me to the love of it became for me the most hateful; such self-conviction bit me at the heart that I fell overcome and what I became then she knows who was the cause of it. Then, when my heart restored my outward sense, the lady I had found alone I saw above me, and she was saying: 'Hold me, hold me!' She had brought me into the river up to the throat and, drawing me after her, was passing over the water light as a shuttle. When I was close to the blessed shore I heard '*Asperges me*'[5] so sweetly sung that I cannot recall, far less write it. The fair lady opened her arms, clasped my head, and plunged me under, where I must swallow the water; then she took me out and led me bathed into the dance of the four fair ones, and each covered me with her arm.

'Here we are nymphs and in heaven are stars. Before Beatrice descended to the world we were ordained to be her handmaids. We will bring thee

Merrenti alli occhi suoi; ma nel giocondo
  lume ch'è dentro aguzzeranno i tuoi   110
  le tre di là, che miran più profondo.'
Così cantando cominciaro; e poi
  al petto del grifon seco menarmi,
  ove Beatrice stava volta a noi,
disser: 'Fa che le viste non risparmi:
  posto t'avem dinanzi alli smeraldi
  ond'Amor già ti trasse le sue armi.'
Mille disiri più che fiamma caldi
  strinsermi li occhi alli occhi rilucenti,
  che pur sopra 'l grifone stavan saldi.   120
Come in lo specchio sol, non altrimenti
  la doppia fiera dentro vi raggiava,
  or con altri, or con altri reggimenti.
Pensa, lettor, s' io mi maravigliava,
  quando vedea la cosa in sè star queta,
  e nell' idolo suo si trasmutava.
Mentre che piena di stupore e lieta
  l'anima mia gustava di quel cibo
  che, saziando di sè, di sè asseta,
sè dimostrando di più alto tribo   130
  nelli atti, l'altre tre si fero avanti,
  danzando al loro angelico caribo.
'Volgi, Beatrice, volgi li occhi santi'
  era la sua canzone 'al tuo fedele
  che, per vederti, ha mossi passi tanti!
Per grazia fa noi grazia che disvele
  a lui la bocca tua, sì che discerna
  la seconda bellezza che tu cele.'
O isplendor di viva luce etterna,
  chi palido si fece sotto l'ombra   140
  sì di Parnaso, o bevve in sua cisterna,
che non paresse aver la mente ingombra,
  tentando a render te qual tu paresti
  là dove armonizzando il ciel t'adombra,
quando nell'aere aperto ti solvesti?

to her eyes; but for the happy light that is within them the three on the other side, who look deeper, shall quicken thine.' Thus they began to sing and then brought me with them to the breast of the Griffin, where Beatrice stood turned to us, and they said: 'See thou do not withhold thy gaze; we have set thee before the emeralds from which love once shot his darts at thee.'

A thousand desires hotter than flame held my eyes on the shining eyes, which remained still fixed on the Griffin, and even like the sun in a mirror the two-fold beast shone within them, now with the one, now with the other nature.[6] Think, reader, if I marvelled when I saw the thing still in itself and in its image changing. While my soul, full of amazement and gladness, tasted of that food which, satisfying with itself, for itself makes appetite,[7] the other three, showing themselves by their bearing to be of a higher order, moved forward, dancing to their angelic roundelay.

'Turn, Beatrice, turn thy holy eyes on thy faithful one,' was their song 'who, for sight of thee, has made so great a journey; of thy grace do us the grace to unveil thy mouth to him, that he may discern the second beauty,[8] which thou concealest.'

O splendour of living light eternal, who has ever grown so pale under Parnassus' shade or drunk so deep of its well that he would not seem to have a mind disabled, trying to render thee as thou appearedst there, heaven with its harmonies overhanging thee, when in the free air thou didst disclose thyself?

PURGATORIO

1. Having spoken of Dante to the angels, she now speaks *to* him.
2. The honorific *your*.
3. In heaven the sword of judgement is blunted by penitence.
4. North or south wind. Iarbas, a legendary king in North Africa.
5. '*Purge me* with hyssop' (*Ps.* li. 7). The verse is used in the giving of absolution.
6. The two Natures; not the unity of the Person, are seen in revelation.

> Wisdom is 'an unspotted mirror of the working of God,
> And an effulgence of his goodness' (*Wisd.* vii. 26).

7.
> 'They that eat me shall yet be hungry.
> And they that drink me shall yet be thirsty' (*Ecclus.* xxiv. 21).

8. Her smile.

NOTE

The twenty-ninth canto is occupied with revelation and the Church; it is all public and impersonal. The next two cantos are the most intimately personal in the *Divine Comedy*. The pageant is held up at a thunder-clap as at a sign from heaven and it is as if forgotten during the interview between Beatrice and Dante. Yet the thirtieth and thirty-first cantos are not only relevant but essential to the matter of the twenty-ninth. Revelation is not revelation unless it reveals a man to himself and it is by a psychological necessity that Dante makes his confession here—like Isaiah when he 'saw the Lord' in the temple and said: 'Woe is me! for I am undone; because I am a man of unclean lips', and then was called to prophecy.

The first part of the thirtieth canto unites Dante's story, in its most intimate and individual quality, with the story of revelation and its splendours. It is from the centre of the pageant that Beatrice speaks to him; for she is at once the divine wisdom for men and the woman Dante had known in Florence and in love for whom he had found his 'new life'. He was as sure as were all the prophets and apostles that his own deepest experience was a part of revelation and had a significance beyond himself which was universal, and he dared to make Beatrice the living spirit of truth, the voice of the ideal Church of his dream, with such a Church's authority for admonition, for chastisement, for absolution, for enlightenment, while she was still the Beatrice who once showed him her youthful eyes, in whose bodily presence he had trembled with awe and for whom he had suffered ten years' thirst. 'This apotheosis of Beatrice, this first appearance of his lady still veiled amid such glory, releases his imagination from the rigidity of symbols and ritual and gives to it the free wings of art; the drama becomes human and images and emotions spring forth' (*F. De Sanctis*). She appears to him 'girt with olive over a white veil, clothed under a green mantle with the colour of living flame', her olive-wreath, 'Minerva's leaves', the sign of peace and of wisdom and her garments in the colours of faith, hope, and love.

He has gone through Hell and climbed Purgatory with the hope of seeing her again, yet his first impulse in her presence is of bewilderment and fear and he turns to Virgil. So moving is the human drama of his grief at the loss of Virgil that the moral symbolism is absorbed and concealed in it; but Beatrice's rebuke proves at once that it is not forgotten. He turned in sudden terror from Beatrice to Virgil, from revelation to his natural and accustomed reason and conscience, for refuge. It was a resource which, in that presence, completely failed him and Beatrice recalled him sternly to herself, using for her first word his name, which occurs here and nowhere else in the *Divine Comedy*. The passage is an example, singular even for Dante, of the *fusing* power of his imagination, his power to tell his great story with complete objectivity and to make it at the same time the symbol and the vehicle of his own inner life and thought. 'Here it is himself who speaks, it is himself who writes, it is he who accuses and bitterly reproaches himself. . . . He returned to Beatrice to return to himself, to recover that better part of himself which his years and his errors had obscured' (*D. Mantovani, L.D.*), and by no other device could he have made the personal and actual character of his confession more plain than by this unique recording of his own name, 'which' he says 'is noted here of necessity'.

On the much-debated question of the faults here charged against him by Beatrice—by himself, that is—the conclusion of Moore and other scholars seems to correspond best with all the evidence: that during some of the years between her death in 1290 and the date of the vision he had lapsed from the devout idealism of his youth into worldly preoccupations and speculative indifference to religion, with something of the moral laxity which is indicated already in the twenty-third and twenty-seventh cantos. How far his 'wandering' carried him we do not know and it is easy for us to exaggerate, but for himself in the imagined presence of Beatrice it was so grave as to call for public repentance and confession.

The *Vita Nuova*, written probably some twenty years before these cantos, is an essential introduction to them, and the language of Beatrice, especially in the thirty-first canto, gains immeasurably in that context. The name of the *Vita Nuova* occurs, incidentally but deliberately, in the thirtieth canto— translated here 'early life'—and it is in these two cantos that Dante begins the fulfilment of the promise with which he had ended the earlier work: 'After this sonnet there appeared to me a wonderful vision in which I saw things that made me purpose to say no more of this blessed one until I should be able to treat of her more worthily, and to attain to this I strive all I can, as she truly knows. So if it shall please Him by whom all things live that my life continue for some years, I hope to say of her that which was never said of any woman. And then may it please Him who is the Lord of courtesy that my soul may go hence to see the glory of its lady, that is, of that blessed Beatrice, who in glory looks on the face of Him who is blessed through all ages.' Moore writes of the *Vita Nuova*: 'We read how the thought of her, and still more her presence, as she moved forth "clothed with humility", expelled every base or unkind thought and filled him with love and goodwill even to his enemies. It killed all vices in him, inspired all virtues. Such a beneficent influence must surely come direct from above. The type thus conceived of perfect Womanhood, bearing the same ideal relation to Woman as the "Son of Man" to humanity at large, could be none other than a revelation vouchsafed to him from heaven. Its embodiment might then aptly symbolize for him the Revelation of God. And when Dante came later on to treat his own experience as typical of that of mankind in general, the significance of this symbol also might be enlarged so as to become typical of Divine Revelation to mankind generally.'

Beatrice's reproaches against Dante are addressed in the thirtieth canto to the angels, 'who keep always in tune with the notes of the eternal spheres', and they are concerned directly with the standards set for him by creation and providence—'the operation of the great wheels', 'largess of divine graces', 'God's high decrees'. In the thirty-first she speaks to Dante himself and tests and judges him, more searchingly, by himself—'the desires for me which were leading thee', 'the hope of going forward', 'the shame of thy wandering', 'the venom of the argument' that in his bearded manhood he has shown the folly of a boy. He has not only come short of the glory of God, he has come short of himself, and in self-conviction he consents to Beatrice's rebukes. It was in the end the sight of Beatrice, even 'beneath her veil and beyond the stream', that humbled him in an effectual penitence, and he was then purged by Matilda of all bitter and shameful memories in the sacramental waters of Lethe.

Few modern readers will take very seriously the detailed symbolism of the passage that follows, though it is very deliberately contrived for Dante's purpose. Matilda, the spirit of the active life, brings him 'bathed' into the company and guardianship of the four cardinal virtues, the appointed 'hand-maids of Beatrice' and guides of men in their earthly activities, and they direct the penitent beyond themselves to the enlighten-ment of revelation—the unveiled eyes of Beatrice—and to the three Christian, contemplative, virtues, 'who see deeper'. Beatrice reflects in her eyes the one and the other aspect of the one Person of Christ, the ultimate insoluble mystery of the Incarnation, and, on the appeal of the Gospel virtues, unveils to Dante her mouth—for 'the eyes of wisdom are her demonstrations and her smile is her persuasions' (*Convito*). Such a statement of spiritual things is unreal for us and at the best ingenious and historically interesting, and it is the more astonishing that the whole passage glows and shines with the 'amazement and gladness' at once of the redeemed and illumined penitent and of the lover gazing on his lady restored to him from death and reconciled.

Dante's final apostrophe to Beatrice: 'O splendour of living light eternal' refers expressly to the imagery of the scene just described of the reflection of the Griffin in her eyes and corresponds with the language of the sacred Wisdom Literature of the Jews which was so much in his mind in the writing of these cantos. The word *splendore* is generally used by Dante for *reflected* light, and in particular for the reflection, as in the stars, of that light which God is.

The *Purgatorio*, the record in symbol of the devout life, has its consummation in the pageant, and it has been suggested that the liturgical, ritual, and sacramental features of which the cantica is full are completed by the symbolical representation of the consecrated Host in the person of Beatrice as the centre of the pageant. The total absence of the Eucharist from the *Purgatorio* would be strange in itself and it would be especially so in the conditions of the time, when the subject was prominently before the mind of the Church, when Aquinas had recently formulated its doctrine with authority and had written the office of Corpus Christi and hymns in honour of the Sacrament, and when, while Dante was writing these last cantos of the *Purgatorio*, the observance of Corpus Christi was authorized anew by Pope Clement V. The one explicit reference to the Eucharist in the *Divine Comedy* is in the passage of the *Paradiso* where Dante denounces the abuse of papal interdict for political ends: 'Once it was the custom to make war with swords, and now it is made with refusing, now here, now there, the bread which the merciful Father bars to none' (*Par.* xviii.), and such a reference would seem to make the absence of the Eucharist elsewhere in the poem the more surprising. The call '*Benedictus qui venis*' from the expectant elders just before Beatrice appears, mysteriously, we cannot tell whence or how, in the car of the Church, would at once suggest to a devout reader the familiar Preface to the Mass and the approach of the elements of the Eucharist. (The words are commonly, in spite of grammar, referred to Beatrice in her own person.) The Corpus Christi procession centred in the Host carried under a baldaquin, as the pageant centred in the car with Beatrice; Corpus Christi, like the pageant, had chants, lights and scattered flowers; the bull of Pope Urban on Corpus Christi says: 'Let faith sing psalms, let hope dance, let charity exult', and in the pageant these virtues as three ladies came 'dancing to their angelic roundelay'. Correspondences so marked between the pageant and the familiar festival of the Host can hardly be other than deliberate in a context so studied. The pageant, in one aspect of it, is the glorification of Beatrice as the spirit of revelation, the voice and embodiment of the truth of God, and it is no departure from that conception but rather an extension of it to regard her here as the Host in which, for the time and for the need of the penitent, is focused the living light eternal. The culminating scene is strangely abstract and unrealizable, of Beatrice reflecting in her eyes 'the two-fold beast, now with the one, now with the other nature', when Dante's 'soul, full of amazement and gladness, tasted of that food which, satisfying with itself, for itself makes appetite', and along with the sustained ritual solemnity of all the circumstances it seems singularly fitted to express, mysteriously, imperfectly, as for a thing that by its nature cannot be plainly told, the beatific vision under the limiting symbolic conditions of the earthly life, the eucharistic presence of Christ. Such a reading of the scene, if it can be made good, adds to it where it stands a high significance and solemnity. It is a fair question whether it is credible that Dante—'a transubstantially-minded man' as he has been well called—should have totally ignored the Eucharist in such a work as the *Purgatorio*; and if the Eucharist is not here it is nowhere in the *Divine Comedy*.

PURGATORIO

TANT'ERAN li occhi miei fissi e attenti
   a disbramarsi la decenne sete,
   che li altri sensi m'eran tutti spenti;
ed essi quinci e quindi avean parete
   di non caler, così lo santo riso
   a sè traèli con l'antica rete;
quando per forza mi fu volto il viso
   ver la sinistra mia da quelle dee,
   perch' io udi' da loro un 'Troppo fiso!';
e la disposizion ch'a veder èe   10
   nelli occhi pur testè dal sol percossi,
   sanza la vista alquanto esser mi fèe.
Ma poi ch'al poco il viso riformossi
   (io dico 'al poco' per rispetto al molto
   sensibile onde a forza mi rimossi),
vidi 'n sul braccio destro esser rivolto
   lo glorïoso essercito, e tornarsi
   col sole e con le sette fiamme al volto.
Come sotto li scudi per salvarsi
   volgesi schiera, e sè gira col segno,   20
   prima che possa tutta in sè mutarsi;
quella milizia del celeste regno
   che procedeva, tutta trapassonne
   pria che piegasse il carro il primo legno.
Indi alle rote si tornar le donne,
   e 'l grifon mosse il benedetto carco
   sì che, però, nulla penna crollonne.
La bella donna che mi trasse al varco
   e Stazio e io seguitavam la rota
   che fè l'orbita sua con minore arco.   30

CANTO XXXII

The wheeling of the pageant; the great tree;
disasters to the car

So fixed and intent were my eyes in satisfying their
ten years' thirst[1] that every other sense was quenched
in me and on the one side and the other they had
a wall of indifference, so did the holy smile draw
them to itself with the old net, when my face was
turned perforce to my left by those divine ones,
for I heard them say: 'Too fixed!' and the con-
dition of the sight that is in eyes just smitten by
the sun left me for a time without vision. But after
my sight had adjusted itself to the lesser object—
lesser, I mean, with regard to the greater from
which I was forced to withdraw—I saw that the
glorious army had wheeled on its right flank and
was returning with the sun and the seven flames
in its face. As under the shields a squadron wheels
about to save itself and turns with the colours
before the whole can change front, all that soldiery
of the celestial kingdom, being in the van, passed
by us before the pole brought round the car.
Then the ladies returned to the wheels and the
Griffin moved the blessed burden, but without
shaking one of its feathers. The fair lady who had
drawn me across and Statius and I followed the
wheel that made its turn with the smaller arc and

Sì passeggiando l'alta selva vota,
   colpa di quella ch'al serpente crese,
   temprava i passi un'angelica nota.
Forse in tre voli tanto spazio prese
   disfrenata saetta, quanto eramo
   rimossi, quando Beatrice scese.
Io senti' mormorare a tutti 'Adamo';
   poi cerchiaro una pianta dispogliata
   di fiori e d'altra fronda in ciascun ramo.
La coma sua, che tanto si dilata   40
   più quanto piu è su, fora dall' Indi
   ne' boschi lor per altezza ammirata.
'Beato se', grifon, che non discindi
   col becco d'esto legno dolce al gusto,
   poscia che mal si torce il ventre quindi.'
Così dintorno all'arbore robusto
   gridaron li altri; e l'animal binato:
   'Sì si conserva il seme d'ogni giusto.'
E volto al temo ch'elli avea tirato,
   trasselo al piè della vedova frasca,   50
   e quel di lei a lei lasciò legato.
Come le nostre piante, quando casca
   giù la gran luce mischiata con quella
   che raggia dietro alla celeste lasca,
turgide fansi, e poi si rinovella
   di suo color ciascuna, pria che 'l sole
   giunga li suoi corsier sotto altra stella;
men che di rose e più che di vïole
   colore aprendo, s' innovò la pianta,
   che prima avea le ramora sì sole.   60
Io non lo 'ntesi, nè qui non si canta
   l' inno che quella gente allor cantaro,
   nè la nota soffersi tutta quanta.
S' io potessi ritrar come assonnaro
   li occhi spietati udendo di Siringa,
   li occhi a cui pur vegghiar costò sì caro;
come pintor che con essemplo pinga,
   disegnerei com' io m'addormentai;
   ma qual vuol sia che l'assonnar ben finga.

as we passed through the lofty wood, empty by
her fault who believed the serpent, an angelic
music timed our steps. Perhaps three flights of an
arrow loosed from the string would cover as much
space as we had gone, when Beatrice descended.
I heard a murmur from them all of 'Adam!' Then
they encircled a tree stripped of its flowers and all
its foliage in every branch; its tresses, which spread
wider as they went higher, would be marvelled at
by the Indians in their woods for height.

'Blessed art thou, Griffin, that dost not pluck
with thy beak from this tree, sweet to the taste,
for the belly writhes in pain from it.' Thus the
others cried round the mighty tree, and the twice-
begotten animal: 'So is preserved the seed of all
righteousness'; and turning to the shaft which he
had pulled he drew it to the foot of the widowed
trunk and left it bound to the tree by a branch of
the tree itself. As our plants, when the great light
falls on them mingled with that which shines
behind the celestial Carp, begin to swell and then
each is renewed in its own colour before the sun
yokes his steeds under other stars,[2] so, showing
colour less than of the rose and more than of the
violet, the tree was renewed which before had its
branches so bare. I did not comprehend, nor is it
sung here, the hymn that company then sang, nor
did I bear to hear the music through.

If I could describe how the pitiless eyes, hearing
of Syrinx, were put to sleep, the eyes whose long
watching cost so dear,[3] I would picture as a painter
paints from a model how I fell asleep; but let who
will rightly set forth slumbering. I pass, therefore,

421

Però trascorro a quando mi svegliai,   70
   e dico ch' un splendor mi squarciò 'l velo
   del sonno e un chiamar: 'Surgi: che fai?'
Quali a veder de' fioretti del melo
   che del suo pome li angeli fa ghiotti
   e perpetüe nozze fa nel cielo,
Pietro e Giovanni e Iacopo condotti
   e vinti ritornaro alla parola
   dalla qual furon maggior sonni rotti,
e videro scemata loro scola
   così di Moïsè come d' Elia,   80
   ed al maestro suo cangiata stola;
tal torna' io, e vidi quella pia
   sovra me starsi che conducitrice
   fu de' miei passi lungo 'l fiume pria.
E tutto in dubbio dissi: 'Ov'è Beatrice?'
   Ond'ella: 'Vedi lei sotto la fronda
   nova sedere in su la sua radice:
vedi la compagnia che la circonda:
   li altri dopo il grifon sen vanno suso
   con più dolce canzone e più profonda.'   90
E se più fu lo suo parlar diffuso
   non so, però che già nelli occhi m'era
   quella ch'ad altro intender m'avea chiuso.
Sola sedeasi in su la terra vera,
   come guardia lasciata lì del plaustro
   che legar vidi alla biforme fera.
In cerchio le facean di sè claustro
   le sette ninfe, con quei lumi in mano
   che son sicuri d'Aquilone e d'Austro.
'Qui sarai tu poco tempo silvano;   100
   e sarai meco sanza fine cive
   di quella Roma onde Cristo è romano.
Però, in pro del mondo che mal vive,
   al carro tieni or li occhi, e quel che vedi,
   ritornato di là, fa che tu scrive.'
Così Beatrice; e io, che tutto ai piedi
   de' suoi comandamenti era divoto,
   la mente e li occhi ov'ella volle diedi.

to when I awoke and tell that a brightness broke
the veil of sleep, and a call: 'Arise, what doest
thou?'

As, when brought to see some of the blossoms
of the apple-tree that makes the angels greedy for
its fruit and makes perpetual marriage-feast in
heaven, Peter and John and James were over-
powered and came to themselves again at the word
by which deeper slumbers were broken and saw
their company diminished by both Moses and
Elias and their Master's raiment changed,⁴ so I
came to myself and saw standing over me that
compassionate lady who was before the guide of
my steps along the river. And all in doubt I said:
'Where is Beatrice?' To which she replied: 'See
her beneath the new foliage, seated upon its root;
see the company that encircles her; the others
take their way above after the Griffin, with a
sweeter and profounder song.'

And if her speech continued longer I do not
know, for already she was before my eyes who had
shut me off from every other care. She sat alone
on the bare ground, left there as guardian of the
chariot I had seen the bi-formed beast make fast.
The seven nymphs in a ring made of themselves a
cloister for her, with those lights in their hands
which are safe from north wind and south.

'Here thou shalt be a little while a forester, and
shalt be with me forever a citizen of that Rome
of which Christ is Roman; therefore, for the
world's good which lives ill, hold thine eyes now
on the car and what thou seest do thou write when
thou hast returned yonder.'⁵ Thus Beatrice; and I,
who at her command was wholly bowed down and
submissive, gave mind and eyes as she wished.

Non scese mai con sì veloce moto
  foco di spessa nube, quando piove   110
  da quel confine che più va remoto,
com' io vidi calar l'uccel di Giove
  per l'alber giù, rompendo della scorza,
  non che de' fiori e delle foglie nove;
e ferì 'l carro di tutta sua forza;
  ond'el piegò come nave in fortuna,
  vinta dall'onda, or da poggia, or da orza.
Poscia vidi avventarsi nella cuna
  del triunfal veiculo una volpe
  che d'ogni pasto buon parea digiuna;   120
ma, riprendendo lei di laide colpe,
  la donna mia la volse in tanta futa
  quanto sofferser l'ossa sanza polpe.
Poscia, per indi ond'era pria venuta,
  l'aguglia vidi scender giù nell'arca
  del carro e lasciar lei di sè pennuta;
e qual esce di cuor che si rammarca,
  tal voce uscì del cielo e cotal disse:
  'O navicella mia, com mal se' carca!'
Poi parve a me che la terra s'aprisse   130
  tr' ambo le ruote, e vidi uscirne un drago
  che per lo carro su la coda fisse;
e come vespa che ritragge l'ago,
  a sè traendo la coda maligna,
  trasse del fondo, e gissen vago vago.
Quel che rimase, come da gramigna
  vivace terra, dalla piuma, offerta
  forse con intenzion sana e benigna,
si ricoperse, e funne ricoperta
  e l'una e l'altra rota e 'l temo, in tanto   140
  che più tiene un sospir la bocca aperta.
Trasformato così 'l dificio santo
  mise fuor teste per le parti sue,
  tre sovra 'l temo e una in ciascun canto:
le prime eran cornute come bue,
  ma le quattro un sol corno avean per fronte:
  simile monstro visto ancor non fue.

Never fire descended so swiftly from dense cloud, falling from the farthest bound, as I saw the bird of Jove swoop down through the tree, tearing not only the flowers and fresh leaves but the bark, and it struck the car with all its force so that it reeled like a ship in storm driven, now leeward, now windward, by the waves.

Then I saw fling itself on the body of the triumphal chariot a fox that seemed starved of all good nourishment; but my lady, rebuking its foul offences, drove it back in such flight as the fleshless bones allowed.

Then, from the place it came from before, I saw the eagle descend into the body of the car and leave it feathered with its plumage; and such a voice as comes from a grieving heart I heard come forth from heaven and it said: 'O my little bark, with how much ill art thou laden!'

Then it seemed to me the earth opened between the two wheels, and I saw a dragon come forth there that drove its tail up through the car, and, as a wasp withdraws its sting, so, drawing back the malignant tail, it dragged out part of the bottom and made off on its wandering way.

What was left was covered again, as fertile soil with dog-grass, with the plumage, offered perhaps with pure and gracious intent, and the one and the other wheel and the shaft were covered with it in less time that a sigh keeps open the lips.

Thus transformed, the holy structure put forth heads on its parts, three on the shaft and one at each corner, the three horned like oxen and the four with a single horn on the forehead; such a monster was never seen.

Sicura, quasi rocca in alto monte,
    seder sovr'esso una puttana sciolta
    m'apparve con le ciglia intorno pronte;   150
e come perchè non li fosse tolta,
    vidi di costa a lei dritto un gigante;
    e baciavansi insieme alcuna volta.
Ma perchè l'occhio cupido e vagante
    a me rivolse, quel feroce drudo
    la flagellò dal capo infin le piante;
poi, di sospetto pieno e d' ira crudo,
    disciolse il monstro, e trassel per la selva,
    tanto che sol di lei mi fece scudo
alla puttana ed alla nova belva.   160

Secure, like a fortress on a high mountain, appeared to me an ungirt harlot seated on it, looking about her with bold brows, and as if that she might not be taken from him I saw a giant standing beside her, and they kissed each other again and again. But because she turned on me her wanton and roving eye that savage lover beat her from head to foot; then, full of suspicion and fierce with rage, he loosed the monster and dragged it through the wood so far that he made the wood itself screen from me the harlot and the strange brute.

1. Since the death of Beatrice.

2. When the sun is in conjunction with the Ram, which follows the Fishes, and before it enters the Bull; that is, in spring.

3. Argos of the hundred eyes was set by Juno to guard Io, loved by Jupiter; Mercury, by Jupiter's orders, lulled him to sleep with the story of Pan's pursuit of the nymph Syrinx and cut off his head.

4. The three at the Transfiguration had a foretaste of Christ's glory. 'As the apple-tree among the trees of the wood, so is my beloved among the sons' (*Song of Sol.* ii. 3). 'And Jesus came and touched them and said, Arise' (*Matt.* xvii. 7). The same word had raised the dead: Jairus's daughter (*Luke* viii. 54) and the widow's son (*Luke* vii. 14).

5. 'What thou seest, write in a book, and send it unto the seven churches' (*Rev.* i. 11).

NOTE

In no other of his hundred cantos is Dante's allegorizing ingenuity more apt to seem to us laboured and unimaginative and lacking even in the superficial qualities of consistency and lucidity; and yet to pass it over is to pass over elements of Dante's thinking which are fundamental for his poem. Without the motives to be found here and in the next canto the *Divine Comedy* would not have been written.

After the long parenthesis of the last two cantos we are recalled to the subject of the twenty-ninth, the pageant of revelation, as Dante himself is recalled by the three gospel virtues, with something of reproach for his 'too fixed' absorption in Beatrice. She is the truth of God for him, the demonstration and persuasion of the things of the spirit; but she is also, standing on the car before him, the reflected 'splendour of living light eternal' for the world, with her place in the centre of the pageant of the Church Militant. In the earlier account of it we have the revelation in its primary and absolute character; we see it now in its relation to the actual world, the institutions and events of history, and Dante's eyes have to be 'adjusted' to the 'lesser' sight after perfect vision.

As in the twenty-ninth canto, the militancy of the Church is stressed; the car is the centre of 'the glorious army' which keeps its stately order on the march, and under Matilda's guidance Dante and Statius take their place in its movement, which is described with military precision.

The members of the pageant are reminded of the Fall as they pass through the lofty wood that is 'empty by her fault who believed the serpent', and they murmur the name of Adam as they approach the tree whose fruit he had eaten and which had been robbed of its flowers and foliage by the generations.

On the meaning of the tree, which is essential to the canto, Parodi, one of the most authoritative of recent Dantists, writes: 'For Adam, as for his descendants in Eden, the tree was intended to symbolize the law under whose authority they were to live, the ordinance to which they were freely to consent, in a word, their righteousness. . . . On earth this natural righteousness, impressed on each individual conscience, is manifested in its ideal unity only in the Empire, one and unique, which is not less holy and not less willed by God, . . . and it forms as it were one thing with its purpose, that is, with the law itself. . . . Symbolizing the idea of right, the tree is also of necessity the symbol of the Empire, because the two things are practically one and the same.' When the pageant gathered about the tree its members praised the Griffin—Christ in His earthly life— for His care not to pluck its fruit, the tasting of which had been the cause of human misery; and the Griffin replied: 'So' —by this obedience to the divine law for men—'is preserved the seed of all righteousness.' The compressed enigmatic language is an echo of the New Testament: Paul's words, 'As by one man's disobedience many were made sinners, so by the obedience of one shall many be made righteous' (*Rom*. v. 19), and Christ's, 'Thus it becometh us to fulfil all righteousness' (*Matt*. iii. 15). It is this primary sense of right, belonging to human nature itself, that has been ravaged and wasted by Adam and his race, that was encircled for its succour by the divine resources of revelation, that was honoured by Christ in its embodiment in the Empire—by His birth and death under the Empire's jurisdiction, by His refusal of 'the kingdoms of the world and the glory of them', by His words, 'Render unto Caesar the things which are Caesar's'—and that bloomed into purple splendour when the car of the Church was joined to it. The vision of the perfected human order of Church and Empire, a thing that never was except in vision, and the hearing of 'the hymn that company then sang' were for Dante like the heaven-wrought wonder of the spring and he was enraptured and overcome as were the three apostles by the sight of 'some of the blossoms of the apple-tree', the foretaste of Christ's glory; and then, like the three, he is summoned to face the bitter, challenging realities of the world.

CANTO XXXII

The scene that follows, of Beatrice cloistered by the seven
nymphs with the seven lights in their hands, while 'she sat
alone on the bare ground' under the tree's new green and
guarded the car that was tied to the tree, is now plain enough.
Divine truth, supported by the seven virtues with the seven
gifts of the Spirit, content in voluntary poverty and protected
by the Empire, watches over the Church, which is itself bound
to the Empire by divine act and authority.

It is here, with that ideal relation of Church and State before
his eyes, the achieved harmony of the life of faith and worship
and inward aspiration with the not less sacred requirements of
social and moral order among men, that Dante is commissioned
by Beatrice as a prophet to his generation. Her promise to him
is not a mere personal assurance of salvation; it is the promise
that he, now 'a forester', a rustic, shall yet be a citizen of
Christ's Rome. Even now his citizenship is in heaven and his
present loyalty to that fatherland is to tell the world his vision.

The last part of the canto is occupied with the representation,
in terms drawn chiefly from the Apocalypse, of seven disasters
which, when Dante wrote, had befallen the Church in the
course of its history. The following may fairly be taken as the
events which Dante intended: (1) the Imperial persecutions of
the early Church under Nero and Domitian; (2) early heresies,
especially Arianism; (3) Constantine's supposed 'Donation' to
the Church of the possessions and jurisdiction of the Empire
in the west (*Inf.* xix), with St Peter's grieving voice from
heaven; (4) the rise of Mohamedanism, regarded as the greatest
of all heresies and schisms in the Church's history (*Inf.* xxviii);
(5) the further enrichment of the Church by the first medieval
Emperors, Pepin and Charlemagne; (6) the consequent cor-
ruption and transformation of the Church, now decked with
the seven deadly sins and conforming to the 'beast with seven
heads and ten horns' of *Revelation* xiii. 1; (7) the events of
Dante's own day—the corrupt alliance of the Papacy with the
French crown, the outrage done by Philip of France to Pope
Boniface at Anagni (*Purg.* xx), and the Papacy's desertion of
Rome for Avignon under Pope Clement (*Inf.* xix) in 1305. To
such abdication of its divine calling and treason to the human
cause and to such moral disaster the Church of Christ had

fallen. It is now no Church of Christ, but a 'monster'—the word is repeated here and in the next canto —and in telling its story in hieroglyphs drawn mainly from Scripture—the tree, the monster with heads and horns, the dragon, the harlot wantoning with kings—Dante used a language which had for himself and his contemporaries the traditional solemn authority of vision and inspiration.

PURGATORIO

'*Deus, venerunt gentes*', alternando
   or tre or quattro, dolce salmodia
   le donne incominciaro, e lacrimando;
e Beatrice, sospirosa e pia,
   quelle ascoltava sì fatta che poco
   più alla croce si cambiò Maria.
Ma poi che l'altre vergini dier loco
   a lei di dir, levata dritta in pè,
   rispuose, colorata come foco:
'*Modicum, et non videbitis me;*   10
   et iterum, sorelle mie dilette,
   modicum, et vos videbitis me.'
Poi le si mise innanzi tutte e sette,
   e dopo sè, solo accennando, mosse
   me e la donna e 'l savio che ristette.
Così sen giva; e non credo che fosse
   lo decimo suo passo in terra posto,
   quando con li occhi li occhi mi percosse;
e con tranquillo aspetto 'Vien più tosto'
   mi disse 'tanto che, s' io parlo teco,   20
   ad ascoltarmi tu sie ben disposto.'
Sì com' io fui, com' io dovea, seco,
   dissemi: 'Frate, perchè non t'attenti
   a domandarmi omai venendo meco?'
Come a color che troppo reverenti
   dinanzi a suo' maggior parlando sono,
   che non traggon la voce viva ai denti,

CANTO XXXIII

*Beatrice's promise of a deliverer; the sanctity
of the tree; the passage through Eunoe*

'*Deus, venerunt gentes*'[1] the ladies, singing now
three now four responsively and weeping, began
sweet psalmody, and Beatrice, sighing and com-
passionate, listened to them, so altered that Mary
changed little more at the cross; but when the
other virgins gave place to her to speak she
answered, rising erect on her feet and glowing
like fire: '*Modicum, et non videbitis me; et iterum,*
my beloved sisters, *modicum, et vos videbitis me.*'[2]
Then she put all seven in front of her, and behind
her, with only a gesture, motioned me and the
lady and the sage who remained. Thus she went
forward, and I do not think she had taken the
tenth step on the ground when with her eyes she
smote on mine and with tranquil look said to me:
'Come more quickly, so that, if I speak with thee,
thou shalt be ready to listen to me.' And as soon
as I was with her, as was my duty, she said to me:
'Brother, why dost thou not venture to question
me, now thou comest with me?'

As with those that are too reverent before their
superiors with whom they speak to bring the voice
distinctly to their lips, so it was with me, and with

avvenne a me, che sanza intero sono
  incominciai: 'Madonna, mia bisogna
  voi conoscete, e ciò ch'ad essa è bono.'   30
Ed ella a me: 'Da tema e da vergogna
  voglio che tu omai ti disviluppe,
  sì che non parli più com'om che sogna.
Sappi che 'l vaso che 'l serpente ruppe
  fu e non è; ma chi n' ha colpa, creda
  che vendetta di Dio non teme suppe.
Non sarà tutto tempo sanza reda
  l'aquila che lasciò le penne al carro,
  per che divenne monstro e poscia preda;
ch' io veggio certamente, e però il narro,   40
  a darne tempo già stelle propinque,
  secure d'ogn' intoppo e d'ogni sbarro,
nel quale un cinquecento diece e cinque,
  messo di Dio, anciderà la fuia
  con quel gigante che con lei delinque.
E forse che la mia narrazion buia,
  qual Temi e Sfinge, men ti persuade,
  perch'a lor modo lo 'ntelletto attuia;
ma tosto fier li fatti le Naiade
  che solveranno questo enigma forte   50
  sanza danno di pecore o di biade.
Tu nota; e sì come da me son porte,
  così queste parole segna a' vivi
  del viver ch'è un correre alla morte.
E aggi a mente, quando tu le scrivi,
  di non celar qual hai vista la pianta
  ch'è or due volte dirubata quivi.
Qualunque ruba quella o quella schianta,
  con bestemmia di fatto offende a Dio,
  che solo all'uso suo la creò santa.   60
Per morder quella, in pena ed in disio
  cinquemilia anni e più l'anima prima
  bramò colui che 'l morso in sè punìo.
Dorme lo 'ngegno tuo, se non estima
  per singular cagione essere eccelsa
  lei tanto e sì travolta nella cima.

imperfect utterance I began: 'My lady, you know my need and what will meet it.'

And she said to me: 'From fear and shame I will have thee free thyself henceforth, that thou mayst no longer speak like one that dreams. Know that the vessel the serpent broke was and is not,[3] but let him that has the blame be assured that God's vengeance fears no sop.[4] Not for all time shall the eagle be without heir that left its feathers on the car so that it became monster and then prey; for I see assuredly, and therefore tell of it, stars already near, to give us the time, secure from all check and hindrance, when a five hundred, ten and five, one sent from God, shall slay the thievish woman and the giant who sins with her. And perhaps my dark tale, like Themis and the Sphinx, persuades thee less because, in their fashion, it clouds thy mind; but soon the facts shall be the Naiads that will solve this hard enigma without loss of flocks and corn.[5] Take note, and even as these words are uttered by me so teach them to those who live the life that is a race to death; and have in mind, when thou writest them, not to hide what thou hast seen of the tree which has now twice over been robbed here. Whoso robs that tree or rends it offends with blasphemy of act against God, who for His own sole use created it holy; for tasting of that tree the first soul longed in pain and in desire five thousand years and more for Him who avenged on Himself that taste.[6] Thy wits sleep if they do not reckon that for some due cause it is of such loftiness and is thus reversed

437

E se stati non fossero acqua d' Elsa
   li pensier vani intorno alla tua mente,
   e 'l piacer loro un Piramo alla gelsa,
per tante circostanze solamente   70
   la giustizia di Dio, nell' interdetto,
   conosceresti all'arbor moralmente.
Ma perch' io veggio te nello 'ntelletto
   fatto di pietra, ed, impetrato, tinto,
   sì che t'abbaglia il lume del mio detto,
voglio anco, e se non scritto, almen dipinto,
   che 'l te ne porti dentro a te per quello
   che si reca il bordon di palma cinto.'
E io: 'Sì come cera da suggello,
   che la figura impressa non trasmuta,   80
   segnato è or da voi lo mio cervello.
Ma perchè tanto sovra mia veduta
   vostra parola disïata vola,
   che più la perde quanto più s'aiuta?'
'Perchè conoschi' disse 'quella scola
   c' hai seguitata, e veggi sua dottrina
   come può seguitar la mia parola;
e veggi vostra via dalla divina
   distar cotanto, quanto si discorda
   da terra il ciel che più alto festina.'   90
Ond' io rispuosi lei: 'Non mi ricorda
   ch' i' stranïasse me già mai da voi,
   nè honne coscïenza che rimorda.'
'E se tu ricordar non te ne puoi'
   sorridendo rispuose 'or ti rammenta
   come bevesti di Letè ancoi;
e se dal fummo foco s'argomenta
   cotesta oblivïon chiaro conchiude
   colpa nella tua voglia altrove attenta.
Veramente oramai saranno nude   100
   le mie parole, quanto converrassi
   quelle scovrire alla tua vista rude.'
E più corusco e con più lenti passi
   teneva il sole il cerchio di merigge,
   che qua e là, come li aspetti, fassi,

at the top, and if vain thoughts had not been water of Elsa[7] about thy mind and thy delight in them a Pyramus to the mulberry,[8] by such features alone thou wouldst recognize in the interdict on the tree, morally, the righteousness of God.[9] But since I see thee turned to stone in thy mind and, being petrified, darkened, so that the light of my speech dazzles thee, I will also that thou bear it away within thee, and if not written at least pictured, for the reason that the staff is brought back wreathed with palm.'[10]

And I: 'Even as by seal the wax, which does not change the imprinted figure, my brain is now stamped by you; but why do your longed-for words fly so far above my sight that the more it strives the more it loses them?'

'So that thou mayst know' she said 'that school which thou hast followed and see if its teaching can follow my words and see your way to be as far from God's way as the heaven that spins highest is parted from the earth.'[11]

To that I replied: 'I have no remembrance that I ever estranged me from you, nor have I conscience of it that pricks me.'

'And if thou canst not remember it' she answered smiling 'recollect now how thou didst drink to-day of Lethe, and if fire is inferred from smoke this forgetfulness clearly proves fault in thy will intent elsewhere.[12] But henceforth my words shall be as simple as may be needful to make them plain to thy rude sight.'

Now more resplendent and with slower steps the sun held the meridian circle which shifts here and there with the point of view,[13] when, just as one

439

quando s'affisser, sì come s'affigge
  chi va dinanzi a gente per iscorta
  se trova novitate a sue vestigge,
le sette donne al fin d' un'ombra smorta,
  qual sotto foglie verdi e rami nigri   110
  sovra suoi freddi rivi l'Alpe porta.
Dinanzi ad esse Eüfratès e Tigri
  veder mi parve uscir d'una fontana,
  e, quasi amici, dipartirsi pigri.
'O luce, o gloria della gente umana,
  che acqua è questa che qui si dispiega
  da un principio e sè da sè lontana?'
Per cotal priego detto mi fu: 'Prega
  Matelda che 'l ti dica.' E qui rispose,
  come fa chi da colpa si dislega,   120
la bella donna: 'Questo e altre cose
  dette li son per me; e son sicura
  che l'acqua di Letè non lil nascose.'
E Beatrice: 'Forse maggior cura,
  che spesse volte la memoria priva,
  fatt' ha la mente sua nelli occhi oscura.
Ma vedi Eünoè che là diriva:
  menalo ad esso, e come tu se' usa,
  la tramortita sua virtù ravviva.'
Come anima gentil, che non fa scusa,   130
  ma fa sua voglia della voglia altrui
  tosto che è per segno fuor dischiusa;
così, poi che da essa preso fui,
  la bella donna mossesi, e a Stazio
  donnescamente disse: 'Vien con lui.'
S' io avessi, lettor, più lungo spazio
  da scrivere i' pur cantere' in parte
  lo dolce ber che mai non m'avrìa sazio;
ma perchè piene son tutte le carte
  ordite a questa cantica seconda,   140
  non mi lascia più ir lo fren dell'arte.
Io ritornai dalla santissima onda
  rifatto sì come piante novelle
  rinovellate di novella fronda,
puro e disposto a salire alle stelle.

going before a company for escort stops if he comes on something strange on his way, the seven ladies stopped at the edge of a dim shade such as under green leaves and black boughs the mountains cast on their cold streams, and in front of them I seemed to see Euphrates and Tigris issue from one spring and, like friends, slowly separate.

'O light, O glory of the human race, what water is this that pours here from one source and parts itself from itself?' When I asked this she said to me: 'Ask Matilda to tell thee'; and then the fair lady answered, as one freeing herself from blame: 'This and other things I have told him and I am certain that Lethe's waters did not hide it from him.'

And Beatrice: 'Perhaps a greater care, which often robs the memory, has darkened the eyes of his mind. But see Eunoe which flows forth there; bring him to it and, as thou art used, revive his weakened faculty.'

As a gentle spirit that makes no excuse but makes its will of another's will as soon as it is disclosed by a sign, so, when she had taken me by the hand, the fair lady moved and with womanly courtesy said to Statius: 'Come with him.'

If, reader, I had more space to write I should sing but in part the sweet draught which never would have sated me; but since all the sheets prepared for this second cantica are full the curb of art does not let me go farther. From the most holy waters I came forth again remade, even as new plants renewed with new leaves, pure and ready to mount to the stars.

1. 'O God, the heathen are come into thine inheritance' (*Ps.* lxxix. 1).

2. 'A little while, and ye shall not see me: and again, a little while, and ye shall see me' (*John* xvi. 16).

3. 'The beast that thou sawest was, and is not' (*Rev.* xvii. 8).

4. A murderer was secure from vengeance if he ate a sop of bread and wine on the grave of his victim.

5. Themis, goddess of justice, whose oracles were obscure, sent a monster to waste the fields of Thebes, being angered at the solution of the Sphinx's riddle; the solution, by a mistaken reading of Ovid, was ascribed to the Naiads.

6. Adam was supposed to have lived 930 years on earth after the Fall and 4302 years in Limbo till the Crucifixion and the Harrowing of Hell.

7. Tributary of the Arno which coats things with carbonate of lime.

8. His mind was stained; cp. *Purg.* xxvii.

9. The 'moral' sense—one of the four recognized senses of Scripture—of the tree of the forbidden fruit is the requirement of submission to God's righteousness.

10. Evidence of pilgrimage to the Holy Land.

11. The Primum Mobile is the highest material heaven.

12. 'As Lethe removes only the memory of *sin*, the fact that he has now forgotten his recreancy to Beatrice, which he remembered just before drinking of the stream, proves that this estrangement was sinful' (*Grandgent*).

13. It is noon of Easter Wednesday. The meridian is relative to the observer's position on the earth.

NOTE

'All the cupidities, all the ambitions, all the sacerdotal world-
liness of the Church are artistically summed up in the harlot—
the Curia committing adultery with kings; all the usurpations,
all the violences, all the frauds of the kings have their artistic
embodiment in the giant—Philip the Fair, the most powerful
and audacious of them, since he could carry off the apostolic
seat from the place where God has set it and the faithful would
see it, from Rome. That remembered, what more is needed
for understanding why the ladies sing with tears *Deus, venerunt
gentes* and why Beatrice, listening to them, is stricken with
grief?' (*G. Manni, L.D.*). She is like Mary at the cross; these
wrongs are like a new Crucifixion. In this time of the
visible Church's absence and suspense—it 'was and is not'—
Beatrice, in her grief, in her anger, in her authority, is the
true soul of the Church, which remains and in 'a little while'
shall be seen again; all this is expressed in the ceremonial
ordering of her diminished procession, in which she is accom-
panied only by the virtues and the few faithful, and in her
use of Latin, the language of the Church's ritual. Meantime,
the Church is lost to the world and Beatrice tells of the world's
recovery.

Her long speech has its main point in the 'hard enigma' of
the 'five hundred and ten and five, one sent from God,' whose
coming is foretold by the stars. The enigma has had nearly as
many solutions as has the number of the beast in the Apocalypse,
which may have suggested this curious device. Both are examples
of the practice of equating the letters of a name with certain
numbers, these numbers being then summed in a total to
represent the name itself. It was a practice deriving from
Jewish antiquity and still used and taken seriously in Dante's
time. It is enough for us to note that the number 515 here

is given by Moore and others the interpretation adopted below. Dramatically, it suited Dante's purpose to use this obscure prophetic diction, which he trusted the facts to make plain. In the visionary manner of prophecy Beatrice speaks in 1300 as if the Papacy's abandonment of Rome for Avignon in 1305 had already happened, and Dante makes her darkly foretell events in the midst of which he wrote some eleven or twelve years after 1300, when the promise of a deliverer could have only one meaning.

For Dante, not only was the Papacy morally vacant at this time, but also the throne of the Empire had been vacant ever since the death of Frederick II in 1250, the nominal Emperors of the past half-century never having appeared in Italy and not having been crowned in Rome. But 'not for all time shall the eagle be without heir', and when Dante wrote a new Emperor, the chivalrous and ambitious Henry of Luxemburg, had been elected, had undertaken his momentous expedition to Italy, and had already crossed the Alps. Many of the lords and communes of distracted Italy had welcomed Henry as the bringer of order and peace and to Dante's high-wrought spirit Henry's coming was the confirmation of his dearest hopes and the assurance of their glorious fulfilment. Dante sent an appeal to the princes and peoples of Italy which began: 'Behold, now is the accepted time, when signs are rising of consolation and of peace; for a new day brightens, showing dawn, which already thins the shades of long calamity.' Guelf Florence was the centre of resistance to Henry and Dante wrote in bitter indignation as 'Florentine and exile undeservedly to the accursed Florentines within', who, 'first and only, fearful of the yoke of liberty, rage against the glory of the Roman Prince, the King of the world and God's minister'. A third letter he wrote to 'the most holy conqueror and sole lord, the Lord Henry, by divine providence King of the Romans, ever Augustus', in his own name and in that of 'all Tuscans everywhere who desire the peace of the land', urging him to haste. 'When my hands touched thy feet and my lips paid their debt, then my spirit exulted in thee and in silence I said within me, "Behold the Lamb of God, behold him who has taken away the sins of the world."' If, as is probable, these last cantos of the *Purgatorio* were written about the same time as these letters, the letters are an essential commentary here and the same outlook and temper are to be found in both.

What might have come of Henry's expedition no one can say, but the new age he was to bring to Italy and to the world was, as Dante conceived of it, such stuff as dreams are made on. Henry was crowned in Rome in 1312 and his death in the following year marked the end of imperial hopes in Italy. Yet Dante's dream of a world-order, august, mighty, inviolable, a tree of God's planting, a living thing rooted in the earth and reaching high heavenward and wide-spreading, is a dream that has inspired the wisest and best men in many ages and inspires them not least to-day—'that on this threshing-floor of mortals men should live freely and at peace' (*De Monarchia*). 'With the Papacy gone astray, the Empire debased and impotent, the religious orders corrupted, power meaning lawlessness, the well-disposed becoming weak and cowardly, religion neither guide nor check to society but only the consolation of its victims, Dante was bold and hopeful enough to believe in the divine appointment, and in the possibility, of law and government, of a State. In his philosophy the institutions that provide for man's peace and liberty in this life are part of God's great order for raising man to perfection. . . . What he yearns after is the predominance of justice in civil society' (*R. W. Church*). That is why Beatrice is so urgent with Dante here and so emphasizes 'that tree', the symbol of all righteous order in the earthly life, the 'robbing' of which is the beginning of all earthly ills. Brought up in the pure Guelf—anti-imperial— tradition of Florence, Dante had not always realized the necessity and the sacredness of such a moral and political order among men; he had failed and slept like Argos set to watch, and in the words of Beatrice he confesses his failure in that larger loyalty. But here, on the summit of Purgatory, his purged and disciplined spirit has its vision of what is meant, of providence and of grace, for men in this 'life that is a race to death'; and he is charged again to make his vision known, bringing it back with him from these heights as a pilgrim his palm-wreathed staff from Palestine. For the whole subject of the *Purgatorio* is the perfecting, by penitence and fellowship and prayer, of the life of man among men.

Beatrice and her little company come to the edge of the shadows of the wood and out into the splendour of the noon-day sun. 'The hour of noon' Dante says in the *Convito* 'is the noblest in the whole day and the one of greatest virtue'; it was then, traditionally, that Christ died and that He ascended, and it was then that Dante's purgation was perfected and he ascended with Beatrice. This is the last mention in the poem of time as reckoned by the sun. When they leave the earth for the spheres of Paradise they pass from earth's time-measurements, and here Dante notes how relative these are: 'The sun held the meridian circle, which shifts here and there with the point of view.'

By Matilda, the spirit of the perfected earthly life, he is plunged in the stream of good memory, that he may take with him all the good this life has given, as a part of a greater whole, into the life of the spirit. Of the sweetness of the draught he cannot speak, 'since all the sheets prepared for this second cantica are full'. It is a strange consideration at such a time; but Dante is one who

> 'freely sings
> In strictest bonds of rhyme and rule,
> And finds in them, not bonds, but wings',

and the cutting short of the narrative conveys to us something of the eagerness, almost the impatience, of one who is filled with the newness of life 'even as new plants renewed with new leaves', and is 'ready to mount to the stars'.

He came forth from Hell 'to see again the stars' and in beginning the *Purgatorio* he promised to 'sing of that second kingdom where the human spirit is purged and becomes fit for the ascent to heaven'. Now he awaits the last fulfilment.